"I'm tempting you?" she cried, face flaming. *"I* want you?"

Her mouth was red from his kiss, her cheeks flushed. The bright green of her eyes had darkened almost to black, and he saw there the mirror of his own desire.

"Ever since I came back you've swung between wanting to kill me and wanting to kiss me," Cal said. "Hell, Mac, a minute ago you would've given me a lot more than a kiss if I'd w[illegible] to take it."

"You're dreaming! If yo[illegible]—!"

"I think that yo[illegible] your mind. This isn't a[illegible]our life and mine. I [illegible]me, once I have you [illegible] of a fight. So be very [illegible]gain."

"You're [illegible] what was between us is over. It [illegible]ed. There's nothing left! This . . . th[illegible]—she drew the back of her hand across her mouth to obliterate the kiss—"this was an accident!" She knew even as she spoke that her words were a lie . . .

* * *

"SUPERBLY WRITTEN, ABSOLUTELY GRIPPING READING . . . A KEEPER!"
—*Affaire de Coeur* on *Visions of the Heart*

"A FINELY HONED PLOT WITH A SENSUOUS LOVE STORY BY A TALENTED AUTHOR."
—*Rendezvous* on *Touch of Fire*

"AN ENGAGING AND ENJOYABLE STORY FOR TRUE WESTERN BUFFS."
—Dorothy Garlock, author of *Tenderness*, on *Lawless*

Also by
Emily Carmichael

TOUCH OF FIRE
VISIONS OF THE HEART

Published by
WARNER BOOKS

EMILY CARMICHAEL

LAWLESS

A Time Warner Company

WARNER BOOKS EDITION

Cover photograph by Herman Estevez
Cover illustration by Jacqueline Goldstein
Cover design by Diane Luger
Turquoise necklace courtesy of David Saity

Warner Books, Inc.
1271 Avenue of the Americas
New York, NY 10020

 A Time Warner Company

Printed in the United States of America

First Printing: October, 1993

10 9 8 7 6 5 4 3 2 1

1

June 1885
Lazy B Ranch
San Pedro Valley, Arizona

The chestnut mare galloped the length of the arena, her long mane whipping back in a furious banner, her nostrils flared in frustration. At the last moment before crashing into the east gate, she slid to a halt, plowing up the soft ground with her hooves and launching clods of dirt into the circular tin water tank in the corner. From a pen in the other corner of the arena, the Lazy B hogs gave several unsympathetic grunts and squinted at the mare through small dark eyes.

She snorted and whirled, facing for a brief moment the woman who leaned against the south gate and the child perched on the fence beside her.

"She looks mad!" The little girl's saucy smile carved dimples in her chubby cheeks and put a sparkle in eyes of emerald green. Her pale-gold hair fell in thick braids halfway to the bow-tied sash of her pinafore.

"She's mad, all right." Mackenzie Butler watched as the mare tossed her splendid head, bucked once, then set off at a fluid trot across the short measure of the ring. Back and forth from the water tank to the hog pen she trotted, ears laid flat to her head, never taking her eyes off the dark whipcord of a man who stood in front of the big sliding doors that led from the arena into the horse barn.

"Today's my day to tame you, eh, wild one?" Tony Herrera raised his coiled rope as if in challenge to the animal.

The mare's ears flicked briefly at the sound of his voice, but her restless motion didn't falter.

"I think the mare has her own idea about who is going to be tamed," Mackenzie commented to her daughter.

Tony continued to woo the mare. "Today is the day I wear you down, pretty senorita." He advanced slowly across the ring. "Come, little wild one. We'll be friends today. You and me. You gonna let me ride you, eh?"

"What do you think, Frankie?" Mackenzie asked.

The child grimaced in thought. "I think the horse is gonna win. Poor Tony," she said with a sigh.

Mackenzie chuckled. "I think you're right."

When Tony reached the middle of the arena, the mare snorted to a halt and turned to face him, ears laid back and nostrils flared. He raised the rope slowly, passing the loop to his right hand. The mare pawed at the ground and flexed her neck in challenge.

Frankie grinned. "I like that horse. I like the white stripe on her nose and her white socks."

"She's a pretty mare," Mackenzie agreed.

"Today's my birthday," the child reminded her mother solemnly.

"I know, Sprout. Today you're five years old. That's a very special age."

"Issy Crosby had a birthday, and she got a pony of her very own. She told me at church."

"Issy is seven. She's much bigger than you are."

With a theatrical sigh, Frankie twisted her little Cupid's-bow mouth to one side. "I sure do like that horse."

Suddenly, the mare exploded from utter stillness into action. With an angry neigh she charged the man with the rope, then dodged to one side at the last moment. Unfortunately, Tony dodged to the same side to avoid her charge. The mare's shoulder connected with Tony's chest and sent him tumbling to the dirt. Squealing, she turned and eyed him malevolently as he gasped for breath and tried to gain his feet. Mackenzie held her breath, but the mare stood still as Tony scrambled for the fence and ducked through the rails.

"Poor Tony." Frankie's giggle belied her expression of sympathy.

"Going to ride her today, are you?" Mackenzie asked Tony with skeptically raised brows.

"That's one bitch of a horse." At Mackenzie's chilly gaze, Tony lowered his eyes. "Sorry. I meant that's one dangerous animal."

"I know what you meant. Find a couple of men to help you put her back into the south pasture. I've got to think about this for a while. She's a beautiful mare. I hate to give up on her."

"This idea of yours about breakin' her gentle is stupid, Mackenzie. We need to tie her to the snubbing post and show her who's boss. That's the only way to break an animal like that."

"I don't want her *broken*; I want her tamed."

"Where'd you get the idea there's a difference?" Tony said sullenly. He turned and stalked toward the barn. Mackenzie sighed and glanced over to where the wild mare cantered back and forth along the arena fence. She recognized the frustration and fear in the horse's eyes as it sought a way out. The beast was penned, nowhere to turn, no escape. Sometimes Mackenzie felt the very same way.

"I could tame her, Ma," Frankie insisted. "I could ride her."

Mackenzie lifted the child from the fence and swung her to the ground. "In a few years you probably could, Sprout. But not this year."

"Yes I could!" Frankie declared. As she skipped beside her mother to the house, she made the words into a chant. "Yes I could. Yes I could. Yes I could."

"Yes you could what?" Andalusia Butler greeted them as Mackenzie opened the gate into the yard. Her slender frame and pale-ivory skin were emphasized by a severe black gown. Since Frank Butler's death six years ago had left her a widow, she'd worn almost nothing but black.

"Yes I could ride a horse!" Frankie sang out. "Oh, Gran! The horse was *so* mad! She bumped Tony right to the ground!"

"Again?" Lu sighed.

Mackenzie shrugged and brushed the dust from her skirt. "Perhaps I should take Tony's advice on how to handle the mare."

Lu gave her a wry smile. "That would please him enormously."

"No doubt. He'd be even more pleased if I let him move into the house and take over everything else as well." She grimaced. "He does have a point, Lu."

"You and I have discussed this before, dear. This ranch was your father's and mine, and now it is yours and mine. Your stepbrother has no part in it. He is merely an employee. I made that clear to him when he came here asking for money. You may follow his advice as you please, but on its own merit—not because he's my son."

"On its own merit his advice isn't worth much."

Frankie tugged at her mother's skirt. "I could ride that

horse," she said, bringing the subject back to where she thought it belonged.

"Not right now you won't. Right now you need to wash for dinner, young lady." Mackenzie took one of her daughter's braids and steered her into the parlor, stopping in front of the cabinet that held Lu's miniature china set. The mirror at the back of the cabinet reflected their images peeking through tiny cups and saucers. "Look at that dirt! Where were you this morning?"

"I was with Gran. We were in the tunnel." The old mine tunnel that Frank Butler had excavated years ago was Frankie's favorite place to play.

"Did you remember to not go beyond the daylight?"

"Yes I did!" Frankie declared smugly.

Mackenzie knelt beside Frankie and looked at them together in the mirror. Frankie's blooming freshness made her feel far older than her twenty-four years. Where was the blithe-spirited young girl who'd come to Arizona from Boston almost seven years ago? Nothing could deflate her spirit then. Her expectations were as bright and wild as an Arizona sunset. Determined to love this land when she finally was allowed to come, she saw adventure and excitement everywhere she looked. The elemental frontier had not intimidated her; it had infused her life with color and magic—rainbows waited behind every mountain and in each sage-colored valley.

How naive she'd been then. How innocent and foolish—until she'd discovered that rainbows often hide tragedy and trust invites betrayal. Now the mirror reflected eyes that were wary, a mouth that had lost its once impetuous smile, and a face that belonged to a woman, not a fresh girl. Her hair still flashed fire in the sunlight that streamed through the parlor window, but now it was neatly braided and wound into a proper chignon at her nape. Her skin was golden from the sun's kiss—she seldom heeded Lu's advice to wear a hat out of doors—and the slightest trace of fine lines fanned from the outer corner of her eyes. She suspected those horrid lines were less from the sun than from fretting over a past that couldn't be undone.

Mackenzie smoothed back unruly golden wisps of Frankie's hair. She could see herself in her daughter's stubborn chin and green eyes, but the Cupid's-bow mouth had the same smile as the girl's father; the unruly, waving hair flashed the same golden sparks in sunlight; the round little cheeks even sported a dimple in the same spot where the father's cheek was dented.

"Go out to the well and wash, Sprout. Gran won't like it if we're late to dinner. She and Carmelita cooked you something very special for your birthday." She smiled as Frankie bounced her way through the parlor exit into the inner court around which the adobe ranch house was built. A hand pump stood amid an array of daffodils, gladiolas, sweet peas, and hibiscus. With her shining yellow hair and blue pinafore, the child looked as bright as any flower in the garden.

Mackenzie was about to join Frankie at the pump when she heard the gate to the yard creak open, followed by a loud knock on the door. She crossed to the door and opened it to face Bull Ferguson, whose hamlike fist was clenched to knock again.

"Miz Butler, there's trouble up on the north range." The man's size had earned him his name. A thick barrel chest and treelike legs lent him the appearance of a meaty square of muscle, but intelligence and a strange gentleness usually softened the rough-cut features of his face. At this moment, however, his face was flushed and sweaty from a fast ride through the day's heat. His eyes were dark with fighting anger.

"What kind of trouble?" Mackenzie asked in a clipped, weary voice.

"Better come see, ma'am, or there's likely to be more of it."

The stiff and bloated bodies of eleven dead cows lay in fly-blown heaps around the salt lick. Ranch hands Crawford and George Keller hovered on the margins of the area like grim vultures, their horses snorting at the stink of the carcasses.

Mackenzie held a cotton kerchief to her nose as she, Bull, and Tony rode up. Keller touched the brim of his hat; Crawford merely nodded, his only hand busy steadying his horse.

"Poison," Keller said gruffly. Lean and leathery, with a gray stubble of beard matching the gray stubble of his hair, he flicked a brief, disapproving glance toward Mackenzie's loose denim trousers. The man didn't approve of women in trousers, Mackenzie knew. In fact, he didn't much approve of women, period.

Mackenzie looked around her and tried to keep her stomach from rising. "These cows have been here for a couple of days." She turned to Tony. "Why wasn't the range checked more often?"

Tony shrugged. "Ask Morgan."

"Jeff Morgan isn't here for me to ask," Mackenzie replied sharply. "You ride this section. I'm asking you."

He shrugged again and spat. "I was busy with that damn mare."

"Watch your language with Miz Butler," Bull rumbled.

Bull and Tony eyed each other hotly until wiry little Sam Crawford rode between them. "Crosby's work," he said.

"Damn right it's Crosby's work," Keller agreed, emphasizing the point by sending a stream of tobacco splatting into the dust. "We're gonna pay that hombre a visit. He needs to learn just who he's messin' with."

"That ain't a bad idea," Crawford said.

Tony joined in. " 'Bout time we did something other than sit on our asses and let Crosby get away with this shit."

Bull simply growled.

Mackenzie clenched her teeth and gathered her courage. "You're not paying anyone a visit." With effort she kept her eyes level as the men looked at her. "Maybe if this section had been ridden every day, as it should have been, this wouldn't have happened."

Keller spat. "Mebbe. Mebbe not."

"Tony," Mackenzie continued doggedly. "You and Mr. Keller replace the salt licks on the public range that our cattle most often use. Mr. Crawford, I want you to make sure that every other section is ridden—today."

Crawford grimaced. "Yes, ma'am," he said, a touch of mockery in his voice.

"I don't want Nathan Crosby to have any other opportunities to damage the herd."

"Jesus, Mackenzie!" Tony complained. "You hire good gunhands and then you won't use them! What's the point of lettin' that . . .that asshole walk all over us?"

Bull rumbled. "Shut up, Herrera."

"It's all right, Mr. Ferguson." Mackenzie kept her voice calm. "I won't start a war over a few cows at a salt lick, Tony, especially when I can't prove anything. Now go do your job. I'll have a talk with Nathan Crosby."

"Talk. Shit!" Tony wheeled his horse and galloped off. Keller shook his head in disgust and followed.

"Go with them, please, Mr. Ferguson."

"Yes, ma'am."

Sam Crawford fell in beside her as Mackenzie kneed her horse into a trot back toward the Lazy B. "The boy has a point," he said.

Mackenzie glanced at him warily. For all his small size, Crawford was an intimidating man. He'd lost his right arm to Apache torture, and his face wore a perpetual grimace, as much from unpleasant habit as from any particular affliction. Sam was better with a gun left-handed than most men were with their right hands, and in a fight, he used his one fist with such efficiency that she'd heard the other cowboys complain that he grew two more when he needed them. Yet of the rowdy crew that worked the Lazy B, Mackenzie trusted Sam more than most, which admittedly wasn't saying much. She was disappointed to hear him take Tony's side.

"So what point do you think Tony has?" she asked, trying to be fair.

"I'll own that youngster don't often say much worth listenin' to, Miz Butler. But mind you, Crosby's been nippin' at our tails ever since I came to work for you two months ago. Even before that, I'd guess. These boys you got here don't take to being nipped at. They got itchy tempers. All this turnin' the other cheek business is makin' 'em touchy as a mean bull."

"They're taking my pay, Mr. Crawford. They'll do what I say."

Sam shrugged, a rather grotesque movement that emphasized his empty shoulder. "Yes, ma'am. But ya know a pot only boils so long before it boils over."

"I'll keep that in mind."

"Well, think I'll go take a gander at the licks down by the river. You okay headin' back alone?"

"I'm fine."

Mackenzie sighed as she watched Crawford trot away. The last few months she had felt besieged from all sides. Nathan Crosby wanted Mackenzie off her land so he could get his hands on the Lazy B's water. The man had driven a large herd of cattle into the valley three years ago and settled on land ten miles northwest of the Lazy B. They'd been amicable neighbors until the current drought had turned Nathan's greedy eyes on Dragoon Springs, one of the most reliable sources of water in the San Pedro Valley. The springs were located not on open range, but squarely on the 160-acre quarter section homesteaded by the Butler family. In the past six months Crosby had driven away her ranch hands, rustled her cattle, torn down her fences, and now he'd poisoned her stock—all for control of three little fountains of water that issued from the foothills of the Dragoon Mountains.

Finally, as if Nathan Crosby weren't enough trouble, her own hands were on the verge of open rebellion. Most of them had worked at the Lazy B for only a short time, replacements for the solid, reliable cowboys that Crosby had driven away with threats and harassment. These new men were drifters and gunhands. She'd hired them because they were fighters; right now the Lazy B needed fighters more than it needed cowboys. Men like George Keller, Sam Crawford, Spit McCullough, Skillet Mahoney, Gid Small, Bull Ferguson, and others of their ilk were the only deterrent she had to Nathan Crosby's running her over like a herd of cattle stampeding through a cornfield. They were the only reason why Crosby limited himself to "nipping at tails" instead of going for the throat.

Mackenzie knew she was sitting on a keg of gunpowder with a flaming match in her hand. She didn't want a war; she wanted to be left in peace to raise her cattle and horses, tend her garden, and watch her daughter grow. But unless Crosby backed off or she could control her own men, this valley that was so parched for water was going to be soaked with blood instead.

As she drew into the court yard, Mackenzie heard a burst of warm laughter from the house. She was in no mood that night to be social, but Thursday night always saw an extra face at their supper table—Dr. Amos Gilbert, physician and established bachelor gentleman of the town of Tombstone. Even had it not been Thursday, he would have come to help the Butlers celebrate Frankie's birthday. Amos was more family than friend, generous not only with advice and moral support, but also cash, when needed. Over the years since Frank Butler's death, Mackenzie had been forced to rely on his generosity more than once to keep the Lazy B afloat. After rubbing down her horse and settling it in the stable, Mackenzie walked wearily to the dining room.

"Well, Mackenzie." Amos settled himself before a plate of Lu's beef roast, early garden peas, steamed potatoes, and fresh-baked bread. "I'm happy to report that your boys are on the mend."

Three of the Lazy B hands had turned their Saturday night off into a saloon brawl in Tombstone—and had come off the worse for it.

"Skillet and Gid should be back in the saddle in a couple of days. Jeff Morgan's going to be laid up for at least six weeks with that broken leg, though." Doc shook his head. "Thought that one had more sense."

Frankie chimed in. "How did Uncle Jeff break his leg?"

"By acting like a fool and getting into a drunken brawl," Mackenzie explained tartly.

Frankie tilted her head thoughtfully. "Did he win?"

"No one ever wins in a brawl. If the crew put half the energy into working that they do into senseless fighting, this place wouldn't be falling apart at the seams."

Amos looked up at her tone. "Problems, Mackenzie?"

"The usual," she said, toying wearily with the food on her plate. "These men think with their trigger fingers, Amos. The only reason they stay here is that the gunfighting business has been in a slump the last few years, and I'm paying them enough to go into Tombstone every Saturday night and get drunk."

Lu shook her head sadly. "Tony is as bad as the rest of them, I know."

Mackenzie didn't remind Lu that Tony was, if anything, worse than the rest. Lu's only child, a product of an earlier marriage to a Tucson hotel owner, Tony had left home shortly after Lu had married Frank Butler. The kid had raised hell for a few years, then had come back to Lu two years ago to ask for money. Lu had taken him back, but she and Mackenzie had agreed that Tony must work for his living. Mackenzie knew that Tony thought he should be bossing the Lazy B. His mother had married Frank Butler, and in Tony's mind that made the ranch his as much as Mackenzie's. His resentment showed in every sullen word he uttered.

"Tony just needs to grow up." Mackenzie was unwilling to add to Lu's already considerable disappointment in her only child. "It's the others that worry me."

"They're dangerous men, Mackenzie." Amos's tone was grave.

"You think I don't know it? I wish I could let them go, but I can't. The law certainly isn't going to keep Nathan off my land!"

Amos shook his head. "Back a few years ago I thought if we could ever get rid of the Clantons, the McLowrys, and the Earps, Tombstone and Cochise County might turn into something besides a haven for rustlers, gamblers, gunfighters, and crooks. But those boys are long gone, and we're still left with characters like Crosby and weak-kneed law officers like Israel Potts."

"Israel's not so bad," Mackenzie commented.

"He's afraid of Crosby," Doc said.

Mackenzie grimaced. "So am I at times."

After finishing her cake, Frankie was dismissed to bed, protesting all the way that a birthday girl should be allowed to stay up however late she wished. The adults stole a few moments of relaxation while Carmelita cleared away the dishes. As they made themselves comfortable in the parlor, Mackenzie noted with amusement the silent glances exchanged between Lu and Amos. Those two were always plotting something for Mackenzie's supposed welfare. By now Lu should have realized that Mackenzie was no longer the green-as-grass girl who had come to Arizona seeing rainbows and magic where there was only danger and hard work. Now she knew that the rainbows were just empty colors in the sky, and that magic didn't exist.

"You look tired, Mackenzie," Amos began. He stoked up his pipe and permitted Lu to hold a match to the aromatic tobacco.

"Is that a medical opinion?" Mackenzie asked with a crooked smile.

"No. It's a friend's opinion."

Mackenzie could well understand why Amos was so successful as a doctor. His fatherly manner combined with his distinguished gray hair and aristocratic features tempted one to think he was right up there with God in working miracles.

"It's been a bad day," she admitted. "Everything will be all right."

"Mackenzie," Amos began with a sigh. "I understand how strongly you feel about this ranch. I know you love it. I know," he said quietly, "that your father loved it. But you're letting it grind you down. Women's votes and suffragettes aside, girl, a ranch in Arizona is no place for a woman to prove her mettle."

Mackenzie rolled her eyes. "I'm not trying to prove my mettle, Amos."

"Then why don't you consider selling the place? You could get a good price for it."

"I can't sell it. This ranch was my father's dream. After Mother went back to Boston and died, he tried to bury himself in every sort of endeavor—mining, storekeeping, freighting. But when he started this ranch he found himself again, I think." She smiled sadly. "I remember the letter he wrote me about it when I was still in Boston with Aunt Prue. He talked about it as if it were paradise. He wanted this place to be the Butler family's special place on this earth. He loved it here; he's buried here. Selling the land would be like selling a piece of my father. Besides, the Lazy B belongs to Lu as much as it does to me. And eventually it will belong to Frankie."

"Don't you think that Frankie might be happier living a comfortable life in a place—"

"Where not everyone is acquainted with the fact that she doesn't have a father?"

"That's not what I was going to say," Amos denied quietly. "But perhaps it is a consideration."

"I'm sorry, Amos. I didn't mean to bite your head off. Maybe I'm more tired than I realize." Mackenzie couldn't resent Amos's words. Of all the people in the San Pedro Valley, he was one of the few who had never raised a brow or given her a disparaging look because she had borne a child out of wedlock. He had stood up for her when the respectable ladies of St. Paul's Episcopal Church in Tombstone petitioned the priest to ban her from services, and as one of Tombstone's most respected citizens, he had done much to ensure her cordial acceptance by the town's merchants and bankers.

"Do you think Frankie is unhappy?" she asked with a concerned frown.

"No, dear. I think Frankie is happy as a mouse in a cheese bin. But in years to come she might have to deal with some awkward situations."

Mackenzie sighed.

"Mac," Amos began gently. He was the only person that Mackenzie allowed to use that nickname. Frank Butler had called her by that name. So had Frankie's father. Memories of both men were painful. "My girl," he continued, "I remember when you first came out to this country. You were anything but what your father expected from a young lady who had grown up in Boston. You were an unconventional scamp, an imp who loved everything you laid eyes on. You seemed to dance on air itself. Look at you now—with lead weights in your feet and your lovely smile all but disappeared."

"I've simply discovered that life is not a dance on air, Amos. Eventually, that's a lesson that Frankie will have to learn also." Even Mackenzie didn't care for the cynical note in her voice. "I'm sorry. Really, I appreciate your concern. But I'm not going to sell the Lazy B."

"Then at least get someone in here who can help you handle the crew and pull this place together. Mackenzie, most *men* would have trouble controlling these yahoos you've got working for you. For a woman . . ."

He left it unsaid, but Mackenzie knew what he feared was a very real danger: her crew was going to explode in her face.

"No one worth his salt will hire on here. Nathan's scared them all away."

"Well . . ." Amos took a long draw on his pipe and slowly exhaled. "I know someone who might. He's a good man, a friend of mine. Rode into town a few days ago looking for a job, and I think he might be just what you need."

Mackenzie caught another silent message between Amos and Lu. What were these two hatching?

"He's not a gunman. In fact, I don't think he's very fast with a revolver, though he's a dead shot with a rifle. But you can be sure these fellows of yours wouldn't mess with him. Or if they did once, they wouldn't twice. And he knows ranching. He's worked for years on the big places in Texas and Kansas."

"I suppose it wouldn't hurt to bring in another foreman while Jeff is laid up."

Lu snorted. "Jeff Morgan! He can't handle this crew you've put together any better than you can!"

"All right. All right! You two win," Mackenzie surrendered with a smile and a shake of her head. "Send this paragon by and I'll talk to him. Satisfied?"

She wondered at the smile the other two exchanged.

Long after Amos had departed and Lu had retired, Mackenzie lay in her bed, restlessly seeking sleep. The closeness between Lu and Amos always made her feel lonely, and loneliness never failed to call up scenes from the past to add to her melancholy mood. Unfortunately, most of them centered around the one man she'd most like to forget.

The first moment she'd seen him was fresh in her mind, even after so many years. A crisp February sky had been as blue as his eyes and the sun as bright as his hair. His strange manner of dress had caught her attention even before she noticed his rugged handsomeness. Tawny hair fell to his shoulders, held off his face by a wide cloth headband. A cotton shirt and sturdy denim trousers were unremarkable—the same sort of clothing every cowboy on the ranch wore—but instead of boots he wore calf-high moccasins with stiffened hide soles that turned up in front to protect his toes. Fresh from Boston, Mackenzie thought he was one of the most curious sights she had ever seen.

Mackenzie had sat on the low wall that surrounded the ranch house yard and watched him in the big arena next to the barn. He worked one of the new foals—a skittish little chestnut filly who danced nervous circles while he coaxed her to follow the lead rope. His movements flowed with grace and exuded a blend of strength and gentleness that would tempt any female to give him her heart. The smile he gave the foal turned Mackenzie's knees to water. If she had been that baby horse, she would have stumbled over her own long legs trying to please that man with the golden hair and gentle smile. And, in fact, that was exactly what she had done over the next months, not caring that he'd been raised by the dreaded Apaches, that almost every white man in Arizona regarded him with suspicion and contempt, that her father forbade her to make a fool of herself over him. Like the cocky, innocent child she was, she thought she knew everything.

Even now Mackenzie could feel the heady joy of his first kiss, the long-awaited declaration of love—and her angry frustration when her father fired the man she was determined to marry. She'd been so damned sure of herself—so ready to prove at any cost that she was a woman who knew her own heart.

Mackenzie turned her face into her pillow with tightly closed eyes, as if the darkness could erase the pain. She would not remember those hours of ultimate foolishness—the look of his face burnished gold and bronze by the lantern light, the feel of his hands on her shivering, untutored flesh. She would not remember.

She closed her eyes more tightly and prayed the past would leave her in peace.

The next morning, first thing after breakfast, Mackenzie rode over to Nathan Crosby's ranch. Frank Butler's Henry rifle rested in its boot by her right stirrup, and a Hamilton twelve-gauge shotgun hung from a thong looped over her saddle horn. In the past few years she had become a fair shot with both. But her most reliable protection was Bull Ferguson, who rode at her side. She wasn't fool enough to ride out alone when she was going any significant distance from the ranch. Geronimo, Natchez, Chihuahua, Mangus, and Nana had fled from the San Carlos Reservation the month before with almost fifty warriors and a hundred women and children. They raided and killed at will both north and south of the border. No less dangerous were most of the white men who roamed the territory. Tombstone wasn't the hotbed of lawlessness that it had been in the early eighties, but it was bad enough.

Crosby's ranch was a good hour's ride from the Lazy B. The time in the saddle gave Mackenzie opportunity to work up a good mad at how Nathan had been plaguing her for the last four months. She had offered him limited use of the springs, thinking that was the neighborly thing to do, but Crosby wanted unrestricted access for his huge herd. Mackenzie wasn't about to let his greediness destroy her own carefully managed range. As it was, the springs were just adequate to water her own small herd, and she had to constantly rotate her cattle between her own range and public range to avoid overgrazing.

The land they rode over was parched; the cattle were lethargic in the June heat. Sage and mesquite dotted a brown landscape where once rich grama grass had stood in waves of undulating green. This was public range, but as the largest rancher in the area, Crosby controlled a good part of it. Mackenzie could work up very little sympathy for the man. Overgrazing and bad management were as much to blame for his troubles as the drought.

Crosby himself greeted them as Mackenzie and Bull rode through the gate in the eight-foot-high adobe wall that guarded his ranch compound. With a battered hat, dusty clothes, a two-day growth of gray beard stubbling his cheeks, and an untidy paunch hanging over his belt, Nathan looked the part he liked to project—a tough old coot who didn't hold with faint hearts, fancy clothes, or soft thinking. He stood on the broad veranda that shaded three sides of his large ranch house, almost as if he were expecting her visit.

"Mornin', Mackenzie," he said in a voice like the grate of metal over unyielding stone. "What brings you out this way?"

Mackenzie swung down from her saddle and looped the reins over the hitching rail. She was ready to give Nathan a piece of her mind when seven-year-old Isabelle Crosby stepped out the front door and shyly came forward, her hands wound nervously in the skirt of her calico dress.

"Hullo, Miz Butler. Did you bring Frankie?"

"Hello, Isabelle. I'm afraid I left Frankie home today."

The two girls were great friends, and whenever they met at Sunday church they chattered like little squirrels.

"Frankie tells me you got a pony for your birthday."

"I did," the girl said solemnly. "Would you like to see her?"

"Sometime I would, dear. But I need to talk to your father right now." What a wonder that a pig like Nathan could have such a sweet child, Mackenzie thought.

"Issy, you run on, now," Crosby said to his daughter. "Ask if Martina needs help with the baking."

"Yes, Pa." She obediently ducked back inside the house.

"She's already quite a cook," Crosby told Mackenzie, granite face cracking in a faint smile. "Only seven years old. Someday she'll make some man a good wife."

His level, mocking gaze reminded Mackenzie that she herself was no man's "good wife."

"Something tells me you didn't ride all the way over here to congratulate Issy on her new pony." Crosby glanced at Bull. "Quite an impressive bodyguard you brought with you, Mackenzie. I'm glad to see you're taking to heart my warning about how dangerous this country is for a woman alone."

Mackenzie bit back a sharp retort. She had come to reason with Crosby, not fight with him. "Nathan, I've got eleven carcasses stinking up the salt lick on the open range just north of my place."

"Is that a fact?"

"That's a fact, and we both know who poisoned that block of salt."

Crosby's eyes shot up. "You accusin' me?"

"Don't be coy, Nathan. You're pushing toward something that's not going to do either of us any good. If you'd cut down on your herd and stop overgrazing the range, you wouldn't need to sabotage my ranch and try to get my water. I'm warning you that I won't put up with any more of this."

Crosby leaned nonchalantly against a pillar of the veranda. "Mackenzie, girl. You're a female, and you don't know what you're gettin' yourself into. I been ranchin' one place or another for the past forty years, and I don't need no snip of a girl to tell me what I should and shouldn't be doin'. Just 'cause you wear those trousers don't make you as tough or as smart as a man, little gal. If you was smart, you'd go back to what a woman's supposed to be doing and save yourself a heap of grief."

Mackenzie flicked her reins loose of the hitching post and swung aboard her saddle. Trying to reason with Crosby was futile. She didn't know why she even tried. A great knot of frustration twisted in her stomach. "Nathan, you've got horse crap for brains. For your sake I hope you start thinking more clearly before you push this situation too far. Come on, Bull, let's go."

As they rode out, Mackenzie felt Crosby's eyes burn holes in her back. Bull's mouth had gone slack in surprise at her unladylike words and still hung open in shock. Her prim aunt Prue had probably just turned over in her grave. The morning had certainly gotten off to a wonderful start.

They rode back to the Lazy B in silence, Mackenzie's spirits dropping with every mile. She was caught in a trap that squeezed tighter every day. One vicious jaw of the trap was Nathan Crosby, and the other, equally vicious, was her own crew. Crosby was determined to poke and prod until the crew she'd hired in her own defense exploded in her face. He didn't want a range war any more than she did, Mackenzie suspected. Nathan counted on fear to drive her off the Lazy B before a war began.

Perhaps Crosby was right. A woman wasn't tough enough to make a go of ranching in this wild country. Mackenzie thought she'd grown tough since her father's death—so tough that her sharp edges chafed even herself. She had kept the Lazy B afloat through Cochise County's most lawless years. She had walked the fine line between rustlers, gunmen, and lawmen who were just as dangerous as the men they hunted. She had fought off Apaches who had raided the ranch three times, and dodged stray bullets from the almost daily gunfights and assassinations in Tombstone. But maybe she still wasn't tough enough. How ironic that she should face defeat at the hands of an insignificant pig like Nathan Crosby. Damn him to hell. Dear Aunt Prue would simply have to continue turning in her grave, because unladylike curses were the only words that came to Mackenzie's mind when she thought about Crosby.

A flashy Appaloosa gelding was tied to the hitching rail outside the yard when they arrived back at the Lazy B. It whickered a greeting at them as they rode up.

"Visitor," Bull growled.

Mackenzie frowned, then remembered the man Amos had mentioned and promised to send by. Her heart lifted just a bit. Perhaps, by some miracle, Amos's friend was the savior she needed.

She dismounted and handed her reins to Bull. "Take my horse and rub her down, would you please, Mr. Ferguson?"

"Yes, ma'am."

Mackenzie dusted her trousers with her hands and brushed back tendrils of hair that had escaped the coiled braid of her bun. "Lu!" she called as she stepped through the gate and headed for the house.

"In the kitchen," came Lu's reply.

Mackenzie veered toward the kitchen building, which was across the dusty yard from the house. The door stood open to reveal Lu kneading bread and cheerfully talking to a man who sat astride a chair with his folded arms resting on the worktable. All Mackenzie could see of him was his back.

"I'm home," Mackenzie announccd.

"So I see." Lu's voice held a quiet tension that brought Mackenzie's senses alert.

The man stood slowly. Mackenzie could see his broad shoulders rise and fall in a deep breath.

"Is this . . .?" she began, then choked on her own words as their visitor turned.

Tawny, windblown hair held back by a wide cloth headband. Eyes the searing blue of the Arizona sky. Skin dark bronze from the hot summer sun. Body tapering from broad shoulders to the toes of dusty, knee-high moccasins. And a face as expressionless as a carved wooden Indian's.

California Smith.

2

For a moment that seemed an eternity, Mackenzie couldn't move, couldn't think, couldn't speak. Images flooded her mind. California Smith, kissing her with a guarded violence that took her breath away. California Smith, his voice firm as he swore that he loved her, his smile lazy and his body golden, lean and naked on the bed beside her. California Smith, etched against an inferno of flames, deep in conversation with a grinning savage.

The world reeled, and six years disappeared in the blink of an eye. Mackenzie once more walked through the unnaturally quiet dawn, feeling Cal's eyes follow her in that nightmare journey from the foreman's shack to the ranch house. The tenderness between her legs from the night's lovemaking was nothing compared to the pain in her heart from the morning's rejection. She'd given him everything she had, and still he was leaving. Head held resolutely high, determined to keep what little dignity she had left, she wondered how a shattered heart could still send blood thundering through her head to pound in her ears.

But the thundering had not been in her head. Memories galloped through her mind as wild as the Apaches who had appeared from nowhere to fill the yard. Roiling dust. Howling war cries. Gunfire. A savagely painted warrior waving a torch. The pungent odor of smoke mixed with dust. Frank Butler stumbling from the house, his boots in one hand, a Henry rifle in the other. Lu aiming a shotgun, and the face of an oncoming warrior dissolving in blood. The terrified screaming of horses and squeals of the hogs. Her own voice screaming Cal's name as he ran into the burning barn to free the horses. The desperate pumping of her heart as she followed.

There the nightmare drew into sharp, horrible focus. She had relived it a thousand times. Jeff Morgan's voice called her name through the choking smoke. She felt his desperate grasp on her arm as he tried to pull her out of the barn. But she resisted, watching in fascinated horror as an Apache nodded solemnly at Cal and then ran toward her, grinning. As if in a dream, the warrior passed by and disappeared. Jeff let go her arm to pursue the Indian, leaving Mackenzie gaping in confusion at Cal's silhouette etched against a backdrop of advancing flame like an image from hell. Calm blue eyes regarded her impassively.

Then came Lu's wail. And burning out of the inferno, Cal's eyes still held hers as an awful premonition told her what she would find when she followed the sounds of her stepmother's screaming.

All the images shattered, exploding into shards of red fury and catapulting her into the present. "Get me a gun!" Mackenzie commanded. She looked around frantically. "Goddammit! Where's a gun?"

"Calm down, Mackenzie." Lu came around the table and reached for her, but not before Mackenzie spotted a revolver on the sideboard. There was a loaded gun in every building of the Lazy B, in almost every room.

With strength born of hysteria, Mackenzie twisted out of Lu's grasp and lunged for the pistol. "Get away from me, Lu. Let me get that piece of snake dung in my sights." Holding the pistol in both hands, she swung it around in an arc that ended level with California Smith's heart—or where his heart should have been if he'd had one. Her own panting breath rasped in her ears. "California Smith, I'm going to shoot you full of holes unless you get off my ranch right now."

Lu gasped. "Mackenzie! Don't be an idiot!"

Mackenzie held the revolver steady, for all that her hands were cold, moist, and trembling.

"Mackenzie, put that gun down right now!" Lu demanded.

Mackenzie watched Cal unhesitatingly advance, her feelings fluctuating between fury and uncertainty. He looked so calm, almost as calm as when, smoke-stained and bloody, he'd knelt beside Frank Butler's body and listened to Jeff Morgan accuse him of sending his Indian friend to do murder as revenge for Frank's firing him. Wooden-faced as a born-and-bred-Apache, he had silently listened to Jeff's near-hysterical shouts. He'd countered with no denial, no defense—only stony calm, just as he was now with Mackenzie's pistol pointed at his chest.

Before she realized his intent, he circled her wrists with one hand, pushed her aim aside, and squeezed. The pistol fell to the plank floor. "You're not going to shoot me, Mackenzie."

Mackenzie struggled against the grip that bound her wrists like a steel manacle. "Let me go, you snake!"

He complied, and she stumbled backward against the sideboard. Eyes on the pistol, she straightened and rubbed her aching wrists.

"Forget it, Mac." He kicked the weapon toward Lu.

"Would you leave us alone for a few minutes?" Cal asked the older woman.

Lu picked up the pistol. "Think you can defend yourself?"

"Don't you dare leave me alone with this bloody-handed savage!" Mackenzie warned. "I'll kill him!"

"With your bare hands?" Cal's wooden face melted into a mocking smile. "I think her bark is worse than her bite. What do you think, Lu?"

Lu shook her head and gave him a sympathetic look. "I wouldn't discount her bite," she warned.

"I'll manage."

"If you say so."

As her stepmother turned to go, Mackenzie followed. "I'm not staying here with the man who—!" The kitchen door slammed just inches from her nose, and at almost the same moment Cal caught her arm and whirled her around. "Don't touch me!" she cried. "How dare you come back here!" She twisted from his grip and retreated out of reach. Cal stayed where he was, but his eyes followed her—measuring, assessing eyes that gave her the uncomfortable feeling that she was the one trespassing, not he. "I don't know why you're here, and I don't care. Get off my land before I call my crew to toss you off."

Cal stood silently and watched Mackenzie fume. This hadn't been a good idea, he mused. Time didn't bury hatred and bitterness; it nurtured them. He ought to know that by now. If he had the brains of a chipmunk he'd be on his horse and out of here before Mackenzie got her hands on another gun. Next time she might pluck up enough resolve to pull the trigger.

"Don't just stand there like a damned deaf tree! Get out!" She made a show of eyeing the cleaver that lay on the table.

Cal didn't recognize the sharp edge to Mackenzie's voice. Six years ago her words had always been light and musical with laughter. That wary, bruised look in her eyes was also new. More familiar was the stubborn set of her chin, the slant of green eyes, the gold highlights in her red hair. She was still beautiful, but the impish gleam was gone, squelched as firmly as the errant curl of her hair was confined in the braided coil at her nape.

Doc Gilbert and Lu Butler were right. Mackenzie needed help—perhaps in ways she scarcely realized.

"I'm here because Doc Gilbert said you needed someone to help out for a while." The truth was that Amos Gilbert had traced Cal to Texas, where Cal had been working as trail boss for the Double R herd, and had persuaded him against his better judgment to come back to the Lazy B. He had written that Mackenzie was going to lose the ranch unless something was done about Nathan Crosby. He also hinted that Mac had been pickling in her own bitterness long enough—and so had Cal.

Coming back was a fool's move, but Cal owed something to the memory of Frank Butler, who had been his friend before he'd stepped out of line with Mackenzie. And then there was Mackenzie. He admitted that he still owed Mackenzie as well.

"Amos Gilbert?" Mackenzie's eyes widened in surprise. "*You* are the man he told me of? Why that . . .that . . .interfering, low-down skunk. And Lu is in on this too, isn't she? I saw the look she gave you! She might as well have said it out loud: 'Pardon Mackenzie's rude behavior. The poor girl's just having a bad day. Please don't be offended'!

"Well, I *am* having a bad day!" She walked slowly forward, pointing at him with a finger that seemed every bit as lethal as the pistol she'd leveled at him a few minutes earlier. "You are the worst part of my day so far, and I don't see how it could get much worse. You can march back to Amos Gilbert and tell him that I don't need your help. I've had a bellyful of your help!"

Cal reached out for the pointing finger that was about to

stab into his face. Mackenzie swatted his hand away. Illogically, he retreated a step—retreated before the advance of a woman half his size who was armed only with a pointing finger and a face full of scorn. How the warriors of the Bedonkohe would laugh to see such a thing. Yet in all this harsh world, Mackenzie Butler was the only thing that had ever truly frightened California Smith, for she was the only person or thing he had permitted past his tough defensive wall. In that instant he realized that old feelings for Frank Butler and the Lazy B were not the only reason he had returned.

He halted with his back against a wall. Mackenzie stopped, even though she looked as if she'd like to stab her finger straight into his heart. She folded her finger back into her fist with the deliberation of a gunfighter holstering his pistol.

"Get off my property and out of my sight," she commanded. "Now." She turned and marched away, jerking the door open so hard it slammed against the adobe wall with a sound like a gunshot. As she headed across the yard toward the house with angry strides, Cal drew a steadying breath and followed. She stopped abruptly, swinging around to face him and nearly causing a collision. "Get off my land!"

She took a step back. Before Cal knew what was happening, her fist swung toward his face. Instinctively he dodged. Her next blow he deflected with his arm.

"Mackenzie!" The plea was two-toned, Lu's higher voice sounding alongside Cal's. The older woman ran from the house and grabbed Mackenzie's arm. Worn out by her own fury, the girl didn't resist.

"Get out of my sight, or I'll call my crew to pack you off my ranch stomach down over a saddle. I swear I will."

"Mackenzie, don't be an idiotic fool!" Lu said sharply. "We need Cal. We need a man to pull the reins in on those trigger-happy scoundrels you hired as range help. We need a man to set this place back on its feet. There's no one else who will mess with Nathan Crosby."

Mackenzie turned on Lu furiously. "You would have him here? After what he did? My father! Your husband!"

"Cal didn't kill Frank," Lu said softly. "I've never held him responsible for Frank's death."

"He might as well have killed him." Mackenzie shot a venomous look toward Cal.

"Still believe that, do you?" Cal smiled bitterly. The deed that Jeff Morgan had charged him with that day six years ago was less criminal than many others he'd been accused of. Because he'd been raised by Apaches, every white man and woman in Arizona Territory seemed to think he ate raw meat for breakfast and ripped the scalps from children for entertainment. But Morgan's accusation hurt most of all, because Mackenzie had believed it. On that bloody morning he'd put aside his gut loyalties to the Indians to defend her and her family, yet she still believed he had her father's blood on his hands. "If I was that determined to get revenge for being fired, I doubt I'd care one way or another if you lost your damned ranch."

Mackenzie gave him a wary look.

"Mackenzie, I came here because Amos said you need help, and I figure I owe you help. Frank Butler once gave me a good job when no other white man would give me the time of day. He was a decent man, and I'd hate to see all his work trampled by scum like Nathan Crosby."

Mackenzie's expression was obstinate. "I don't believe you."

"Mackenzie, this ranch is as much mine as yours," Lu reminded her. "I want you to listen to me now. We're in a fix, and we both know it. Nathan Crosby knows it. Mercy! Everyone in the valley knows it. Give Cal a chance, *niña*."

Mackenzie hesitated, then a wicked smile slowly bloomed on her face. "All right, Lu, if you're so anxious to give the skunk a chance, then we'll give him a chance. Will that satisfy you?"

Lu looked surprised. She glanced quickly at Cal. "This is for all of us, Mackenzie, not just for me. I think it's for the best."

"Good, then. He's hired. On trial."

Lu gave her stepdaughter a suspicious look.

"And you can feel perfectly safe leaving us alone to discuss the terms of his employment." Mackenzie raised a brow and jerked her head toward the house. "I promise I won't shoot him."

Lu left with obvious reluctance, and Mackenzie crossed her arms and turned her attention back to Cal. "Doc hasn't done you a favor, Smith. You won't last two days here. The Lazy B crew will have you for dinner."

Cal shrugged. "That ought to make you feel better." He gave her a wry smile.

Mackenzie bristled. "Go ahead and laugh. You might not get the chance later. Dealing with the men here is going to be a bit tougher than seducing a green girl who doesn't know crosswise from straight."

Cal shook his head and smiled. "Seduced you, did I?"

She had the grace to flush under his steady gaze.

"I think I just might make you eat those words, Mackenzie Butler."

"You won't be here long enough," she told him, but the hint of doubt in her voice made him smile.

As if sensing her advantage was eroding, Mackenzie straightened and looked him coolly in the eye. "You know where the bunkhouse is," she said. "You can put your kit there. If you can stick it out until the end of the week, you can move into the foreman's shack.

He chuckled at her grim tone. "You're certain I'm that easy to chase off?"

"You weren't that hard to chase off six years ago, Smith.

As I recall, all it took to start you running was the idea of marriage to me."

Cal had to grin as he watched Mackenzie turn and march stiffly toward the house. The kitten of six years ago had grown into a she-lion, and he was likely to get clawed but good before this was over.

The sun had set before Cal returned from Tombstone, where he'd gathered his things and settled his hotel bill. His possessions consisted of two blankets, an extra pair of moccasins, two changes of clothes, a comb, and a small antelope-skin "medicine bag" that his Apache father had given him the day he had left the Bedonkohe with General Howard, fourteen long years ago. The bag contained Hoddentin, sacred meal used for morning and evening sacrifice to the sun. His father had also included a small piece of lightning-charred wood and a crystal of quartz the size of Cal's little fingernail. The amulets were supposed to protect him from harm, both from earthly weapons and evil spirits. Cal didn't believe in such things anymore, but before he had left his hotel room, he had hung the bag around his neck just the same and wondered if anything in it would protect him from a bad-tempered woman who was testy as a wounded bear about a host of things she little understood.

Cal admitted that Mackenzie had a right to be bitter. He, too, bore wounds from that tragic morning. She couldn't know how hard it had been to leave her after a night of lying in her arms. The reality that innocent, openhearted Mackenzie could never be happy as the wife of the despised "yellow-haired Apache" was the toughest thing he'd ever had to face. The night before, with passion thundering through his veins, convincing himself that the two of them could make a life together had been easy. But the clear light of dawn had brought the real world back into focus. A woman like Mackenzie needed a man who could protect her from life's cruelties—not a man whose only possessions were a razor and an extra pair of moccasins. Even his name wasn't his own, but a concoction of the Army troop who'd "rescued" him from the Apaches.

When he'd told her he was leaving, the pain in her eyes had nearly torn the heart from him. Bloody hours later, after the Apache raid had decimated the ranch and left her father dead, Mac had grasped at Jeff's accusations as an excuse to hate him—and he'd let her. He'd owed her the chance to hate him as much as he hated himself right then.

When Cal arrived back at the Lazy B, the air smelled of dust, mesquite smoke, and fried chiles. Windows in the ranch house, bunkhouse, and foreman's shack glowed with yellow lamplight, and from the bunkhouse came the tinny wail of a harmonica punctuated by gusts of raucous laughter. He found an empty stall in the barn to stable his big Appaloosa gelding, hefted his saddlebags and spare blankets over his shoulder, and headed for the bunkhouse.

When he walked through the door the harmonica trailed off into a discordant whine. The men playing cards at the table stopped their conversation and looked up. A bewhiskered gent lounging in his bunk put down the piece of wood he whittled and warily wiped the blade of his knife on his trousers. Another glanced up from hammering the sole of a boot, missed the boot, and landed the next blow on his own shin.

"Shit!" He hurled the offending hammer to the floor.

The small commotion broke the momentary silence. One of the cardplayers, tall and lean, with dirty gray stubble on his chin matching the equally gray stubble on his scalp, got to his feet and stuck his thumbs in his belt. "Who might this be?" he drawled.

Cal slung his kit into the nearest empty bunk. "This might be your new foreman," he drawled back.

The man's eyes narrowed. "Do tell. Seems to me we already got a foreman. With a broke leg."

"Then I'd say you need another one. Got any objections?" Cal inquired, though he already knew the answer.

The rest of the Lazy B hands settled back and watched with enjoyment as their spokesman eyed the newcomer scornfully. "What's your name, Mr. Foreman?"

"California Smith."

"California Smith. I heard a ya." He spat a good-sized wad of tobacco juice into a spittoon beside the table, then looked pointedly at Cal's shoulder-length hair and dusty moccasins. "You're the fella who lived with the Apaches when he was a kid, ain't ya?"

"That's right."

"Well, I'm George Keller, and I don't much cotton to Apaches or them what has truck with 'em. In that getup ya look more Injun than white to me. Betcha like to eat dog meat for dinner, huh?"

The audience laughed, and Keller warmed to his subject. "Ya know, I always figgered Apache bucks like horses better'n wimmen. Course, lookin' at an Apache squaw, who could blame 'em? Tell me, Smith, do Apache bucks mount their squaws from the back, like a stud horse? Is that the way your Apache daddy taught you to stick it to a squaw—so's you wouldn't have ter see 'er face?"

Keller's guffaws joined the general laughter. Cal's gaze didn't flinch as he assessed the snickering hands one by one. One by one they looked at his hard, impassive face, felt the weight of his glittering blue eyes, and stopped laughing.

Keller was the last to fall silent. He stepped forward and walked a wide circle around Cal, grinning as he examined the newcomer from every angle. "Ya know, Smith? I don't much like cowpokin'. I'm a gunhand by trade. I don't like workin' fer no uppity woman, neither. But what the hell. I need the money, and Miz Butler's money is as good as anybody else's." His circle completed, Keller leaned back against the table and regarded Cal with eyes full of malice. "I'll tell ya where I draw the line, though, Smith. I draw the line at takin' orders from a goddamned Apache. And every man here feels the same. That right, boys?"

The hands rumbled cautious assent.

Cal replied calmly. "I figured we'd have to fight about it."

The scene was always the same, no matter where he went. Cal was accustomed to the white man's hatred. For years it had pressed in upon him like a solid wall—from all directions, wherever he went. The whites would never forgive him the sin of being raised by Apaches. The white people of Arizona Territory hated anything that was Apache—even if it had yellow hair and blue eyes.

"You going to be the first?" Cal asked Keller with expressionless calm.

"Reckon I will be."

The hands eagerly shoved back the table and benches and hooted encouragement to their leader. Cal and Keller circled warily, each looking for an opening in the other's defense. Keller made the first strike, jabbing at Cal's middle with a vicious uppercut of his fist. Cal sidestepped and slammed his fist into Keller's jaw. Keller recovered quickly, landing a blow to Cal's head. He paid for it by tripping over Cal's outstretched foot.

Cal dove for his adversary even before Keller hit the floor. From that point Cal had the advantage, because no one could outtwist, outmuscle, or outlast an Apache in wrestling. Keller struggled to land a blow in defense, but his arms were too busy fending off the grips that threatened to pin him to the floor and make him helpless against whatever nastiness Cal might intend. The older man struggled against certain defeat—until he managed to free a knife from its sheath inside his boot.

The onlookers roared approval as the wicked-looking

blade caught the lantern light and curved in a gleaming arc toward Cal's back. But Cal twisted; his hand sliced at Keller's wrist. Suddenly the knife was Cal's, and Keller lay impotently trying to break the strength of the newcomer's hold.

Cal sat on the downed man's chest and brought the blade to where Keller could watch his own panting breath fog its gleaming surface. The onlookers took a collective breath, not moving for fear of what that knife could do to Keller before they could pull Smith from his body.

"The Apaches taught me to fight man to man," Cal told Keller. "And when an enemy fights with honor, an Apache allows him honor in defeat." He grabbed the short stubble of Keller's hair. Keller mouthed a wordless plea, and his eyes grew wide as Cal grinned. "But I learned to fight dirty from the U.S. Cavalry." He slammed Keller's head against the plank floor with a satisfying thunk. Keller's eyes rolled back in their sockets.

Cal got to his feet and tossed the knife on the bunk beside his kit. "Spoils of war," he explained to the silent hands. "Who's next?"

For a moment uneasy silence reigned. Then a man with a tobacco-stained beard and bowed legs stepped out of the group.

"Name's Spit McCullough," he said to Cal. "I don't care much who gives the orders, 'slong as I get paid. But I reckon I owe it to ol' Keller there to take you down a peg or two, Smith. Keller's got me out of a bad scrape or two. Cain't jest let 'im lie there and not try to make good for 'im."

"Suit yourself," Cal said.

Spit didn't have a knife or the power of Keller's punch. But he was fast. Before Cal knew what had happened, a roundhouse swing caught him full in the face. He retaliated with a fist to Spit's hard middle and an uppercut to his chin. Spit coughed and staggered, but came back with a charge like a bull, head lowered and legs pumping. He drove Cal back against the wall with a force that sent black spots swimming before Cal's eyes.

The audience hooted in appreciation, expecting Cal to slide down the wall into a limp heap, as had other men who'd been unfortunate enough to be on the receiving end of Spit McCullough's famous "mad bull charge," but Cal merely shook his head and lunged forward with a series of punches that made Spit stagger. The fight degenerated into a punching match until Cal landed a well-aimed fist alongside McCullough's temple. Spit swayed a moment, then fell flat.

Breathing hard, Cal surveyed the hands grimly. "Anyone else want to try?"

A few feet shuffled. No one met his eyes. Then Tony Herrera pounded a fist on the table.

"What the hell are we doin'?" he challenged his comrades. "Smith's *one* man, for Chrissakes! You want to take him out? Let's take him on all at once!"

The hands shifted uneasily.

"Come on! Bull! Sam!" He scowled at their inaction. "Gid. Harve? Shit! Goddamned yellowbellies!

Sam Crawford turned his perpetual grimace Tony's way. "Don't get yer spit up over nuthin', boy. The man's earned his place—for now. Let 'im be."

Tony looked at them one by one, seeing the retreat in each face. He turned his scowl back toward Cal. "Let the goddamned Apache be?" he snarled. "Like hell!"

Cal braced himself as Tony lunged.

Mackenzie toyed with her supper. Carmelita's special enchiladas—usually Mackenzie's favorite—tasted like cardboard, the refried beans like paste, although Lu and Frankie were certainly doing justice to the meal. But Mackenzie's insides were twisted so tightly that the very sight of food made her ill.

"What's wrong, Ma?" Frankie asked. The girl eyed Mackenzie's plate. "If you're not gonna eat your beans, can I have 'em?"

"Nothing's wrong, Frankie. I'm *fine*," she declared with more than necessary emphasis. "And no, you may not have my beans. You've already eaten so much, you're bound to explode at any minute."

"No I won't explode!"

Frankie's happy giggle was usually balm for the worst of Mackenzie's moods, but tonight it didn't do the job. Neither did the faint notes of Carmelita singing in the kitchen building. Any sign of happiness grated across her inflamed nerves and sent her spirits plunging to even blacker depths.

"If I can't have your beans, can I have dessert?"

Mackenzie made an effort to smile. "Yes. I suppose. Run out to the kitchen and ask Carmelita to give you a treat. Ask nicely."

"Yes, ma'am!"

Mackenzie watched her daughter bounce out of the dining room, then met Lu's disapproving gaze with flashing eyes. "What do you want me to do? Take her out and introduce her to her father? Then tell her that her father was responsible for her grandfather's murder?"

"California Smith did not murder your father, Mackenzie."

"Not with his own hand. But he stood by and let him be murdered by the savages *he* calls friends and brothers."

"You don't really believe that," Lu said with quiet certainty.

Mackenzie had certainly believed it six years ago when kneeling over her father's bullet-torn body, when the image of Cal chatting with a savage was fresh in her mind's eye—and the pain of his rejection still raw in her heart. There had been that, too, she admitted. Cal's guilt had fit perfectly with the nightmare that had so suddenly descended upon her. Now, after so much time had passed, Mackenzie no longer knew what she believed. She closed her eyes, visualizing that morning just as she'd done hundreds of times before, trying desperately to pluck truth from confusion. She remembered waking up in Cal's arms, their bodies fitted closely together against the morning chill, bare flesh gleaming in the faint dawn light streaming through the window of the foreman's shack. Her memories were exquisite in their detail. She turned toward him. Crisp hair tickled her cheek when she pillowed her head upon his chest. Her hand slid over the hard muscle of his stomach. He clasped her gently, but other than that, she got no response. She could feel the tension in his body and sense the wariness of his mood.

Even as they lay together in naked, intimate entanglement he had planned his getaway. She had given him her heart and soul; he had wanted only her body, and that only for a night. Still, she might have continued to foolishly love him if he hadn't shown his true colors during the Apache raid.

Mackenzie opened her eyes on the present, on Lu watching her sadly from across the table, on her daughter—Cal Smith's daughter—skipping through the pantry door and setting a plate of fried and sugared tortillas on the table. With a flash of insight she suddenly knew that some illogical part of her still cherished that magical night with California Smith, even knowing what came after. The frustrated romantic in her still remembered the miracle of how he'd made her feel. Would the magic he'd woven around her in the past reach across the years and make her vulnerable once again? She couldn't allow it. He'd hornswaggled Amos and Lu; he wouldn't do the same to her. Not this time.

"You want one of these, Gran? Ma?" Frankie asked, her mouth full of sugared treats.

"Frances Sophia, you're going to rot your teeth!" Lu began. "I don't know why your mother . . ." Lu's scolding trailed away as the sound of faint shouts drifted to their ears.

Mackenzie got up and grabbed the Hamilton twelve-gauge

that was propped against the wall in the corner. "Stay here," she told Lu and Frankie. "I'll see what's going on."

Shouts were still coming from the bunkhouse as Mackenzie hurried across the stretch of dirt that separated the house from the ranch buildings. The night was moonless, and the stars gave just enough light for Mackenzie to see Tony Herrera catapult from the bunkhouse door and slide a considerable distance on his backside to land practically at her feet. Cal hurtled out after him and halted as Tony struggled to his feet, staggered a few steps toward Cal, then sank to the ground in a limp heap.

"What the . . .! What is going on here?" Mackenzie demanded furiously.

Cal ran his fingers through his tangled hair and grinned. "I figure you know what's going on, Mackenzie."

He looked a bit the worse for wear. Mackenzie tried to find satisfaction in his bruises and swelling eye, but found only a prick of guilt. Her prediction that the hands would have him for dinner had come uncomfortably close to the truth. She marched over to the bunkhouse door and looked in. George Keller was picking himself up off the floor gingerly—and Spit McCullough was flat on his back with a trickle of blood running from the corner of his mouth into his shaggy hair. Mackenzie promptly lost all sympathy for Cal. Her rowdy hands might have taken a few bites out of his hide, but it looked as though he'd made mincemeat of them.

Bull and Sam both shrugged when subjected to Mackenzie's indignant glare; the others simply looked sheepish. With rapidly building vexation, she turned on her heel and almost collided with Cal, who had silently moved to stand behind her. Stifling the urge to jump back, she whispered scathingly, "The foreman's job is to control them! Not kill them!"

Cal's grin fanned the fires of her anger.

"We'll just see if you're still grinning like a jackass by the end of the week!"

Cal's eyes crinkled in silent laughter as he watched Mackenzie stalk toward the house. "And good night to you also, Miss Butler," he said softly.

3

The next morning dawned with a bloodred sky that was a fit reflection for Mackenzie's mood. She emerged from her bedroom with shadowed eyes in a pale face. Walking past the inner court's flower garden without her usual greeting to the gladiolas and sweet peas, she marched through double doors into the dining room, where Lu and Frankie were already seated at the big oak table.

"Do I have to eat this?" Frankie said in greeting. She spooned up a doughy mass of oatmeal to show her mother.

"You do," Mackenzie answered tersely.

"Yuk!"

"Put some sugar and milk on it; it'll taste better."

"The milk's sour." Frankie made a face.

"Then ask Carmelita for some fresh."

Carmelita bustled through the pantry door, a cheerful smile lighting up her plump brown face. "Good morning, senorita!"

Good morning, indeed! Mackenzie mused bitterly. "Carmelita, is there any milk fresher than what's in the pitcher?"

"*Si.*" She picked up the pitcher, sniffed at the contents, and made a face. "I will get some."

"And Carmelita?" Mackenzie sighed. "There's one additional mouth to feed in the bunkhouse this morning."

"*Si.*" The Mexican woman's face lit with a grin. "Senor California is back!" She rolled her eyes expressively. "He is still very handsome hombre! No more boy! Now he is all man, *si*?"

Mackenzie pulled out her chair so that it scraped across the floor with a grating squeal. "He's only here for a few days, so don't get all soupy about it." Even six years ago Carmelita had been ecstatic over California Smith. Mackenzie remembered feeling quite jealous at the time. Now the woman's attitude was simply irritating. The only interest Mackenzie had in the man was getting rid of him.

Carmelita put on a sober face and went back into the pantry. As Mackenzie sat down and poured herself a cup of coffee, Lu raised a brow in her direction. "A few days?"

"I'd be surprised if he lasts that long. The men don't like him."

"The men don't like anything they can't eat, drink, shoot, or beat up. Of course"—she raised a brow—"you wouldn't consider making it easier for him by backing up his authority."

Mackenzie simply studied the glob of oatmeal she'd dished up for herself.

"You're hardly giving him a fair chance, Mackenzie."

"I don't especially want to give him a fair chance. I'm surprised I let you talk me into giving him a chance at all." Mackenzie felt a surge of renewed anger as a vision of her father's face flashed through her mind. Where had been the fairness in his murder? Where had been the fairness in California Smith aiding, perhaps even inciting, the savages who had slaughtered him? "Don't defend the man to me!"

"We need him, Mackenzie. Would you sacrifice this ranch because of a six-year-old grudge—a grudge based on nothing other than wild conjecture?"

"I saw him talking to that Apache just before the Indian ran out of the barn with a bloodthirsty grin on his face."

"Did you understand what they said to each other?"

Frankie's bright eyes moved back and forth between Mackenzie and Lu. "Who's California Smith?" she asked.

"He's—"

"No one you need to know." Mackenzie cut Lu off with a glare. "He's a new hand."

"Carmelita knows him? He must be handsome, 'cause Carmelita gets soupy and giggles when she talks about him." Frankie ended her sentence with a sneeze, then grinned.

"Use your hankie, not your napkin," Lu instructed as the little girl wiped her nose.

"I don't have a hankie."

"Then go fetch one." Mackenzie told her.

Frankie slid off her chair and ran into the court.

"I don't want to talk about Cal around Frankie. There's no sense in getting her curiosity up."

"He's her father," Lu reminded Mackenzie.

"Something I'd like to forget. And something she doesn't need to know. Frankie's just fine thinking her father is dead." She spooned her oatmeal with a vengeance.

"You think Cal's not going to know when he sees her? She's his very image."

"He won't see her."

Lu sniffed in disbelief. Frankie ran back into the room, hankie in hand.

"Don't wave it in the air like a flag," Mackenzie admonished. "Wipe your nose with it."

"I already wiped my nose on my napkin."

Mackenzie sighed. Frankie obligingly sneezed again and wiped her nose on the handkerchief.

"Do you have a chill?" Mackenzie asked in a calculating tone.

"My nose just tickles."

"You have a chill," Mackenzie decided. "I think you'd better stay indoors for a few days."

"No!" Frankie wailed. She plunked her spoon angrily into her cereal. "I don't have a chill!"

"I don't want you to take sick. You can stay in for a little while."

"No!"

"Don't use that tone with me, young lady!"

"You're not fair!"

"Life isn't fair!" Mackenzie snapped. First Lu. Now Frankie.

"You'll have to forgive your mother," Lu told Frankie. "She's not feeling well today."

"Well, *I* feel fine!" Frankie insisted.

"Your mother's only thinking of your own good. She's right. Stay in for a few days and that nasty sneeze will go away."

The sneeze would go away. Mackenzie could only hope that California Smith would go away as well.

Mackenzie's day did not improve when she finished her oatmeal, toast, and coffee and walked to the arena to watch the daily morning ritual of Tony working the wild mare. The red dawn had faded into a warm, blue sky, but Mackenzie's mood hadn't made a similar transformation.

Sam Crawford and Spit McCullough, his face black and blue, leaned on the arena fence watching the show. Jeff Morgan, crutch under one arm and broken leg held carefully off the ground, also awaited her. She greeted him warmly. This morning was the first she'd seen of him since she'd helped Amos set his leg.

"Are you feeling better?" she asked him.

He grimaced, appearing to be in much the same mood as she was. "What happened to Spit's face?"

"A fight in the bunkhouse."

"Sounds like I'd better get back on the job."

Mackenzie refrained from reminding him that even without a broken leg he'd had little success in controlling the Lazy B crew.

Sam Crawford ambled over. "Bull and George are out ridin' fence, Miz Butler. Spit and me, we're gonna take the rest of the boys over to the south horse pasture and cut out the two-year-olds to deliver on that Army contract. But first we figgered to stick around to see Tony break his fool neck with that mare."

"If Tony can't ride her," Mackenzie speculated, "I don't imagine anyone can." Tony was a troublemaker and hothead, but he had a way with horses.

This particular horse seemed to be the exception, however. As Tony stalked the mare around the arena, she stayed just out of his reach. Every time he raised his rope, her nostrils dilated and her ears flattened against her head in angry warning. Several times she charged, and Tony dove out of her way just in time to avoid injury.

After ten minutes of this fruitless game, Tony headed for the side of the arena, slapping the coiled rope against his leg in angry impatience. The moment he turned his back, the mare gave a whicker of satisfaction and tossed her head in triumph. Mackenzie smiled wryly at the mare's antics. She herself often felt the same way after a disagreement with Lu's son.

"I've had about enough of this," Tony said to Mackenzie over the fence. "I know you wanted to break the mare gentle, but she's not gonna have it. Let Sam and Spit get in here with a couple of ropes and we'll tie her to the snubbing post. That'll fix her." He gave Jeff a brief nod. "Mornin'."

Mackenzie sighed. Tony was right. The mare wasn't responding to kindness, and she was too valuable to turn loose. "You be careful," Mackenzie warned. "I don't want anyone hurt."

"You worried about me or the mare?" Tony returned.

"Looks like somebody already used your face as a sledgehammer," Jeff commented with a grin.

Tony gave him a sour look and turned away.

"Another fight?" Jeff asked.

"Same one," Mackenzie said.

"Spit and Tony?"

"And George Keller and . . .a new hand."

"Must have been quite a welcoming party."

Mackenzie kept her face expressionless. "I guess so."

Spit, Sam, and Tony moved in on the horse from three sides, just as they did when they had to drive her back to the pasture. This time, though, she wasn't headed for a rest—she was headed for a showdown. The mare tossed her head and snorted. She whirled, but her escape was cut off on every side. Tony tossed his rope, looping it around her head and cinching it tight. Sam's rope followed, and Spit lassoed her from the third direction.

"That's what happens when you get stubborn," Tony gloated as the three men maneuvered the horse toward the snubbing post at the far end of the arena. The mare squealed and attempted to rear, striking out with her front legs. The men deftly avoided the slashing hooves and forced her up against the post, tying her so securely that only her hindquarters could move. She kicked out futilely, snorting with frustration.

"Gotcha now!" Tony told the mare. "Spit. Bring me the saddle that's over there on the rail."

"This is gonna be sumpthin'!" Sam Crawford chortled.

The mare squealed in anger when Tony lifted the saddle

onto her back and jerked the cinch tight. " 'Bout time you learned some manners," he told her with a triumphant smile.

Grabbing the bridle, Tony forced the steel bit to the back of the mare's mouth and yanked down hard.

Mackenzie felt uneasy as she watched the horse's struggles.

"Wouldn't wanna be that horse," Jeff said. "Ol' Tony's got a temper."

"That mare's got a temper, too," Mackenzie replied.

Tony swung aboard, settled firmly down in the saddle, and signaled Spit and Sam to ease the ropes from the mare's head. As soon as the mare felt the release of tension she exploded into action. She launched herself into the air, twisted, and came down hard on all fours.

"Yee-haaa!" Sam shouted.

The mare crowhopped, bucked, reared, and twisted. Although his hat flew off his head, Tony held on, grim-faced and silent. Sam and Spit scrabbled out of the way to avoid being trampled.

"Tony! Don't use your spurs!" Mackenzie called out. "Darn him anyway! How does he expect to settle her down if he's raking her sides!"

"Like I said," Jeff reminded her, "the boy's got a temper."

"Well, he's not going to use it on that mare!"

Heedless of danger, Mackenzie ducked between the fence rails to put an end to the contest just as the mare accomplished the job for her. With a squeal, the horse rose up on rear legs and pawed at the air.

"She's going over!" Sam shouted. "Jump, Tony!"

Tony cursed and launched himself out of the saddle only seconds before the mare lost her balance and tumbled backward. He rolled as he hit the ground, narrowly avoiding the mare as she crashed to earth on the very spot he had landed. Her thrashing hooves caught him a glancing blow on the back as he scrambled out of the way.

"Damned vicious she-bitch of a killer horse! I oughta get a gun and fix you good. Somebody get me a gun, dammit!"

Mackenzie beat Sam and Spit to Tony. She offered her hand to help him up, but he was too busy cursing to notice. "Are you hurt?" she demanded.

"Goddammit to hell, of course I'm hurt! I'm gonna get a gun and . . ."

His cursing was too voluble for him to really be hurt, Mackenzie decided with relief. She turned her attention to the mare, who had struggled to her feet. Her sides heaving, she held a front leg off the ground. Foam flecked her neck and flanks, where it was pinkened by the bloody stripes inflicted by Tony's spurs. The saddle cinch had loosened and the saddle had slipped beneath her now swollen belly. Mackenzie's heart ached in sympathy. She heartily regretted giving in to Tony's advice.

Spit advanced toward the mare, rope in hand. She threw her head up, eyes wide. Still favoring one leg, she shied away. Her hindquarters slammed in to the arena fence. Squealing in panic, she plunged forward and scattered her would-be captors in a rush.

Sam drew his pistol. "Her leg's broke. Ain't nothing to do but shoot her."

Mackenzie grabbed his wrist. "Don't you dare, Mr. Crawford! It might be just sore or sprained."

"She's a killer," Tony growled. "Go ahead and shoot her."

Mackenzie whirled to face him. "I give the orders here!"

"What's going on?" A new voice entered the fray.

Mackenzie's heart jumped. She had refrained earlier from asking the men where Cal was, as if he might disappear if she didn't mention him. She'd hoped that by some stroke of good fortune he'd seen the folly of staying where he wasn't wanted and lit out for friendlier territory. No such luck, apparently. Steeling herself, she turned to face California. He stood straight and tall in his damned Apache moccasins and headband, his hair the same sunlit tawny gold that had caught her attention when she'd first seen him in this very arena six years ago. He, too, bore a few marks from the night's altercation, Mackenzie noted.

Sam and Spit eyed Cal warily, while Tony regarded him with open hostility. Still propped against the fence twenty feet away, Jeff stared in Cal's direction. Mackenzie wasn't looking forward to explaining the situation to Jeff when he recognized the newcomer, and of course he would recognize him when he saw him up close. Who could forget that shoulder-length tawny hair and those crystal-blue eyes?

"Ain't nuthin' to concern our new *foreman*." Spit punctuated the last word with the well-aimed stream of tobacco juice that had earned him his name.

A wicked idea suddenly raised Mackenzie's spirits as Spit and Cal exchanged measuring looks. "Mr. Smith, maybe you would like to try your hand at settling her down." She nodded toward the mare. "She's hurt herself . . ."

"And damned near killed me!" Tony interjected.

" . . .and we can't help her because she's in a panic," Mackenzie finished, a challenge in her voice.

Cal eyed the mare and Mackenzie both. The wooden expression didn't soften.

"What did you do to her?" he asked.

"Tried to ride her like a horse should be rid!" Tony answered belligerently. "Mackenzie, gimme a gun and I'll take care of the problem."

Mackenzie wasn't sure which problem Tony meant to take care of—the mare or the new foreman. She certainly didn't want him shooting her mare. "Go ask Lu for some salve for those bruises, Tony."

"Crap!"

Cal ignored the argument. Slowly he walked toward the mare as Spit, Sam and Mackenzie perched themselves on the fence to watch. Sullenly, Tony climbed through the fence and stood a good distance away from them. One part of Mackenzie wanted Cal to fail, to see the mare kick the stuffings out of him. Another part was frightened for both him and the mare.

Jeff hobbled indignantly over to where Mackenzie sat. "Is that who I think it is? And if it is, what in dagblasted hell is he doing on the Lazy B and still standing on his two feet? Mackenzie, you've—"

"I'll explain in a moment," she said, her eyes glued on what had become a staring contest between man and horse.

"Did Spit call him foreman? Have you—"

"Hush, Jeff. Later."

The mare shied away when Cal was about five feet away from her.

"You should be able to do better than that!" Spit shouted. "Ain't you Apache boys supposed to be half horse?"

Cal's eyes never left the mare. His face, wooden only moments before, had softened with a gentle smile. She remembered that smile. Long ago he had used the same smile on her when she was stubborn or argumentative.

"They oughta be half horse," Sam joined in. "Or half mule. They eat enough of 'em."

"Hell!" Spit continued. "Those Injuns screw 'em, too. That horse is a damn sight prettier 'n most squaws I've seen."

Jeff scowled. "Watch your language, boys."

"Shit! Miz Butler's heard worse."

"I said—"

"You wanna make somethin' of it, Morgan?" Spit always ready for a fight, balled his fists.

"Don't you have enough black and blue on your face?" Jeff shot back.

Mackenzie snapped. "Cut it out, you two. Sam, you and Spit take the men and go bring in those two-year-olds. Now."

Jeff was ominously silent as the two men left.

Mackenzie turned her attention back to the corral. Cal was talking to the horse in strange, soft words that Mackenzie couldn't understand. Maybe the mare did. She laid back her ears, then pricked them up and forward. Cal stretched out his hand. The mare snorted in alarm and arched her neck warily.

Mackenzie felt as if she'd flown back in time. The first time she had seen Cal he had been working with a horse in this same arena. She'd watched him charm a skittish little filly, much as he was now charming this frightened mare. At the time she'd thought his gentle wooing of the little creature's trust was one of the most beautiful things she'd ever seen. How gullible she had been! Gullible and naive!

The mare retreated as Cal moved slowly toward her. Keeping his hand outstretched, he didn't rush. Slowly he backed her into a corner where her sides were blocked, stopping before she backed into the fence. She had nowhere to go except forward.

Cal's hushed Apache words fell softly on Mackenzie's ears. His voice wove a seductive spell—so potent in its magic that it summoned memories of a night long ago, when he'd been so patient with her shyness, so gentle in his restraint, and finally, when passion took them beyond gentleness, so beautifully loving in the strength of his desire. How could she have known that the gentleness and patience were a mask for a savage heart?

Her reflections skidded to a sharp halt as she realized where they led. She should remember that romance was a fantasy and stupid delusions led to disaster.

The mare whickered plaintively and stretched out her nose. Ever so gently Cal took hold of the bridle and, still murmuring to the horse, ran his hand along her foam-flecked neck, over her trembling shoulder, and down the injured leg.

"It's not broken," he called to Mackenzie.

Still holding the bridle, he examined the mare for other injuries, stopping at the wounds inflicted by Tony's spurs. The mare laid back her ears and switched her tail.

"She's in foal, I think."

No wonder she fought so for her freedom, Mackenzie thought with sudden sympathy.

"I'll put her in a stall and poultice that leg," Cal said. "It should be better in a few days."

Mackenzie watched as Cal worked with slow deliberation to free the mare from the cockeyed saddle. She felt the angry heat of Jeff Morgan's eyes.

"He's only here to help while you're laid up," she explained, not looking Jeff's way.

"I can't believe you would take him back!"

"I'm not exactly taking him back. Amos Gilbert sent him, and Lu wants me to give him a chance."

"After what he did? Jesus, Mackenzie! He shoulda been swinging from the nearest tree the morning of the raid. You and I both saw him talking with that Apache!"

"Nobody knows for sure that Cal had anything to do with the raid, or Pa's death." She tried Lu's arguments on for size, and found that the words did sound reasonable, even though she herself was reluctant to believe them.

"We both know better!" Jeff declared. "I should've shot the yellow-haired savage when I had the chance."

Mackenzie jumped down from the fence and met Jeff's angry gaze. She couldn't tell him that it wasn't his business. Jeff had been on the Lazy B longer than she'd been. Her father had made him foreman when he'd fired Cal. He'd been a good and loyal friend; he had a right to be angry.

"Look, Jeff. I don't like this any more than you do, but Lu wants him here. This is her ranch as much as it is mine—more, maybe. To tell the truth, we need *someone* who can control these men, because I can't, and you're no good to me hobbling around on a crutch."

"There's other men you could hire!"

"No there's not. Crosby's got everyone thinking we're about to go under, Jeff. No one worth a plugged nickel will work here.

"And why do you suppose Smith will?" Jeff asked sourly.

"Maybe he gets a kick out of me having to take him back."

"Or maybe he's after something else. He was mighty sweet on you. Maybe he still is."

Mackenzie didn't bother to tell Jeff that he needn't worry about Cal's pursuing her. She had served herself to him on a silver platter six years ago and he'd declined the offer.

"If he makes a move toward you, I'll kill him."

"Don't be an idiot," she said sharply. "He's not coming anywhere near me, and if he did, it would be my responsibility to take care of the situation. You're not my keeper, Jeff. I can take care of myself."

"Don't trust him, Mackenzie. You'll be sorry if you do."

The contempt in Jeff's voice was laced with fear. Jeff was afraid of Cal also, just like everyone else. "Go rest your leg," she said in a more conciliatory tone. "I need you back on your feet again so I can get rid of California Smith."

Jeff's mouth drew into a tight, sullen line as he withdrew into silence. Turning stiffly, he hobbled back toward the foreman's shack. Mackenzie looked toward Cal, only to find his eyes were on her, not the mare. She wondered if his sharp, Apache-trained ears had picked up their low-voiced argument.

"I'll get a stall ready to restrain her. She should be all right here for a few minutes."

Mackenzie didn't answer. She watched as he looped the bridle over one shoulder, hefted the saddle over the other, and headed through the big double doors into the barn. The mare's gaze followed him until he disappeared, then swung around to rest nervously upon Mackenzie.

Mackenzie returned the mare's look with a scowl. "Like him, do you?" she asked sharply. "If you do, you're a fool."

The rest of the week went no more smoothly as far as Mackenzie was concerned. She was at cross-purposes with herself; even though she wanted Cal gone, she recognized the need for him to stay. But his presence dredged up memories that Mackenzie had almost succeeded in burying. Every place on the ranch suddenly became a reminder of something they had shared—the arena where he had spent so many mornings teaching her to ride; the barn where she'd first lured him into kissing her; the foreman's shack, where she had surrendered her innocence, where he had lain with her the next dawn while his savage brothers prepared to attack; the ranch yard, where her father had bled out his life and Cal had answered Jeff Morgan's charges with cold, proud silence. The memories hurt. They reminded her of her own foolishness, of a bright future that had turned to blood and ashes, of a lively, imprudent girl who had become a woman all too fast. They distracted her during the day and invaded her dreams at night. Every morning she woke with a twinge of guilt that the man who bore responsibility for Frank Butler's death was on the Lazy B and still alive.

Why had he come back? Mackenzie wondered almost every hour, and why did he insist on staying? Once, when her father had warned her that Cal was a loner set apart from society, Mackenzie had foolishly boasted that she understood the man. She'd been sadly wrong. Cal was an enigma, and his heart was as hidden as that of a statue carved from stone. He'd been molded by a people she had learned to fear and by forces she didn't understand.

One possible motive for Cal's return frightened Mackenzie more than any other—the possibility that Amos Gilbert, in his well-meaning meddling, had told Cal about Frankie. Would a man like California Smith care that he'd fathered a child? Would he want that child, perhaps? The very idea gave Mackenzie nightmares. Somehow she had to get rid of him before he could come face-to-face with the daughter he'd sired.

Mackenzie made sure the rest of the week sorely tried Cal's patience. By midweek the Lazy B crew rumbled resentfully about the long shifts and hard work. Part of the crew—Sam Crawford, Bill Darnell, Skillet Mahoney, Bull Ferguson, Gid Small, and George Keller—spent three days dawn to sundown riding fences, checking salt licks, and inspecting watering ponds to ensure that Nathan Crosby would have no more opportunity to damage the Lazy B herd. The rest of the crew—Spit McCullough, Harve Kendall, Charley Black, and Tony Herrera—performed the sweaty, dusty task of green-breaking the two-year-old horses that were due to be delivered to Fort Buchanan in three weeks. Cal spent his time riding between both groups and prodding them to do their jobs.

As the crews headed out on Thursday morning, Mackenzie motioned Cal over to where she stood by the ranchyard wall.

"I want some men to go up to Dragoon Springs and repair the dam at the pond. I rode up there yesterday and noticed that one side has been trampled pretty badly by the cattle. I want it fixed before it gives away completely."

"I'll send Bill Darnell up with a crew."

"No. Send George and Spit. And maybe two others. That's all we can spare."

Cal's face remained irritatingly expressionless. "Whatever you say."

Mackenzie grimaced as he walked away. Just once it would be nice to get a rise out of him, to see in his face or his eyes an acknowledgment that she was making his life difficult.

"You're inviting trouble." Lu walked up and brushed the dust from her black skirt. She still held the basket of scraps she'd been throwing to the hogs. "George and Spit are probably the two who will resent that job the worst. They think manual labor is beneath their dignity as gunslingers. They'll give Cal a hard time."

Mackenzie grinned wickedly. "I know."

Lu's dark eyes narrowed with disapproval. "You're making this as unpleasant as possible for him, aren't you?"

"Yes," Mackenzie answered without hesitation.

"We need him, Mackenzie." Lu's voice, usually so gentle, was as sharp as Mackenzie had ever heard it. "The ranch needs him, and you're behaving like a fool—worse, like a petulant child. Your father would not approve of what you're doing. Not at all."

Mackenzie physically recoiled from Lu's words. "If not for California Smith, my father would be here today, not lying in the ground beneath the cottonwood grove!"

"Why do you cling to that fantasy?" Lu demanded. "Is it because you need to blame someone for what happened, someone to be a target for your anger? You should learn that fastening blame doesn't ease hurt."

"Why do you defend him? You know as well as I what happened."

"I know very little of what happened, and neither do you. Perhaps that Apache did dash from the barn and kill Frank. I don't know. Perhaps if Cal had killed the Indian when you saw them together in the barn, your father would still be alive. I don't know that, either. Such details are part of God's design, and no one can say that an action done one moment won't precipitate a disaster in the next. And you don't really believe after all these years that Cal deliberately incited that warrior to kill Frank."

"Don't I?" Mackenzie challenged.

"No. You don't. Because if you believed that in your heart, you never would have let him come back. My wanting him here wouldn't have mattered."

"I don't want him here!" Mackenzie insisted. How could

Lu claim to know her heart better than she did herself? "He never even denied Jeff's charge."

"Some things shouldn't have to be denied, Mackenzie. Especially to someone who claims to love you."

"I *did* love him, but he certainly didn't love me! Do you know that he was going to leave the ranch that morning anyway? Even after . . .after . . ."

"After you gave him what every woman considers her most precious gift?"

Mackenzie returned Lu's level gaze. "Yes."

"Have you ever considered that hurt feelings might have swayed your judgment that morning?"

"No." Mackenzie had had enough of this nonsense. Lu was proficient at slipping through her defenses and striking a chord of doubt that Mackenzie's didn't want to admit, even to herself. She marched into the yard, slammed the gate behind her, whirled back toward Lu, and glared accusingly. "You've defended him from the first. You think I was wrong to ever throw him off the ranch."

"I think you're too quick to anger," Lu answered calmly. "You judged Cal's guilt with very little evidence except your own pain."

Mackenzie turned on her heel and stormed into the house. She didn't know what made her angrier, Lu's calm insistence on such heresy, or her own niggling fear that her stepmother might be right.

The next day Mackenzie realized she had gone too far. It seemed George Keller had been so angry about having to sling dirt onto the dam that he'd drawn his pistol on California Smith. Bull Ferguson recounted the story to Lu and Mackenzie when he came to the kitchen building for Carmelita to dress a nasty cut he'd received stringing barbed wire. (Bull often brought his cuts, scratches, and bee stings to Carmelita to cure, Mackenzie had noted with amusement over the past weeks.) He told the story with relish, especially when plump little Carmelita's eyes grew widc with excitement.

According to Bull, Spit McCullough picked a fight with Cal. Cal promptly "knocked Spit on his can" and then somehow miraculously disarmed Keller when Keller drew his pistol.

"Didn't the other men help Mr. Keller?" Mackenzie asked.

"No, ma'am," Bull chortled. "Sure as heck not. Not after they seen Smith take that gun away and whip ol' Keller like he was a snot-nosed kid."

"California Smith could whip all of them together!" Carmelita claimed extravagantly.

Mackenzie gave Carmelita an annoyed look.

Hoofbeats and a whirlwind of dust outside kept Bull from elaborating on his story. The dust settled as Sam Crawford slid from his horse, vaulted the low wall, and trotted toward the kitchen door. His one hand grabbed a kerchief from his pocket and mopped the sweat that streamed down his face and neck.

"Crosby hands are gettin' ready to drive cattle through the fence toward Dragoon Springs," he announced. "Leastways, that's what it appears."

"Good Lord!" Mackenzie cried. "Get the men and—"

"Smith's already rounded up the crew. He's on his way. Sent me to tell ya what's goin' on. Gotta go! Can't miss a good fight!" He headed back toward his horse before Mackenzie could answer.

"Talk!" she shouted after him. "Don't shoot! Talk!" Mackenzie ran out of the kitchen toward the house to get her riding trousers and boots. Damn Nathan Crosby! Damn him to hell! What was he trying to do? Start a war?

4

As the Lazy B crew galloped toward Dragoon Springs, Cal was almost glad that Nathan Crosby had finally made a move. After a week on the Lazy B, he needed someone on whom to vent his frustration. More than once he'd almost saddled his horse and ridden away, leaving Mackenzie to fight her own battles. Frank Butler was dead, and no service Cal did for the Lazy B was going to erase the part he'd played in the old man's death. Paying such a debt of honor was hardly worth putting up with a woman who would just as soon spit on him as look at him, and a ranch crew who nipped at him like coyotes whenever he turned his back.

Only the pride of challenge kept him from giving up. Cal's Apache father, Daklugie, had warned him more than once that pride should be tempered with good sense, that when a battle was not worth the price, a smart warrior retreated rather than allowing himself to be killed for the sake of pride. Only white men were stupid enough to think they gained honor by sacrificing their lives in hopeless defeat.

Still, he discovered he couldn't do the wise thing and leave. Every time Mackenzie turned her eyes upon him, he could see in their bright-green depths the courageous and passionate girl who'd once forced him to believe in love and hope for the future. She'd grown weary, disillusioned, and perhaps wiser than the girl he'd loved six years ago, but the courage, the strength, the natural grace and sensuality were still there, as was the bright, bold spirit that had once made her laugh at what she'd called his "taciturn dignity." Amos had hinted that Cal and Mac might still be able to patch up their differences. Not until Cal saw her again did he realize how much he hoped Amos was right. Mackenzie was the reason he stayed. Mackenzie was the reason he was determined to save the Lazy B. She was the one good thing that had happened in his life since he left his home with the Apaches, and he had stupidly given her up because of pride, hurt dignity, and self-pity—a result, no doubt, of his white blood tainting his good Apache training.

In the meantime, life at the Lazy B had driven Cal to the point of needing a good fight—a fight against a real enemy, which was the Apache idea of the best part of life. His minor battles with the crew didn't count. Their petty blustering wasn't worthy even of unblooded boys. He hoped that when they met the Crosby hands, the Lazy B crew would prove they were men, not children.

When Cal and the crew rode over the rise just north of the springs and the pond, three Crosby cowboys were bringing the last of a sizable bunch of cattle through the south fence, firing their pistols into the air to stampede the animals toward the dam. The lead cattle were already at the pond, and those behind them bawled and pressed forward as they caught the scent of water. More than a hundred head of Herefords, once prime cattle, but now leaned by the parched range, thundered in dusty confusion toward the springs and Mackenzie's newly repaired earth-and-stone dam.

"Let's go get 'em!" George Keller shouted to the Lazy B hands. He slid his Winchester from its saddle boot and raised it to his shoulder, aiming for the closest Crosby man. Before he could fire, the barrel of Cal's rifle slid under the Winchester and raised the muzzle toward the sky.

"Fire into the air!" Cal Shouted. "All of you! Turn the cattle, dammit! The first man who fires at anything besides the sky answers to me!"

The crew were more interested in blood than saving the springs and the pond from damage, but in the interest of their own skins they did as Cal ordered—until a new player added to the confusion of the dangerous game. Mackenzie rode up at a full gallop, her gold-red hair flashing in the sunlight like a bright beacon.

"What the hell is *she* doing here?" Cal demanded of no one in particular. "Goddammit!"

Mackenzie reined her horse to a halt beside Spit McCullough, who shouted a greeting as he continued to fire into the air. Cal spurred his horse in their direction. As he slid to a halt beside Mackenzie, a bullet whined off a nearby rock and plowed into the ground behind them.

"Hell!" Spit shouted. "Those bastards are shootin' for real." He leveled his pistol. Mackenzie grabbed his wrist and shoved it upward.

"In the air, Mr. McCullough, or I'll have your ears roasted over a slow fire!"

At her vehement threat, Spit's face went blank with surprise. Cal almost had to grin. Suddenly, amid all the gunfire, Mackenzie's horse screamed, rose up on its hind legs, and slowly toppled. Cal saw Mackenzie's lips form a cry of alarm, but he couldn't hear her voice above the gunshots and the bawling of panicky cattle. Time slowed to a nightmare pace. He saw blood spatter from a bullet hole in the horse's neck, saw Mackenzie's knuckles go white as she grasped the saddle horn to keep from falling into the confusion of hooves below her, saw her mouth open in a scream when she realized the horse was going to tumble backward on top of her. Feeling as though he moved in slow motion, Cal leaned over, circled her waist with his arm, and dragged her across the front of his saddle as her horse twisted in a final, grotesque dance, then crashed to the ground.

The air whooshed out of Mackenzie's lungs as she landed stomach down across the front of Cal's saddle. She struggled to slide to the ground, but his hand pressed down firmly on her back to hold her in place.

"Just stay put," he ordered.

She had a splendid view of his muscular thigh and the soft leather of a calf-high moccasin as he whirled his horse and galloped up the rocky rise from which Dragoon Springs flowed. The hard pommel of the saddle jarred rhythmically into her ribs, and with every stride her behind bounced higher into the air. As the horse slid to a halt, Cal's hand came down upon her buttocks in a stinging slap—ostensibly to steady her.

"Put me down!" she choked. "Get your hands off me!"

He allowed her to slide to the ground. "Couldn't let you fall," he explained, one brow arched in unperturbed mockery.

She hastily straightened her clothes, trying not to squirm under the weight of his steady gaze. He had probably saved her life by his quick action. She should thank him, but she felt like shouting at him for the indignity he'd made her endure. "I suppose I should thank you," she said ungraciously. "I . . . well . . . "

His calm, unreadable face seemed to mock her by its very lack of expression. "I do thank you. You saved me from a very bad fall."

"Mackenzie, I don't know what you think you're doing

here, but stay up in these rocks out of the way until I tell you to come down."

His dictatorial tone pushed every thought of gratitude from her mind. "Don't you tell me what to do! Those Crosby hands are wrecking a month's worth of work, and I'm—"

"Those Crosby hands are going to be taken care of just as soon as you let me get back to doing the job you hired me to do. Now stay here. That bullet that hit your horse just might have been meant for you."

That silenced her.

"By the way," he continued, and Mackenzie was surprised to see a slow smile spread across his face, "that was an impressive threat you made to Spit. Is that what they teach in that fancy ladies' school you attended back east?"

"No!" she snapped. "That's what they teach in thc great territory of Arizona."

He grinned and reined his horse around. "You would have made a good Apache," he said over his shoulder.

As he galloped down the hill and back into the fray, Mackenzie rubbed her still-stinging backside. "Couldn't let you fall, indeed!" she muttered.

The battle at Dragoon Springs shortly turned into a free-for-all. Cattle milled and bawled; cowboys yipped, shouted, cursed, and fired their weapons into the air for the sheer hell of it. There was no hope of turning the cattle once they had scented water. The beasts heedlessly trampled every obstacle between them and the pond. The stone retaining walls around the pond caved in in a dozen places, and the dam, sagging under the weight of so much beef, broke through in two spots.

Mackenzie watched helplessly from the rocks above the springs. The Lazy B had eight men on the scene to Crosby's three, but the number of men made no difference, for the cattle were in control. The cowboys on both sides, high on the sound of gunfire and the smell of gunsmoke, were ready for a fight. A bloody range war was about to start right here, Mackenzie feared. Thc Crosby hands, outnumbered as they were, had no desire to start a gunbattle, but the Lazy B crew itched for blood. Even from her perch on the rocks, Mackenzie could see it in their faces. She also saw them glance at Cal. Bill Darnell, a drifter who had signed on three weeks ago, cocked his rifle and aimed it level and deadly in the direction of one Crosby cowhand, but at a shout from Cal he fired in the air. The men were afraid of Cal, Mackenzie realized, not only because of his Apache background, but because he'd proved himself tougher than they were.

Finally the gunfire ceased. The cattle crowded the pond, drinking, muzzles dripping, only occasionally raising their heads to give the cowboys uninterested looks. Lazy B and Crosby men eyed each other with restive hostility. Mackenzie recognized the Crosby hands: Hank Miller, Speed Bowers, and Kelly Overmire—the worst of the Bar Cross men.

She stood up on her high rock and called down to Overmire, who she knew would be the men's leader. "Get your cattle off my property, Overmire! And you can send a crew out to fix my fence and my pond while you're at it."

Overmire grinned when he swung around and saw her. He spurred his horse toward her perch, pushing through a sea of cattle. Looking up at Mackenzie, he tipped his hat in a gesture that was more insolence than courtesy. "Hullo there, Miz Butler. We're sorry as hell about these here beeves breaking down your fence. We tried to turn 'em, but you know how ornery thirsty beeves can be."

"You tried to turn them toward my springs, you mean."

Scrambling from her rock, she half-slid down the hill, feeling at a disadvantage being on foot while everyone else was mounted. Out of the corner of her eye she saw Cal urge his horse forward. He stopped beside her. The rest of the Lazy B crew fanned out behind him.

"Don't play coy with me, Mr. Overmire," she snapped.

"We both know what happened. You can get your beeves out of here and then tell your boss that if he doesn't start behaving himself I'll have the law down upon him."

Overmire sucked in his breath in mock alarm. "She sounds fierce boys!" he said to the other two Crosby hands, who had ridden up beside him. "In fact, she sounds jest like an old schoolmarm who used to rap my noggin with a stick ever' damn chance she got."

Mackenzie's eyes narrowed. "I mean it. Don't think I don't."

Overmire chuckled. "I'm sure you do, Miz Butler. It jest so happens that the law and Mr. Crosby are real close. Real close."

"Get off my land, you swaggering lout."

"Whooee! You are a mean one, ain't cha? But maybe you jest oughta settle down and be a mite more neighborly." He chuckled. "By the way, Miz Butler, I'm right sorry about the bullet that caught your horse. Too bad about my boys being careless like that. It's jest plumb awful to think that it coulda hit you instead."

Mackenzie felt a chill go down her spine. Cal had been right. That bullet had been meant for her. Either that or it was meant as a deadly warning. If she were taken out of the picture, Nathan Crosby would have only Lu to contend with in his attempt to get the Lazy B land and water.

"Take your men and your cattle and get out of my sight," she ordered in disgust.

Overmire just grinned.

"Do what the lady says." Cal's voice was quiet, but the hands of all three Crosby men jerked up to look at him.

"And who might you be?" Overmire asked.

A humorless smile pulled at Cal's mouth. "Miss Butler's foreman. Name's California Smith."

The cocky grin left Overmire's face. "I've heard the name."

"Figured you had."

"We don't much like Apaches around here, Smith, even when they're colored white and yella."

Cal's expression didn't change. "You heard what Miss Butler said. Move your cattle out. If any Bar Cross beeves are found on this side of the fence again, they'll belong to the Lazy B."

"Suppose I don't like takin' orders from the likes of you?"

"We could fight about it, if it comes to that. But I doubt you'd like the outcome."

Overmire flexed the fingers of his right hand. He glanced toward the gun that was holstered against Cal's thigh. "I could take you."

"Maybe," Cal agreed. "but I wouldn't try."

For a moment the tension between the two men stretched tight. Then Overmire's hand relaxed and dropped onto his saddle horn. Mackenzie let out the breath that she only then realized she'd been holding.

"You can also tell Mr. Crosby that the next time a Bar Cross man makes any mischief on the Lazy B or threatens Miss Butler in any way, he'll regret it. You can tell that to the hands as well."

"Sure thing. We'll all be shakin' in our boots," Overmire said with a sneer.

When the Crosby hands started to herd the now sated cattle away from the springs, Mackenzie felt like a puppet whose string had been suddenly cut. "Go help them," she directed her men. Her shoulders sagged.

"Are you okay?" Cal asked.

"Sure." She sighed. "Fine." She looked up at his wooden face, and wondered if he'd been even a fraction as frightened as she had been. "Could you have outdrawn him?"

"Not unless he's a lot slower than I think he is."

She closed her eyes, not wanting to think about what could have happened. If Overmire had called Cal's bluff, bullets would have been flying though the air like mosquitoes on a summer evening. The first bullet would have downed Cal, and the others . . . She didn't want to think about it.

"He wasn't going to push it," Cal assured her. "Not as outnumbered as they were."

Irritated by his imperturbability, she flashed him a sharp glance. "You're made of stone, aren't you?"

The wooden face melted enough to allow a sight smile. "No, Mackenzie, I'm not." He reached out his hand. "I'll give you a ride home."

Ignoring his offer, she walked over to her horse. "Poor Dusty. She was a good mare."

"I'd rather see her on the ground than you."

She was silent.

"Come on, Mac. Mount up. It's a long walk back to the house."

The nickname startled her. He had called her that when she had finally gotten him to say he loved her, and again on the night they had made love.

"Don't call me that," she snapped.

"Are you going to walk?"

"No."

He was laughing inside, Mackenzie suspected. Laughing at her, in spite of that blasted wooden face. Well, if he thought she was afraid of him, if he thought his touch or his nearness made her the least bit uneasy, she would show him how wrong his was. Ignoring his outstretched hand, she grabbed the saddle cantle and swung up behind him.

Sam Crawford rode up beside them. "They're headed out," he reported. He gave Cal an assessing look. "That was a fine bluff you pulled. Unless you're a whole lot faster than I think you are, Overmire woulda blowed your brains out."

"Maybe."

"You got guts, Smith. I'll give you that."

Mackenzie heard the tone of grudging respect in Sam's

voice. She'd lost—this round, at least. The week was over. Cal had proven he could handle her crew, and he'd thrown out a challenge to Crosby that made this war his fight as well as hers.

"Have two of the men bury Miss Butler's horse. The rest of them can start to work repairing the fence and the pond. Bill, Skillet, and George can split up and ride the fences around the rest of the property, just in case Crosby decides he hasn't caused enough trouble for one day."

"Figger the men would rather pay a little call on Crosby."

"That's just what Crosby wants us to do—ride onto his property and start something. He'd have every man on his ranch waiting for us with a gun in his hand."

Crawford spat. "Don't scare us none."

"A smart man doesn't let the enemy set the place and time of battle," Cal told him.

"Guess you're callin' the shots," Crawford said.

"That's a fact. I'm glad we both understand."

"Mr. Crawford," Mackenzie added. "Have someone bring my tack back to the barn, please."

"I'll do that, ma'am."

She wished she could think of some relevant orders to add to Cal's, but he'd thought of everything. What's more, he'd clamped a lid on her men before they could explode. Lu would no doubt be delighted that he was proving so efficient. Damn him.

"I'll be back after I've taken Miss Butler home."

Cal nudged his horse with his heels. The Appaloosa lurched forward into a brisk trot, and to keep her seat Mackenzie clamped her arms around Cal's lean-muscled middle before she realized what she was doing. "Hold on," Cal warned as the gelding broke into a gentle canter. Mackenzie could almost hear a grin in his voice.

They rode for a few moments in silence. After Mackenzie established her balance with the rhythm of the horse's gait, she loosed her hold on Cal, but his nearness still made her uncomfortable. Riding double on the back of a horse didn't permit much distance between the riders. Cal's body blocked the view to the front. Her vision was full of his broad shoulders and head of tawny hair. A cotton shirt stretched across his back and displayed the flex and roll of muscles as he moved in easy rhythm with the horse. Rolled-up shirtsleeves revealed bronzed, sinew-corded arms. The masculine scent of leather and clean sweat assaulted her nostrils. It was the scent of him that brought the memories flooding into her mind—those strong arms cradling her securely, the play of muscle and sinew as he arched above her.

Mackenzie swallowed hard and shrank from touching the body in front of her—a difficult task, since only scant inches separated her breasts from Cal's back. She worked so hard at her task that she was caught off guard when the beat of the Appaloosa's gait changed and Cal reined the gelding to a halt. The sudden stop threw her forward.

"Easy there." Cal reached back to steady her. "Thought I taught you how to ride better than that."

"Why did we stop?" she demanded irritably.

"Runner's limping." He swung his leg over the front of the saddle and dropped lightly to the ground.

"Wonderful," Mackenzie muttered to herself as she slid down. She was stuck on the far reaches of the ranch with California Smith for company. "I'll walk to the house and have another horse sent out," she volunteered quickly.

His eyes crinkled in amusement. "Don't be so anxious to strike out alone, Mac. We might as well walk together."

Mackenzie folded her arms across her chest and watched as he lifted the Appaloosa's right front foot and examined the underside of the hoof.

"Picked up a stone. His foot's bruised. That's all." Cal slipped a long-bladed knife from a sheath at his waist and pried the rock free. "He shouldn't be carrying our weight, though. We're only a mile or so from the barn." He tied the reins around the saddle horn and gave thc horse an affectionate slap on the shoulder. "You'll be sound enough after a day's rest."

Neither spoke as they began to walk. The Appaloosa followed after them like a well-trained dog. Mackenzie, uncomfortably conscious of the man walking beside her, just concentrated on putting one foot in front of the other. She almost jumped when Cal broke the silence.

"A week's over," he reminded her. "Can we call a truce between us?"

"I said you could stay if you were still here at the end of a week," she admitted. "So you can stay, if that's what you want."

"And a truce?"

Mackenzie hesitated. "It was Lu's idea to have you here, not mine."

"What are you afraid of, Mackenzie? Do you think because I was raised Apache that I'm going to murder you all in your beds? You once had more sense than that."

She gave him a look that frosted the air between them. "Once I was a fool. I'm not a fool any longer. I've survived your Apaches, not only the raid that killed my father but three others besides. Victorio, Loco, Geronimo—they've all sent their savages here at one time or another. I've survived the war between the Clantons and McLowrys and the Earps. I've survived walking down Allen Street in Tombstone and dodging bullets from someone else's fight. And I can probably survive Nathan Crosby without your help."

"If you've got any brains, Mac, you know that you don't stand any chance at all against Crosby without my help."

"Don't call me that!" she snapped.

"You don't still believe I was in cahoots with the Apache that killed your pa, do you?"

She felt his steady gaze upon her but refused to meet his eyes.

"Do you think I would come back here if I'd done that?"

"I can't imagine why you came back," she said. "And you can't deny that instead of fighting you were having a friendly chat with the savage who murdered my father."

"We weren't exactly having a friendly chat."

"I saw you. Jeff Morgan saw you. You didn't even bother to deny it when Jeff accused you of ordering that savage to kill my father."

Cal sighed wearily. "Mac, that Apache warrior was my brother. His name is Yahnozha. When I went into the barn to free your father's horses, he jumped me, and until we recognized each other, we were set to fight until one of us was dead."

"Your brother?"

"Apaches figure family a bit differently from whites, but yes, he was my brother."

"Well, your 'brother' left you and went directly to kill my father."

"Do you know that for sure?"

"Jeff saw him."

"Can Morgan tell one black-haired, half-naked Apache from another? Can you?"

She retreated into an uncertain silence.

He stopped, took her arm, and turned her to face him. "Answer me, Mackenzie. Don't substitute your imagination for the truth."

His steady gaze burned through her anger to the uncertainties beneath. "I guess . . . I guess I don't know what I believe," she admitted. "If you didn't send that Indian to kill my father, why didn't you deny Jeff's charge?"

Cal sighed. "If you've really got to know, I stayed quiet because I figured it would do you good to really hate me for a while. I thought it might help you get over what I'd done to you." He shook his head sadly. "Mac, I never meant to hurt you back then. No matter what you think, I did love you, and I never meant to hurt you."

Mackenzie was silent for a moment while she digested his words. She wanted to believe him. Lord, how she wanted to believe him!

"If you'd known that Yahnozha was going to kill my father, would you still have let him go?" she asked softly.

Cal expelled a long, slow breath. "I can't answer that. What man could? I loved my brother. We grew up together, endured the trials of boyhood together. We fought together." He looked up at the sky, as if the answer might be written there. "I loved Frank Butler, too. Before I met him, I was a drifter. He was one of the few white men in Arizona who treated me like a man instead of an animal."

Mackenzie was surprised to hear pain in Cal's words. She's almost forgotten that he had feelings, so well did he hide them.

"Where did you go after . . . after you left."

"To the San Carlos Reservation. My father—my Apache father—was there. He died of the smallpox a few days after I got there."

Did the savage Apaches love their parents as civilized people did? Mackenzie wondered. It was hard to imagine tenderness having any place in an Apache's heart.

"Then?" she asked.

"Then I drifted for a while. I worked as a drover in Kansas, and finally signed on with a big outfit in Texas as trail boss."

"Sounds like a good job."

"It wasn't bad."

She hesitated a moment, then asked him the question that had been plaguing her all week. "Why *did* you come back, Cal? Why would you want to stay at a place where both the crew and I have tried everything in our power to make your life miserable? What's in it for you to help us fight a war we could very well lose?"

He shoved his hands in his pockets. "I have my reasons."

"Like?"

"Like I owe your pa for treating me decently when no one else would. I figure I had a hand in his death."

She looked at him sharply.

"Maybe if I hadn't run off to save his damned horses I could've kept him from getting shot. Or maybe it was Yahnozha who killed him. In that case I owe a blood debt."

"To a dead man?" she asked bitterly.

"Death doesn't cancel the debt. One who wrongs a man is responsible for his family."

"How admirable." She lifted one brow in a sarcastic arch. "Suppose this part of the family declines your noble sacrifice."

He smiled. "Then there's the other reason. At some point in his life a man has to decide what he wants and then stand firm until he gets it."

The look he gave her threatened to stop her heart. "What is it you want?"

"I haven't quite decided what I want, Mac. But I'm closer to it here than I was in Texas. Maybe I figure that if I owe the Lazy B, you owe me something as well."

"What do you think I owe you?"

Cal simply smiled.

For one fanciful moment, Mackenzie remembered how sweet it had been to be in love with this man, then she discarded the foolish thought. The two of them had nothing left between them. If what Cal said about that horrible day was true, then she had wronged him terribly. Surely, the only feeling he could have left for her was contempt—perhaps laced with pity. Besides, even before the Indian attack he had been preparing to leave her. How could he claim to have truly loved her when he'd taken all she'd offered and thrown it back in her face?

Mackenzie scowled, trying to call up the old anger at the memory of his rejection but not quite able to light the fire. The older she got, the more she realized that things were seldom as simple or straightforward as they seemed. Black and white had merged to numerous shades of gray.

She sighed. "Cal, what happened between us in the past was a foolish mistake. It's gone. I've forgotten it. It never existed. You don't owe anything to me or the Lazy B for blood debt or honor or anything else. Once I was foolish enough to believe in honor, right and wrong, magic, rainbows and . . . and love. But not any longer." A hot stinging in her eyes warned of imminent tears, and Mackenzie fought against them. She thought she'd exorcised these emotions long ago. Damn California Smith for bringing them to the surface.

"That doesn't sound like the Mackenzie Butler I knew."

"The girl you knew is dead, Cal. I've learned that magic doesn't exist, rainbows are just empty colors in the sky, and hate is far stronger than love."

"Then you're not as smart as I thought you were," Cal said softly. "Hatred is a crippling disease, Mac."

With a short, bitter laugh, Mac turned to face Cal. "Then why does everyone in Arizona—white and Indian alike—seem to thrive on it?"

"You don't look like you're thriving, Mac. I haven't seen you laugh once since I came. Or even smile."

"I didn't say that *I* hated anyone."

He gave her a twisted smile. "I could have sworn you hated me."

She answered him with silence.

"Or maybe you're just afraid of me."

"I'm not afraid of anyone," she snapped.

The ranch compound was in sight. Mackenzie increased

her pace, anxious to be home where she could shut herself away from California Smith. He had a way of stripping away a person's mask and reading the feelings beneath, even though he kept himself as well hidden as a turtle inside its shell. Six years ago she hadn't minded his uncanny insight. Now it frightened her. She didn't want to examine her hates and fears; she didn't want to think about what had happened on that horrible day six years ago. That horror was already settled in her mind. She had learned to live with it. Stirring up questions and doubts was like roiling the slime in the bottom of a pond—before long what was once clear and calm became a whirlpool of confusion.

Cal dropped behind at the barn. She left him without a word. Suddenly a little voice piped from the arena and struck an icicle of fear through Mackenzie's heart.

"Ma!" Frankie's voice called. "Did you know Daisy's gonna have little pigs? Gran told me that's why she's so fat and grunty!" The little girl trotted over to Mackenzie, pigtails bouncing in a merry dance on her back, a ragged doll held in one hand. "I'm not sneezing anymore, Ma," she said, looking up at her mother's rigid face. "I shouldn't hafta stay in!"

A soft moccasin tread behind Mackenzie completed her nightmare. Cal came up beside her. He smiled at Frankie, his face for once transparent. Mackenzie could see a deep inner light burn in his eyes.

"My name's Frances Sophia," Frankie told him in her most grown-up voice. "Are you the Mr. Smith that makes my mom mad all the time?"

"That's me," Cal affirmed, grinning down at the child.

"Go in the house, Frankie." Mackenzie's voice was taut.

"I've been in the house forever!" Frankie objected.

"Frankie!" came a call from the house. Lu appeared at the gate to the yard. "Oh, dear!" she exclaimed.

"I went to the tunnel to find my doll," Frankie explained.

"All right, Sprout. Go on, now." Mackenzie thought her nerves just might snap under Cal's knowing gaze.

Frankie didn't go; she continued to look up at Cal in fascinated curiosity. Even Lu didn't move. Everyone seemed frozen in place by the intensity of the gaze Cal fastened on the child.

He finally tore his gaze from the little girl and turned to Mackenzie. An ominous smile played about his lips. "For something that didn't exist, Mac, whatever that was between us all those years ago certainly produced interesting results."

5

"I'm five," Frankie explained proudly to the man who towered above her. The man didn't look like a wolf in sheep's clothing. That was one of the things her mother had said about him. Frankie had seen a picture of a wolf in a book, and this fellow didn't resemble one at all. No pointy ears. No fur. No long snout nor lolling tongue. And he wasn't dressed like a sheep, either. Her mother must have been funning. There were other names her mother had used for him when she didn't think Frankie was listening, but Frankie didn't understand them. She didn't understand why her mother thought he was so nasty. He looked like a very nice man to Frankie. He had hair the color of the sun, just like hers.

"I'm five," she repeated, for she wasn't sure he had heard her. He stared at her as though she'd said something amazing. While being five was very special, she didn't expect a grown-up man to be quite so spellbound by the news. She held up five chubby fingers to make sure he understood.

"Five," she repeated. "And soon I'm going to have a pony of my very own."

The tall man smiled, and the sun suddenly seemed to light his face as well as his hair. He squatted down on his heels so he could talk to Frankie from her level. His face was nice, Frankie decided. His teeth were shiny and white, not black, like the teeth of some of the cowboys. Better yet, his breath didn't stink.

"A fine girl like you deserves a pony of her own," he said.

Frankie was in full agreement. She wished the man would tell that to her mother. "Did you have a pony when you were five?"

"Yes, I did. He was black with white stockings, and he could run like the wind all day long."

"I have a doll with white stockings," Frankie told him solemnly. She showed him the soiled rag doll clutched in one hand. "I left her in Grampa's tunnel, and all week I couldn't find her, 'cause I had to stay in the house. I was sneezing. But I'm not sneezing anymore, so I went out to get her. Then I went to see the hogs. Did you know Daisy is gonna have little pigs?"

He grinned, seeming to find all this interesting, so she went on. "Would you like to see my grampa's tunnel? It's nice and cool, and Ma lets me play there if I don't go where the light runs out or get too dusty. It goes all the way through the mountain."

Cal's eyes and ears were filled with Frankie. He could see Mackenzie in the little girl's green eyes, the winged delicacy of her brows, the stubborn set of her chin. The dimples in each cheek were his, though, as was the gold of her hair."I'd like to see your grandpa's tunnel someday."

If Cal had needed another reason to stay at the Lazy B, here she stood. In an amazing trick of fate, one moment he was a man alone, a man with nothing and no one, and in the next moment he had a daughter with dimples and golden hair, a child with intelligence shining in lively green eyes and spirit glowing in a mischievous smile. She had existed for five years without his knowing her. He had missed her baby gurgles, her first words, first steps. A flood of sadness engulfed him. He had lost more than he'd known when he had turned his back on the Lazy B and left Mackenzie's anger—and her love—behind him.

Frankie tugged at Cal's shirtsleeve. "We could go to the tunnel now," Frankie suggested hopefully. "Okay, Ma?"

"No."

Cal heard the tension in Mackenzie's voice and added to her anxiety by looking up at her with a wicked grin. Her eyes darkened in anger, but the anger didn't compare to his own. She hadn't intended to tell him he had a daughter.

Mackenzie clasped her hands uneasily. "Go back in the house with Gran, Frankie. It's almost dinnertime."

"Do I hafta stay in?"

"No," Mackenzie answered softly. "You don't have to stay in anymore."

"Good!" Instantly bright again, Frankie flashed her dimples at Cal. "We're having chili for dinner. Do you want to eat with us?"

"Frankie," Mackenzie hastened to object. "Mr. Smith is a hired man. He eats in the chow hall."

"Oh."

Frankie looked at Cal with a momentary solemnity. The child couldn't know the bonds that linked them, but all the same Cal felt something special pass between them. He was a good deal more than just a hired man to both Frankie and Mackenzie, and sooner or later he would force Mac to acknowledge it.

"Come along, Frankie." Lu took the little girl's hand and gently tugged her toward the house.

Cal slowly straightened. His eyes didn't leave the child who had started to skip and bounce at Lu's side. Only when the two of them had disappeared into the house did he meet Mackenzie's glacial green gaze.

"Stay away from her," Mackenzie warned. Icicles hung from every word.

"Not a chance, Mac. She's my daughter."

"She's *not* your daughter!" Mackenzie declared. "You may have sired her—like any animal following blind instinct—but you haven't been a father to her, and you won't. You won't be here that long, only until Jeff Morgan can get back in a saddle."

As if responding to the mention of his name, Jeff emerged from the foreman's shack. He swung toward them on his crutches. "Mackenzie, Lu said there was trouble out at the . . . " He looked from Mackenzie to Cal and hesitated.

Mackenzie welcomed Jeff with undisguised relief. "How long did Doc say it would be before you can ride?"

"Heck, Mackenzie." Jeff fixed a hostile gaze on Cal. "I'll get up in the saddle today if you want me to."

Cal ignored him. "Who does Frankie think is her father?"

"Frankie's father is dead," Mackenzie answered. "She doesn't just think he's dead. He *is* dead."

Cal stared at her until he could see her composure start to crack and her cheeks warm to a faint blush.

Morgan interrupted the awkward silence. "Mackenzie, let me—"

"I can take care of this, Jeff. No, stay," she ordered as he threw her a hurt look and turned to go. "I want to talk to you."

She regarded Cal with an expression that pleaded for understanding. "Do you think I could tell her the truth?"

Cal just looked at her.

"What am I supposed to tell her? 'Frankie, meet your father. He'll be here a few weeks. Maybe a month. And then you'll never see him again.' How do you think that would make her feel?"

"It's only you who thinks she'll never see me again."

"She won't. You gave up Frankie—and anything else you had at this ranch—when you left. Cal, you know that even if I hadn't thrown you off the ranch, you wouldn't have stayed. You had already told me that you were going and there was no place for me in your life."

"That isn't exactly what I said. I told you I couldn't give you the life you needed. You've held a place in my life since I first saw you."

Mackenzie took a deep breath and willed good sense to conquer emotion. "There's no place for you in Frankie's life, Cal. Not now, not ever. Leave her alone."

"No, Mackenzie. I won't tell her the truth, not now, at least; but I won't stay away from her."

"Then she'll stay away from you. I'll keep her away."

"I imagine that might be like trying to stop a rockslide once it's begun." He smiled. "She likes me."

"Frankie likes everyone. Don't think you're special."

Mackenzie hated him with the same intensity with which she'd once loved him, Cal realized. Or was it fear that colored her voice and darkened the green of her eyes? She was like that wild mare of hers—wary, snorting, and full of vinegar. Yet like the wild mare, she had a heart that would tame under the right hand.

"I'm not going to take her away from you, Mac."

Mackenzie flushed to instant fury at the very mention. "Damn right you're not going to take her away from me! If I see you even say hello to Frankie I'll boot you off this place so fast—"

"Firing me won't do any good," he warned. "I won't go." Mackenzie opened her mouth to protest, but Cal cut her off. "Don't decide to test which of us has more control of the crew, Mac. You might lose."

Jeff Morgan clumped forward on his crutches. "Get off this ranch, you bastard."

"You speaking for Mackenzie now?"

"It's not healthy to stay where you're not wanted, Smith."

Cal smiled. Jeff Morgan was as transparent as ever. It was wonder Mackenzie couldn't see what he was after. "It's not a good idea to pick a fight when you're on crutches, Morgan—or maybe you figure it's safer that way."

Crutches and all, Jeff surged forward. "I'll make you eat those words."

Mackenzie grabbed Morgan's arm. "Don't be a fool! I told you I could take care of this!"

"I'll be moving my kit into the foreman's shack," Cal announced. "Find somewhere else to stay, Morgan."

He saw a gleam of stubborn challenge ignite in Mackenzie's eyes, much as it had on a day long ago when she'd told him she would marry him with or without her father's consent—probably with or without his own consent as well, Cal reflected with wry amusement. Now she wanted to get rid of him as intensely as once she'd wanted to keep him. This was going to be an interesting war, he thought, and the war he contemplated had nothing to do with Nathan Crosby.

"See you later, Mac." He gave her a grin that met her challenge and walked off, leaving her to cook in her own steam.

Mackenzie watched silently as Cal walked toward the barn with his Appaloosa following patiently behind. She recalled what he'd said about why he'd come back—a man had to decide what he wanted and stand firm until he got it. California Smith had just found what he wanted, Mackenzie feared.

Jeff shook off Mackenzie's hold and looked at her in injured indignation. "Are you gonna let him get away with this?"

"Don't worry, Jeff. You can stay in the guest house until he leaves. I'll ask Carmelita to move your belongings. It won't be for long." She headed for the house. Jeff hobbled angrily after her, his crutches thumping in the dirt. He followed her into the entrance hall, past the gun case, and into the office.

"Dammit, Mackenzie! I can't believe you're gonna let Smith get away with this! He shoulda hanged six years ago. He shoulda been shot the day he had the nerve to set foot back on this ranch. And you're gonna let the bastard stay? After what he did!"

"What did he do?" Mackenzie snapped.

She opened a ledger, then slammed it shut, tired of being told what she should and shouldn't do, should and shouldn't believe. The confused muddle of uncertainties eddied into a whirlpool in her mind, and she realized that through all that hatred and anger of the past years, she had been waiting for Cal to defend himself—to tell her that he had no part in Frank Butler's murder. Now he had. His words had rung with honesty. He hadn't told her exactly what she wanted to hear, and perhaps that was why she believed him. Belief had been growing stronger within her until now, faced with Jeff's vitriol, the belief blossomed into certainty.

"Just what did Cal do? You're the only one who claims the Apache in the barn went directly out to kill my father. Can you really tell one Apache from another, Jeff? Did you have him in sight all the way from the barn to his horse to where he shot Pa?"

Jeff flushed. "I tell you, California Smith planned the whole thing! Mackenzie, that man is as much Apache as any savage on the reservation. He grew up Apache. He thinks Apache. Do you really believe it was a coincidence that Apaches killed Frank Butler just after your father fired him?"

Lu came through the doorway. "You two can be heard all the way out to the kitchen," she said, then gave Jeff a frown. "Are you spouting that nonsense again?"

"It's not nonsense!"

"Apaches raid and kill all over southern Arizona, Jeff.

There isn't a place for miles around that hasn't been hit at least once."

Jeff scowled. "I know what I saw. And so does Mackenzie."

"Neither of you saw enough to make that kind of accusation. Don't you think you've made enough trouble for the poor man?"

"Lu's right. I did tell Cal I would hire him if he was still here at the end of a week. We need him."

Jeff snorted contemptuously.

"And the foreman shouldn't bunk with the crew," Mackenzie continued. "He should be in the foreman's shack."

Lu nodded approval. Mackenzie didn't bother to add that she wasn't at all sure she could get Cal off the ranch even if she tried.

"He's doing a good job." Lu gave Jeff a smug look. The two of them glared at each other until Mackenzie broke in.

"Jeff, you know you always have a job here."

"Don't bother with your handouts!" he snapped. "I'll get my kit out of the foreman's shack and off the ranch. You and that yellow-haired Apache are welcome to each other."

"Jeff! I said you could have the guest house! We need you to stay. For pity's sake, you've been here since before I came. You can't go!"

"The hell I can't! I'm not staying on with that murdering savage running things." He turned and stalked out into the yard, as much as one can stalk on crutches. Mackenzie pursued him through the gate and toward the foreman's shack.

"Jeff. Cal's not running things! I run things here. And I need you."

"It doesn't look that way to me. It looks to me like California Smith's got everything going his way. He's even got you forgetting he had a bullet put in your pa."

Mackenzie halted with a soft curse and let Jeff storm on his way. The man obviously wasn't going to listen to reason.

She hated the thought of his leaving. Since her father's death Jeff had always been there, almost like family—always lending a shoulder for support and never demanding anything in return except friendship. Why on earth did he have to choose now to get temperamental? If she could put up with California Smith, certainly Jeff could!

Reluctant to face Lu's "I told you so" that awaited her in the house, she wandered over to the arena and leaned against the fence. From the far corner the wild mare regarded her suspiciously. Cal must have turned her out for exercise. He seemed to have adopted the mare as a special project. Mackenzie had heard some of the crew laughing about how Cal spent so many of the evening hours talking to the mare in Apache, giving her treats, or just sitting with her.

"Men are snakes," she told the mare. "Arrogant, stubborn, and just plain stupid."

The mare merely flicked her ears. Only yesterday Mackenzie had watched from the window of the office while Cal mounted the horse for the first time. The mare had allowed him in the saddle and carried him around the ring twice without tossing him off. Mackenzie had scarcely believed that anyone could make such rapid progress with an animal that just over a week ago had almost killed Tony Herrera.

"You're just as gullible as the rest of the world's females, aren't you?" she accused the mare. "Charmed by a handsome face and soft words. You should be more careful about whom you trust," she warned.

If Mackenzie had wronged California Smith, he had wronged her as well. She wondered if that made them even.

The Fourth of July was hot and dusty, with the temperature in Tombstone climbing with each passing moment. By midmorning a man couldn't take an easy stroll down Allen Street without soaking himself in sweat. The dazzling sun turned the sky almost white and beat down with unrelenting intensity. The cicadas sang busily in the sage and mesquite, and dust roiled from beneath trundling wagon wheels and hung in the still air. All in all it was a typical summer day in Tombstone, and a perfect day for a picnic.

Tombstone occupied almost the entire area of a small mesa that fell away on all sides to reveal dramatic vistas over the sage-green floor of the San Pedro Valley. The rugged Dragoon Mountains rose in the distance, and on a clear day one could stand on the outskirts of Tombstone and look through Mule Pass as far as Sulphur Springs Valley on the eastern side of the Dragoons.

Long and narrow, the town of Tombstone filled the width of the mesa with only a few dusty streets. On the west side, just as the mesa started to slope down toward the valley, a scrub-grass covered field stretched from behind the Bird Cage Theater to the back of the Bloody Bucket Saloon. It was in this field that the good citizens of Tombstone celebrated their country's birth. A few piñons, junipers, and scrub oaks provided shade; everything else needed for a picnic was supplied by the miners, ranchers, shopkeepers, lawyers, housewives, bootmakers, seamstresses, dressmakers, accountants, and whoever else wished to make a fine day of it.

Mackenzie, Frankie, Lu and Carmelita took their place in the wagon cavalcade that was headed for the picnic site. The entire San Pedro Valley and much of Sulphur Springs Valley was descending upon Tombstone for a day of celebration. As soon as they neared town, Mackenzie's escort of ranch hands galloped off for their own celebration in the bars along Allen Street. While the more respectable citizens of Tombstone enjoyed lemonade, fireworks, barbecued beef, and games in the field outside of town, the rowdier elements would be enjoying the bars, gambling tables, and the whores only a stone's throw away. For the entirety of its young life Tombstone had been split into two worlds. Respectable matrons gave musicales, teas, and poetry readings within shouting distance of bawdyhouses; Schiefflin Hall imported the finest plays, operettas, and minstrel shows for a cultured audience; while just a few blocks away the infamous Bird Cage Theater entertained miners, gamblers, and gunmen with leg shows and rowdy skits. Both elements of the town had learned to ignore the existence of the other.

As they parked their wagon next to a host of others at the north end of the field, a self-conscious young man whose usual job was sweeping out the Occidental Hotel lobby approached with an apologetic air. "I don't suppose you ladies have any firearms?"

Mackenzie smiled. As he did every year, Marshal Creel had deputized a horde of youngsters to guarantee that no guns got into the picnic site.

"We have a shotgun under the seat," she admitted. "But it'll stay right here."

"Yes, ma'am. Just don't take it onto the field."

Frankie's eyes grew large as she surveyed the excitement and confusion. "They've started fireworks!" she exclaimed. "I hear the fireworks."

Mackenzie chuckled. "Not yet, Sprout. That's just the cowboys in town."

Lu climbed gracefully down from the wagon and lifted their picnic basket from the back. "I've never understood why men find fun in all that yelling and shooting into the air."

"And shooting at each other," Carmelita added darkly. "Men are children," she concluded.

"I don't shoot at anyone," Frankie protested.

"Ah, *chica*!" Carmelita soothed. "I was talking about another kind of child. Of course you don't shoot at anyone."

"I'm just grateful this valley isn't what it was four years ago," Lu commented.

Mackenzie was grateful as well. A few years back, one

couldn't walk the streets of Tombstone without the danger of becoming embroiled in someone else's gunfight. At one point assassinations were almost daily occurrences. And the lawmen had been as dangerous as the outlaws—money, power, greed, and violence had formed the basis of government. Personally, Mackenzie had believed that Deputy U.S. Marshal Wyatt Earp and his brothers had been almost as bad as the men they'd claimed were outlaws and murderers—the Clantons and McLowrys. Sheriff John Behan of Cochise County had been another dangerous character. Mild-looking, affable, but able to hold his own with the most vicious of Arizona's badmen, Behan had sided with the Clantons in Tombstone's little war. With the law fighting the law and every bloodthirsty gunman, con artist, rustler, and murderer migrating to southern Arizona—the last refuge of the Wild West—honest ranchers and miners had pulled their heads inside their shells like turtles in a shooting gallery. Mackenzie, for one, was glad things had finally quieted down.

Tombstone was more sedate now, even on wild days like the Fourth. The town was dying, though it still struggled for life. The year before, the price of silver had dropped, forcing mine owners to lower wages. Irate miners had staged a violent strike that closed many of the mines, and although most had reopened, mining was no longer king in the San Pedro and Sulpher Springs valleys. Ranching was fast taking over this wide-open land. It was a quieter, steadier industry than mining, and one that attracted fewer get-rich-quick opportunists. The badmen that had made Tombstone live up to its grim name were mostly dead or gone, and the staid voices in town that had been so long drowned out by rowdy lawlessness were steadily gaining in volume.

The field was already crowded when the Butler party arrived. Picnic blankets formed a bright patchwork on the clumpy grass. Children dodged between and around people, blankets, vendors' booths, and anything else that got in the way of their games. Men gathered in groups to smoke and talk while their wives laid out the contents of picnic baskets, minded children, and visited with neighbors they might not have seen for months. Dress ranged from suits and silks to miners' flannels and calico.

Mackenzie inhaled a deep breath of air. It smelled of sage and mesquite, dust, smoke, and the delicious odor of the barbecue that had been turning on a spit since early morning. "I see a nice grassy spot under that tree," she said. "Let's spread the blanket there."

"Do you see Amos?" Lu asked. "He said that he'd meet us here."

Mackenzie looked around. "I don't see . . . yes I do. There he is. Over by the barbecue spit. You can't miss that head of white hair."

Amos and another man were snitching samples from the side of beef that turned over the fire, burning their fingers in the process.

"Mercy!" Lu said with a tolerant smile. "He's no better than a little boy who can't wait for dinner."

Amos looked up, saw Lu, and waved. He gestured his companion to come along as he started toward them. Mackenzie caught the flash of sunlight on tawny gold hair, and her heart sank.

"It's California!" Frankie crowed in delight. "He's with Uncle Amos!"

Mackenzie sighed as Frankie ran to greet the two men. In the two days since Frankie had met Cal, Mackenzie hadn't been able to keep the little girl from running his way every time he appeared. She had always followed, afraid to leave them alone together, and thus had been unwilling witness to the growing bond between them.

Frankie surrounded Amos's legs in a quick hug, then held up her arms to Cal. When he lifted her from the ground and settled her onto his broad shoulders, she squealed in delight.

"Hello, Amos." Mackenzie's tone was barely civil. "I thought you were staying at the ranch, Mr. Smith." She itched to give him a taste of her temper for flaunting his conquest of Frankie's affection, but she couldn't very well give him a tongue-lashing with Frankie perched on his shoulders.

"Skillet volunteered to stay to keep an eye on things, so I figured I'd come into town and join the hoopla."

"I would've thought the celebration on Allen Street would be more to your taste," she said acidly.

He grinned. "Now, Mac, you know that booze doesn't mix well with us savages."

Mackenzie decided she preferred his "Indian face" to an expression that gloated of triumph in every line.

"Giddyup!" Frankie bounced her feet against Cal's chest and tugged on his hair, trying to guide him like a horse. "Let's go see everything!"

"Yes," Lu agreed, taking Amos's arm. "Let's walk around and see who's here. It'll be a long time before that barbecue is done."

Carmelita hastened to claim the spot beside Cal as they strolled the field. Mackenzie silently welcomed Amos and took his other arm.

"Are you speaking to me?" Amos inquired in a whisper, his eyes twinkling.

"Just barely," Mackenzie told him sourly. "You don't know what you've done, you old meddler." She couldn't keep the affection from her voice, however. Amos meant well, no matter what the results.

"Perhaps I do know what I've done," he whispered back.

As they walked, Frankie treated Cal to a preview of the delights to be found at a Fourth of July picnic, repeating what Lu had been telling her for the past two weeks. "There'll be horse races," she told him, "and funny people races and shooting contests. And there's a prize for the best pie—Lita's gonna win, huh, Lita?"

Carmelita giggled and smiled up at Cal. Mackenzie thought her terribly obvious.

"Lita makes the best pies ever." As if talking of pie had awakened her stomach, Frankie's eyes lit upon the bakery stand. "Could we get some cookies, Ma? And look! They're selling lemonade!"

They were buying their glasses of lemonade when Frankie spied an even greater delight. "Look, Ma! Ice cream!"

Ice cream was a confectionery treat that was rare, expensive, and delicious. Bowls of the stuff were being sold by a Chinaman—Quong Kee, owner of the prosperous Can-Can Restaurant.

"He must have hauled in ice all the way from Tucson," Amos commented.

"Can I have some?" Frankie pleaded. "Can I have some?"

Amos laughed. "I'll treat you this time, you little minx. Next time you have to buy it for me."

"Oh, Uncle Amos!" Frankie scolded as Cal lifted her down from his shoulders.

Mackenzie declined to join Amos and Lu in the crowd around the ice-cream booth. They agreed to meet back at their picnic blanket in an hour. To Mackenzie's dismay, Cal stayed with her instead of joining the crowd for ice cream, and Carmelita stuck with Cal. The Mexican girl chattered merrily about her chances in the pie contest until she saw Bull Ferguson in the crowd a short distance away. Bull spotted her at the same time, grinned, and doffed his hat. Carmelita's dusky cheeks grew rosy.

"Go on, Carmelita," Mackenzie said. "Just remember that we eat in an hour."

Carmelita went off on Bull's arm, apparently thinking a fish already hooked was worth more than one still in the river.

Mackenzie found herself alone in the crowd with Cal. What she had looked forward to as a bright, relaxing day had become tense the moment he appeared. "You're not going to give me any peace, are you?" she accused.

"Peace is something you have to find for yourself, Mac."

"What would you know about peace?"

A faint, crooked smile curved his lips. "More than you, I'd guess. I'm not the one at war with myself."

"Me? At war with myself? You're imagining things."

They were drawing interested glances from some of the other picnickers, Mackenzie noticed. She wondered how many of these good citizens recognized Cal as the infamous "yellow-haired Apache." Some of them certainly did, and they would hasten to tell others.

"Well, now, hello there, Mackenzie." Deputy Sheriff Israel Potts fell into step beside them. "I saw Andalusia and Frankie over by the ice-cream crowd and figgered you'd be here somewhere too. Glad ya'll could make it this year."

"Hello, Israel."

The Cochise County deputy sheriff for the Tombstone area was an amiable man who resembled a clown more than he did a lawman. Gray wisps of curly hair fringed his balding pate, and every few moments he took off his hat to wipe his brow and carefully rearrange the few remaining hairs. Spindly legs seemed barely able to hold up the round belly drooping over his belt, and a fine red tracery of broken blood vessels in his face bore witness to his prodigious drinking habits. Still, Israel was competent at his job when he felt so inclined. Mackenzie's chief objection to him was that he seldom felt inclined.

"You a stranger in these parts?" Israel regarded Cal with professional suspicion.

"This is my new foreman," Mackenzie said. "Cal Smith."

"Cal Smith," Israel repeated thoughtfully. "Cal Smith. Seems I've heard the name. Cal for Calhoun, Calvin, Caleb, Calum?"

"California," Cal said.

Israel's brows shot up. "Seems I'd remember a name like that. You ain't the fellow who was marshal over in Yuma a few years back, was ya?"

"Nope."

"California. I know I've heard the name." The dome of his brow wrinkled. "I know! You're the gunhand who killed ol' Matt Jenkins up in Tucson last year."

"Sorry. Last year I was in Texas."

A short, dapper man with neatly combed gray hair and a goatee emerged from the crowd, a young woman on his arm. The man tipped his hat. "Morning, Mackenzie. Israel."

"Good morning, John, Viola." Mackenzie smiled.

Israel tipped his hat to Viola and nodded to John. "John. Ma'am. I'll see you folks later, I hope. Have to get back to business now. A lawman never gets a day off, ya know."

Israel ambled off and Mackenzie performed the introductions. "California Smith, meet John and Viola Slaughter. About the same time my pa was setting up the Lazy B, John drove a big herd of longhorns out from Texas. He's got the San Bernadino Ranch down on the border."

The two men shook hands. "I've heard a lot about you, Mr. Slaughter."

John smiled and assessed Cal with hard, canny eyes. Despite his short stature, Texas John Slaughter was hard to mistake for anything but a tough and dangerous man. "I've heard a bit about you too, Smith. I remember reading about you in the papers back in '72 when you came out of Chochise's stronghold with General Howard. The general must've been quite a talker to talk Cochise into peace and you into rejoining the white world all in the same day."

Cal's expression closed. "That was a long time ago."

"Glad to see you've done all right for yourself."

"Can't complain."

Viola Slaughter smiled at Mackenzie. "You ought to come down to San Bernardino and pay us a visit, Mackenzie. I get lonely for a woman my own age—especially one who can talk about something other than cooking and babies and needlepoint."

John grinned. "Viola spends more time in the saddle than I do."

"That's not quite true, dear. Almost, but not quite."

"You really should come down," John agreed. "Bring Cal with you." He winked. "I'd wager I could teach you a thing or two about these new Herefords we're trying to raise."

"Probably you could," Cal acknowledged. "Though I worked with them a bit over in Texas."

After a few more minutes of small talk the Slaughters moved on, leaving Mackenzie once again in Cal's company. When she lapsed into stony silence, Cal chuckled. "Not in much of a picnic mood today, are you?"

"Not as long as you're around," she said truthfully.

"Well, in that case I think I'll join Frankie and the others. I've never had ice cream."

Mackenzie watched him walk away with a jaundiced eye. Of course, the skunk knew that his joining Frankie would make her even more uncomfortable than his staying with her.

"Hello, Mackenzie."

The day turned even grimmer. She had been so intent on watching Cal that she hadn't noticed Nathan Crosby's approach. As usual he was dressed in dusty denim trousers and shirt. The hat pulled down low over his brow was sweat-stained and shapeless.

"Taking a day off from working mischief?" Mackenzie inquired with icy politeness.

"Now, you're not holding that incident the other day against me, are you? Accidents like that happen on the range. I'd think you woulda learned that by now."

"You and I both know it wasn't an accident that your cattle crashed through my fence and trampled my pond. Don't push me too hard, Nathan."

He shrugged. "This is a hard business, a hard country, with hard men. No place for a woman to be hornin' in where even a man can get in trouble right quick."

"So you've told me."

"Jeff Morgan tells me some interesting stories about your new foreman."

Mackenzie looked at him in surprise.

Crosby grinned unpleasantly. "Morgan's workin' for me now. Expect him to be a big help, even with that bum leg. Yessir. A big help. He's told me all about that yella-haired fella who backed down Overmire the other day. All about him."

Mackenzie was more hurt than alarmed by Jeff's defection. She knew he was angry, but she hadn't guessed he would go over to the enemy.

"Sweet young woman like you shouldn't have to be associatin' with a dangerous man like California Smith. Must put you in a real awkward position."

Nathan's mocking tone told Mackenzie that Jeff had indeed told all—not only Cal's supposed part in the Apache raid on the Lazy B, but also Cal's part in Frankie's birth. She cursed silently. "You'd best be concerned about the awkward position you're in, Nathan. California Smith seems to think he has a lot invested in the Lazy B, and he isn't going to tolerate your shenanigans. You'd better think twice before going up against him."

"Well, now, there's no reason to get mean-tempered about it, Mackenzie. I'm prepared to make you a right generous offer for that place of yours—enough money to take you back east and set you up in a nice house. You and Andalusia both. Live the gentle life. Catch yourself a husband." He smirked. "After all, no one back east would know about that kid of yours being born on the wrong side of the bed."

"The Lazy B isn't for sale," Mackenzie said curtly. "and you're not going to drive me off with threats, Nathan."

"Well, now, Mackenzie, I wouldn't put any great hopes in that Smith fellow, if I was you. Remember what happened to your daddy."

"Cal didn't have anything to do with what happened to my father," Mackenzie snapped. Inside, however, Crosby's comments gave her pause. It was true Cal had so far gained an uncomfortable amount of power over her. He had her trigger-happy crew in the palm of his hand, had Lu and Frankie and Amos thinking he was some sort of paragon, even had Mackenzie herself defending him to Jeff Morgan and Nathan Crosby. For a moment she was almost tempted to say yes to Nathan's offer. It would get Cal out of her life once and for all. If it weren't for her father's dream . . .

This is where I'll stay, Frank Butler had written his daughter when he first started the Lazy B. *This is my legacy to you and to your children and their children.* How could she let his dream be killed by a greedy troublemaker like Crosby?

"Think about it, Mackenzie. The offer's still open."

A distraction a short distance away rescued Mackenzie from Nathan's further importunings. Shouts carried above picnic conversations. A high-pitched scream rose and then faded. The picnic crowd, Nathan and Mackenzie included, flowed toward the trouble.

Nathan craned to look over the heads in front of him to see what was going on. With a grin splitting his weather-worn face, he chuckled, then turned to Mackenzie.

"If you're bound and determined to stay on that ranch of yours, girl, you'd better hire someone who can control those hotheaded men of yours. Looks to me like that Smith fellow is better at picking fights than stopping them."

6

Cal watched his adversary, trying to gauge when Tony Herrera would make his first move. A ring of avid onlookers encircled them, but he could still hear the girl in the blue calico dress weeping some twenty feet away. Cal guessed she was about sixteen, with disheveled brown hair that fell over her face. Another girl, only slightly older, had pushed her way through the crowd to put her arms around the girl's shoulders and lead her away.

"Goddamned murderin' Apache. I'll teach you to butt in where you're not wanted."

Tony's face was flushed, his gaze intense as he circled warily, waiting to spot an opening where he could strike.

"Seems that's a lesson you haven't learned, either." Cal felt icy coolness flood his veins. His mind centered and focused with steely control, alert to everything around him but still concentrating on his adversary. This was the only way he knew how to fight, the way his father Daklugie and his

Uncle Geronimo had taught him to fight. No anger, no distraction. Make a knife of your mind and heart. Make your body a rock that feels no fatigue, no pain.

Tony charged with a roar of rage. Like a bull he aimed his head at Cal's middle. Cal stepped cooly aside. He could easily have brought his knee up to connect with Tony's chest as he stumbled by, but he didn't. Nor did he follow up his advantage while Tony was off balance. A celebration was no place to kill a man.

The young Mexican recovered in seconds, turned, and closed in with fists flying. A blow glanced off Cal's jaw, but he ignored it and answered with a right hook that made Tony stagger. When Herrera recovered, blood trickled from the corner of his mouth. He spat a crimson-tinged glob of saliva into the dust.

"Dog-eatin' Injun. That's what you are, Smith! Why don't you go back to the reservation where you belong?"

Cal had been hearing these same insults for so long that they no longer meant a thing; he'd closed off his mind and heart. Tony had no such protection, however. His anger and frustration had obviously been growing since Cal had stepped into the little stand of concealing piñon pines and pulled him off Letty Greene—and Cal knew that anger and frustration would drain Tony's energy and lead him to make rash mistakes.

"You act like a child," Cal told him, "not a man."

With a snarl Tony lunged forward. Cal avoided his fists and caught him in a nearly unbreakable grip. "I think you should apologize to the girl you insulted."

Tony twisted in Cal's grip. "No fuckin' Apache tells me what to do! I'll teach you to mind your own damned business!" He twisted free, ducked down, and pulled a knife from his boot. Aiming for Cal's gut, Tony sliced the knife upward in a deadly arc. With seemingly effortless ease Cal caught his wrist and twisted. The knife fell to the ground, and Cal brought up a hard fist onto Tony's jaw. Tony jerked back, tottered, then dropped senseless facedown in the scrub grass.

Cal shook his head as he rolled Tony over with his foot. "Foolish boy," he said to the unconscious Mexican. "If I were a real Apache, you would be dead."

Mackenzie, who had elbowed her way to the front of the crowd, had hardly breathed while watching the fight, not knowing whether she should fear for Tony or for Cal. Surprised by the depth of her concern, she exhaled a long, slow breath of relief when Tony hit the ground.

Before Mackenzie could gather her wits, Lu pushed through the circle of onlookers, ran to her downed son, and knelt beside him. Doc Gilbert was close behind her. Mackenzie joined them and put a comforting arm around her stepmother's shoulders.

"Lu," Cal said softly. "I'm sorry."

Lu shook her head, refusing his apology. "I just hope you hit him hard enough to knock some sense into his head. Mercy, smell the liquor on him!"

"What's goin' on here, people?" Israel Potts pushed a path through the spectators, who were starting to drift away now that the entertainment was over. As usual, Potts had timed his entrance soon enough to play the officious lawman and late enough to eliminate the need for any strenuous action on his part. He glared at Cal. "Brawls aren't allowed on the picnic field, Smith. I'm gonna have to fine ya or throw ya in the clink."

"Now just a minute, Israel!" Mackenzie shot to her feet in indignation. Cal threw her a surprised look. She was rather surprised herself. "Why don't you find out what happened before you fix the blame?"

"I'll say, Sheriff." John Slaughter stepped forward. "The law ought to thank Mr. Smith, not fine him. He prevented an assault on a young lady."

Out of courtesy, Slaughter didn't elaborate on which young lady, but her identity was obvious to all. Leticia Greene wept nearby on her father's shoulder. Her sister, the girl Cal had seen lead Letty away from the fight, still glared at Tony's supine form.

"Well now," Israel insisted, "seems like he got a mite carried away." He glared up at Cal, who overshadowed him by a foot. "Now I remember where I heard that name! California Smith. You was the kid who was livin' with that ol' devil Cochise!" He shot a concerned look toward Tony. "He still alive?" Israel asked, as though Cal's association with the Apaches reduced Tony's chances of survival.

"He'll be all right," Doc Gilbert said.

What few spectators remained commented among themselves. They had heard Tony's wild name-calling and had dismissed it as drunken rage. After all, what worse name could one call an enemy than Apache? But now Deputy Sheriff Potts had confirmed the truth. A few of them remembered the newspaper stories of fourteen years ago and other tales since then from less reliable sources. "Once a savage always a savage," a man remarked to his wife. She nodded sagely, as did several others.

Mackenzie caught the murmurs of outrage and distress that rippled through the onlookers. The glares were not directed at Tony, who'd been caught behaving like a rutting pig, but at Cal. For the first time she understood what her father had tried to tell her so many years ago. People hated anything Apache. She herself had learned to hate and fear the Apaches over the last years. If she hadn't good reason already to be cautious of California Smith, would his being raised Apache make her fear him? She didn't know.

Israel harrumphed officiously. "No matter what happened, I'm not sure these good folks here want to picnic with an Apache whelp. Maybe for your own good you oughta go on your way, son."

"Now wait just a damned minute, Israel!" Ted Greene left his weeping daughter in her sister's arms and strode to the deputy sheriff. "That lout"—he pointed to Tony—"drunkenly insulted my poor Letty and was about to attack her when Smith here dragged him off. Letty told me the whole thing. I think he's owed some thanks from you, Israel, not insults. *I* sure ain't afraid to thank him." He turned to Cal, who watched the debate impassively. "Thank you, Mr. Smith, for bein' man enough to help my girl. I'm in your debt." He offered his hand for a handshake.

A hint of surprise flickered in Cal's eyes as he took the man's hand. Greene shook hands firmly, then clapped Cal on the shoulder. "My thanks, friend." The outraged father cast Israel and the spectators a withering look, collected his daughters, and stiffly walked away.

"Goodness! I also think Mr. Smith should be lauded." Millicent Bigley wobbled her double chins at Israel in indignation. Millicent was founder of the Tombstone Ladies' Musicale Society and a pillar of St. Paul's Episcopal Church. Mackenzie held her in fond regard, despite Millicent's occasional pompousness. She was one of the few respectable ladies who had defended her five years ago when Mackenzie had almost been banned from that church. "Tombstone needs more men who are willing to defend women instead of despoil them. Laudably done, sir!"

Although Cal had received all the insults without the flick on an eye, he looked uneasy now. Mackenzie guessed that approbation didn't often come his way.

"Thank the man, Israel!" Millicent instructed.

Israel cleared his throat and gave the woman a cautious look. Puffed up like an indignant hen, Millicent outweighed him in both bulk and determination. He took the better part of valor and retreated. "Well, now, I suppose I'll let you off with just a warning . . . "

"Thank him, Israel!" Millicent insisted.

"Well, of course, you got our thanks for helping Miss Greene. But if you're foreman of the Lazy B, I'd appreciate your riding herd on your men. The peace-loving citizens of this county don't want no trouble."

"Lazy B men won't give you or the town marshal any more trouble, Deputy Potts," Cal promised.

Millicent nodded her satisfaction. Israel sighed in relief. "Let's just move on, now," he commanded the few spectators who remained. "Move on. We got some serious picnickin' to do."

Amos recruited several men to carry Tony to his surgery, where he could be examined. Lu followed them. As Mackenzie and Cal stood looking at each other in silence, Mackenzie still felt the weight of the crowd's hostility toward him.

"You really do get bedeviled for something that wasn't your fault, don't you?" she said softly.

He blinked in surprise.

"You can hardly be held responsible for being taken by the Apaches when you were a child."

Cal gave her a cynical grin. "Any normal, God-fearing kid would have had the decency to die."

They walked toward the spot where Mackenzie's blanket was spread under a tree. Eyes followed them, everything from surreptitious glances to blatant stares—curious, hostile, a very few admiring. "It seems unfair," Mackenzie remarked.

"Why should you care if they hate me?"

"I don't care," she said, as much a reminder to herself as to him. "If you hadn't been raised Apache, perhaps you would have killed that Apache in the barn. Perhaps my father wouldn't have died."

"Dont fool yourself. If I hadn't been trained in the Apache way of fighting, Yahnozha would have killed me, not the other way around." He chuckled, a bitter sound with little humor. "If he had killed me, you might have mourned me for months."

Or years, Mackenzie thought silently, remembering the intensity of her feelings for him six years ago.

"Senor!" Carmelita cautiously approached, holding an impatient Frankie by the hand. "Is it over, senor?"

"It's over." Cal wiped a trickle of blood on his cheek.

"The little one did not see," Carmelita assured them. "I took her to the bakery wagon. But she did have three pastries."

Mackenzie rolled her eyes. "Only three?"

"California!" Frankie pronounced his name with glee, looking proud of the way the syllables flowed off her tongue. She let go of Carmelita's hand, ran to Cal, and latched on to his leg. "We had ice cream!" she informed him, tilting her head back to look up at him. "And Lita bought me cookies and sticky rolls, and we looked at Lita's pie on the pie table. Did you know they're gonna have a horse race? They're gonna go down the field and all the way around town and back. Are you gonna race?"

"That Appaloosa of mine's not fast enough to race," he told her. "He's a darned good horse who can go all day at a trot, but he's not fast."

"I like fast horses," Frankie told him. "Don't you like fast horses?"

Cal squatted down on his heels. "When I was just a little older than you I loved fast horses. I had a horse who could outrun the lightning, whose hooves pounding over the ground sounded like a roll of thunder."

Frankie's eyes opened wide. "Really? I bet the wild mare is that fast! I bet she could win the race!"

"Maybe she could. Maybe next year she will."

Frankie squealed in delight. Over her head Mackenzie scowled at Cal. She lifted her daughter into her arms. "How about watching the footraces?" she proposed.

The Fouth of July footraces were more a matter of fun than competition. In one race contestants sashayed to the finish line with an egg balanced on a spoon. In the next the brave contenders ran, stumbled, and scrambled backward to the line. As the third race was called, Frankie jumped up and down. "I know this one! I know this one! This is where they tie people together! You and Uncle Jeff won this last year, Ma!"

Cal looked curious.

"The three-legged race," Mackenzie explained. "We got lucky."

"Go again, Ma!"

"Uncle Jeff isn't here, Sprout."

"You could go with California!"

"Frankie . . . "

"You could win! Couldn't you, California?"

He grinned. "Sure we could."

"You can't be serious!" said Mackenzie.

Cal took Mackenzie by the arm and steered her toward the starting line. "You wouldn't want to disappoint your daughter, would you, Mac?"

Mackenzie's arm burned in Cal's grasp, and her face heated with anger—at least she told herself that was the cause. "Just let me go!" She jerked her arm from his hold, but a glance back at Frankie's eager face told her she was trapped. "You'll pay for this!"

Cal just grinned at her scowl.

At the starting line, they were given a length of rope to tie themselves together. Cal knelt down to bind their ankles, but Mackenzie snatched the rope from his hands and did the job herself, not wanting his hands under her skirts. She didn't like the smirk on his face.

A little man whom she recognized as the assistant in Phister's General Mercantile fired the starting gunshot, and the racers leapt forward in great awkward bounds. Cal grabbed Mackenzie by the waist to help her along, and she instantly jerked away.

"Come on, Mac. Left, right, left, right, left. Oh, hell! If you won't hold on to me you'll—"

"Just shut up and run," Mackenzie warned him. She concentrated so intently on not holding on to Cal that she nearly lost her balance and toppled them both. They progressed in a series of awkward lurches, but the other contestants—three teams of men, a team of adolescent girls, and another mixed team, did just as badly.

Halfway to the finish line Mackenzie stumbled, grabbed for Cal, then jerked away from him as though he were a hot stove. She tripped, nearly bringing Cal down on top of her. Only Cal's catlike balance kept them from collapsing into a tangle of arms and legs. With scarcely a missed beat he pulled her up and, before she knew what was happening, lifted her bodily with one arm wrapped around her waist. Spectators hooted and laughed as she moved in a parody of running, her bound leg carried along by his. They finished second.

Laughing, Cal set her back on her feet. The arm still wrapped around her waist sent shivers down her spine. She jerked away, lost balance, and ended up on her backside. Unprepared, Cal came down on top of her. Their bound ankles held them in an intimate tangle, his knee pressing against the inside of her thigh through the material of her skirt. He balanced on his arms, caging her beneath him. His warm breath caressed her face, and a sudden glint of desire in his eyes made Mackenzie's insides clench in a spasm of uncontrolled, unwanted response. The years suddenly fell away, and the hard ground became the lumpy cot of the foreman's shack. Once again she felt the shivery, vulnerable feel of her legs so gently being coaxed apart by his thigh, heard his quick breathing as he lowered himself on her.

Past and present seemed to blur as Cal's lips parted and inched infinitesimally toward hers. For a moment she was sure he would kiss her—in broad daylight and under the eyes of anyone who cared to watch. The moment stretched to eternity as he poised above her, muscles taut, eyes gleaming, chest heaving with more than the race's exertion.

Cal grinned suddenly and pushed away. "It's hard to believe you won last year."

Mackenzie flushed under his wicked grin, but she was breathing too hard to reply with a fittingly scornful answer.

Frankie ran up to help Cal unwind the rope that tied their ankles. "You didn't win," she said forlornly.

Free at last, Cal disentangled them. The sudden absence of his touch left Mackenzie feeling unexpectedly bereft. Her knees were weak and her heart raced. Worst of all, he was looking down at her with an expression that told her he knew *exactly* what she was feeling.

Frankie tugged on Cal's hand. "Come on, California! There's a shooting contest now. You can win that."

Cal offered Mackenzie a hand up, but she waved it away. As she watched him walk away, Frankie's little hand tucked into his large one, her stomach fluttered with a peculiar weakness. Her heart still raced from their sudden unexpected intimacy, from the savage longing she'd seen in his eyes, and the ache of irrational craving in her own traitorous body.

The Fourth of July marksmanship contests were much more serious business than the footraces. Almost the entire picnic crowd gathered to watch the menfolk, and occasionally womenfolk as well, display their speed in drawing and firing a pistol and their marksmanship with a rifle.

Cal resisted Frankie's effort to push him into the fast-draw contest. The pistol was not his favorite weapon. His aim with a revolver was true, but he had put little effort into developing speed because one needed a fast draw only in a face-to-face duel, and Cal saw no sense in such contests. If men wanted to fight face-to-face, they should contend with muscle or knives in a true test of courage and skill. Pistols were for raids or battles, where slow, deliberate marksmanship counted much more than speed.

The rifle contest was a different story, however. To Frankie's delight, Cal fetched his rifle and joined the other men at the firing line, cautioning Carmelita, who had joined them, to keep an eye on Frankie. As he took his place among the contestants, Cal saw Mackenzie join the spectators and take Frankie's hand in hers. He looked away to the targets at the other end of the field. Through some sixth sense he felt her eyes upon him. He still burned from their contact. Her slim waist has been pliant beneath his hand, her flesh where he had touched it as smooth and soft as he remembered. Her hair had smelled of the sun, and the heady scent of her body had filled his head, not cloyingly sweet with artificial perfumes like most other white women, but a tangy, fresh-air scent with a hint of sage and soap.

Mackenzie Butler was a woman to make any man ache from the wanting of her. Cal ached. He had dragged Mackenzie into that race because he enjoyed seeing her icy composure upset. Perhaps he'd also wanted to prove that her denial of their relationship—past and present—was a lie. He had caught himself in his own trap, though. Being so close to her only demonstrated with unmerciful ferocity just how much he wanted her.

"Contestants ready?"

Ten of them stood at the firing line. At the far end of the field, ten tin cans waited to be demolished.

"Aim!"

A ridiculously easy exercise. Cal raised his rifle to his shoulder and smoothly took aim. He could feel Mackenzie's eyes upon him. Was it his imagination that sensed the confusion and uncertainty of her gaze?

"Fire!"

Ten simultaneous explosions rattled the crockery at the lemonade stand and shook the pies on the contest table. Eight cans flew into the air. Two stayed put; two contestants shook their heads and moved off the firing line.

Cal glanced over at Frankie, who jumped up and down clapping her hands. Behind her, Mackenzie smiled and ran a gentle hand over the pigtailed hair that glowed gold in the sunlight. The expression on her face was warm with affection. Could any mother so love a child and have no feeling for the father? Cal wondered.

"Ready!"

The cans had been moved back fifty feet. More of a challenge, but not much. Cal remembered the hours at Fort Buchanan when Josh Cameron had made him fire at barely visible twigs, tiny clods of dirt flying through the air, a distant bucket tied to a rope behind a swiftly galloping horse.

"Aim!"

He lifted the rifle to his shoulder. He hadn't thought of Josh Cameron in a long time. The gruff old Army sergeant had been almost as much of a pariah as Cal. When he'd "adopted" Cal during his stint at Fort Buchanan, his compassion hadn't made him popular with his fellow soldiers. Josh hadn't cared. In the six months since Cal had left the Apaches, he'd gone through three families who had tried to give him a home. A sullen, rebellious, and dangerous youth, Cal had been just the kind of near-impossible challenge that old Josh thrived upon. The old sergeant had used tactics that Cal understood and respected—iron discipline tempered with caring concern. He'd managed to stuff some civilized manners into Cal's head and give him a rough understanding of the white man's ways—not an easy task. He'd also taught him to be a crack shot with a rifle.

Old Josh would have liked Mackenzie. "She's a difficult woman," Cal could almost hear the old man say. "Just right for a big ornery cuss like you."

"Fire!"

Eight rifle shots cracked through the air. Five cans flew

from their perches, and three more of the contenders departed from the line.

The cans were moved back again, and then again, until only Cal and one other man were left. Then two cans were hung by string from juniper branches and set to swinging. After two rounds only Cal remained. The defeated man reached out to shake his hand.

"I never thought I'd see the day," he said with an amiable gruffness. "I've won this here contest five years in a row. Mister, you're the best shot I ever seen." He grimaced. "Hope the damned Apaches didn't teach you to shoot like that, or we're in a heap more trouble than we thought."

"An old Army sergeant taught me to shoot," Cal told him.

"Well, God bless the Army." The man spat a dark brown stream and gave Cal a tobacco-stained grin. "That do be a relief to hear."

A few others came over to congratulate him, shaking his hand or complimenting his skill. Frankie escaped from Mackenzie's hold and tackled him around the knees, almost knocking him off balance with her enthusiasm. Carmelita pursued the little girl, but her eyes were only for Cal.

"You won!" Frankie squealed.

"Yes, I did." He answered her grin with a wide smile of his own.

"What did you get?"

"I think I win a pie from the contest."

"Choose Lita's! It's the best!"

"And have you eat it all?"

"Not *all* of it! I'll leave some for you."

"All right, then. I guess we'll choose Carmelita's pie."

Listening from a few feet away, Carmelita blushed. Most of the other spectators regarded him with a mixture of hostility and admiration. The only regard he was interested in, however, was Mackenzie's. Her eyes were hooded and unreadable, a trick she might have learned from him. But he felt her confusion almost as if it were his own. Perhaps it was his own.

When had he decided that he still loved her? Cal wondered. He had come back to the Lazy B to repay a debt of honor—or so he'd thought. All these years he had thought the only thing he felt for her was regret, regret that he'd hurt her, regret that he'd left her with a lie, without an explanation or defense. What a jolt to discover, over these days, that passion was still there, along with the peculiar joy that had always warmed him when he looked at her.

"Nice shootin', young man."

Cal's mind snapped back into focus. He'd been concentrating so hard on Mackenzie that he hadn't heard Nathan Crosby come up beside him. A lapse like that might get him killed someday, he reflected.

"You as good with a pistol?"

Cal took a good look at the man before him. Earlier, Amos Gilbert had pointed out Crosby from a distance. Studying the rancher from up close, Cal didn't much like what he saw. The old man was carelessly dressed and only haphazardly shaven, but there was nothing careless in his sharp blue eyes and nothing haphazard in the determined thrust of his jaw. This man was an enemy to watch.

"I can get by with a pistol," Cal replied.

"I'll just bet you can." Crosby smiled like a fox and took Cal's measure. "You don't look like a man who likes takin' orders from a female. You get tired of workin' on the Lazy B, then come over to the Bar Cross. I can always use a man who's good with a gun."

"I'll stay where I am," Cal replied calmly.

Crosby grunted. "Loyalty's a thing to admire when it's not misplaced. Give it some thought, son. Meantime, watch yourself. That Miz Butler's a sweet-lookin' gal, but she could get you in trouble." He looked down at Frankie, who still clung to Cal's leg, then he looked back up at Cal, studying his face. Chuckling, he walked away.

"What did Nathan say to you?" Mackenzie asked sharply, walking over to him as Nathan left. She took Frankie's hand and pulled her gently away from Cal's leg.

"He offered me a job," Cal told her with a taunting grin.

Though her face paled momentarily, her gaze was level and unflinching. "Fine. Go work for him."

"Not today."

Without a word Mackenzie led Frankie away. Cal shook his head. Mackenzie was little better at hiding her feelings than she'd been six years ago. She didn't really want him to leave.

Carmelita touched his arm. "Come, Senor California. It is time to eat." Still thinking of Mackenzie, Cal allowed the Mexican woman to lead him away.

"Mackenzie Butler! You never cease to amaze me!" Nellie Cashman walked into the hotel's private parlor, gracefully balancing two china cups on their saucers. "Have some tea and tell me all about this new cowboy of yours that the whole picnic was buzzing about."

"I didn't know you went to the picnic." Mackenzie leaned wearily back on the pillows of the horsehair sofa.

"I was there just for a bit." Nellie handed her a cup and sat down beside her. "I'm afraid running a hotel and restaurant calls for my attention even on the Fourth of July. "Now stop changing the subject and tell me about this man." Her small oval face was alight with friendly curiosity.

Mackenzie sighed. This was the first moment of the day she'd had any peace. Lu had gone to dinner with Amos. Frankie was safely tucked away in bed, and Carmelita was off somewhere with Cal. She had seen them leave the picnic field together after the barbecue.

"My goodness!" Nellie declared. "What a frown! Was your day that bad?"

"It wasn't good. Nathan Crosby offered to buy the Lazy B and then made some not very veiled threats when I refused to sell. I found out that Jeff Morgan has gone to work for the Bar Cross, and Lu's son Tony got into a drunken brawl over Letty Greene."

"*And* you got beat in the three-legged race," Nellie added with a smile. "That I saw. Now, tell me about California Smith. I've heard some outrageous stories about him. How well do you know this person?"

"Too well."

Nellie raised a brow.

"California Smith is Frankie's father." Mackenzie saw neither shock nor disapproval on Nellie's fine features. "You're the only one other than Lu that I would ever tell this to, Nellie—though Jeff Morgan guessed a long time ago, and now probably Nathan Crosby knows as well. I suppose anyone with eyes in their head who sees them together could come to the same conclusion."

Nellie was silent for a moment. Some time ago Mackenzie had confided the story of her father's betrayal by the man Mackenzie thought she loved. Her story had been colored with bitterness and anger, and they had not spoken of it but one time. Often Nellie had wondered how much the bitterness had twisted what Mackenzie thought of as truth.

"So *he* is the one," she said softly. "They do look quite a bit alike."

"You'd already guessed," Mackenzie accused.

"I had a good idea. John Slaughter mentioned to me that Mr. Smith once worked for your father. Why did you take him back, Mackenzie? I thought he was the one man in the world you would gladly push off a cliff."

"I hired him back because Lu wanted him, and because I needed someone who can make my hired men stand up and pay attention. No one else worth his salt is going to hire on at the Lazy B as long as Crosby is putting the pressure on." She sighed and pushed absently at a stray wisp of hair along her cheek. "It . . . it seems so long ago that my father died. I guess it was a horrible day for Cal as well as me. I don't know why I was so ready to believe that he was responsible for everything that happened." She grimaced. "That's not true. I do know why I blamed him, and it's not to my credit. I realize now that Cal wasn't responsible for my father's death, at least not directly, so I really don't have any call to push him off a cliff. But if there were someone else who could help me with the ranch, I wouldn't hesitate to push him off the Lazy B and out of my life—more important, out of Frankie's life."

"Does Frankie know?"

"Of course not!"

Nellie smiled at her friend's discomfiture. "He seems like a good man, Mackenzie, despite people holding their breath when he appears."

Mackenzie shook her head and laughed, a sound that held no hint of humor. "I said I don't blame him anymore for Pa's death. I don't know that I'd describe him as a good man." She studied her teacup, frowned, then looked up almost sheepishly. "What makes you think he's a good man?"

"From the way he looks at you." Nell took a sip of tea and gave Mackenzie a knowing glance over the china cup. "And the way he looks at Frankie. People in this country are so steeped in hatred for the Apaches that they forget that it must have taken extraordinary strength and courage for a little white child to survive among such a savage race. They also forget that Mr. Smith chose to leave the Apache life behind and rejoin civilization. That must have been very difficult for him. I'm guessing he must have a very strong character indeed."

Mackenzie set her cup down on its saucer. It rattled with the shaking of her hand. She got up, walked to the big, empty fireplace, and, leaning against the split-log mantel, frowned at the trace of cold ashes on the grate. "Amos, Lu, and now you," she said with a sigh. "Why does everyone want me to believe that California Smith is such a paragon?"

"Lu loves you. Maybe she's concerned about your being alone for the rest of your life."

"Cal isn't the answer to that problem. He never really loved me. Even before the Apache raid he was going to leave that morning without me." Mackenzie colored slightly. "Even though we'd just spent the night together."

Nell gave her a patient look. "Are you so sure that means he didn't love you?"

Mackenzie hesitated, than returned to the sofa and collapsed wearily with a sigh. "Even if he loved me then, Nell, he couldn't love me now—not after what I believed of him, what I did to him."

"Love can sometimes surprise us."

Mackenzie felt a flash of irritation. Once she'd thought love could conquer all, but she didn't believe that any longer, no more than she believed in magic. "What's wrong with a woman choosing not to complicate her life with a man?" She gave Nell a steady look. "You live *your* life without a man."

Nellie laughed. "But I'm not you, dear. I'm naught but an Irishwoman with a wanderlust. I follow the boomtowns and the miners—I suppose because I like to feel needed, and they always have such a need. Before Tombstone it was the gold rush in Cassiar, British Columbia. Soon I'll leave Tombstone and follow the miners somewhere else, to give them decent food and a sympathetic woman's ear and be a nurse when they need one. These men pretend to be so strong, but really, so many of them are in need of a gentle, civilizing touch. I don't need one man when I have so many."

"You'll spend your life on them and get nothing in return," Mackenzie warned. Nellie Cashman, known as the Miners' Angel, was the one woman in town who could walk the streets of Tombstone without fear of being insulted or harassed. She had a soul as beautiful as her perfect oval face. Any man or woman in need could come to her and receive food, a place to sleep, or a gentle healing hand on wounds of both body and spirit. She worked diligently to raise funds for churches and charities of all kinds. Mackenzie envied her her gentle soul, and sometimes felt hard and cynical in comparison.

"In return, I get everything I need, Mackenzie. I need to be needed. But you . . . " she continued before Mackenzie could change the subject. "I don't think you have what you need. Please, don't let the past tarnish your future. Why fight the battle alone if you can find a good, strong man to fight beside you?"

That image brought a smile to Mackenzie's face. "If that good, strong man you're thinking of is Cal Smith, I assure you most of the battling we'd do would be with each other. Besides, I've told you. The whole thing's impossible. The sooner he goes, the better for me, for Frankie—and for him, too."

"Well," Nell said, a twinkle in her eye. "I suppose you know what's best for you and Frankie, and I should get down from my soapbox. But you can't blame those of us who love you for butting into your life now and then."

Just then Carmelita walked through the front door and into the parlor. She was quietly singing a happy, tuneless song in Spanish. Mackenzie felt a flash of sharp annoyance that irritated her even more because it was senseless. The girl had done nothing wrong in leaving the picnic grounds to cavort with California Smith.

"Oh, senoritas, hello," the Mexican woman said. "Is a lovely evening!"

Carmelita floated up the stairs to the room she shared with Frankie. Mackenzie stared at her with narrowed eyes gone even greener than usual, and Nellie observed Mackenzie's expression with a satisfied smile.

* * *

Despite the gaslights along Allen Street, the alley alongside the livery at the OK Corral was dark enough to completely hide the three men waiting there. The sound of liquor sloshing in the bottle they passed among them was the only clue to their presence.

"Be quiet, you drunken lout! D'you want him to hear us?" Tony Herrera glared through the darkness at Spit McCullough.

"M'not drunk, you Mex bastard. At least not so drunk I can't split a skull or two."

"Just shut up! Both of you!" Bill Darnell demanded in a harsh whisper. "He's comin' outta the saloon. Walkin' this way."

"Headed for beddie-bye with his horse," Tony sneered.

Split and Bill didn't care to remind Tony that Cal wouldn't be the only Lazy B cowboy sleeping in the livery that night; bedding down in the straw had more to do with empty pockets than anything else. The kid was in a sour mood, and he had a habit of meeting such comments with his fists. Better to remain on Herrera's good side.

Not that the two cowboys minded Tony taking California Smith down a peg or two. The sonofabitch had been asking to get his blood spilled, what with his overbearing, pushy ways. Bill and Spit had been more than willing to offer their services when Tony thundered into the saloon straight from Doc Gilbert's office. The damned yellow-haired Apache had jumped him, Tony claimed—jumped him without good cause or reason just for the plain mean cussedness of it. Plain mean cussedness was something with which Bill and Spit were well acquainted, but they'd rather use it on someone else than have someone use it on them.

"Get ready!" Tony warned them. "Spit! Put down the damn bottle. You'll need both fists with this guy."

"Hell. I'll hit 'im over the head with the bottle."

"Goddammit!" Tony cursed. "Ted Greene just came out of his gunshop and Smith stopped to talk to him."

The waiting men could hear the snatches of the words between Ted Greene and their intended victim—a rifle ordered, not yet in. The conversation lasted only a moment before Greene locked the door of his shop. "You have a good night, now. That rifle should be here in a week or so. Drop back by then."

"I'll do that."

The men parted with a friendly wave.

"Okay," Tony snarled, savoring the moment. "Get ready. Here the bastard comes."

7

Cal set off toward the livery barn at the OK Corral, where Runner was stabled, and cautioned himself not to let Ted Greene's friendliness once again raise hopes of someday being treated like a normal, run-of-the-mill man. Fourteen years ago when he left behind all he knew and rode out of Cochise's camp with General Howard, he had thought in youthful innocence that once he learned the white man's ways and became more proficient at the white man's language, he'd be just like all other white men. He had hoped that he would fit in with the white men as he had never quite fit in with the Apaches.

The Apaches had always treated him with scrupulous fairness. They were a people accustomed to taking the offspring of other races and cultures and molding them into one of the *Dine*, the People. But somehow Cal's light hair and eyes had set him apart. The di-yin, or shaman, of the Bedonkohe had named him Goshk'an after the yellow fruit of the yucca. The name had reminded the whole band that his hair and coloring were not Apache, even though, as his father Daklugie had often reminded him, his heart was Apache.

A few years in civilization had taught Cal that he fit in no better with whites than he did with Apaches. There had been several open-minded whites who almost convinced him that wasn't true. Josh Cameron had been one, Frank Butler another. But it was Mackenzie Butler who'd almost given him a true place among the white men. She'd been temptation almost beyond his power to resist, but fate and circumstance had snatched her away. Now he knew better than to expect anything from white society other than fear, contempt, curiosity, or caution. He was, and always would be, an outsider.

As Cal's thoughts drifted toward Mackenzie, he deliberately steered them away. He conjured up an image of Carmelita—sweet, obliging, uncomplicated. She had invited him to spend the evening with her family, who lived in a two-room adobe house at the edge of town. For lack of anything better to do, he had accepted. The girl's family had been reserved but cordial. Her three younger sisters had smiled and giggled behind their hands, and a ten-year-old brother had done his best to play the role of his sister's stalwart guardian. Carmelita had positively oozed with sensual invitation. He ought to take her up on her offer, Cal mused. Carmelita was pleasant, clean, and refreshingly honest about her needs. Cal hadn't had a woman in a long time, and he might be celibate the rest of his life if he waited for the one he truly desired. He smiled wryly at the direction of his thoughts. Mackenzie again, sneaking into his mind even as he contemplated lust with another woman.

The OK Corral and Livery Stable loomed up in front of him. He was more than ready for a good night's sleep. The tequila that Carmelita's father had pressed upon him had just about done him in. Cal didn't often drink, and when he did, the alcohol seemed to go straight from his mouth to his brain.

As he neared the corral, he thought he spotted a movement in the alley between the livery and the saddlery next door. He slowed his stride and carefully took in the sounds of the night. All was quiet. Not the slightest breeze stirred the warm, dusty air. The faint tinkling of music from the saloons farther up the street only emphasized the silence near the livery. The gas lamps with which Tombstone so proudly illuminated Allen Street served only to cast the alley into impenetrably black shadow.

A cautious sixth sense that had been tuned to perfection during his years with the Apaches warned Cal that the flicker of movement hadn't been a stray dog or a staggering drunk. He could have turned and walked away. He could have gone back to the Bloody Bucket Saloon and sat in the relative safety of noise and a raucous crowd. He walked on, however. Daklugie had once told him that trouble could not be ducked or eluded. If a man ran, trouble followed; if he hid, trouble would search until it found him. Far better, his father had told him, to use one's strength to defeat trouble when it first appeared than waste one's strength running.

The ambush came as no surprise. When three men leapt from the darkness of an alley and descended upon Cal in silent ferocity, he was ready to fight. The night suddenly exploded into flailing fists and clutching hands. The air stank of liquor fumes and sour breath. Cal could recognize none of his assailants in the darkness. There were three of them, he realized grimly, and they were not amateurs in delivering a beating. The familiar cold clarity of battle settled upon him as he eluded grasping hands, dodged flying fists, and delivered a few blows of his own. He tripped one attacker by kicking the legs out from under him. A second later his fist slammed against someone's jaw with a satisfying crack.

The ambushers had the numbers on him, however. While

Cal fended off an attack from the front, another assailant struck at his back. Steadily they maneuvered him deeper into the pitch-black alley until he was pinned against a wall. Someone took a swipe at his head with a whiskey bottle. Cal ducked just in time and the bottle shattered against the adobe.

"Shoot 'im!"

Cal recognized Spit McCullough's nasal voice.

"Naw. Just let me at the bastard with my fists!"

Tony Herrera. The hothead couldn't beat him alone, so he'd enlisted friends. Cal should have known.

"Hold 'im," Tony ordered his cohorts. "I'll break every bone in his body."

Cal crouched against the wall with his assailants ranged in front of him. Spit inched forward. "Take his other arm, Bill."

Bill Darnell. Three Lazy B hands. For one wild moment Cal wondered if Mackenzie knew anything about this attack, then dismissed the notion. Ambushes from dark alleys weren't Mackenzie's style. When that lady wanted to take a man down, she didn't sneak around about it.

Spit and Bill moved in warily from both sides while Tony waited with doubled fists. Cal was almost tempted to reach for his gun, but knew one of the three would certainly nail him before his hand had even reached his holster.

"You're gonna be sorry you messed with me by the time I'm through with you," Tony promised grimly. "We'll see how tough you really are, California Smith."

Spit lunged at him from one side, Bill Darnell from the other. Cal ducked and sent his right shoulder into Bill's chest. At the same time, Spit grabbed Cal's left arm and gave it a vicious twist, but he was unable to hold on when Cal lowered his head and charged Tony. Cal ignored the pain of his wrenched arm and shoulder. A man's body was a weapon—a block of wood, a stone, a club. Pain was irrelevant.

"Goddamn—ooof!" Tony cried when Cal rammed him. The Mexican staggered back. Cal's fists pounded his face. "Shoot the bastard!" Tony choked out between blows.

"The hell you say!" A new voice entered the fray. Cal recognized Ted Greene as the gunsmith shouldered into the fight. His new ally grabbed Spit by the collar and slammed hard knuckles into his jaw. Spit hit the ground, bounced once, then lay still.

"Damn!" Bill Darnell's voice cracked with panic. He slid a knife from his belt and sliced it in an arc toward Ted's stomach. Cal shoved Tony aside, grabbed Bill's wrist and twisted. The knife fell to the ground. Hardly missing a beat in the violent dance, Cal stepped between Ted and Bill to deliver a knee to Bill's groin. As if their moves had been choreographed, Ted brought his fist up into Bill's face just as he doubled over in pain. Bill fell facedown in the dirt.

Tony watched groggily as Bill hit the dirt. When Ted and Cal turned their attention toward him, his eyes grew wide and flashed white in the darkness. He reached for his gun. Cal's foot was faster than Tony's draw. He kicked the pistol from the Mexican's hand to send it flying into the darkness.

"Waste of a good pistol," the gunsmith remarked coolly. "Never find it in the dark."

"Come back and get it tomorrow," Cal invited. "Herrera's not going to be in any shape to use it."

Tony turned to run, but Cal was on him in three long strides. They tumbled to the dirt, Tony on the bottom. Cal's fist came down once, hard, and Tony lay still.

Cal shook his head. "That's twice today. You'd think he'd learn."

"You'd think," Ted agreed. "The sonofabitch. I went back to the store to get the ledger to work on at home, and I heard the ruckus."

"Glad you came," Cal admitted. "I'd be lying in the dust right now if you hadn't."

"And I'd be spillin' my guts out all over this alley if you hadn't stopped that bastard's knife. Guess I've gotta thank you again, Smith." Ted grinned. "Why don't you let me buy you a drink."

"Let's wake these fellows up, first. I have a thing or two to say to them."

"There's a watering trough by the corral."

"Good enough."

Tony, Spit, and Bill all came awake sputtering and flailing their fists. Cal smiled at them as they retched out the slime-coated water of the trough. When they raised their faces they stared down the long barrel of his Colt .44. "You're fired," Cal told them calmly.

"You can't fire us," Tony coughed out.

"You're lucky that's all I'm doing." He gave them all a look intended to remind them of Apache inventiveness in revenge. "If I see any of your faces around the Lazy B, you'll regret your mother ever gave birth."

"Jesus!" Spit whined. "Let's get outta here. Herrera, you bastard, you can take Smith on if you wanna, but I'm headin' out."

"Same here." Darnell wiped his face with the tails of his dirty shirt and backed away. Spit retreated at his side. "You won't see us again," Darnell assured Cal.

Tony spat blood into the dirt by the side of the trough. "Mackenzie's gonna twist you inside out when she hears what you done. She's my stepsister. You can't fire me."

"Maybe you're right," Cal mused aloud. "Maybe I ought to just stake you out on an anthill somewhere so she won't ever know what happened to you."

Even in the dark Cal could see Tony's brown skin turn a shade paler.

"Apache bastard." Herrera turned and stalked away.

Ted Greene grinned at Cal. "They looked suitably impressed."

Sometimes it helps to have a reputation, Cal acknowledged wryly.

"I can see it does. How 'bout that drink, my friend."

Cal nodded. He didn't particularly want a drink, but he didn't have so many friends that he could turn down making a new one.

Mackenzie was in the kitchen stirring up a batch of biscuits for dinner when Bull Ferguson rode up, dismounted, and tied his horse to a hitching ring in the ranch-yard wall. He lumbered through the gate and looked around. Behind Mackenzie, Carmelita hastily washed flour from her hands and smoothed the wrinkles from her skirt.

"We're in here, Mr. Ferguson," Mackenzie called. She wondered what excuse he'd dreamed up this time to visit Carmelita in the middle of the workday. Dinner wouldn't be served in the chow hall for at least another hour.

Bull stopped short of the kitchen door and took off his dusty hat. "Miz Butler," he greeted her with a nod. Peering around her, he smiled at Carmelita. "Hullo, Lita."

"Hullo, Bull."

"Uh . . . " For a moment he lost his train of thought. "Miz Butler," he finally recalled. "There's a rider comin' in from the north. Look's like Smith's Appaloosa."

Mackenzie's mouth drew into a tight line. "And does it look like Mr. Smith riding the Appaloosa?"

"Can't say, ma'am. Me and the boys was about a mile away when we spotted him. Figgered I'd ride back and let you know."

"Hello, Mr. Ferguson," Lu said as she crossed the yard, her black skirts lifted daintily above the dust. "What is this you say about Mr. Smith?"

Mackenzie didn't give Bull time to answer. "Well, you can ride back out and see if it truly is him. If it is, tell him he needn't bother to stop. I'll have his belongings sent to him in town."

"Uh . . . " Bull twisted his hat in his hands.

"Don't pay any mind to her," Lu said with an airy wave of her hand. "She's only joking."

"Uh . . . yes, ma'am." With an apologetic grin to Carmelita, Bull slapped his hat back on his head and backed away. When the ranch-yard wall stopped his retreat, he hastily made for the gate and the safety of his horse.

As Bull galloped back toward the north range, Lu folded her arms across her chest and regarded Mackenzie with a stern gaze. Mackenzie refused to meet her eyes and turned back to the biscuit dough.

For three days the entire Lazy B, ranch hands as well as household, had tiptoed around Mackenzie's foul mood. In Tombstone the morning after the picnic, California Smith and three of the Lazy B hands—Tony Herrera, Spit McCullough, and Bill Darnell—had been nowhere to be found. Her temper in a slow boil because of the mass defection, Mackenzie had gathered her other men and headed home. During the entire dusty ten miles to the ranch she had tried to convince herself that she was glad that Cal was gone. Losing Spit and Bill was what made her mad, and she was concerned about Tony, or rather, she was concerned about Lu's worry over Tony. She had also dreaded the disappointment in Frankie's eyes when the little girl learned that her adored California had taken a powder.

Frankie, however, hadn't batted an eye at Cal's loss. He'd come back, she assured her mother. Mackenzie told herself that she didn't want him to come back. He could stay away forever—and she hoped he did. But as one day passed and then another, her mood had deteriorated.

Her foul humor had not been improved by Tony's return to the ranch a full twenty-four hours after he had disappeared. Bruised and still hung over, he whined about him,

Spit, and Bill having a little fun with the new foreman the night of the picnic—a joke, he had claimed. But Smith had gotten on his high horse and fired them all.

"He's been just itchin' to get rid of me one way or another ever since he came to this place!" Tony had complained. "He's scared the men'd side with me if it ever came to a showdown."

Mackenzie had thought that claim rather farfetched, but for Lu's sake she had been ready to give Tony back his job. Lu, however had been adamant about supporting Cal's authority. She'd told her son to get off the Lazy B and not come back until he could act like a man instead of a child.

Finally, Mackenzie ended the long silence that had fallen upon the kitchen. "I won't take California Smith back," she told Lu, still stirring the overworked biscuit dough.

Lu fixed her with a steady gaze. "So," she commented, her serenity ruffling Mackenzie's feathers all the more. "What excuse have you concocted this time?"

"Excuse?" Mackenzie upended the mixing bowl with a clatter and turned the dough onto the worktable. "You call it an *excuse* that Cal got into two brawls on the Fourth, far exceeded his authority in dismissing three of *my*—not his, but *my*—employees, and then disappears for three days? You think that's responsible behavior for a foreman?"

Carmelita eyed Mackenzie and Lu uneasily. She dusted her hands upon her apron and flashed them a quick, nervous smile. "I must go fetch more water, senorita, senora. Excuse, please."

Lu gave Carmelita a sympathetic look as she hurried out. "See, *niña*? You've even made Lita jumpy with your snapping and growling. The poor woman thinks you've been possessed by a devil, I'm sure. I know you've been worried about Cal these past three days, but you really shouldn't take your foul mood out on others, dear."

"I am *not* in a foul mood!" Mackenzie snapped. "And I certainly haven't been worried about that man!"

"Aren't you at all curious about what's kept him away for three days? I know that I am."

Mackenzie harrumphed and attacked the biscuit dough with a rolling pin. "I suppose I can at least hear what he has to say."

Lu answered with a knowing smile.

The Appaloosa that trotted up to the house thirty minutes later did indeed carry California Smith. Frankie, who was busily making mud pies in the arena, ran over and greeted him in delight, jumping up and down and waving muddy hands in the air. At the water pump by the arena tank, the ranch hands stopped their washing for dinner to stare, eager to see the new foreman taken down a peg or two. They hadn't been able to get the best of him, but they expected the boss lady could do the job. For the past few days her temper had matched the color of her hair.

Mackenzie waited for Cal by the watering trough in front of the ranch house. Hands on hips and eyes like sharp emerald knives, she watched as he trotted casually up to the house, swung down from his saddle, and braced himself for Frankie's muddy tackle. She hadn't been at all worried about him, Mac told herself. All the same, she noted the signs that Tony's "joke" had been more vicious than he had claimed. Cal's cheek was discolored by a fading bruise, and the corner of his mouth was split by a cut that hadn't been there last time she saw him. Other than that, however, her prodigal foreman looked good. Tanned and lean, he happily endured Frankie's muddy greeting. His hair ruffled in the slight breeze, shining in a sun-colored halo about his head and shoulders. Mackenzie cursed silently. Why did California Smith always have to look so appealing, even when he'd been riding through the dust and sun all morning?

"Frankie," she said in a taut voice. "Go help Lita put the men's dinner on the table in the chow hall."

"Okay," Frankie answered. "Bye, California!"

"Wash your hands first," Mackenzie instructed.

As Frankie bounced away, Mackenzie fixed Cal with a sour gaze. "Good afternoon to you, too," he said with a hint of a smile.

Carmelita came out into the yard, saw Mackenzie and Cal facing off on the other side of the wall, and hastily ducked back into the house.

"Where in the blazes have you been?" Mackenzie demanded. "And where do you get off—"

He held up a hand to interrupt the potential tirade. Mackenzie surprised herself by falling silent and waiting for him to speak.

"I see you didn't get my message."

"What message?" she asked suspiciously.

"I asked Ted Greene to let you know I'd be gone a few days trying to round up some more help. I guess you know by now that I fired McCullough and Darnell. Herrera, too."

"No, I didn't get your message. We left town before anybody was up and around. And yes," she hissed angrily, "I know you fired three of my employees out of hand. Where do you get off letting my men go without consulting me? Just who do you think you are?"

"Your foreman." His face settled into its usual, irritating, emotionless mask.

"That doesn't give you the right to make such a decision."

The dinner bell on the chow house clanged, but the hands who lounged against the arena fence and the side of the barn didn't move. Their grins showed how much they were enjoying the confrontation between the boss lady and her new foreman. Mackenzie noticed their attention, and her irritation increased a notch.

"Mac," Cal said in a reasonable tone. "I don't mind a man

not liking me and telling me to my face. I don't even much quibble about a man picking a fight with me, as long as he does it out in the open where I can see him coming. But a man who attacks from ambush with the odds three to one in his favor isn't worth keeping around."

Mackenzie hesitated an instant. "Tony insisted they were playing a prank—a practical joke."

"Only if you consider murder a joke. Darnell tried to cut Ted Greene with a knife."

"What's Ted got to do with this?"

"He dove into the fight to try to help me. He wanted to even the odds a bit."

If Ted Greene could vouch for Cal's story, that changed things. Mackenzie hated to be wrong, especially when California Smith was right. There wasn't any help for it, though. With the men watching, with her foot in her mouth, she had plainly jumped to the wrong conclusion. "I'm sorry," she gritted out. "Obviously I got the wrong story."

He cocked his head in mild surprise. "What did you say?"

She set her jaw and forced the words out once again. "I said I'm sorry. Clearly you did the right thing. We'll just have to make do with three less men."

"I hired three more men," Cal told her calmly.

Regarding him with narrowed eyes, Mackenzie sat back against the tin watering trough and folded her arms across her chest. "You hired more hands without getting my approval? Where did you get them?" She was vexed that he'd taken that decision from her as well, but curious about how he'd found anyone willing to work for the Lazy B. "We don't need any more men who deal better with guns than with cattle," she reminded him in a low voice that wouldn't carry to the listening men. "Don't you have your hands full enough as it is?"

"These men I hired know cattle well enough," he answered with an enigmatic smile. "And they're better with horses than anyone I've seen. You can trust them. I trust them."

A touch of suspicion brought a frown to Mackenzie's face. This sounded too good to be true. "Where are these fellows you hired?"

Cal raised an arm in a signal, then let it drop. "They're riding in."

Mackenzie felt more uncertain about this by the second, and when she saw three riders detach themselves from the foothills that bordered the ranch on the east, her heart began to pound. More than once she had seen similar riders come down from the Dragoons, men who could blend in with the rocks and dirt until they wished to be seen, men who rode as though they were part of their horses, men whose faces held the wide-open sky, the ruggedness of the mountains, and the cunning of wolves: Apaches.

"Is this some kind of a joke?" she demanded in a sharp voice. A surge of panic flooded her veins. Jeff had been right, the panic screamed within her. Cal had brought the savages down upon them once again.

"Mackenzie," Cal answered softly, "these men are friends."

"They're Apaches!"

"They're White Mountain Apaches from the San Carlos Reservation. They're not Chiricahua."

The ranch hands followed the direction of her stare and straightened abruptly from their relaxed positions against the arena fence. Like puppets controlled by the same puppeteer, all went for their guns simultaneously.

"Put down your guns!" Cal shouted to them. His eyes swung around to Mackenzie, silently asking for her support.

Mackenzie's heart thudded wildly in her chest. It might be that these three were only the point of the spear. More might follow to catch them with guns still holstered. She looked at

Cal and was caught by his steady gaze. She saw no deception there, but then, who could read California Smith?

"Mackenzie . . . "

How could she trust him? His eyes held hers. For a moment she felt giddy, lost in the blue-crystal coolness of his scrutiny.

"Put the guns down," she told the men, then realized she had merely whispered. "Put your guns down!" she commanded, louder this time.

Mackenzie thought she saw a flash of warmth in Cal's eyes before he looked away—or was it a gleam of triumph? Whatever it was, she wasn't through with him yet. She moved closer so that she could speak without the hands hearing. "You expect me to let Apaches work on this ranch? Are you crazy?"

He looked down at her, towering over her in a way that made her realize she was much too close, but she refused to back off.

"White Mountain Apaches haven't been on the warpath in years," he said. "These are reservation Indians, Mac. They're peaceful."

The three savages reined in their ponies in front of the house, twenty feet from where Mackenzie and Cal stood. The very sight of them made Mackenzie want to retreat. Coarse black hair, held off their faces with wide cloth headbands, fell to the middle of their backs. Their cotton shirts and trousers were similar to local Mexican garb, the only distinction the narrow breechclouts that reached to their knees. Soft hide moccasin boots were exactly like the ones Cal always wore. Their expressions, also, were very like the impassive mask that Cal so often assumed. Unemotional, granite hard, patient, waiting.

Each Indian wore a single-holster gunbelt and carried a rifle. Bandoliers of ammunition crisscrossed their chests.

Peaceful Apaches, indeed! "They're reservation Indians. Fine. They can just go back to the reservation."

"The Apache war is just about over, Mac. When a war ends, enemies have to learn to live together."

"Tell that to Geronimo and Natchez."

"These men aren't renegades. The San Carlos agent will let them work here as long as you'll take responsibility for them."

"Responsibility! For these . . . for these . . . ?" Mackenzie was speechless.

Lu chose that moment to come out into the yard from the house. She gasped when she saw their visitors. "Mackenzie!"

"It's all right, Lu. These are 'peaceful' Indians," Mackenzie said sarcastically.

"Mercy! Lord help us!" Lu grabbed the top of the yard wall as if for support and watched the Indians with narrowed eyes.

"This is an insane idea!" Mackenzie told Cal in an emphatic, low-pitched voice. The Apaches watched their conversation impassively; the cowboys watched with scowls and mutterings. "Even if I permitted these Indians to stay, the men would never work with them. They'd sooner kill them than ride with them. Can't you see that?"

"Apaches aren't that easy to kill," Cal told her with and upward twitch of one brow.

"That's not the point!"

"The men will do what I tell them to do," he assured her.

"We could hire white men and avoid the whole problem."

Cal shook his head. "Try to find someone to work on the Lazy B other than some gunslinging yahoo who's going to cause more trouble than he's worth. Crosby's put out the word that anyone who wants to stay in one piece had better find work elsewhere."

Mackenzie scowled in frustration. What Cal said was true. She couldn't very well deny it.

"We need the help, Mac. Do you think I'd bring these men here if I thought they were any danger to you, or to Frankie?"

They did sorely need the help, and once again she was furious with him for being right. "Are these your brothers too?" she asked sourly.

He smiled, and she could see in his eyes that he knew he'd won. "Not exactly brothers. Mahko"—the burliest of the Apache trio fixed his eyes upon her as he was introduced—"is brother to the wife of Dohn-say's nephew. Dohn-say was my mother."

Mackenzie gave the savage a weak smile.

"Istee is to Mahko's right." At the mention of his name, Istee actually smiled. His face lit up with boyish charm. "He and Bay-chen-day-sen are good friends of Mahko's."

All three Apaches gazed at her with what seemed intense curiosity. Mackenzie squirmed mentally. Did one say "pleased to meet you" or "how do you do" to a savage? "Do they speak English?"

"Some," Cal told her.

"This would not be easy work," she told the Apaches, trying to sound as discouraging as possible. Istee smiled and nodded. The others just continued to look at her.

"Cal, they'll be trusting their lives to those men." She gestured toward the hands, who were still straining to listen. "You know they think the only good Apache's a dead one."

"These three can handle themselves," he replied. "and I can handle the men."

"Why do they want to do this?" she asked, at a loss.

"Because I asked them to. And because they're tired of the reservation."

Mackenzie shook her head. "California Smith, sometimes I think you're from another world. You take insanity and make it seem like irrefutable logic."

His mouth twisted into a slight smile.

"I guess you win," she conceded reluctantly. "Get your 'peaceful Indians' settled, and get those loitering cowboys into dinner so they can go out and do some work this afternoon."

Cal's eyes crinkled as his smile deepened.

"Don't look so pleased with yourself. I think you're asking for trouble. Whatever happens is on your head." She stalked through the gate into the yard and took Lu's arm. "Come on, Lu. Let's let our foreman get about his work. Carmelita probably needs help in the kitchen. I'm sure Frankie's driving her crazy by now." She glanced back at Cal with an annoyed look as she pulled her still-staring stepmother toward the kitchen.

The Apaches watched with frank curiosity as Mackenzie strode toward the kitchen building with Lu in tow. Istee chuckled quietly. "Your woman has an angry mouth," he commented to Cal in Apache.

Cal grinned and shook his head. "That's not the only part of her that's angry."

Mahko nodded solemnly. "She does as you tell her. That is good."

Cal almost laughed at the pronouncement. He wouldn't want these three to get the idea that Mackenzie was the sort of female who could be depended upon to be tractable. They would be sorely disappointed if they did. "She does as I say only because she's caught in a trap and she can't see any escape. She has much bitterness against the Apache and against me, but at heart she's a good woman."

Mahko and Bay-chen-day-sen nodded sagely; Istee grinned and said, "I think you also are in a trap you cannot escape. Women have a way of doing that to a man if he is not very careful."

Mackenzie shut the yard gate behind her and walked with purposeful strides toward the barn, where the hands were gathering to mount up for the morning's work. She glanced uneasily at the gray thread of smoke that curled up from the foothills. Her new "cowboys" had declined to settle into the bunkhouse—granted, a wise decision—and had quickly and efficiently set up a camp just behind the first rise of land to the east, less than a quarter mile from the ranch buildings. Mackenzie had been shocked to learn they'd brought their wives with them. Cal had explained that Apache men felt quite at loss without a wife to tend to home fires, thus Apache women often traveled with their men, even at times on the warpath.

Lu had been broodingly silent most of the previous afternoon. Her stepmother was as uneasy as she about having Apaches on the ranch, Mackenzie realized. She resisted the urge to say "I told you so" and point out that she had said all along that Cal would bring trouble to the Lazy B. Against all common sense and better judgement, Mackenzie had chosen to trust Cal on this, and she didn't even know why. The afternoon before, when his gaze had trapped hers and held her eyes with almost painful honesty, something had turned in her mind. Just as she no longer believed that Cal had brought his savage brother down upon the Lazy B six years ago, she also had faith that he would not deliberately bring trouble upon them now. He would never take the chance of Frankie's being hurt.

Lord, but she hoped she was right.

The men gathered just outside the barn. They were not yet mounted. Some of their horses were still unsaddled and hitched by halters and lead ropes to the arena fence. What sounded to be a heated discussion fell abruptly into silence when Mackenzie walked up. None of the men met her eyes. Even Bull, usually the most amiable of the lot, fixed his gaze on the dusty ground.

"Mornin', Miz Butler." Sam Crawford stepped out of the

group and touched his one hand to the brim of his battered hat.

"Mr. Crawford." She glanced at the sullen men. "Is there a problem?"

"It's them Injuns, Miz Butler."

Mackenzie felt her stomach twist. She'd suspected her unruly men were going to dig their heels about the Apaches. "Those are reservation Indians, Mr. Crawford. They know horses, and they know cattle." Which was more that she could credit most of her cowboys, Mackenzie reflected silently. "They have the San Carlos agents' permission to be here. Since we're shorthanded, they'll be helping out for a while."

Sam's perpetual grimace turned even nastier than usual.

"Don't worry, Mr. Crawford," Mackenzie said. "They're tame. Friendly."

Sam spat into the dirt. "I'll tell you true, Miz Butler, tame or not, they're still Apaches, ain't they? No man here's gonna dirty hisself by working alongside them filthy savages."

Her hands calling the Apaches filthy was rather like the pot calling the kettle black. "Mr. Crawford . . . !"

"No ifs, and, or buts, Miz Butler."

The other men nodded agreement. Seven surly faces regarded her with obdurate rebellion, but Mackenzie could almost smell their fear. The men might complain that they were too proud to work alongside "dirty" Apaches, but what they really were was scared stiff.

"We ain't doin' a lick of work till those Injuns are gone," George Keller added.

The men looked up as a soft footfall scuffed the dirt behind Mackenzie. The rock-hard determination in their faces faded to uncertainty.

"Just who's not going to work?"

Mackenzie jumped at the sound of Cal's voice.

"We ain't," Keller told him. The others dropped their gazes and stared at the floor.

Cal seemed to ignore Keller's answer. He came up beside Mackenzie and nodded a greeting, his wooden face in place and not looking a bit daunted. "You want the fences ridden today?" he asked, just as if everything were normal.

"I want some of the men to ride along the San Pedro to see how many of our beeves are down there. The others can work with the horses. Your . . . uh . . . the new hands can go wherever you think best."

An unfriendly murmur rose from the listening men.

"Yes, ma'am." Cal smiled, almost as though he were enjoying himself. "Saddle up, men."

The hands stood rock still.

"Anyone who doesn't ride can pack his kit and be on his way." He targeted Keller with his eyes. "Mr. Keller, do you want to scratch out your living with a gun again? You hand's gotten a bit slow for that kind or work. When you drew on me a few days ago I had time to grab your wrist before you could get a single shot off."

Keller reluctantly dropped his eyes.

"Mr.Crawford." Cal turned to Sam. "You don't cowboy worth a damn. No other ranch in Arizona is going to hire you. And Mr. Ferguson, you eat too much to give up your two regular meals a day."

Bull chuckled, nodded his head, and turned to tighten the cinch on his mount.

"Gid Small." A blond youth jerked his head up to look at Cal. He had the mien of a sullen child told to do his chores. "I thought you were saving up to buy that new Winchester in Gus Bigley's gunshop."

"Shit!" Gid cursed in an emphatic whisper. Mackenzie felt the resistance start to dissolve. The men shuffled toward their mounts.

"We'd do a lot better with a foreman who don't have red

skin under the white," someone muttered just loud enough to be heard.

Cal's eyes swept over the group in a calm, cold glance. "Someone want to prove he'd make a better foreman?" he challenged.

Suddenly, every man present seemed to find something to study on the ground. "Guess I'd rather have them Apaches ridin' with me than against me," Bull conceded.

The men mounted up and Cal swung aboard his Appaloosa. Mackenzie couldn't help but note the powerful grace of his movement, the breadth of his shoulders, the sun gleaming off his tawny, hatless head. As if on cue, Mahko, Istee, and Bay-chen-day-sen trotted up to join the group just as the hands set out. Cal sat his mount with the same suppleness and skill as the Apaches did. The four of them made the rest of the group look clumsy.

Mackenzie allowed herself a moment of sour resentment at Cal's deftness in handling her employees, her stepmother, her horses, her cattle, her enemies . . . her daughter. She had struggled hard to save this ranch, to deal with its rough, dangerous men, to be a good mother in a land that was no more merciful to children than to adults—and California Smith breezed in and made everything look so easy, made Mackenzie feel almost unnecessary. Lu would tell her she was being unreasonable; and she *was* being unreasonable, Mackenzie acknowledged. Where Cal was concerned, she had a habit of throwing reason out the window.

The object of Mackenzie's malice wheeled his horse about and trotted back to her while the hands continued under the Lazy B arch. He admonished her in a tone her father might have used had he still been alive. "Stay away from these men, Mac. You're only going to get yourself in trouble. You hired *me* to handle them. Let me do my job."

As he wheeled his horse and followed the crew amid a swirl of dust, Mackenzie leaned back against the open barn door. Narrow-eyed, she looked toward the stall where the wild mare placidly munched the extra ration of grain that Cal gave her every morning. "Did you hear the arrogance of the man?" she asked the horse. " 'You hired *me* to handle the men. Let me do my job,' " she mimicked.

The mare snorted.

"I forgot," Mackenzie said. "You like the big jackass. So sorry."

She started back toward the house, no longer feeling like riding out to check the springs, as had been her intention. She felt herself being sucked into a current like a twig in a torrent—losing control of the ranch, struggling for control of herself. She hated to admit it, but Cal just might win this struggle. His strength and confidence made other men obey him—and so far Mackenzie had obeyed him also. It would be easy to depend on his strength and let the Lazy B's problems rest on his broad shoulders rather than bear the burden herself. It would also be easy to let the carefully nurtured ice melt from around her heart and forget the past, forget that six years ago, trusting California Smith had led to disaster. Cal might not have killed her father, but he certainly had killed her heart.

She reached the yard wall and turned to look at the column of dust raised by the departing hands. They had split into two groups. Some headed toward the river. Another group—including the Apaches—rode toward the field where the green-broke two-year-olds were pastured. Even at such a distance she could spot Cal riding near his Apaches.

Mackenzie swallowed hard. She felt an attack of utter foolishness stalking her. God help her if she forgot the lessons of the past.

8

The Butler ranch house seemed the same and yet not the same, Cal mused as he stepped into the dim entrance hall. The hatrack still stood in the corner, though Frank Butler's hat no longer hung there. The glassed-in guncase still bristled with weapons. Frank's old Henry rifle stood in line beside a twelve-gauge shotgun and two Winchesters. Not a smudge or a speck of dust marred the shiny blue metal of the barrels, and the wooden stocks were oiled and polished. Apparently, Mackenzie had learned the value of a good weapon. Or perhaps Lu was the one who kept them in such good condition.

Straight ahead of him, Cal glimpsed Frank's office through a half-open door. The oak desk and bookcases were tidy, not cluttered as they had been when Frank had been in residence. The air was no longer blue and pungent with cigar smoke. In that office Frank had asked Cal to leave the Lazy B—gently, without rancor, and wishing him the best of all things. The best of all things, that is, except Mackenzie. Cal was a good man, Frank had explained, but Mackenzie was very young and very green. She didn't even know what love was. She didn't know what she was letting herself in for, thinking she was in love with a man such as California Smith.

Cal smiled, even though the memory pricked with pain. Frank had known less about his daughter than even Cal had. Certainly neither of them had known her very well. He remembered his shock when Mackenzie had come to him that night demanding that he marry her. Green though she'd been, she had known instinctively just how to get what she wanted. Cal had been quick to discard his honorable intent to leave her be. Wanting her the way he had, he hadn't been hard to seduce. If the next morning hadn't brought a harsh dose of reality, if they'd left together as Mac had wanted, Cal wondered where they would be now. Would Mackenzie have tired of being the wife of a man branded a renegade and savage? Would her first joy at their union have faded in the harsh reality of being the yellow-haired Apache's woman?

A giggle from the direction of the parlor brought him back to the present. He moved silently to where he could look into the room through the half-open door. Frankie sat beside her mother on the window seat. The afternoon light slanted through the window behind them and illuminated mother and child in a golden haze. Their heads—one a rich red, the other bright gold—bent together over a book that lay open in Mackenzie's lap. As Mackenzie read aloud, Frankie pointed at the page and giggled. They were both so absorbed in the story that they took no notice of Cal standing in the doorway.

Certainly one good thing had come of his brief time with Mackenzie, Cal thought. Frankie was a beam of sunlight distilled to its brightest and molded into a child. She was light, laughter, fragile innocence, and guileless, untarnished wisdom. On that violent day when Mackenzie had been robbed of her joyous spirit, her laughter and trusting love had passed to the child she cradled within. A love that had died so soon after blossoming at least had borne one beautiful fruit.

Cal continued to watch, drinking in the sight of Mackenzie for once unguarded and smiling, but only a few short moments were granted him before she looked up. For an instant her eyes seemed to light at the sight of him. Then the hint of brightness darkened almost as if she had forced it away.

"I . . . uh . . . knocked," he explained rather lamely, "but no one answered."

For a moment Mackenzie was silent. She seemed to have trouble gathering enough composure to speak. "I suppose I wasn't paying attention." she finally said. "What is it, Cal?"

"George and Gid found twenty-five steers down by the San Pedro with Lazy B brands changed to the RA brand. It was a pretty good job, but they could still recognize the change." He didn't need to add that George Keller and Gideon Smith both had done a bit of brand-changing themselves in years past and therefore had an expert's eye for what a modified brand looked like.

Mackenzie closed her book and frowned. "RA," she said thoughtfully. "I don't recognize the brand—but I'd lay a good wager that whoever RA is, Nathan Crosby is behind this somehow. Rustlers would've run the cattle off before changing the brands." Giving Frankie's knee an affectionate pat, she stood up. "Let me go to the office and check the brand's registry."

"Aren't we gonna finish the story?" Frankie asked in a disappointed voice.

"We'll finish it, Sprout. I'll be right back."

Frankie permitted herself a tiny frown of annoyance as Mackenzie left the room. Her mother said that pouting was for babies, and whenever Frankie pouted, her mother imitated her sullen expression until Frankie had to laugh at such a ridiculous face. Therefore, Frankie was careful not to let the frown get too bad, just in case her mother should come back in and start making foolish faces in front of California. She didn't want her mother to look foolish in front of California. She wanted Cal to like her mother so he would stay at the Lazy B.

Frankie liked California. The other men who worked on the ranch were a little bit scary. Well, maybe not really scary. After all, Frankie was five, and five-year-olds didn't get scared like little babies. But those other men smelled bad and spit a lot and didn't smile at Frankie like California did. She wanted California to stay. If he married her mother, then he'd have to stay.

Frankie bounced off the window seat, walked over to Cal, and tugged on his trouser leg. "Ma was reading me a story," she explained, and handed him the book. He was looking at the doorway where her mother had left; his expression made Frankie hope that he did like her mother after all. She wouldn't tell him some of the bad names she'd heard her mother call him when she thought Frankie wasn't listening. He might not like Ma if he knew she'd called him a puffed-up snake's behind—only, her mother had used another word for behind. Frankie would get sent to the corner if she so much as thought that word. She didn't even know that snakes had behinds, but she had an idea that California wouldn't like being called one.

"Do you like to read stories?"

He looked down at her and smiled. California had a nice smile, she decided. His teeth were all there, and they were white. When he smiled, his eyes crinkled and got an even deeper blue.

"Ma was reading fairy stories that a man named Aesop made up. And it's spelled with an *A*, not an *E*. Even though it sounds like an *E*. I'm learning to read," she informed him proudly. "Did your ma read you stories when you were little?"

Cal sat down on the window seat and seemed to give her question a good deal of thought. She didn't think the question was that hard.

"My mother's name was Dohn-say. She told me many stories, but the stories weren't written down like Mr. E . . . ."

"Aesop. A-E-S-O-P." She spelled it out proudly.

"Right. The people I lived with when I was your age—the Apaches—don't write their stories. They speak a language that is only in the head, not on paper."

"You mean Indians don't know how to read?"

"They don't have to read. Their stories and laws and customs are passed from parents to their children in spoken words, and many of the old people among the Apaches are great storytellers who will entertain the children and their parents for hours at a time telling the stories of the *Dine*, the People."

Frankie thought this was a wonderful idea. "What are the stories about?"

"Would you like to hear one?"

"Oh yes!" She climbed up on the window seat beside him. "Please, California!" Frankie assumed her usual story-listening position by dragging Cal's arm across her shoulders and snuggling up to his side. Snuggling up to California was very different than snuggling up to her mother. He was like a warm rock and smelled of sunlight and leather. Being this close to him filled a place in Frankie's heart that she didn't know needed filling. Being this close to him, Frankie decided, was nice. She looked up at him expectantly. "You can start now," she told him. "I'm ready."

"All right," he said. He held her so lightly that he must think she would break, Frankie decided. The eyes that looked down at her glowed with the same warm light she so often saw in her mother's when they sat together like this. "This is a story my father used to tell me."

"Your father told you stories?" she asked. The few Apache

men Frankie had seen in her young life didn't appear to be the sort of men who would tell stories to little boys and girls.

"My father was a wonderful storyteller. He told me many times the story of a great quarrel between the lightning and the wind. Would you like to hear that one?"

"Yes, please."

"One day long ago Lightning and Wind were talking between them."

"Lightning and wind can't talk!" Frankie scoffed.

"In this tale they can. They are two very powerful beings with very powerful tempers."

"Oh. All right. What did they say?"

"They had a big fight over who did the most good on the earth and who was the strongest. Wind got very angry when Lightning said that *he* was the most powerful and he could do very well without Wind."

"Ooooh! What did Wind do?" Frankie could just imagine the wind throwing a fit like the cowboys did when they got mad.

"Wind hid. He ran away and hid from the earth so that no one could find him. The people were frightened, and soon they learned how important Wind was, for without Wind, no rain fell on the earth and everything started to dry up."

"That's terrible!"

"So they hired all the hawks and other birds to search for Wind. They even asked the yellow and black bee to search, because the bee could fly into very small spaces where perhaps Wind was hiding."

"I got stung by a bee once. It hurt a lot."

"This bee wouldn't have stung you," Cal said. "He was too busy looking for Wind."

"Did he find him?"

"Bee found him. Wind was hiding in a very far place on the earth. At first Wind was angry that Bee had found him and wouldn't listen to what Bee said, but then Bee called the Wind's name right to his face."

Frankie gave a delighted gasp. "Did Bee call Wind a bad name?"

"No," Cal explained. "Bee called Wind by Wind's own name. Among the Apache, a person is not called by his personal name except when it's very important to get his attention. So when Bee called Wind's name to his face and asked him to come back, Wind had to listen, for he knew then that what Bee said was very important."

"Did he come back?" Frankie asked, entranced.

"Wind pouted," Cal told her with raised brows. " 'Lightning said he could do very well without me. Why do the people want me back now?' " Cal did an imitation of Wind's blustery voice that made Frankie dissolve into giggles.

"What happened? What happened?" she pleaded after her giggling fit ended.

"Bee told Wind that the people were suffering greatly. No rain had fallen because Wind was hiding, and the earth was so hot and dry it was about to burn away."

"Oooooh!"

"When Wind heard this, he said he would speak to Lightning in four days and that Lightning should meet him at a certain mountaintop. Wind told Bee that Lightning should wait for him on top of a rainbow. Four days passed, and when Wind went to the mountaintop, he found not only Lightning awaiting him, but Earth and Sun as well. Sun had come from the east in the form of a little whirlwind."

"Like the dust devils on the valley floor?" Frankie asked.

"Just like that, only this was a sun devil."

She giggled.

"Well, on top of that rainbow, Wind and Lightning embraced and made up. Together they made the earth as it once was, with green grass and plenty of water. Then Lightning breathed a mighty breath and created four persons who they sent in the four directions: east—"

"West, north, and south," Frankie provided proudly.

"That's right. And these four persons were the seasons, so now we have summer, winter, fall, and spring."

Frankie clapped her hands with glee.

"Sun gave Wind and Lightning a pipe to smoke. They smoked the pipe and made peace, and ever after that they were friends."

"That's a pretty good story," Frankie agreed wholeheartedly. "Now finish the story that Ma was reading to me. Please?"

Cal looked ruefully at the book. "To tell the truth, Frankie, I don't read very well."

Frankie was amazed. All grown-up people knew how to read, or at least, most grown-up people. Her ma had told her some of the men in the bunkhouse didn't know how to read. California said that Indians didn't read either, but California wasn't really an Indian, because he had yellow hair, and she knew he was smarter and better than the men in the bunkhouse. So he really ought to know how to read. "You mean nobody ever taught you how to read?"

"Well, I lived with a family in Tucson when I first left the Indians." He smiled, and Frankie thought the smile had a funny twist to it. "A school there tried to teach me to read but they gave up. Not too long after that I lived with a soldier at Fort Buchanan named Josh Cameron. He taught me to read and do sums enough to get by. But I'd be so slow at the reading, you'd forget the story."

"Oh." Frankie's face fell, then the perfect scheme blinked into her head like a gift from a guardian fairy—an impish one with a nose for trouble. "I could maybe teach you to read, California! And you could teach me how to ride a horse. Ma won't, but you could!"

"You ma won't teach you to ride?"

"Oh, she wouldn't mind!" Frankie rushed to forestall the objection she saw coming. "She wouldn't. Really! She just . . . uh . . . doesn't have the time, but Ma knows that I'm really big enough to ride a horse."

"Oh, I'm sure she does." The smile on California's face looked as if he was laughing inside, Frankie thought. But at least he hadn't said no. Yet.

"I taught your mother how to ride a horse long before you were born."

Frankie narrowed her eyes in disbelief. "You came to live here after I was born."

"That's right," Cal agreed. "But a long time ago I used to work for your grandfather, when your mother first came to the valley to live. She didn't know how to ride a horse either, and she asked me to teach her, just like you asked me to teach you. Only she didn't offer to teach me to read in return."

Frankie thought California's face looked odd, just as though he had stuck something into his mouth that was sweet and bitter at the same time. "Didn't she give you anything?"

"Oh, yes," he said in an odd tone. "She gave me something. She gave me . . . a lot."

"What did she give you?"

Cal's expression took on a familiar cast, the look that adults have when they're not going to tell what they're thinking. Frankie saw that expression a lot.

"She gave me . . . something wonderful that was a secret between your mother and me."

"Oh." How disappointing. Frankie wondered if she should tell California the naked truth. "California?"

"Yes?"

"I probably don't read good enough yet to really teach you. Ma's still teaching me. But when I get good enough, I'll teach you."

Cal smiled. "I'd like that."

"But I'm big enough to learn to ride a horse, aren't I? I would really like to ride a horse."

Mackenzie stood in the parlor doorway listening to Frankie cajole and bargain with Cal to get her dearest wish. Her heart squeezed at the sight of them together. Cal's arm was draped across Frankie's shoulder in a hold that was both protective and possessive, and Frankie looked up at him with eyes warm with hero worship.

She never should have left the two of them together, Mackenzie thought. Her heart, however, had difficulty resenting how naturally they fit together. After all, they were father and daughter. Frankie might not know it—Mackenzie might deny it if her daughter ever questioned her on the subject—but all the denials with the world wouldn't change the truth. The warmth in Cal's eyes when he looked at his daughter rivaled the warmth in which he'd once looked at her.

Standing in the doorway, spying like an intruder on a private little world that had been born in the brief minutes she'd been gone, Mackenzie suffered an irrational pang of loss, a mad yearning for California Smith to once again look at her with such love in his eyes. Up from the depths of her mind rose the memory of how content she had felt lying in his arms. Content, protected, cherished, loved. And Mackenzie had loved in return. Oh, how she had loved.

Love had died a bitter death in both of them, Mackenzie reminded herself sternly, and the bitterness now stood between them like a solid wall. For all that Cal thought he owed a blood debt to the Lazy B, he had no place in her life, no place in her daughter's life. Mackenzie tried to steel her heart against the light she saw in Frankie's eyes when the little girl looked at Cal. The joyful glow was more than a child's delight in the prospect of riding lessons. Did some instinct tell Frankie that this man was more to her than just another one of the Lazy B's cowboys?

Mackenzie decided that she'd best halt their conversation before it went too far.

"Don't you think you should grow another couple of inches before you become a horsewoman?" she chided her daughter gently.

Frankie looked around in surprise at Mackenzie's voice. Cal didn't look startled at all. He had known from the first that she was watching, Mackenzie realized. A man who had lived much of his life among the Apaches was difficult to sneak up on.

"Oh, Ma!" came Frankie's exasperated objection. "Issy has her very own pony. I could learn to ride!"

"Isabelle is two years older and three inches taller than you, Sprout."

"California had his own horse when he was as little as me!"

Mackenzie gave Cal a stern look, but his eyes were on Frankie.

"Pleeeease!" Frankie pleaded. "California said he would teach me!"

Frankie's excitement and the caring warmth in Cal's eyes was hard to resist. "Well . . . if you promise to do everything that Mr. Smith tells you to do and be very careful."

"Oh, I will! I will!" Frankie sprang up from the window seat and hopped around the room clapping her hands in delight. "Can we start now, California? Can we?"

"Mr. Smith has work to do this afternoon, Frankie. You mustn't pester him while he's working."

Frankie clamped a lid on her excitement with visible effort. "Yes, ma'am."

"Now, you go out to the court and water the flowers for me, will you, please? Then help Gran in the garden. She's picking fresh vegetables for dinner."

"Yes, ma'am." Frankie started to bounce toward the door that led to the inner court, but immediately slowed to a more sedate pace, obviously trying hard to please her mother and not risk her fragile victory. When she was out of sight, Mackenzie turned a stern eye on California.

"Don't worry, Mac," he said with a grin. "I wouldn't let her get hurt. After all, you should know I'm a good teacher."

The memory of all the early mornings and late evenings they'd spent together in the arena flashed into her mind—bouncing along on a placidly trotting horse while Cal, patient beyond the limits that any man should be expected to be patient, coached her on how to sit the flow and rhythm of the horse and how to let her body relax. Mackenzie hadn't really cared about riding; she'd simply wanted to be near him. She had certainly gotten her wish. His instruction hadn't stopped at horsemanship; Cal had also been a devastatingly superb instructor in bed.

Her face heated at the unwelcome recollection, and Cal's smile bore witness that he thought along the same intimate lines.

"I found the RA brand in the registry," Mackenzie said briskly, banishing the unwanted images from her mind. "It belongs to Raitt Armstrong. He ranches a spread across the river to the northwest. He's friends with Crosby, but I wouldn't have thought that Raitt would fall in with Crosby's tricks. He's always seemed to me to be an honest man. But then," she added, a hint of bitterness sharpening her voice, "I'm not noted as a good judge of character, am I?"

"It's not hard to be fooled about a man's nature," Cal replied. "Sometimes we see people for what we want them to be rather than for what they are."

Mackenzie didn't like this turn of the conversation either. "Well, in any case, I don't think we need to make an issue of this with Raitt. Mostly because I suspect Crosby is behind it, not him. Though I can't imagine why Crosby wouldn't use his own brand if he's gone into brand-switching."

"Lazy B changes a lot easier to RA than Bar Cross," Cal

pointed out. "Maybe he thought you wouldn't notice the changes. You're operating this ranch pretty much on the edge as far as herd size, Mac. It wouldn't take much of a loss to make this a very bad market year."

Mackenzie sighed wearily. "What do you think we should do?"

"Right now? Nothing. We didn't see the brands being changed, so it's going to be difficult to prove any accusations. Besides, if you accuse Armstrong, you might be barking up the wrong tree. And you have only suspicions about Crosby. I'll tell the crew to keep a sharp eye out. If we can catch these brand-changers in the act, then you'll have the law on your side."

"And if we can't? As you say, I can't afford to lose many cattle."

"During roundup we'll take all the beeves that are ours, including the ones that are wearing changed brands. If Crosby or his friend Armstrong wants to fight about it, we face that when the time comes."

"Lord, but I'm tired of being pushed around and forever trying to cut my losses!"

"It'll end, Mac." Cal's voice was sympathetic. "Crosby's only hauling in the rope to hang himself. You've done a good job with the Lazy B, and it couldn't have been easy. Don't give up now."

Mackenzie tried to fight down a flush of pleasure at his compliment. The reservoir of her anger against him was close to running dry, and that was dangerous. She conjured up memories of how she'd felt waking up in his bed to be told that he was leaving without her. But this time the incantation of bitterness couldn't quite still the stirrings of her heart.

"I'm not about to give up," she assured him.

He smiled as he turned to leave. "If you send Frankie out

to the arena after supper tonight, I'll put her up on old Traveller. Very carefully," he promised.

"If Frankie gets hurt, I'll hang your skin out to dry," Mackenzie warned with a lifted brow.

Cal grinned at her as they walked to the door. "Thought you'd already tried that a time or two."

Mackenzie couldn't even work up a good mad at that unmannerly remark. Partly because it was very true. Also because she just then realized that all through their conversation, Cal had regarded her with a look every bit as warm as the one he'd turned on Frankie. Cal took hold of her arm when they reached the door. All teasing was gone from his voice when he spoke. "Mac. Frankie is really something. What we created together, you and I . . . "

Mackenzie drew back and found herself trapped between the wall and Cal's body. He didn't look as though he was thinking of their daughter. A hot, predatory glint in his eyes was all too familiar. She didn't move, dangling in the limbo between longing and fear.

Cal's mouth lowered gently to hers. He urged her lips apart, stroking her mouth with his tongue and stealing her breath. His touch sent shivers of response along her spine. When the kiss ended as gently as it had begun, Mackenzie's heart raced, and her hands shook.

"Thank you for that one night, and thank you for Frankie." His breath played against her wet lips, and then the door closed quietly behind him. Mackenzie rushed to the window to watch him walk toward the barn. She stood as if in a trance until he disappeared behind the big wooden door.

When Amos Gilbert arrived fifteen minutes later, Mac was still sitting bemused on the parlor sofa. He stuck his head into the room and asked, "Lu did tell you I was coming for dinner instead of supper, didn't she?"

Mackenzie jumped.

"Carmelita let me in."

"Oh, Amos. Yes, of course Lu told me. It's Thursday, isn't it?" She stood abruptly and tricd to gather her wits. How could she have let one stupid kiss derail her mind into such fanciful, ridiculous, downright wicked thoughts. "I think Lu is out in the garden with Frankie picking some fresh vegetables."

Amos gave her a quizzical look. Mackenzie wondered if something in her face revealed that she'd just allowed herself to be thoroughly kissed by California Smith. Not only allowed it, but enjoyed it.

"I see Cal is back," he remarked. "He rode out just as I pulled up."

Mackenzie smiled what she was sure was an idiotic smile. "Yes, he came back. He'd left a message in town that he'd gone to hire some more help for us. We left too early to get the message."

Amos grinned and gave her an "I told you so" look. "I didn't think he was the type to run off without leaving word."

"Don't rub it in, Amos."

"Would I do such a thing?"

"With great relish."

Amos chuckled. "Well, I'm glad it's straightened out, anyway. How is your new foreman getting along?"

"Nothing has changed, Amos." She flushed slightly at the fib and knew that Amos read her accurately. Things *had* changed; Mackenzie simply hadn't decided if they had changed for the better or worse.

Amos smiled slowly at her discomfiture. "Well now, I think I'll just go see if Lu and Frankie need help picking those vegetables. There's nothing quite like fresh-cooked carrots and peas to liven up a meal."

All through dinner Mackenzie felt as if half her mind were somewhere else, stuck somewhere in the past when she and California Smith had both been younger and, for her part at least, a good deal more foolish. She relived his kiss over and over, telling herself that Cal was entranced with Frankie and the kiss had come from his delight with the child—not with the mother. Her denial was a lie, though, and Mackenzie knew it. That kiss hadn't been a mere thank-you; it had been a caress of male desire and passionate tenderness. Perhaps Cal did still care for her, despite all the years and bitterness that lay between them.

Suddenly Mackenzie felt out of control. Invocation of the old hurtful images no longer fired the anger as it once had. She was thinking thoughts she shouldn't, feeling emotions that were far too dangerous.

"Mackenzie?"

She looked up from her plate. From the tone of Lu's voice, this wasn't the first time her stepmother had tried to get her attention. "Yes?"

"I said Amos is going to drive me into town this afternoon. Is there anything we need that that I should pick up?"

"No," Mackenzie said vaguely. "I don't think so. Are you coming back to spend the evening, Amos? I can have Carmelita prepare the guest house."

"No, thanks. We won't be late. In fact, would Frankie like to come with us?"

"I can't," Frankie hastened to tell him. "Tonight California's going to teach me to ride a horse!"

"You don't say!" Amos smiled broadly. His enthusiasm elicited a pleased grin from Frankie. "California must like you very much to go to that trouble."

"He does," Frankie assured him. "He likes me a lot."

Amos and Lu both gave Mackenzie satisfied looks.

"Don't jump to any conclusions," she warned them.

As Amos had promised, they were back early. An hour after supper, just as the long summer shadows were turning the valley purple, Amos's buggy pulled up in front of the house. Hearing the rattle of wheels on the gravel, Mackenzie set aside the book she had been trying to read.

Lu swept into the parlor. "I see Frankie is having her first riding lesson."

"Yes. She's ecstatic."

"You don't sound very happy about it."

"I don't like Frankie's becoming so attached to Cal. It's not a good idea."

Lu shrugged, her mind obviously elsewhere. When Mackenzie looked at her stepmother more closely, she noticed a rare flush glowing on Lu's cheeks.

"Where's Amos?" Mackenzie asked.

"He's putting the buggy in the barn. He decided to spend the night after all."

"That's good. He shouldn't be driving back to town in the dark."

Lu's face glowed even brighter. "Mackenzie. I have something to tell you."

Mackenzie smiled. "You look like someone set off fireworks behind your eyes. What's happened?"

"Amos proposed."

This was no great announcement. Amos proposed in jest every couple of weeks, and Lu regularly turned him down with a stern warning to behave himself.

"Mackenzie! He really proposed!"

"You mean he meant it?"

"Every word."

Mackenzie held her breath, even though the expression on Lu's face told her the answer. "Did you accept?"

"Yes! Yes, I did!"

Mackenzie was dumbfounded. She should say something, she knew. Congratulations, best wishes, what a wonderful surprise. But she couldn't quite.

"Oh, my dear! I know how you must feel. It's not that I don't still love your father. I will always love the memory of

Frank Butler. But I also love Amos, and he's alive, and here. Mackenzie, *niña*, I'm not a woman who is happy living without a man."

Mackenzie rose and gave her stepmother a hug. "Lu, that's not it at all! I was just . . . surprised. I love Amos. He's one of the finest men in the world, and I'm delighted that you're so happy."

"Oh, I am happy." Lu spread her arms and did a pirouette. "I am so very happy."

Bemused, Mackenzie couldn't help but smile. What had happened to her sober, sensible, dignified stepmother?

"Tomorrow you and I must start planning the wedding. Not tonight while Amos is still here." She smiled in blissful tolerance. "Men get so bored with that sort of thing. You and I and Frankie will decide who we must invite and what we shall have to eat. Oh, it's past time we had a party at the Lazy B! A wedding will be just the thing."

Mackenzie's face fell as she remembered that six years ago, she also had dreamed of a wedding at the Lazy B. Lu misinterpreted her sudden stillness.

"Oh, my dear. I don't want you to think that Amos would ever try to interfere in the ranch. No. In fact, I plan to sign the entire ranch over to you. Amos is quite well fixed and can provide for me very nicely."

"You helped my father start this ranch," Mackenzie objected.

A hint of sorrow didn't take the glow from Lu's face. "Frank passed his dream on to you, *niña*, not to me. Come, now, show a happy face. Amos will be in any minute, and he was afraid you might disapprove of his stealing me away."

Mackenzie could hardly disapprove when Lu was obviously so content—she seemed to have lost ten years in one day. Amos seemed equally pleased. He had always treated Lu with warm affection, but now that their future was settled, a heat shone from his eyes that was almost painful for

Mackenzie to see. She had almost forgotten what love looked like, what miracles it wrought in the spirit as well as the body.

She went to bed that night ashamed to admit she was jealous of her stepmother. Compared to Lu, a woman twenty years her senior, Mackenzie felt like a dried-out spinster, a prune with none of the juices of life flowing through her veins. She fell asleep and dreamed of weddings. Not Lu's, but hers—the wedding she'd been so determined to have six years ago. She tossed uneasily as sleep magnified and added to her memories of the one night of passion she had known with California Smith. She relived the nervousness of her amateurish seduction, the fear that had so quickly been soothed by Cal's gentleness, the sweet fulfillment of his possession. In vivid detail she felt the bliss of his body moving on her and inside her, smelled the sweet musk of their lovemaking, heard the sounds of her own cries of release. The dreams did not end in such exhilaration, however. Still burning with desire in Cal's embrace, Mackenzie looked toward a window, where dawn broke through the magic, comforting darkness of the night. She could see the dust swirl from beneath pounding hooves and hear the shrill, chilling war cries as wild savages rode directly toward the room where she lay with her lover. Cal looked down at her and smiled. Mackenzie clung to the man who still covered her body, knowing she would lose him. A brown Apache face grinned at her from the window, and then the window exploded in blood.

Mackenzie woke, drenched with sweat, her heart slamming desperately against her ribs and the hot trace of tears still wet on her cheeks.

9

Mackenzie had stayed away from Frankie's first riding lesson, but she couldn't stay away from the second. Her daughter's ecstatic account of the lesson the day before was too much of a lure.

First thing after supper, Frankie rushed out to the barn and pulled Cal away from the conversation with the wild mare. Mackenzie followed not far behind, watching with mixed feelings as Frankie tugged on Cal's trouser leg.

"What are you saying to her?" Frankie inquired, cocking her head curiously at the strange words he spoke so softly to the horse.

"I'm telling her what a beautiful lady she is and what a fine baby she'll soon have."

"Then why don't you say that?"

"Horses understand Apache better than English."

"Oh." Frankie accepted the declaration without question. "Can I ride her sometime?"

Cal smiled down at her. "I figure you will, sometime. But not real soon. You need to grow bigger, and she needs to tame down a bit."

"*You* ride her," she said with a bit of defiance.

"That's different. It doesn't matter if she throws me on my backside, but your little backside is a lot more breakable than mine." He reached down and gave her a pinch to demonstrate, and Frankie burst into a fit of giggles. "Suppose we get that beautiful bay mare of yours saddled?"

Frankie's "beautiful bay mare" had been Frank Butler's favorite cutting horse in her day. Even when Mackenzie's father had last mounted her she had been rather long in the tooth, and for the last two years she'd been a pensioner at the Lazy B, contentedly staying in the pasture while her younger comrades worked each day from sunup to sundown. She didn't seem to mind Frankie's bouncing along on her back, though. Sleepy-eyed and fat, the old mare plodded around the arena in a placid shuffle.

Mackenzie leaned on the arena fence and watched. Perched on top of the mare's broad back, Frankie looked as small as a little elf. The Lazy B tack room had yielded no saddle small enough for Frankie's short legs, so Cal was teaching her to ride bareback. If a person could ride bareback, Frankie had boasted to Mackenzie the night before, a person could ride anything. That was how California had learned to ride.

Mackenzie had been alarmed at the idea. Saddles, after all, were what kept one from falling off a horse, or so she had always thought. But her little daughter looked perfectly at home astraddle the mare's back, even though her legs stuck almost straight out. One little hand was wrapped in the thick black mane while the other held the reins jauntily above the mare's neck. Mackenzie could tell Frankie was having the time of her life.

"Look at me, Ma!" Frankie gave Mackenzie a big grin as the horse shuffled by.

"Relax your back, Frankie," Cal advised. "Go with the motion of the horse. There's a rhythm to the gait, just like in a song. You have to find it."

Cal's patient instructions reminded Mackenzie of those evenings long ago when she had been the one lurching along atop a creature who seemed to move in four different directions at once. She hadn't been as apt a student as Frankie, but then, her mind had been on conquering someone other than the horse.

"Grip with your legs, Frankie," Cal coached the little girl. "I know it feels awkward. When your legs grow longer it'll be easier, but you can do it now, too."

Frankie laughed in delight as the mare picked up her pace from a shuffle to a real walk. Cal grinned, deepening the sun lines that fanned out from his eyes. The years showed on him, Mackenzie reflected. When she'd first known him he'd been a boy just grown into manhood with a promise of power and virility; now that promise had been amply fulfilled.

The years showed on her also, Mackenzie acknowledged to herself, only their mark was not so complimentary. Women were supposed to be gentle and feminine. Mackenzie felt that she was neither. The necessities of survival in Arizona had robbed her of both. Instead, she'd gained independence, a certain competence in doing a man's portion of work, a down-to-earth caution, and common sense. Mackenzie was no longer the girl who went after what she wanted with no thought to the consequences; she was a woman who struggled for what she needed to survive. What she wanted no longer had any relevance to her life.

Mackenzie felt a familiar tugging at her heart as she stood watching Cal teach her daughter—his daughter also—how to manage a horse. She felt utterly wicked and weak to still have any feelings for the man, but part of her felt like basking in the glow of remembered passion—or was it only remembered?

She gave Frankie an encouraging wave and headed for the house. As she left, she could feel Cal's eyes burn into her back. The tension within her tightened another twist. All along she'd known Cal had returned for something other than to repay a debt of honor to Frank Butler, but this moment was the first time she considered that he might have come back for her.

Mackenzie spent the next few days fighting an inner battle. Her sensible, cautious self watched helplessly as a part of her that had been long buried—an impetuous, reckless, bolder, and much less wise Mackenzie—battled for control. She felt split in two, at war with herself, and the sensible Mackenzie was losing. The unwise child of six years past was still alive within her, still longing for a man she couldn't, and shouldn't, have. Avoiding Cal did no good. He simply popped up in dreams and idle thoughts as Mackenzie's mental discipline deteriorated along with her good sense.

The surrender came on an unusually gray afternoon after the hands had ridden in to wash for supper. Frankie was in her room, engrossed in making dolls out of rags and string—a craft Lu had taught her. Lu was occupied with Carmelita in the kitchen, the two women preparing supper and entertaining themselves with plans for the coming wedding. Mackenzie had spent the day working at the huge pile of mending that had accumulated over the last two months. The task kept her hands busy and her mind idle, making her easy prey for an attack of impetuosity when she saw Cal cross from the foreman's shack to the barn.

The light was too dim for any more mending to be done, Mackenzie told herself; the sun was veiled by clouds and about to sink below the Huachuca Mountains in the west. Heart beating strangely fast, she put down the mending and went to her room to don a fresh dress. The Mexican-style bodice that she chose was embroidered in a shade of green that complemented her eyes. The skirt was full and colorful, not too fine to be worn in a barn, but feminine and graceful just the same.

Satisfied with her attire, Mackenzie loosed her hair from its coiled braid, brushed the fiery kinked mass, pulled it away from her face, and fastened it so that it cascaded down her shoulders and back in waves. The severe bun was giving her a headache, she told herself. She pinched her cheeks and regarded herself in the mirror with critical concern. Not that she was overly troubled about her appearance, but a lady did need to maintain at least a modicum of grooming, even on the frontier.

Satisfied at last, she strolled out to the kitchen building and stuck her head in the door.

"I'm going to the barn to check on the wild mare," Mackenzie told Lu and Carmelita. She didn't add that Cal was also in the barn. Cal was not whom she wanted to see, Mackenzie assured herself. She was simply concerned about the mare, who was nearing her term. "Did you hear me?" she asked uneasily.

"What?" Lu looked up from peeling carrots. "Oh, yes, dear. I'll keep an ear tuned for Frankie."

Mackenzie almost wished Lu would ask her to stay, help with supper, help plan the wedding—anything to keep her out of the barn. But her stepmother merely tossed cut carrots into the stewpot and continued her conversation with Carmelita.

"Supper will be ready soon, senorita," Carmelita told her absently. "Be careful with that horse."

Be careful. Be careful. The warning echoed in her mind, but the horse was not the one she should be careful of. Mackenzie shook her head ruefully and headed out of the house.

The barn was dimly lit by a kerosene lantern hanging from an overhead beam. It smelled warmly of horseflesh, hay, and leather. The wild mare—no longer so wild—occupied the second in the row of stalls that stretched along the left side of the barn. The other side sheltered three wagons and the covered buggy that Frank Butler had bought when he'd first moved to the ranch. The vehicle was ill-suited for the rough roads in the San Pedro Valley, and Mackenzie seldom used it. When she had first come to the ranch from Boston, Mackenzie had thought her father's buggy very plain. Now the vehicle seemed fancy, fragile, and rather useless. The buggy hadn't changed, though; Mackenzie was the one who had changed. She was no longer the girl fresh from Boston. Then she'd had ignorance and naïveté to excuse her mistake in pursuing Cal. What justification did she have now?

She wasn't pursuing California Smith, Mackenzie reminded herself sternly. She had come to the barn to check on the wild mare.

Liar! her conscience chided.

Cal leaned on the mare's stall, rubbing her velvety nose and talking softly to her in Apache. Mackenzie watched from the shadows by the door, reluctant to make herself known and trigger the wooden Indian face, or worse still, the mocking smile she saw so often on Cal's lips. The mare nuzzled Cal's fingers. Mackenzie smiled in wonder at his progress with this "untamable" horse. Ever since the day the mare had first let Cal ride her, they seemed to have a special rapport. Sometimes, watching them together, Mackenzie almost thought the mare understood Cal's words. Maybe horses did understand Apache, she mused, remembering Cal's outrageous claim to Frankie. The Apaches certainly were some of the best horsemen in the world, and Cal for many years had been Apache in everything but blood.

The reminder of Cal's background made her uncomfortable. She didn't regard Cal in the same light that she regarded the brown-skinned savage warriors who were the subjects of most of the horror tales that came out of the southwestern frontier. But she should, her conscience reminded her. Childhood and youth were a person's foundation. Just as Mackenzie, for all that she'd adapted to frontier life, was still a product of Boston society and her aunt's upbringing, Cal was and always would be what the Apaches had made him.

"Are you going to come in?" Cal said without turning toward her.

He'd known all along that she was there. She should have known better than to think she was unobserved. "I never could sneak up on you," she admitted with a smile, emerging from the shadows.

He turned around and gave her a lazy smile. "Were you trying to sneak?"

"Not really." She came forward hesitantly, hating her own diffidence. "I just came in to check on the mare, and . . . well, there you were. It seemed like a rather private conversation you were having with her." She looked over the stall partition at the mare.

"It's hard to come up on an Apache without being heard," Cal admitted.

Mackenzie thought she heard a hint of pride in his voice. His father had once told her that Cal's Apache arrogance and pride made whites hate him all the more. He refused to be ashamed of the years he spent with the savages.

Mackenzie leaned back against the stall door—far enough away from Cal to be decent, close enough to speed the pace of her heart. There really wasn't much room available for leaning when one considered all the space taken up with latches and iron hitching rings and hooks for bridles and halters. "Do you still think of yourself as Apache, Cal?"

The shadowy warmth of the barn seemed to wrap them both in a cocoon of intimacy, isolated from the real world in a space that held only the two of them. Here the past didn't intrude, the future had no meaning. Mackenzie felt her defenses against her own feelings surely and irreparably erode. She shouldn't have come, but she was glad she had.

"Sometimes," Cal admitted. "Not as often as I used to. It's been fourteen years since I lived with the Bedonkohe band. I've lived as a white man longer than I lived as an Apache."

"They say the years of your childhood and youth are the most important in determining how you look at the world, though. It must be hard for you to live in one world when you were raised in another."

He regarded her with what might have been surprise—or perhaps suspicion.

"It's hard to think of Apaches as people," she continued. "One can think with one's brain that an Apache warrior has children that he loves, that he has friends, maybe a wife, a mother, a grandmother, that he has weaknesses and strengths and likes and dislikes just like everyone else in the world. One can reason that an Apache warrior was once a baby in some loving mother's arms, or a little boy racing with other children around their mothers' skirts. But it's easier to see an Apache only as a monster. I realize that's a heartless thing to say, but people at war learn to hate the enemy. You aren't really Apache, yet in a way you are, and sometimes that makes me afraid now that I know what an Apache is."

"The war is almost over," Cal said quietly. Mackenzie didn't know if he referred to the war between the Apaches and whites or the war between Mackenzie Butler and California Smith.

"Are you glad after all these years that you left the Apaches?"

"A man should always be glad to be on the winning side of a war." She halfway expected him to retreat behind his wooden mask, but he didn't. His eyes glinted in the lantern light and focused somewhere far away both in space and time. "When General Howard told me that I should leave my people and come with him, I didn't want to. But I had an uncle, or at least to the Apache way of thinking he was sort of an uncle. He was older than me and a good deal wiser. His heart had much bitterness toward the white man, and he thought Cochise was foolish for making peace with General Howard. This uncle told me I should go with the general because the Apache world would soon die. Some would fight to keep it alive, but it would die just the same. He was known to have a gift that sometimes revealed the future. I believed him."

"Did he hate you for your white blood? Is that why he told you to leave?"

"No. He didn't hate me for my white blood. He liked me well enough. I had a chance to escape, and he thought I should take that chance. He was right. The Apaches have lost. The renegades who still fight on refer to themselves as 'The Dead'. I'm lucky my blood is white, or I might be fighting the losing battle with them. I can't see myself submitting to being a prisoner on the reservation like those who've made peace."

Mackenzie couldn't see him surrendering to such a life either. The very thought made her sad. Cal was too much a lone wolf to be caged with the pack, forced to live within someone else's boundaries, obeying someone else's rules. Uncomfortable with such a mental image, she labored to change the subject by turning her attention to the mare in the stall. "I saw you riding her yesterday without a bridle or saddle, yet she looked perfectly under control. How do you do that?"

Cal also turned so that he was looking into the stall. The shift in position brought them closer together. "I was teaching her to respond to changes in weight and leg pressure. She's a good horse. Learns fast."

Mackenzie smiled. "She seemed to be listening to every word you said when I came in."

"Horses understand Apache—"

"Better than English," Mackenzie finished for him with a laugh. "I heard you tell Frankie."

"She is a fine mare, Mac. I think we should put you up on her soon."

"What?"

"Who do you think I've been training her for?"

"I . . . well, I . . . didn't think about it."

"She is your horse, and you're a good rider. I should know. I taught you."

He'd taught her more than how to ride, Mackenzie remembered. Suddenly she felt awkward. "Isn't it awfully near her time? Maybe we should stop riding her altogether until she delivers." She remembered how miserable she had felt when pregnant with Frankie.

"She's got a few weeks yet." Cal reached over the stall door to rub the mare's neck. "Mares aren't like people. They usually don't have the same problems delivering their babies." He grinned wickedly. "Apache women are like mares in some ways—they deliver babies easily and recover fast. Of course, you might expect that. Most white men think that Apaches are half horse."

"No one actually believes that," Mackenzie scoffed.

Cal raised one brow in a cynical slant. Abruptly his grin faded. "I hear white women aren't as lucky as Apaches in giving birth. Did you have a hard time delivering Frankie?"

Mackenzie recoiled both physically and mentally. His question pulled them into a realm of intimacy and memory that she was not ready to accept. Frankie's birth had been all the more painful for the hollow feeling of betrayal and anger that had accompanied the agony of childbirth. While Cal's child had struggled for freedom from her body, memories of the babe's father had crowded her consciousness, bringing wrath, outrage, and a queer, undefined longing that sprang from her foolish heart. And now California Smith dared to ask if she'd had a hard time delivering Frankie. She flushed with anger, and yet a mocking voice in her head asked her if she hadn't been inviting this kind of intimacy.

"Too personal a question for the child's father to ask?" Cal's voice held a hint of sarcasm, as if he had sensed her sudden withdrawal. Mackenzie returned to the present—the warm barn, the wild mare, and Cal. Not the same California Smith who had made love to her so many years ago. Not the same California Smith whom she had created out of her anger and hurt. Neither of those men, Mackenzie realized, had been real. They were figures she had concocted from her own needs—a need to love, a need to hate. Perhaps the real California Smith was the man who had come to save the ranch of an old friend, even though that friend was dead and gone. Perhaps he was the man who'd saved Letty Greene, the man who so gently had coaxed the wild mare into submission, the man who took hours out of his free time to teach a little girl to ride. Did she really know California Smith? Mackenzie wondered.

"No," she answered with a sigh. "The question is not too personal. The . . . the labor was difficult, though I suppose it wasn't any more difficult than most women's labor." She smiled and corrected herself. "*White* women's labor, that is. I certainly wasn't very brave or stoic about it, but we got through it all right, Frankie and me. My aunt Prue in Boston told me once that when a woman first touches her newborn child, all memory of pain flees. She should have known," Mackenzie said with a quiet chuckle. "She had five children, all daughters." She was silent for a moment, her eyes softening as she remembered the moment that Frances Sophia Butler had been laid in her arms for the very first time. "Aunt Prue was right. When I first saw Frankie, first touched her and saw her little hands and feet wave in the air, all the pain left, even though a moment before I'd been hurting so bad I wanted to cry. I can't describe it."

Mackenzie saw a flash of envy in Cal's eyes and suddenly

felt his loss at missing Frankie's first five years. Until a few weeks ago he hadn't even known they had a child. A wave of sympathy made her long to reach out and touch him in understanding. She resisted, however. He wouldn't want her compassion, she told herself.

Abruptly Mackenzie turned her attention back to the mare, whose sleek reddish coat glimmered in the lantern light. The horse regarded her with wary caution, and once again Mackenzie found herself feeling kinship with the animal. "She's a beautiful creature, isn't she?"

"Yes," Cal agreed, his eyes still on Mackenzie. She felt a disturbing tingle where those eyes touched her. Surely she was imagining things. They were, after all, talking about a horse.

"Sometimes I feel guilty for ever bringing her in from the mountains. She's so magnificent. Perhaps she deserves to be free."

"Freedom is as much a fairy story as those tales you read to Frankie. Everyone is a slave to something—loneliness, pride, loyalty, hunger. Survival itself is a harsh master."

Mackenzie regarded him in surprise, one brow lifting. "That's a very bitter thing to say."

"Not really. A creature without a master has nothing to fight for, nothing to love."

"Who or what is your master, California Smith?" she asked softly.

He smiled, but didn't answer her question. "That mare is better off with you than in the wild."

One could get only so far into California Smith without coming up against that private wall, Mackenzie mused. She'd thought she'd known him so well six years ago. She hadn't known him at all. "Do you think she would let me pet her?" she asked, looking at the mare.

"Probably."

Mackenzie's eyes lit with a glint of her old mischief. "Perhaps she'd like to hear what a woman has to say instead of having to listen to a man all the time."

"Maybe she would," Cal agreed amiably. "Why don't you try it?"

Mackenzie reached out her hand. The mare flicked her ears and moved away.

"Let's go into the stall," Cal invited. At Mackenzie's grimace of doubt, he assured her, "The mare's not going to hurt you. She's not angry any more, just a bit frightened."

"You think so?"

"Come on," Cal urged with a smile.

Cal unlatched the stall door and they carefully slipped inside. The mare retreated but didn't lay back her ears or show any indication of the hostility that had accompanied her every move just two weeks ago.

"Talk to her," Cal advised.

"I don't speak Apache," she said, slanting a brow.

"Try speaking female. She ought to understand that well enough."

Mackenzie stepped forward hesitantly. The mare laid back her ears, then flicked them forward uncertainly. "Hello there, girl. You don't even have a name, do you? We can't call you wild mare when you've been such a lamb these past days, can we? What shall we name you?" She continued to croon as she moved very slowly forward. Cal's intent regard was a weight she tried to ignore.

The mare flicked her ears again, then gave a plaintive whicker. She arched her graceful neck and cautiously stretched out her nose. Mackenzie slowly raised her hand and touched the velvet of her lips. Delighted, she laughed softly. "Oh, she's so beautiful."

Cal didn't answer, and Mackenzie didn't turn to look at him, but she felt the power of his gaze. She shouldn't be here; she certainly shouldn't be acting like a foolish coquette, but somehow the sprite of a girl that she once had been had flown across the years and taken control.

"How did you tame her, Cal? Look at her. She's so gentle. A little scared, maybe, but there's a gentle look in her eyes. I can hardly believe this is the same horse that almost killed Tony. Did you work with wild horses when you were with the Indians?"

"Some," Cal admitted, coming forward to stroke the mare's nose. "Horses are a lot like people. You meet their needs, soothe their fears, show them a little consideration, and generally they turn out to be decent animals. Mares are easier to work with than stallions. Mares respond to a gentle hand."

"Stallions don't?"

"Some do—like that big gray you have that sires most of your foals." He grinned. "Others are so ornery, they never learn any manners. It's all a part of being male, I think."

Being male, like Cal. California Smith was male enough to set any woman's nerves humming. Mackenzie felt her face heat and turned away to hide her flush. As if sensing Mackenzie's sudden discomfiture, the mare blew impatiently and tossed her head. "I think we've overstayed our welcome," Mackenzie said. She gave the mare a farewell pat and tried to slip out of the stall. Cal moved toward the door also. In her haste to leave, Mackenzie brushed quickly past him. Just that brief moment of contact released a flood of warmth into her veins.

"No," Cal commanded as she opened the stall door. He reached across her and refastened the latch.

Panic fluttered through Mackenzie's stomach as he grasped her by the arms.

"You've been asking for this, Mac, so you must want it."

His mouth descended on hers, warm, insistent, demanding. Arms pinned at her sides by his strong grip, Mackenzie twisted to escape, but he held her still while his mouth gently plundered. He tasted good. He smelled of mesquite, hay, and masculinity. The feel of his lips moving on hers and his tongue playfully darting in and out in intimate possession ignited a fire in Mackenzie's belly that slowly burned its way through her resistance. Even the rough stubble on Cal's jaw felt erotic as it brushed against her face and woke passions that had long since been put to rest. Her body was not untutored. It knew what it desired and ignored the warnings of the little good sense she had left.

Mackenzie moaned low in her throat and gave up the fight, splaying her hands against Cal's chest in blissful surrender. She couldn't get enough of touching him—his ribs, his shoulders, his back, the thick mane of hair that looked sunlit even when the sky was gray and dark. The feel of him made her wet with raw hunger. The world narrowed down to the two of them, here, now, in this moment. Nothing else mattered.

"Mackenzie," Cal whispered against her cheek, his voice hoarse. She had eaten away at his heart too long, and now his desire was like a starved wolf suddenly released from a cage. It threatened to devour until hunger was sated without thought of consequences. "Mackenzie . . . " He set her back from him, though he still ached with the craving to take what she offered. Right now she was his for the taking. Mackenzie might not even be aware of the invitation that her body blatantly extended, but he could sense that she was no longer in control of needs buried so long ago.

"What?" She looked bewildered. Her mouth was red from his kiss, her cheeks flushed. The bright green of her eyes had darkened almost to black, and he saw there the mirror of his own desire.

"You've got to be sure."

Confusion clouded her eyes.

"Is your anger at me so weak that it can be defeated by one kiss?"

Her mouth dropped in surprised and her eyes sharpened as fury swept away the sweet.confusion of desire. Cal felt the loss of her passion like a cold wind blowing through his soul. He had to be sure, he told himself. She had to be sure as well. Mackenzie could be like the wind inside a summer storm, first blowing one way, then another, sometimes fierce, sometimes gentle and warm. "What do you want, Mac? Do you want to love me or push me away?"

Her face flamed.

"Ever since I came back you've swung between wanting to spit on me and wanting to kiss me. Hell, Mac, a minute ago you would've given me a lot more than a kiss if I'd wanted to take it."

"You're dreaming! If you think that I—"

"I think that you need to make up your mind. This isn't a game we're playing. It's your life, and mine. I still love you, Mac, and this time, once I have you I won't let you go. Not without a hell of a fight. So be very sure before you tempt me past where I can keep a leash on myself."

"Leave me alone! Just leave me alone!" She drew the back of her hand across her mouth as if she could obliterate their kiss. "I hated you once. Lord, I wish I still hated you."

"Hatred at least is honest."

He didn't give Mackenzie the reaction she wanted. She wanted him to do something that would destroy the foolish softness that was overtaking her soul, provide ammunition to use against him as he once again invaded her heart. He had broken that heart once; she wouldn't give him a chance to break it once again.

Cal's voice was calm, his eyes all too knowing. "Love can be honest too, Mac, if you have the courage. But when you walk the narrow ridge between love and hate, sometimes the heart itself becomes a lie. I'm not afraid to admit that I still love you, that I made a mistake in ever leaving you. And I think you still love me. But if you want us to be together, you're going to have to be very sure that you can forgive me for the past and live with a present where most people still regard me as a savage."

Mackenzie prayed for anger—enough anger to erase the foolish urge to throw herself back into his arms. "You arrogant jackass! You have a nerve making demands of me!"

He merely smiled, pushing her ire to a new level.

"You *are* an ass!" She jerked open the stall and stalked toward the barn door, her stride so angry her footsteps might have left singed straw in her path. Her wrath was fueled by the knowledge that Cal was right. She'd come to the barn hoping to find solace for the needs he stirred without having to give an inch in return. Cal had known exactly what she was doing, almost as if he could look into her eyes and read her mind.

She stormed out of the barn. The bright dusk dazzled her eyes, blinding her temporarily. Halfway to the house she stopped in her tracks. On the foothills that rose from behind the guest house, a figure on horseback sat silhouetted against the scarlet sky. Another joined him, then more, until there was a row of silent, motionless specters looking down upon the Lazy B.

For a moment Mackenzie was stunned by her own fear. She had fought Apaches before and won, but familiarity didn't dilute the terror. She choked, then found her voice, but before she could call out the alarm, hands landed heavily on her shoulders.

"Be quiet," Cal commanded.

Mackenzie didn't want to believe it. She had accepted that Cal was innocent of collusion with the Indians, and now Cal himself proved her wrong. The Apaches were casually riding down the hill, confident of their welcome, and Cal was telling her to submit. Why didn't he just put a knife in her back and be done with it?

"Another brother?" she asked cynically.

"Not exactly. The uncle I told you about. His name is Geronimo."

10

Geronimo. The very name chilled Mackenzie's blood. She knew his history. What Arizonan—white, Mexican, or Indian—didn't? Although not a hereditary chief of the warring Chiricahua Apaches, he'd nevertheless battled his way to leadership since the death of Cochise. Chief Juh and Cochise's son Natchez accepted him as an equal and often bowed to his counsel—counsel that had left a crimson streak of murder and thievery across Arizona and northern Mexico. To whites and Mexicans, the name Geronimo was synonymous with violence.

The band of Apaches numbered fourteen. Mackenzie counted and compared the force to the number of her own men, who were streaming out of the bunkhouse as if even inside they had sensed the threat descending upon the ranch. When they saw what the threat was, the ranch hands exploded with alarm and frantically went for their guns.

"Put down your guns," Cal commanded them. He

squeezed Mackenzie's shoulder and whispered. "Back me up, Mac."

Mackenzie shivered. She felt as though she'd just stepped off a cliff into empty space. The men froze in place, guns in their hands, confused and near panic.

"Back me up," he repeated calmly. "Do you want this little visit to turn into a bloodbath?"

"Put . . . put down your guns," she ordered the hands. "What in blazes is going on?" she demanded of Cal in a soft, vehement hiss.

His only answer was a gentle squeeze of her shoulders.

The hands looked at her with incredulous expressions on their faces. "Put down your guns," she repeated.

Reluctant and muttering, the hands holstered their pistols and lowered their rifles. Mackenzie hoped that Lu and Carmelita were so engrossed in the kitchen that they hadn't noticed the visitors. Lu, gentle lady that she was, was a bit bloodthirsty when it came to shooting Apache raiders, and Carmelita tended toward noisy hysteria. Neither reaction would help the situation right now.

Not deigning to even glance at the men clustered in front of the bunkhouse, the band of Indians reined to a halt ten feet from where Mackenzie stood in Cal's grasp. They formed a rough wedge at whose point was mounted a stocky man in a stained red cotton shirt and dirty white trousers. A cloth band held back coarse black hair that reached past his shoulders. His face, shrewd and furrowed with deep creases, bore a stripe of white paint from one cheekbone across the prominent bridge of his nose to the other cheekbone, a stark slash against the brown of his skin. His eyes were like shiny black marbles—cold, hard, glittering with menace.

Geronimo. Mackenzie had never seen him, but she had seen daguerreotypes. In pictures he looked menacing—in person he looked like the devil himself.

Geronimo regarded them both with a lethally penetrating

gaze while his band, similarly dressed and painted, surveyed the ranch with alert, cautious glances. When he finally spoke, it was to Cal, not to Mackenzie.

"*Shil na'ash!*" he greeted Cal. The slash of his mouth twitched into a grim-looking smile.

"*Shil na'ash,*" Cal returned, his voice deathly calm.

Mackenzie could only stand in tense agony as the conversation continued in rapid Apache. Cal's hand slipped possessively to her upper arm and closed around it tightly in warning. She longed to shake herself free of his touch. Had Cal betrayed them? Was he even now telling Geronimo to wreak whatever havoc he pleased on the ranch and livestock? She didn't want to believe it, couldn't believe it. And yet the evidence was before her eyes.

Finally, Geronimo gave a satisfied grunt and signaled his warriors to dismount. Cal gestured toward the arena for them to corral their horses. As soon as Geronimo turned away, Mackenzie twisted out of Cal's grasp.

"What is going on?" she whispered fiercely. "You can't claim that Geronimo is a reservation Indian! What were you talking about with that savage?"

The cowboys gathered around them, eyes darting fearfully to where the Indians went about the business of turning their mounts into the arena. Mahko, Istee, and Bay had slipped in from their camp, apparently having spied on the doings from the foothills. They looked every bit as uneasy at Geronimo's visit as the rest of the hands.

"Calm down," Cal told them all. "I knew Geronimo when I was a boy with the Bedonkohe. He heard a rumor that I was ranching where we had once ridden together with Cochise. He wanted to see if it was true, so he's paying us a visit. A friendly visit."

"I'd like to give the murderin' sonofabitch a friendly slug between the eyes," Sam Crawford muttered.

"Anyone who reaches for a gun is going to start a bloodbath," Cal warned. "The best thing you men can do is go back to the bunkhouse and stay there until I tell you something different. Mahko, Istee, Bay—for now you go back to your camp and tell your wives to stay out of sight. We wouldn't want any of our guests to get the idea that your women could brew a batch of tizwin and serve it around."

The three White Mountain Apaches wore the same wooden face that Cal so often donned, but Mackenzie could read resentment in their black eyes. They were no more pleased with Geronimo's presence than she was, Mackenzie realized.

"You mean to tell me Geronimo is here on a neighborly visit?" she asked Cal incredulously.

"He wanted to make sure his band didn't raid within the family, so to speak."

Her eyes grew wide. "He thinks the Lazy B is your ranch?"

"And that you're my wife," he added. "Would you rather he know the ranch belongs to an Apache-hating white woman and burn it to the ground?"

"No." Mackenzie realized she'd almost accused him falsely once again. How quickly her fragile trust turned to fear. "I almost thought . . . well, I guess I owe you another apology."

He smile wryly. "I don't remember getting a first one."

Mackenzie tried to hold back her fear. She hated the helplessness she felt. Right now all their lives depended on Cal's goodwill. The ranch hands milled uneasily, darting distrustful glances both at the Apaches in the arena and at Cal.

"Nothing's going to happen if you yahoos keep your heads," Cal told them. "Go back to the bunkhouse."

The hands sullenly dispersed.

"Are they going to leave soon?" Mackenzie glanced uneasily at the Indians in the arena.

Cal took her arm and guided her back toward the house. "Soon enough."

"When?"

"Don't be so impatient, Mac. Apaches set great store by hospitality, and these are definitely men you don't want to insult."

She cast an anxious look over her shoulder at the arena. "Now that they know you're here, what else do they want? They look like they're settling in for the night!"

"I asked them to supper," Cal admitted.

"You what?"

He hustled her through the gate and into the house. "I asked them to supper. If your uncle came calling, wouldn't you invite him to eat?"

As a social event, the evening that followed was not a huge success. Geronimo's band refused to eat in the house, or even at a table. They set up camp between the guest house and the foothills. Mackenzie, Lu, and a very nervous Carmelita brought food into the yard, where Cal made a campfire to stave off the darkness. Everyone on the ranch sat around the fire to eat. Fearing trouble, Mackenzie argued about having the ranch hands present, but Cal insisted. He sent for the three White Mountain Apaches to attend as well. If everyone on the ranch was in the yard, he told her, Geronimo would have no fear of being betrayed. The less nervous Geronimo was, the safer they were.

So they all sat in an uneasy circle around the fire. The renegades ate voraciously. The hearty beef stew, corn tortillas, and chile sauce that the women served disappeared almost as soon as it was ladled into the Indian's bowls. Conversation was limited by both language and the hostility that lured just below the surface of everyone present. Frankie seemed to be the only one who wasn't affected by it.

When Frankie first came out of the ranch house accompanied by both Mackenzie and Cal, Geronimo's eyes swung to the child in curiosity.

"He likes children," Cal assured Mackenzie. "Don't worry about Frankie."

Mackenzie held her silence, fear twisting her stomach. Cal was right, though. When he introduced Frankie to the fierce renegade leader, something very close to a smile appeared on the Apache's face. Frankie was not fearful at all, only curious. She gave Geronimo her widest grin, bent her knee, and spread her skirt in a little curtsy. Grinning, Geronimo copied her greeting, bringing a hearty laugh from his band. Mackenzie hadn't known that Apaches could laugh.

While Mackenzie helped Lu and Carmelita keep up with the ravenous Apache appetites, Frankie sat close beside Cal. She giggled at the sight of the Indians eating with their hands, and Mackenzie held her breath.

"You're supposed to eat with a fork," she announced to Geronimo, and held up her own utensil.

"Hands just as good." Geronimo held his hand with fingers pointing up to copy the position of Frankie's fork. When he grinned, his face became a wreath of deeply scored lines.

"It's not polite," the child informed him solemnly. "My mother says that only babies and monkeys eat with their hands."

"Frankie!" Mackenzie scolded. Her heartbeat could have started an earthquake. "Mind your manners!"

Geronimo actually laughed and picked up the fork that had up until now gone unused. He made a joke of stabbing at the tortillas. Grinning, his warriors took up the game.

"You could use some practice," Frankie told them.

Geronimo made a comment in Apache that made his warriors guffaw with laughter.

"What did he say?" Mackenzie whispered to Cal as she filled his bowl with stew.

"He says that Goshk'an's daughter already thinks like a wife," Cal told her. "He likes her. Don't worry."

Don't worry. Impossible advice. Mackenzie was sick with worry. Though Geronimo laughed at Frankie, his conversation with Cal sounded solemn indeed. Mackenzie could only wonder at what they spoke of, as their words were all in Apache. The ranch hands were ominously silent, their eyes regarding the "guests" with unconcealed rancor. Infrequently one of Geronimo's band contributed a word or two to the conversation, and even more rarely, one of the White Mountain Apaches would growl out a comment. At one precarious point sparks flew between one of the renegade band and Istee, but, to Mackenzie's surprise, Geronimo put an end to the argument before it got out of hand.

By the time the women sat down to eat, only the dregs of supper remained and the Indians were belching their appreciation.

"Got whiskey?" Geronimo asked Cal.

Mackenzie's heart sank.

"No whiskey," Cal replied firmly.

Geronimo nodded without argument. Mackenzie let out a silent sigh of relief. She marveled at how comfortable Cal seemed with the savages. It was no wonder, she acknowledged. After all, he'd been raised in their company. But she'd never pictured him sitting around a fire conversing with the most dangerous Apache of all. This California Smith who seemed right at home among these savage raiders was the same man who had the nerve to tell her she didn't know her own mind, her own soul. Did he know his? she wondered. Did he truly know if he was Apache or white? And would she ever understand him or herself well enough to know why California Smith, infuriating as he was, still had a claim on her heart?

The evening continued without serious incident, but by the time the moon had risen and the plates, bowls, and mostly unused silverware had been cleared away, Mackenzie's nerves were as taut as a bowstring. The renegades and the Lazy B hands eyed each other with loathing, and the three White Mountain Apaches regarded both groups with disdain. Cal's face was calm and unreadable, and Geronimo, except for a rare smile or frown, maintained an impassive mask that put even Cal's wooden Indian face to shame. To add more difficulty to the evening, Carmelita performed her chores with tears in her eyes, so close to hysteria that Mackenzie could almost see the screams building in her throat. Lu sustained a rigid composure that was brittle enough to splinter. The only one who seemed at all relaxed was Frankie, who chattered to Lu, to Cal, to Geronimo, and to anyone else who would listen to her. Someday soon, Mackenzie thought, she needed to educate her daughter on who was a friend in this world and who wasn't.

Finally, Geronimo rose from his cross-legged position to indicate that the evening was over. Mackenzie almost allowed herself to feel relief, until she noticed that the renegades ambled off toward the camp behind the guest house instead of toward the horses that milled in the arena.

"Don't tell me they're not leaving," she said to Cal.

"Apaches don't like to travel after dark," Cal explained as he escorted her toward the house. "Night is the time when the spirits of the evil dead roam the earth, usually in the form of owls."

"I can't imagine an Apache being afraid of anything," she said with a weak smile. "Especially an owl."

"Everybody's afraid of something."

"Even you?"

"Yeah. Even me."

Lu met them in the entrance of the house, her backbone a rigid column of tension. "Have they left?"

"No," Mackenzie said grimly.

"They'll be gone by morning," Cal told her.

Lu managed a bleak smile. "California, no offense, but I do wish you would tell your friends and relatives to stay on the reservation."

Cal shook his head ruefully. "I don't think anyone will ever convince Geronimo to stay on the reservation. To tell the truth, I can't really blame him. Not that I like all the blood he's been spilling, but he has been robbed of a home."

"Just so he doesn't rob us of ours," Lu replied.

"Did you get Frankie to bed?" Mackenzie asked.

"Frankie and Carmelita both. Lita asked to sleep with me in my room tonight. Frankly, I'm glad of the company. I think I'll go to bed myself and hope when I wake up this will all be over."

Lu gave Mackenzie a goodnight hug and went to find the oblivion of sleep. Mackenzie slumped down on the sofa and stared out the window into the dark inner court. Cal made no move to leave. She could feel his eyes regarding her in an almost proprietary manner.

"Geronimo thinks this is my ranch and you're my wife," he explained when she threw him an inquiring look. "He might be a bit puzzled if I were to sleep in the foreman's shack. Believe me, we don't want him to find out I lied to him."

Mackenzie sighed. "I see your point. You can sleep on the couch in the office. I'm certainly not going to bed while those renegades are camped behind my guest house."

He dropped down in a chair and ran his hand through the bronze tousle of his hair above the cloth headband. "Nothing's going to happen, Mac. Geronimo is a dangerous man—even a vicious man, I suppose. But he would die before he would betray his own sense of honor. He wouldn't abuse our hospitality by turning on us. As long as there are no women in camp to make tizwin to get the warriors drunk, he'll keep our own private little peace."

"Tizwin?"

"The Apaches' favorite liquor," he explained with a rueful smile. "Home-brewed by the women. Some women have recipes passed down through generations—the pride of their family. I hear there's been a lot of unrest on the reservation because the whites have put an end to brewing tizwin."

"Do the wives of *our* Apaches know how to make the stuff?"

Cal smiled at her personal claim to the White Mountain men. "I imagine so, but they won't make it for Geronimo. Just to be safe, I told Mahko, Istee, and Bay that their wives were to stay out of sight. You notice that they weren't any happier to see the renegades than you were. The white men's opinion that all Apaches are the same under that brown skin is a myth."

Mackenzie shook her head. "I still won't sleep."

"Then I'll stay up with you."

The night was long, the hours of darkness torturous in their slow passing. Mackenzie tried to occupy the time with a book, but her mind couldn't focus. Cal sat opposite her in the chair that was once Frank Butler's favorite, head tilted back upon the headrest. His eyes were closed, his face relaxed, but Mackenzie could feel his alertness; his strength was a palpable presence in the room. As the hours ticked slowly by, they didn't speak or look at each other. Cal's eyes remained closed, seemingly oblivious to anything around him. All the same, Mackenzie had to admit that having him in the room with her was a comfort. She wondered if he believed his own assurances about Geronimo's sense of honor.

Midnight was long past when Mackenzie finally surrendered to sleep. One moment she was fighting exhaustion and worrying about what the Apaches were up to in the darkness beyond the guest house, the next moment early-morning sunlight streamed through the windows. Someone had covered her with the quilt that had lain across the back of Cal's chair. The room was empty and quiet. She was alone. The house had not been burned down around her, nor had she been murdered in her sleep. Perhaps Cal had been right about Geronimo's peculiar sense of honor.

When she hurried out of the house into the cool morning air, she discovered that Cal had been right about something else as well. The clearing beyond the guest house was empty. Geronimo and his men were gone, leaving no trace behind.

The days that followed Geronimo's visit were strangely peaceful, but it was a peace that Mackenzie didn't trust. Harsh experience had taught her that true peace didn't exist. Tranquility was merely the calm between storms.

The days were busy, however, and Mackenzie didn't have much time to worry about when the next storm would come or what it would be. She rode with the hands to check on the calves and foals that had been born in spring and early summer; she traveled with Cal, the three White Mountain Apaches, and Bull Ferguson to deliver twenty green-broke two-year-old horses to Fort Buchanan; and in her few moments of spare time, she read to Frankie, helped Lu and Carmelita tend the chickens, pigs and a burgeoning vegetable garden—Daisy had farrowed a fine litter of piglets, much to Frankie's delight. She left the supervision of the hands to Cal. As always, the men were dissatisfied with their lot, grumbling about the work, the lack of gunplay and general hell-raising, the presence of the White Mountain Apaches, and the indignity of working for a woman and an Apache-lover. Geronimo's visit hadn't endeared Cal to the Lazy B crew. If they'd feared the taint of Apache about him before, they feared it even more after Geronimo greeted him as part of the renegade's family. The hands weren't willing to mess with him, though. A look from Cal could stop a brawl in mid-explosion, and his frown put a halt to insurrections before they were well started. Mackenzie watched as he used the crew's fear against them. They were men accustomed to ruling and being ruled by fear, and in Cal's hands fear proved a very effective weapon—not abused, simply recognized and wielded efficiently.

Cal's position was rather sad, Mackenzie reflected. He'd been hired reluctantly out of desperate need and was obeyed reluctantly out of genuine fear. A man like California Smith deserved something better.

Mackenzie surprised herself by such musings. The humiliating episode in the barn should have fueled her anger, but all she could remember was Cal's admission that he still loved her. Her foolish heart wouldn't allow her to ignore or forget him.

Recognizing her own weakness, Mackenzie kept her distance from Cal, though she suspected she was in more danger from herself than from him. Since their encounter in the barn, he behaved with perfect decorum toward her—even on their trip with the horses to Fort Buchanan. His behavior was so proper, in fact, that it was annoying. After the words he'd said to her in the barn, she had expected at least some indication of his continuing passion. How could he kiss her with such delicious ardor, say such words of love, then simply ignore her as he had done since? Had he realized the hopelessness of his demand? Was he waiting for her to come to him and surrender? Or had he been merely mocking her?

Whatever the answer, Mackenzie found herself unreasonably self-conscious when she was around Cal. On the ride to Fort Buchanan to deliver the two-year-olds, she had positioned the horse herd between them for the entire trip. On the Lazy B, she made sure that she tended to chores in a direction opposite from the one Cal took in the morning. The only time she absolutely couldn't avoid him was every evening for supper when he gave Frankie her riding lesson.

The evening riding lesson had become a nightly ritual, and Frankie would have been terribly disappointed if her mother had missed even one moment of her performance on the back of the amiably ambling bay mare. So Mackenzie spent an hour every evening watching Cal coach their daughter in the basics of survival on top of a horse. The hour was the high point of Frankie's day, but certainly not of Mackenzie's.

Mackenzie admitted she was jealous of the way Frankie responded to Cal, almost as if her daughter knew without being told that the man with the golden hair so like her own was her father. Cal's patience with Frankie's energetic antics was a marvel to watch. Mackenzie could understand why Frankie loved him. She even understood how, six years ago, a green girl from Boston with not much more sense than Frankie had come to love him.

What Mackenzie didn't understand was why she should still be attracted to him after all that had happened and all the good, solid, down-to-earth sense she had so painfully acquired over the last years. Her anger had not been hot enough to burn him out of her heart, and the years not long enough to bury him.

July passed slowly into August. The wild mare was no longer wild, but weighed down by the burden of impending birth. Frankie graduated from the placid bay mare to a gentle buckskin pony. Cal brought the horse back from Tombstone one Saturday afternoon, along with a child-sized saddle that a five-year-old girl could lift up on a pony's back all by herself—with the help of a step stool. On the same visit to town Cal purchased a stocky blood-bay mare for Mackenzie, a replacement for the horse she had lost in the skirmish with the Bar Cross hands. Frankie promptly named her pony Goldie and her mother's new mare Dolly. Lu was happily planning her wedding, which was scheduled for September after fall roundup. Amos's visits increased from once weekly to twice. Watching Lu with Amos was a bittersweet experience for Mackenzie. Lu's happiness gave her joy, but it also underscored her own increasing loneliness. The earth was meant to be walked on two by two, Mackenzie concluded.

The days passed calmly. Mackenzie divided her time between the ranch, the house, and motherhood while waiting for something to break the unusual peace—for Crosby to renew his nastiness, for the Apaches to return, or for the drought to finally reach Dragoon Springs and stop the Lazy B's lifeblood water from flowing out of the rocks. She was prepared for any number of calamities to occur, but the disaster that did befall came from an unexpected direction.

One Saturday afternoon in early August, Mackenzie accompanied Cal, Bull Ferguson, and Gideon Small into town to pick up supplies. While Cal went to the mercantile, Small to the gunsmith's, and Bull to the harnessry and bootmaker, Mackenzie took some time to seek out Israel Potts. More changed brands were showing up on the open range—all Lazy B's changed to RA. More than fifty of the Lazy B herd that Mackenzie had rotated onto her own land to water at the springs bore the RA brand. She might not have recognized them as her own cattle if the men working for her hadn't had experience themselves in altering brands. The law should be able to do something about such underhanded goings-on, she reasoned. But Israel was quick to set her straight.

"If you catch 'em in the act, haul 'em in here and I'll jail 'em," he offered magnanimously. "Or if you can identify 'em and tell me their names, I'll even go after 'em, Mackenzie."

"Israel, you know I can't give you names," Mackenzie complained. "None of my men have been able to catch the thieves in the act—though they have come across burned-out fires a couple of times."

"Ashes don't prove nothing. Just what makes you so sure these brands have been changed? Maybe some of Armstrong's cattle wandered across the river. The San Pedro's low enough. And that is open range, ya know."

"My hands can tell the brands have been changed."

"Well now, that might come down to your word against

Armstrong's. Raitt Armstrong's a fairly respected man in these parts."

"I didn't mean to imply that Raitt was behind this."

"Who else would want to change brands to RA?" Israel asked with exaggerated patience.

"You know who," Mackenzie accused.

"Now, don't be expectin' me to follow your female kinda reasonin'. As deputy sheriff for the Tombstone area of Cochise County, I gotta base my doin's on good sense and logic, not some female emotional suspicion."

Mackenzie scowled in exasperation.

"If I was you," Israel continued blithely, "I would just handle the situation yourself. Bringin' the law in on it might get the cattle confiscated until the matter gets settled. And no tellin' how it might get settled. Like I said, right now it's your word against Armstrong's—or whoever," he added when she started to object.

The conversation with Israel started Mackenzie's day on the downswing, but matters were to get much worse. When they arrived back at the Lazy B, Lu came running to meet them even before they stopped the wagon at the barn. One look at her face sent a stab of fear through Mackenzie's middle.

"Thank God you're back!" Lu exclaimed. "Frankie's gone. The hands are out searching, but so far"—her voice broke—"so far no luck."

The fear in Mackenzie's middle exploded into panic. "What do you mean Frankie's gone? How could she be gone?"

"She decided to go for a ride on that pony of hers. Lita was watching her and thought she'd gone to the tunnel to play. Oh, Mackenzie! I don't believe this is happening! I thought at first she'd be just down the road or in one of the pastures, but it's been an hour and a half!"

The open range held gopher holes, ditches, the boggy

river, snakes, cactus, stray Apaches, and any number of dangers for a little girl. What's more, there was a lightning-streaked thunderstorm building over the mountains that might bring torrential rain, hail, frightening thunder, and even flash floods in the drought-dry gullies. Frankie could have lost her way. With so much open space in the valley they might never find her. Even now she might be hurt, frightened, crying.

The sick panic in Mackenzie's stomach sharpened to a cramp of desperate fear. It immobilized her just when she needed most to spring into action. Her chest tightened until she could scarcely breathe. Then a voice intruded into her terror.

"We'll find her, Mac."

Cal was still beside her on the wagon seat. As it was so often, his face was an impassive mask of emotionless calm, but his clear blue eyes glittered with a hard strength that was somehow comforting. For the first time since California Smith had come back to the Lazy B, Mackenzie was unequivocally glad that he was here.

11

They found Goldie munching brittle grass on the banks of the San Pedro River. Cal had easily picked the pony's tracks out of the confusion of hoofprints surrounding the ranch and unerringly followed them down the road that ran besides the pastures, through ravines, over sage-covered hillocks, down dry sandy washes, and out onto the flat floodplain of the river. He knew just where Frankie had gotten off her horse—or rather, been lifted off. For no little bootprints mixed in with the man-sized prints in the sand of the floodplain. The buckskin pony, making shallower prints now that Frankie's weight was off its back, ambled a few hundred feet to the riverbank, while two other horses galloped off toward the north.

All this Cal read from the sand, from broken twigs and crushed sage. He wasn't surprised to find a rolled-up message tied to Frankie's child-sized saddle when they found her pony. Only MacKenzie was surprised.

"Where is she?" Mackenzie cried as she jumped from her horse. "This is her pony! Where's Frankie?" Her eyes searched the rugged landscape desperately.

"She's not here, Mac."

"How do you know? She must be here!"

Still mounted, Cal nodded toward the roll of paper tied behind the saddle cantle. Mackenzie's eyes grew wide. She snatched the paper from the leather tie-thongs and unrolled it. "No," she cried softly. "Oh, no."

"Is it Crosby?" Cal asked, certain of the answer.

"How did you know?"

"I saw the signs back a ways. Two men took her and headed north. Figured they'd leave somthing telling us what to do to get her back."

"Crosby. He's made what he wants very plain." She slumped back against the pony as if she could no longer stand without aid. "He says Frankie's visiting Isabelle, and I can fetch her when I go to the Bar Cross to sign the bill of sale for the Lazy B."

Cal had never seen Mackenzie so defeated. All life had drained from her face. Her eyes closed, as if to block out the world and its pain. Slumped against the patient pony, she looked like a puppet held up by only one string. His heart ached for her. Frankie was probably having a fine time with Isabelle, unaware that anything was amiss. But Mackenzie had just entered the gates to her own private hell.

"He's won," Mackenzie conceded dismally. "He can have the Lazy B and to hell with both the ranch and Nathan Crosby."

"Mackenzie," Cal said softly. "You can't give in. Start giving in now, to something like this, and you'll find yourself giving in for the rest of your life."

Mackenzie's eyes came to blazing life. "How can you say that?" she demanded hotly. "Do you think for one minute that the Lazy B, that anything, is worth Frankie being put at risk? You hardhearted, calculating, sonofa—"

"Nothing's going to happen to Frankie, Mac. I'll get her back." He swung down from his horse and took the pony's reins from where they trailed on the ground. Mackenzie looked as if she was about to attack him, but she satisfied herself with a black glare. Cal decided he preferred her angry to defeated.

"I won't have it, Cal! I don't want you to do anything! I'm going to do exactly what Crosby tells me to do."

"No, you're not," Cal told her calmly."You're going to ride with me back to the ranch and stay there while I go after Frankie."

"Like hell! I will *not* have Frankie endangered. The ranch isn't worth a single hair on her head."

"What are *you* worth?" he demanded harshly. "Your pride, what you think of yourself—what is that worth? What is it worth for Frankie to spend her life knowing that she lost her grandfather's ranch because she was a foolish little kid? Bullies are something you never give in to, Mac, or you find yourself running scared and giving in every time you should be standing up for yourself."

"It doesn't matter!" she almost screamed. "All that matters is Frankie!"

Cal wanted to reach out and gather her into his arms for comfort, but he doubted she would allow it. The only comfort he could provide was retrieving their daughter, safe and sound. "Do you really believe I would let anything happen to Frankie?" he asked softly. "You might not trust me with anything else in your life, Mac, but you should know I can be trusted with our daughter."

Mist brightened Mackenzie's eyes, then spilled over onto her cheeks in dribbling tears. Cal could see her fight for control. "Frankie . . . I . . . " The dam burst and a deluge poured down her face.

Cal gently pulled Mackenzie into his arms. In her misery she didn't resist. He felt her body shake with huge sobs and wondered if she cried only for Frankie or for Frankie and herself both, for six years of bitterness and dry loneliness that had taken her girlhood and given her so little in return. Frankie was the brightest light in Mackenzie's life, one of the brightest in Cal's life as well. He wasn't about to let his daughter go just when he'd discovered her. Neither was he willing to let Mackenzie go now that he'd found her again.

"I'll bring her home, Mac." He tightened his hold. "And if Crosby has hurt a hair on her little head, I'll make him wish he'd never been born."

Cal took only the White Mountain Apaches with him when he left for Crosby's ranch. Mackenzie tried to accompany him, but he flatly refused.

"Can you sneak up on a house surrounded by guards without being seen or heard?" he asked her.

Mackenzie didn't need to respond. They both knew the answer.

"Can you slit a man's throat if need be, without him making a sound?"

Even in the fast-fading dusk he could see her face pale.

"You're not going. And don't try to follow behind us, Mac. You'll only hurt my chances of getting Frankie out without a ruckus. You don't want her to be frightened, do you?"

"No," Mackenzie said quietly.

"This is something you're going to have to trust me with."

"At least take more men."

Cal shook his head. "Three Apaches are worth at least ten of any other men."

As they rode under the Lazy B arch, Cal felt Mackenzie's eyes burn holes in his back. He felt her agony and let it merge with his own, then set it aside—something acknowledged but not felt. To accomplish the task he'd set himself, he had to once more become Apache. An Apache would never let pain, fear, or grief distract him from single-minded concentration. An Apache became one with the land he rode across, part of the horse he rode, part of the sage, the sand, the rocks, the wind. The enemy wouldn't see or hear him come, wouldn't feel his presence, wouldn't sense anything wrong with the world until it exploded around him. Soon, Cal vowed, Nathan Crosby would have reason to regret touching California Smith's daughter.

By the time Cal and his little band reached Crosby territory, the sun had set and stars were popping out in a deep-purple sky. Just out of sight of the Bar Cross ranch house, Cal motioned a halt. He signaled Bay to stay with the horses while Mahko and Istee dismounted and slipped with Cal past the line of sentries that guarded the ranch compound. The house was protected by an encircling adobe wall. First they had to get past the wall through the closed wooden gate. Then they had to find out where Frankie was being kept, slip into the house, and spirit her to safety. When that was accomplished, Cal could finish his business with Nathan Crosby.

Cal led the way toward the ranch compound, sometimes slithering on his belly to take advantage of low cover, sometimes clinging to the shadows of rocks or a stand of juniper. The moon had risen in the east, but he knew how to avoid its revealing light and make himself invisible. Regressing back to his Apache days was almost too easy. California Smith receded to the back of his mind as Goshk'an came to life again. Once again he was the youth who had to be better than all the other youths at anything they did: hunting, riding, wrestling, running, endurance. He was the one who beat his fellow apprentice warriors when they were instructed to run up a mountain and back down with a mouthful of water—without losing a drop. He was the one who stepped in where the other boys feared to go, who volunteered for the toughest tasks and worked until he conquered them. He was the one who drilled himself in the arts of war until they were second nature, as much as part of him as eating and sleeping. Fourteen years hadn't dulled the skills he had learned.

Cal and the three Apaches reached the wall, disappeared into the shadows at its base, and slipped unnoticed through the unlocked gate. The house loomed in front of them, a sprawling adobe building with a tile roof and a wide covered porch that wrapped round three sides. All was quiet. Lantern light glowed behind the shutters along the front and one room on the side.

Cal motioned Mahko and Istee into the shadows while he stole silently to the lit side window. He guessed that the window along the front opened from a parlor or office. The side window, he hoped, might be Isabelle's bedroom or Frankie's prison.

He was right. The room was both. When he peered through the slats of the shutter he saw Isabelle and Frankie seated cross-legged on a braided rag rug beside a bed. Frankie was showing her friend how to make dolls from rags and string. In this case the rags were linen handkerchiefs and the string was the green ribbons that had fastened Frankie's pigtails. Both girls were engrossed.

Cal waited for ten minutes, crouched in the shadow of the house, hoping Isabelle would leave. She didn't, and every minute increased his chances of being discovered. He would have to deal with Isabelle as well as Frankie.

Fortunately, the window was open to admit the cool night air. All Cal had to do was push the shutter and it slid back. The girls didn't even notice until he tapped lightly on the window casement.

"California!" Frankie cried in delight. "It's California!"

Cal raised a finger to his lips for silence. Frankie's voice immediately dropped to an excited whisper. "What are you doing at the window? Is Ma here? Are you going to spend the night, too?"

"We're going home, Frankie," he told her quietly.

Isabelle glared at him. "Men aren't supposed to be looking into my window," she declared. "I'm going to call my father."

In one lithe motion Cal hoisted himself through the window and dropped lightly into the bedroom. Isabelle backed away in alarm.

"Don't be a 'fraidy-cat, Issy!" Frankie giggled at her friend's behavior. "It's okay. This is my friend California. He taught me to ride a horse."

In spite of Frankie's assurance, Issy looked ready to carry out her threat and call her father. Cal dropped to one knee. "Don't be afraid, Issy. I've just come to take Frankie home."

"My father said she could spend the night," Issy declared sullenly.

"Frankie's mother decided that she should come home."

Frankie tapped Cal on the shoulder. "Do I have to go home now?" she asked. This time the whisper was a bit plaintive. "I would like to spend the night. Issy and me are making dolls."

"Maybe Issy can come over in a few days and you can finish making dolls," Cal offered. "And you could both eat some of Carmelita's prickly-pear pie."

"Oh, yes!" Frankie forgot to whisper.

"My father would never let me," Issy complained.

"I'm going to talk to your father," Cal promised, somewhat grimly. He rose, crossed to the window, and gave a soft owl's hoot.

The implication that Cal knew her father seemed to set Issy at ease. "I would come over if Pa said I could."

"I'll show you my new pony." Frankie's face clouded. "Is Goldie all right, California? Mr. Crosby said I should ride on his horse so we could go faster. He said Goldie would go back home by himself."

"Goldie's fine. He's eating grain, safe in his stall."

Frankie smiled brightly and gave Issy a superior look. "Goldie's really pretty. He's all yellow except for a black mane and a black stripe down his back and black socks. I'll let you ride him if you come over."

"We've got to go now, Frankie."

"Oh." Her voice dropped with disappointment.

"You get to climb out the window," he told her.

"Okay!"

He hoisted her up through the window. Sinewy brown arms reached out to take her. "This is Mahko," Cal explained to Frankie. "Mahko's going to take you home while I talk to Mr. Crosby and tell him why you had to leave."

Frankie went unhesitatingly into the Apache's embrace. Issy stuttered a complaint, but Cal hushed her with a finger to his lips. "Shall we go talk to your father?" he asked her.

"O . . . okay."

Cal waited for a few moments, his hand on Issy's shoulder, until another owl's hoot assured him that Frankie was safely on her way. Mahko had successfully worked his way through the sentries and given the child to Bay-chen-day-sen to take home. He waited another few moments to give Istee time to make his way to the bunkhouse, as they had planned.

"Okay, Issy," he finally said. "Let's go see your pa."

Nathan Crosby was in the parlor, leaning comfortably against the mantel of the unlit fireplace. In conference with him were Kelly Overmire, Hank Miller, Jeff Morgan, and Tony Herrera. So Tony had gone to work for Crosby, Cal thought with wry amusement. He hoped the boy gave Nathan as much trouble as he'd given Mackenzie.

"Pa." Isabelle announced hesitantly. "Mr. California's here to see you. He sent Frankie home."

Crosby's head jerked up. His face twisted with anger, then alarm. Overmire and Herrera clutched at their pistols.

"Put the guns away, you fools!" Crosby snarled.

"Go back to your room, Issy." Cal gave the girl's shoulder a gentle squeeze.

"Will you ask him if I can visit Frankie?" she asked anxiously.

"Sure I will."

When Isabelle was gone, Crosby motioned to his men. Grinning, they unholstered their guns. "You're not as smart as I thought you were, Smith," Crosby sneered.

"What are you going to do?" Cal asked with a cold smile. "Shoot me down for coming to fetch Mackenzie Butler's daughter? Seems to me the law might ask some questions about that. Besides, you're in deeper trouble than you know, Nathan. I've got a few men outside."

Tony snickered. "You might have gotten past the guards, Smith, but those oafs that work for Mackenzie never could've slipped through."

Cal's expression didn't change. "Mahko!" he called softly.

The front door opened and Mahko took a step inside, a savage figure with rifle held ready. Tony raised his pistol, but Crosby motioned him to be still.

"Once an Apache bastard, always an Apache bastard, eh?" Crosby said. "How many you got out there?"

"Enough," Cal lied coolly. "Have your men put their guns on the floor."

Crosby gestured, and guns dropped to the floor.

"I want you to think about how easily I got through your guards and into your house, Crosby. Think about that next time you plan mischief against Mackenzie Butler."

"Mischief?" Crosby asked innocently. "The only mischief I see is you sneakin' into my house like some sort of thief."

"We all know what I'm talking about."

Crosby smiled slyly. "Frankie was here on a visit to Isabelle. They're good friends. Everyone in the valley knows that. Mackenzie can't complain. I even left her a note telling her where her daughter was." His tone grew condescending. "If I were her, I would be ashamed to let my kid ride around alone with all the things that can happen to a body in this country."

Cal's face grew grim. "If I were you, Crosby, I'd think carefully on some of those things that can happen. Could be that I'm a man who isn't concerned with the legalities of a matter like this. I might get carried away if anything happened to Mackenzie Butler or her daughter or anyone else at the Lazy B. I don't think you'd want me to get carried away, Crosby."

A shadow of fear flickered in Crosby's eyes at Cal's softly spoken threat.

"You're makin' a heap too much of this thing, Smith." Jeff Morgan held his hands out in a conciliatory gesture as Cal flickered a glance his way. "Mr. Crosby didn't mean Frankie no harm, nor Mackenzie neither. He's just trying to convince that stubborn woman of what's really best for her. You know as well as I do that this ain't no country for a woman living alone trying to make a go of a ranch like the Lazy B."

Cal heard the note of sincerity in Jeff's voice. The man was actually naive enough to believe what he said.

"I think Mr. Crosby and everyone else needs to let the lady make her own decision on that," Cal replied. "Just remember that anyone who touches Mackenzie Butler or her family answers to me."

"Oh, now don't that just make us shake in our boots!" Tony Herrera had been sullen and silent until now, but the prospect of Cal getting away with his audaciousness was just too much for him to tolerate. "Mackenzie can make her own decisions, all right," he said with a sneer. "Just look at how well she's done! She breeds a kid with this yellow-haired

Apache, stands by while he murders her father—my mother's husband—and then she takes the sonofbitch back in and lets him yahoo around threatening law-abiding, upstanding citizens like Mr. Crosby here. The only decisions that bitch can make is when to get on her back and how wide to spread her legs."

"Shut your filthy mouth, Tony!" Jeff Morgan's face turned a livid, angry red.

"It's true! You can't say that any of it isn't true! She's had you wrapped around her finger so long that you don't know up from down!"

Nathan watched with an amused glint in his eye as his men sparred and hissed. Cal watched with quickly building rage. Tony's malicious slurs grated against his temper, and a scalding flood of anger threatened his self-control. He spoke one harsh word in Apache. As if cut off by a sharp knife, the blustering between Morgan and Herrera stopped. Mahko appeared once again in the doorway.

Cal's eyes narrowed. "You don't want to fight with Morgan, Herrera. You want to fight with me."

Tony grinned.

"Come ahead, boy." Cal unbuckled his gunbelt and threw it to Mahko. He spoke to the Indian in English to make sure that all the occupants of the room understood. "Any of these skunks tries to interfere, shoot him."

Mahko nodded, giving each man in turn a measuring, predatory look.

"How many times do you have to be pounded before you learn what's good for you?" Cal taunted Tony.

"I ain't learnin' from no goddamned, piss-drinkin' Apache!"

Tony lunged and threw his arms around Cal's torso, pinning Cal's arms to his side. With a quick burst of strength, Cal broke the hold. Tony lashed out with a right hook. Cal ducked and returned a fist to the gut. While Tony staggered and gasped for breath, Cal caught him in a wrestle hold and they tumbled together to the floor. Tony flailed. Desperately he grabbed at the leather thong that held the Apache medicine bag around Cal's neck, twisting it, trying to cut off Cal's breath. The thong broke. Tony tried to reach Cal's throat with his hands, but Cal fended him off.

Crosby, Miller, and Overmire watched avidly while laying wagers on the outcome. Jeff Morgan fidgeted in indecision, his eyes traveling from the fight to Mahko and back again. Mahko watched the Bar Cross men and the fight with equal dispassion, his rifle held ready to make sure none of Herrera's allies decided to up the odds in the Mexican's favor.

"I got five says Smith takes 'im," Overmire told Crosby.

"Raise to twenty," Miller demanded.

"Done," Crosby said.

Morgan looked at them all in disgust.

"How 'bout you, Injun?" Crosby mocked. "Speak English? Got money to lay on your man, there?"

Mahko gave him an impassive stare. "Bet good knife against Colt pistol that Goshk'an sit on Big Mouth."

Nathan cackled. "Done. Come on, Herrera. I got my pistol ridin' on your whippin' that yella-haired Apache!"

Tony grunted as he struggled in Cal's grip. "Lemme up, ya bastard, and I'll show you how a man fights."

"All right." Cal grinned wolfishly and let Tony up. "We'll fight your way."

"You'd be better off gettin' outta this valley," Tony growled.

"Think so?"

"Think that slut at the Lazy B is worth dyin' for? That's what's gonna happen one of these days when you stick your nose in where it doesn't belong."

Tony lashed out with a right hook. Cal dodged, then moved in with his own attack. He felt his anger flow like molten steel to every muscle of his body. When a few of

Tony's blows landed, he scarcely felt them. They tumbled out the door, onto the porch, and into the dirt. Out of the corner of his eye Cal saw the Bar Cross crew cringing against the bunkhouse wall under the watchful eyes of Istee, who looked as though he hoped that one of the men would try something.

Tony struggled to his feet. Cal crouched in a predatory stance and smiled coldly. "You just leave Mackenzie Butler out of your conversation from now on."

"Like hell!" Tony spat from lips that were already beginning to swell.

"You should learn to admit it when you're beaten," Cal commented.

Tony snarled and lunged forward. Cal met him halfway with a shoulder to his middle, lifting him like a sack of flour—a cursing sack of flour. Wheeling rapidly around, Cal found what he needed.

"Might as well put the rest of you where your mouth is." He launched the Mexican into a fresh pile of horse droppings by the hitching rail. Tony's curses slammed to surprised silence as the greenish, fragrant goo splashed up around him, then they doubled in vigor. But he didn't get up.

Cal turned to Crosby, who watched stonily. "Remember what I said, old man, because I meant every word."

Mahko gave Crosby a triumphant grin and held out his hand for the Colt. "Goshk'an sit on Big Mouth, I win," he reminded Nathan.

"Get down on your faces," Cal ordered the Bar Cross men. "All of you."

Crosby and his men gave no argument. As they lay prone on the ground, Istee and Mahko collected their weapons and threw them down the well that abutted the guard wall. Cal motioned the two Apaches to leave. When they were safely out of the gate, he backed away to follow.

"You owe me twenty," Miller growled to Crosby.

* * *

Mackenzie was beside herself the moment the rescue party left. She prowled the house, the yard, the inner court, driving both Lu and Carmelita to distraction with her verbal worrying. She shouldn't have let Cal go. She should have given Crosby what he wanted. What had made her trust Cal and a band of Apaches to rescue her daughter, for God's sake?

Carmelita tried to comfort Mackenzie with assurances that Cal would bring Frankie back. California Smith could do anything, the Mexican woman exclaimed confidently. She got only an impatient frown from Mackenzie for her effort.

As time dragged by, Mackenzie paced and cursed herself for giving in to Cal's scheme. She'd been swept away by Cal's seeming command over the horrible situation. How often had she allowed herself to be swept away by him? Too many—starting with six years ago. She wondered if she'd had a choice this time, though. Cal had been determined to go. The expression on his face when he'd left had made Mackenzie shiver. She almost felt sorry for Nathan Crosby. Almost, but not quite.

Mackenzie was alone in the parlor when a prickling ran along her spine. No sound alerted her, but all the same she crossed to the window. Her breath stuck in her throat when she looked outside. There beside the yard wall, bathed eerily in the moonlight, a tall figure sat astride a horse—a tall, lean figure with a squirming bundle of little girl on the saddle in front of him. Mackenzie hadn't heard the horse come in and the sentries had given no alarm. She wondered if she was dreaming. Then the figure turned his face toward her. The moon illuminated Bay's angular features.

"Lu! Lita! It's Frankie!"

Mackenzie ran for the door. Seconds later she was kneeling in the dirt of the yard and squeezing Frankie in a bear hug that made the little girl squeak in complaint. Lu and

Carmelita both stood by with tears streaming down their cheeks.

"I was just visiting Issy," Frankie told her mother. "Her pa invited me. I didn't get to show her my new pony, though. Is Goldie all right?"

"Goldie's fine," Mackenzie said, scarcely able to choke out the words. She didn't know whether she wanted to scold Frankie or shower her with assurances of love, but she could do neither—only sob, the tears burning hot trails down her cheeks. "Never, never go riding alone again! Promise me!"

Frankie looked wide-eyed at her mother's tear-stained face. "I just wanted to show my pony to Issy. Her pa said Goldie's not fast enough to go to their house!" she said indignantly. "He made me ride with him like I was a baby!"

Mackenzie pushed her daughter to arm's length and gave her a gentle shake. "Promise me!"

"Okay." A confused frown puckered Frankie's brow and tears welled in her eyes.

"No, no. Don't cry." Mackenzie pulled her daughter back into her arms. "Everything's all right, Sprout. Just don't go visiting alone again." She glanced at Bay-chen-day-sen, who watched impassively from atop his horse. His face was almost invisible in the night, only the whites of his eyes gleaming in the moonlight. "Thank you for bringing her back."

"Goshk'an get girl. I just arms that carry back."

"Thank you anyway."

He nodded solemnly.

George Keller trotted in, reining up beside Bay and giving the Indian a startled look.

"He came in a few minutes ago," Mackenzie explained, a hint of censure for the sentries in her voice.

"Well, there's more comin' in," Keller told Mackenzie. "Looks like Smith and the . . . uh . . . the rest of the tribe.

Damned if they didn't manage to pull it off." His tone hinted at grudging respect.

Mackenzie closed her eyes, relieved. Even when she had seen Bay with Frankie, a burden of worry still weighed her down. It hadn't lifted until Keller's announcement confirmed that Cal was also safe. She rose to her feet and pointed Frankie toward the house. "Go to the office and fetch the little leather pouch in the top right-hand drawer. Can you do that?"

"Sure!" Frankie bounded off with her usual vigor. Half a minute later she came running back with the item Mackenzie had indicated. Mackenzie checked inside the pouch and sniffed the rich aroma of the pipe tobacco that Lu kept on hand for Amos Gilbert's visits. She closed the pouch and handed it to Bay.

"We would like you to have this tobacco and share with the others of your camp. A small gift of thanks."

Bay accepted the pouch with a solemn nod, then smiled. It was the first time Mackenzie had seen Bay-chen-day-sen smile.

"You'll also get a bonus in next week's pay—though there is nothing I can do to tell you how grateful I am."

"Your words enough," Bay assured her.

Mackenzie laid a hand on her daughter's shoulder. "Frankie, thank Bay-chen-day-sen for letting you ride home with him."

"Thank you, Mr. Daysen," Frankie chirped. "I liked riding home with you. And I really like your horse."

Another smile softened the Apache's face. "You are welcome, Goshk'an's daughter."

Frankie gave him a puzzled look. Mackenzie smiled awkwardly and turned her daughter toward the house. "Lu, I think we should get Frankie inside now."

"Does Mr. Daysen know my father?" Frankie asked as she

was escorted toward the door. "Was my father's name Gosh . . . uh . . . ?"

"It's just a saying for little girls." Mackenzie urged Frankie through the front door. "To the pump with you, Sprout. After you've washed off all that dirt, you can eat the supper that Gran saved for you. Then to bed."

"Aw, Ma!"

"The sun's been down for hours, and you've had a big day."

"I'm not tired!"

Mackenzie gave her a look that quelled all argument. Frankie obediently marched off to the inner court. Lu and Carmelita followed. They had just disappeared when hoof-beats pounded outside. Before Mackenzie could hurry to the door, Cal strode in, a cloud of dust rising from his clothing at every step. He'd ridden hard, and it showed.

"Frankie?" he demanded.

"She's fine. She's at the pump washing."

Cal nodded.

"Nathan?" she asked.

"Still alive," he assured her. "Though I'd imagine right now he's cranky as hell. Morgan and Herrera better stay out of his way for a few days."

"Tony was there?"

"He found himself a new job."

Mackenzie wasn't really interested, not in how cranky Nathan was, nor that Lu's wild son now worked for the Bar Cross. All that mattered was that Frankie was safe—and Cal. She couldn't deny that she'd been desperately worried about him. Something inside her wanted to tell him. She wanted to tell him more—that whatever else stood between them, she would always owe him for Frankie's safety. Looking at his impassive face, Mackenzie realized he didn't expect thanks. He didn't expect anything from her, and suddenly that made her ashamed.

"I . . . I thank you, Cal. I don't know what to say."

"You don't need to say anything," he said softly. "Frankie's my daughter too."

"I know. I know you didn't go out there for me. You went for Frankie."

His eyes flickered, but whatever went through his mind remained unspoken. Mackenzie felt her control falter. It had severely eroded over the past few hours.

"I was so frightened," she admitted, not able to meet his eyes. "Frankie is my whole life. Without her I would want to die." Tears overflowed onto her cheeks. She didn't attempt to evade Cal's arms as he gently pulled her against his chest. He didn't speak; he simply held her, steady and hard as a rock, safe, comforting.

Mackenzie cried for a moment, relieved to let go for once. But such weakness couldn't be indulged for long. In a few moments she pulled away.

"I'm sorry." She sniffed, then sneezed from the dirt on his shirt.

Cal grinned and touched her cheek with one finger. "I've gotten dust all over your face, and you turned it to mud."

"Oh." She stepped back, embarrassed.

Just then a pigtailed whirlwind flew into the room and tackled Cal's knees. "California! You're back. Did you talk to Issy's pa? Can she come over and make dolls and meet Goldie?"

Cal smiled and lifted Frankie into his arms. "Issy can't come over for a while yet."

Poor Frankie, Mackenzie reflected. She and Isabelle Crosby got on so well, but after today's work, Nathan Crosby wasn't likely to let his daughter get within a mile of Mackenzie or Cal.

"Oh." Frankie's face fell, then brightened as Cal playfully tweaked her nose.

"But when she does come over you're going to show her

some of that best riding this side of Texas, 'cause you and I are going to work very hard on making you a horsewoman even better than your ma."

"Okay!" Frankie squealed in delight.

Mackenzie watched them together. They were so much alike. Two heads of tawny hair reflected the lantern light, two sets of identical dimples flashed as they smiled at each other. So happy with each other and so alike. Mackenzie watched them and felt her defenses dissolve. Her painfully built walls, her caution, her good sense, her heart itself was crumbling, and she couldn't do a thing to stop them.

12

"Lightning's having her baby!" Frankie burst into the court and bounced along the curved brick path to where Mackenzie knelt weeding the flower garden. Bits of straw decorated the little girl's pinafore and clung to the calf-high moccasins Cal had made her a few days before. Since he'd given her the little deerhide Apache-style boots, she'd refused to wear any other shoes. Mackenzie almost had to pry them off when Frankie went to bed at night. "California says it'll be few hours yet, but she's starting her con . . . con . . ."

"Contractions," Mackenzie provided.

"Yeah! She's starting those! And he said I could name the baby horse, if it's all right with you."

Mackenzie sat back in the dirt and laid aside her spade. "Well, you named the mare, didn't you? And you named Goldie and Dolly. Maybe we should let somebody else have a turn at naming the baby."

Frankie's face immediately fell.

Mackenzie gave her a quick smile. "I was just teasing, Sprout. Of course you can name Lightning's baby."

"Okay! I want to name it Wind!"

"Wind?"

"Yeah! California told me a story about Lightning and Wind. They were two people who had this talk on top of a rainbow. And if I named the baby Wind, it wouldn't matter if it's a girl or a boy."

"I think Wind is a very nice name," Mackenzie told her.

"I'm going to go tell California! I bet he likes the name!"

"I'll go with you." Mackenzie got up and dusted off her skirt. "I'd like to say hello to the mother-to-be."

The barn was lit by a lone lantern that cast a dull-yellow glow over the maternity stall. The mare stood with her head down, restlessly shifting her weight from one side to the other. Cal was in the stall with her. A barrel of fresh wash water stood outside the stall door, and towels hung over the partition.

The other inhabitants of the barn were restless as well, as if they anticipated the coming birth. Two stalls down, Goldie rustled around his box and strained his neck to see over the partition. Cal's Runner and Mackenzie's Dolly both had their noses pointed in the direction of Lightning's stall, and in the small fenced pasture just outside the west barn doors, the Lazy B's big gray stallion neighed and pranced back and forth.

Mackenzie grinned at the racket the gray was making. "You'd think this was his baby about to come into the world," she commented to Cal.

"Maybe it is," Cal said.

"I don't think so. We found this girl way back in the Dragoons running with a group of mares that belonged to the most magnificent red-coated stallion you've ever seen. He managed to get most of his harem away from our roundup, but Lightning and three yearlings came home with us."

The mare swung her head toward Mackenzie and huffed out a little moan.

"Oh, come on, Lightning! It hasn't been all that bad!"

Frankie giggled. "Oh, Ma! She doesn't speak English!"

"I suppose she speaks Apache?" Mackenzie slanted a look at Cal.

"Most horses do," he said with a teasing smile.

Mackenzie had intended to stay only a few minutes, but once she was with the laboring mare, she couldn't tear herself away. Just as she had sympathized with Lightning when the mare had so valiantly struggled for freedom, she ached with her now in the effort to give birth. The contractions were scarcely visible and still spaced at long intervals, but every time the mare grew glassy-eyed and pushed, Mackenzie wanted to push with her, just to make things easier.

Shortly after the sun went down, Lu brought a basket of fried chicken, fried potatoes, and baked squash to the barn. "I didn't think any of you were going to leave this barn to eat," she said briskly, but when she looked over the partition at Lightning, her eyes softened. "Going to be a mother, are you, dear?"

The mare whickered at the sound of a new voice.

"That's all right, dear. Keep up the good work and you'll have your baby here in no time."

Cal pulled over a worktable and Lu set out food, tableware, and plates.

"A picnic!" Frankie exclaimed. "Okay!"

Lightning looked on placidly as they filled their plates. "Hard to believe she was such a nasty creature not so long ago," Lu commented.

Mackenzie looked up sharply. "Who?"

"The mare, of course. California's done a marvelous job of calming her down, don't you think?"

"She wasn't nasty," Mackenzie said somewhat defensively. "She was just scared."

"Don't take it personally, Mackenzie dear, but she was nasty, whatever the reason. You're to be congratulated, California. She's a horse that would have made even my father take a second look, and he had the finest stable in Mexico City at one time. It seems you have a touch with hard-to-handle ladies."

Mackenzie shot her a lethal glance.

The four of them sat together and watched while Lightning progressed in her labor. The mare seemed to know exactly what she was doing and had no concern over their presence, but all the same, as the contractions grew more intense and closer together, they spoke in whispers and took care to make no sudden movements. Even Frankie was quiet, her eyes wide and solemn in a worried face.

Finally Lightning lay down on her side and started working in earnest. Cal went into the stall and knelt at her head, speaking to her in soft tones. Mackenzie had always thought that the Apache language was a harsh tongue until she heard Cal speaking it. Apache was a beautiful language, she discovered as she listened, or perhaps, Cal's voice was the thing that was beautiful. It had a deep, soft resonance that could make a woman lose herself and forget where and who she was.

Cal had left the stall door open—escape was not one of the things on Lightning's mind right now—and Frankie tiptoed over to stand at the mare's nose. "Does she hurt?" She asked her mother, not Cal, as if instinct told her that even her hero California could only intrude so far into this female domain.

Touched, Mackenzie knelt down beside her daughter. The mare heaved a labored sigh. "She might hurt a little," Mackenzie told Frankie. "But when she has her new baby she'll forget all about the hurting."

Lightning heaved up. Her body contracted into an arc of strain. Frankie stepped back in alarm. "Is she all right?"

"She's fine, Frankie," Cal answered, but Mackenzie didn't like the look on his face as he palpated the mare's abdomen.

Lu apparently didn't like it either. She took Frankie's hand. "Come on, Sprout. Your bedtime came and went an hour ago. Time to go in."

"But I wanna stay! Can't I stay, Ma?"

"Do as Gran says, Frankie."

The rebellious pout on Frankie's face slowly faded under Mackenzie's steady gaze. "I still get to name the baby horse?"

"Of course you do. First thing in the morning, you can come out to the barn and tell the new baby its name."

"Okay. I will!"

"Come along." Lu tugged Frankie toward the barn door.

"She wouldn't have been any trouble," Cal said when they had gone.

"She's much too young to witness something like this. Let her have her illusions for a while yet."

Cal shook his head and ran a gentle hand along the mare's sweating neck. "White women have strange ideas. Birth is not something that shatters illusions—it's the grandest thing in the world. Foals, puppies, babies. I've delivered a lot of foals, a few litters of puppies, and I watched my Apache mother Dohn-say give birth to two of her children. The miracle of it never ceases to amaze me." He gave Mackenzie an enigmatic look. "Did birthing Frankie shatter your illusions?"

Mackenzie fastened her eyes upon the mare, not able to look up and meet Cal's direct gaze. "My illusions were shattered long before that," she told him softly.

"I suppose I did that."

"No," Mackenzie told him honestly. "People who live in this territory learn to accept losing loved ones to outlaws, gunmen, crooked lawmen, range wars . . . Apaches. Six years ago I hadn't learned to accept that. I released all my anger upon you." She shook her head at the bitter memory. "Back then I still believed that the good were always rewarded, right always won, and the world was filled with love and magic. I was too stubborn and ignorant to know how incredibly stupid I was."

"You weren't stupid," Cal denied in the same soothing tone he used with the mare. "You were young, green, and unlucky."

"I was stupid," Mackenzie repeated. "But now I've learned some things, I hope." She gave him a faint, apologetic smile. "Still stubborn, but not stupid. I no longer believe in love or magic, Cal."

Cal caught her eyes in a gaze of strange intensity. "If that's true, then you're not as smart now as you were six years ago. The world is full of magic, Mac. People who don't believe in it just don't see it."

Mackenzie didn't get a chance to answer, for just then the mare started to struggle in earnest. For the next hour she labored mightily to deliver her foal—with no results. The very air of the barn was heavy with the certainty that something was terribly wrong. Even the other horses were quiet and anxious.

At the end of an hour, Cal stripped off his shirt and went to the water barrel to wash his arms and chest.

"Something's wrong, isn't it?" Mackenzie asked. Her heart sank. This mare had become very special to her.

"'Fraid so. I was hoping the foal would turn by itself, but it hasn't. She can't deliver it the way it's sitting inside her."

"What . . . what are you going to do?"

"Turn it."

"Do you know how to do that?"

"I've done it before a couple of times." He took a rope from its hook on the door. "It isn't easy, and it doesn't always work. Moving things around inside a mare is more risky than poking around inside a cow. If you're not careful, you can tear something that won't heal."

"What happens if you do?"

"Then the horse dies," he said matter-of-factly. "But she'll die if I don't help her, Mac," he added at her look of horror. "That foal's not going to turn around by itself."

The task wasn't easy. Mackenzie had to subdue a queasy stomach as Cal maneuvered his arm inside the mare and tried to reposition the foal. Her job was to hold the mare's tail out of Cal's way, so she had a much better view of the procedure than she cared to have. Lightning was exhausted, but she still tried valiantly to deliver the baby. Mackenzie saw Cal's face whiten with pain as the mare bore down again and again, her powerful muscles squeezing his arm.

Cal was filthy with greenish mucus by the time he stopped to catch his breath. His arm still reached into the mare. "I've got the rope looped around a front foot," he told Mackenzie. "Come over here and take the end of it."

Mackenzie cautiously picked up the end of the rope that extended from the mare's birth canal.

"When I tell you, pull with all your strength. It's going to take a good tug to get this baby turned around. While you pull, I'll try to get the little guy where he oughta be. Ready?"

Mackenzie's heart pounded. "Ready."

"Pull."

She braced herself and pulled. Years of doing ranch work had honed her to lean muscle and wiry strength, but it wasn't enough. Nothing budged.

"Keep pulling."

Mackenzie braced her feet against the uneven floorboards and leaned her entire weight against the rope. Slowly, ever so slowly, something gave.

Cal grunted, twisting as he tried to push the foal around. "There it goes," he gritted out. "Whoa!"

Mackenzie let the rope go slack. The mare renewed her efforts. Cal took the rope from Mackenzie's shaking hand and gently pulled, helping the mare in her effort. Within half a minute out slid the foal, slippery and plastered with mucus. Lightning twisted her head to look, gave the baby a single nuzzle, then whuffed and lay her head down in exhaustion. The mother left the task of cleaning her baby to Cal, who carefully wiped the mucus from the foal's nose and toweled it dry.

"It's a boy," he announced as proudly as if he himself were the papa. Mackenzie watched in wonder as Cal ever so gently cleaned the baby's eyes and face. When Lightning obeyed instinct and staggered to her feet, he urged the infant to find the mare's teat. Mackenzie stood at Lightning's head and crooned to her what a fine mother she was. Soon the foal was noisily suckling and Lightning gave a great sigh of contentment. "Welcome to the world, Wind," Cal said softly.

Mackenzie chuckled. "You weren't supposed to tell him his name. That's Frankie's privilege."

Cal grinned. "Don't worry. He'll have forgotten it by morning."

Five minutes later, while washing at the water tank in the arena, they were still laughing at the joke, small as it was. Exhausted from the long ordeal, they both needed the release of laughter. Even the slightly sour-smelling birth fluid that spattered them both seemed a reason for humor.

Mackenzie was dirty enough to prove she'd been working hard. Her skirt was spotted with slime and blood and the sleeves of her bodice stained with mucus, even though she had rolled them up past her elbows. Cal laid claim to far more damage, however. He was soaked with his own sweat and the mess that had accompanied birth. He no sooner reached the water tank than he stripped off his shirt, pulled off his moccasins, jumped in the water, and came up sputtering. Mackenzie didn't blame him. She supposed she should be grateful he had left his trousers on. If she hadn't been with him, he no doubt would have plunged in buck naked.

When Cal stood up, water cascaded from his naked torso and shimmered in the light cast by the waning moon. Mackenzie tried to ignore a tightness that gripped her stomach at the splendid sight.

"Feel better?" she asked with a hint of envy in her voice.

"Much!"

"You make me sorry it's too late to drag the tub in from the yard." A bath would feel wonderful, but it was much too late. Hauling the tub into her room and filling it, even if she didn't heat the water on the stove, would surely wake the whole household. Maybe she should take the tub to the kitchen instead. The water that came from the well just outside the kitchen building was chilly, but cold and clean was still far better than . . . She suddenly noticed the wicked gleam in Cal's eyes.

Without a word, he vaulted from the tank, his eyes never leaving her. "What are you thinking, California Smith?" She held out an arm to ward him off.

"I'm thinking that you need a bath as much as I do."

She backed away as he advanced. "Oh, now wait a moment. This isn't at all proper! What're you—?" Mackenzie couldn't evade him. She dodged his grasp, but he anticipated her every move and moved faster.

"Don't squeal!" he warned her with a grin as he grabbed her arm. "The whole ranch will turn out in their nightshirts thinking the Apaches are raiding again."

The Apaches *were* raiding again, Mackenzie thought wryly as Cal swung her lightly up into his arms and marched toward the tank. "This is no way to treat your boss," she complained, a smile tugging at her mouth.

"Only when the boss is covered with muck. Hold your breath!" With a mighty heave he launched her into the tank. Her entry into the water was not graceful, but it was refreshing. She came up spitting, her hair plastered to her face in front of her eyes and spreading down over her shoulders like a sleek, wet shawl.

"That was . . . that was most unnecessary," she choked.

"Do you feel better?" he inquired with a grin.

She grimaced, then sighed. "Yes." Mackenzie did her best to look innocent. "Help me out?"

Cal laughed softly. "No, Mac. I'm not that stupid. I remember that you're the devil's very daughter when it comes to water fights."

What other man would remember such a detail? On a day many years ago she'd soaked him with a bucket of dirty wash water, horse wash water at that, to provoke him into chasing her. "Well, if you're not going to be a gentleman . . . " she began in her best Boston society voice. Then she made a fountain with both hands and sent a stream of water straight into his face.

"You little witch!" He choked as another stream found its target.

Mackenzie giggled musically—a happy sound much like her daughter's laughter.

"I think you need help getting properly clean," Cal said, advancing toward the water tank with a predatory stride.

"No, no!" Mackenzie warned, sending another blast of water his way. It didn't stop him. He jumped agilely over the side of the tank and wasted no time in reaching for her. Mackenzie ducked under his arm, stepped behind him, and gave him a push. Caught off balance, he plunged forward face first, starting a tidal wave that sloshed water over the sides of the metal tank. When he surfaced she dunked him again, laughing like a girl.

Suddenly Mackenzie's legs were flipped from under her. She sank, her laughter surfacing as bubbles. Cal pulled her up again and pinned her against the side of the tank. Slowly, their laughter died. Their eyes met and held, neither of them able to look away to break the suddenly irresistible spell.

Mackenzie felt a flush of heat prickle her skin despite the coolness of the water sloshing back and forth against her body. The world narrowed to encompass only Cal, his face transformed abruptly from teasing boyish laughter to erotic intensity. His eyes were pure heat, like the blue cone of a calm, unwavering flame. In the pale moonlight she could see the taut expectation in the line of his mouth, the rapid pulse in his jaw. Her own blood raced along with his.

Caged by his arms, she had no escape. Not that she wanted to escape, Mackenzie admitted. Slowly one of his hands moved from the rim of the tub. Gently, tentatively, his fingers brushed her breast. She closed her eyes, unable to resist the flood of desire that rushed through her veins. His hands curled, cupped, lifted, and primitive need coiled inside her belly.

"Mackenzie . . . " He pressed against her, his body hard and glowing with male heat. She couldn't mistake the urgent state of his arousal.

"Oh, please . . . " Mackenzie didn't know what she asked of him—to let her be or to press forward and finish what they both had started. She ached so that she didn't think she could stand it. Something was going to break—her will, her heart, every flaming nerve in her body.

Slowly his mouth descended for a kiss, moving languorously as in a dream. He hovered above her lips, waiting. . . . "Mackenzie," he whispered. "Come to me."

He waited only for her to be sure, to commit herself irrevocably, to take the initiative in closing the distance. Just a few inches separated them—a few inches, an injured heart, and six years of anger, bitterness, and misunderstanding. Her lips parted. Her breath came in short bursts. Just a few inches.

A few inches only. How she wanted to reach up and pull him to her, to feel his mouth take hers in a victory of possession, a victory for them both. But something inside her refused to take that step. Some frightened part of her still refused to relinquish her defensive shell. To love again, to trust again, that was the road that led to pain.

"No," she whispered. "I'm sorry. No." She ducked under his arm and scrambled from the tank. Trailing a river of water, she ran to the house, barring the door behind her and then collapsing back against it with great gasps. All the way Cal's eyes had followed her with such heat that she was surprised her clothing didn't steam.

Although exhausted, Mackenzie didn't sleep well that night. Her mind was awhirl with regret, speculation, shame, and embarrassment, while her body still ached with unfulfilled desire. She'd been scarce inches from giving in to Cal, a scant breath away from asking him—begging him—to make love to her. Somewhere inside of her still resided the foolish, careless, naive girl she'd been six years ago.

But she was older now, and wiser. Six years ago Cal had been the one who doubted her ability to live with a man who was tainted by his connections to the Apache. Now she was the doubter. She would be subjecting not only herself but also Frankie to scorn. And Cal—did she really know him? Did she trust him with her heart? When he'd sat with Geronimo it had been clear that much of him was alien to her.

Six years ago she had believed that love could conquer anything. Now she knew that love was a fragile thing that easily foundered in mistrust and anger. Love brought as much pain as happiness, and when it died its death could be ugly.

Long before dawn Mackenzie resigned herself to sleeplessness. She got up, donned a loose shirt and a pair of trousers, and walked to the barn to greet Lightning and her new foal. The foal slept folded into a corner of the stall. Dry and clean, his dark coat shone with brilliant red highlights in the light of Mackenzie's lantern. A copy of his mother's white blaze marked his nose. Close by her baby, the mare dozed on her feet. When Mackenzie walked up, the new mother raised her head and whickered a friendly greeting, as if she remembered the help Mackenzie had given her during the night's travail.

"You're very welcome," Mackenzie answered her, "but it's Cal you should be thanking, not me."

She wondered at the ache of disappointment inside her, then realized that without really being aware of her expectation, she had thought that Cal would be out in the barn to say good morning to the new foal. What a very sad case she was to put herself deliberately in the way of such temptation! Where was her self-control, her determination, her good sense?

Mackenzie sighed and leaned on the stall partition, her arms stacked one on top of the other to pillow her chin. Wind woke with a little snort, blew indignantly into the straw, and gave her a curious look. She remembered how close they'd come to losing both him and his mother. If not for Cal's strength and expertise, they would have been burying Lightning this morning instead of admiring her new baby. Cal had worked hard to save them when he could have more easily given up. He admired the mare, just as Mackenzie did, and he hated to see a life wasted—even the life of an animal.

That was something about him that certainly wasn't Apache. Beneath the hard, impassive exterior was gentleness, humor, compassion, and patience. For all his Apache ways—his moccasin boots, headband, and shoulder-length hair—Cal was more civilized than most of the white men in Arizona, Mackenzie realized.

She had perceived that six years ago. It was one of the reasons she had loved him. It was one of the reasons she still loved him.

The admission sent a shock wave through her mind. She still loved California Smith. In spite of everything—her father, the years that had passed, Cal's savage background. All this time she had fought to keep her heart to herself, fearing the pain of loving again, but Cal had owned her heart all along. Even though Mackenzie's feelings had been shrouded in bitterness for a long, long time, she'd never really stopped loving him.

Mackenzie suddenly felt as though someone had lifted a ton of weight off her shoulders. Loneliness was a terrible thing. It colored the world gray and blinded one to the sheer joy of being alive. Right now she felt so light that her feet would leave the ground if she so much as moved. "I guess you had better judgment than I did," she told Lightning. "You liked him all along, didn't you? Maybe what I need is a good dose of horse sense."

Mackenzie felt like a bird suddenly liberated from a cage. She loved California Smith, and that love felt good. It felt sure, and it felt sane. Six years ago Cal had done what he thought he had to do. So had she. It hadn't been his fault or hers. Both of them had paid a price for their choices. Now was the time to go forward. Only a coward let misgivings and uncertainties rule the conduct of life—and Mackenzie had never considered herself a coward.

The raucous crow of the Lazy B cock reminded her that the ranch would soon be stirring; a hint of dawn grayed the darkness. She didn't feel like dealing with everyday problems, so she took leave of Lightning and her baby, saddled Dolly, and headed out toward the south pasture. Lu wouldn't worry at finding her gone. When she was pregnant with Frankie, Mackenzie had often spent the early-morning hours in this same pasture trying to find courage to deal with the problems that beset her. It was the prettiest and most peaceful spot on the ranch, a place where earth and sky seemed in perfect harmony. In her more fanciful moments, Mackenzie speculated that some special spirit dwelt there, a guardian to Dragoon Springs. The spirit had given her solace many times before. Maybe it would help her decide what to do about loving California Smith.

Riding north to south on Lazy B property was like riding from the desert into paradise. Close to the northern boundary of their homesteaded acres, the ranch compound stood among sage, mesquite, and grass. In normal years the grass was abundant; this year it was dry and brittle. A thousand feet south of the ranch one could see the first trace of the little stream that led from Dragoon Springs and the dammed pond. To the north the stream sank under the valley's sandy soil, but to the south, as the stream approached its source, it grew wider and deeper. Nourished by precious water, the valley grew more lush. Mesquite and chaparral gave way to tall grama grass that Frank Butler had declared the best grazing grass in the whole United States. Wildflowers decorated the greenery with splashes of color. Live oaks and juniper marched beside the little stream like dark-green guardians of the priceless water.

By the time Mackenzie reached the springs and the pond, the valley was bathed in rosy light. To the east glowed the Dragoons, their outline etched in bright white-gold, a promise of the still-hidden sun. Two days ago the herd mares had been turned out into the pasture with their foals to graze on lush grass around the springs. A few cattle kept them company. Some of the animals were still bedded down on the ground. Others slept on their feet, but for the most part the herd was beginning to stir. Mares watched sleepily as their foals tested spindly legs in the cool morning air. Others dozed as their offspring suckled their breakfast or raced through the dew-soaked grass, while cattle watched the antics with sleepy disinterest.

Mackenzie dismounted and tied her mare to a juniper. She knelt beside the stream and splashed her face with cool water. Then she sat with her back against a tree to watch the sunrise—and think about what she wanted for the future.

The Lazy B had been her future ever since she had first set foot on its dusty ground. Now the ranch seemed incomplete without California Smith. Yet how could she justify risking her future and—more important, Frankie's future—on a man who'd wandered all his life, who didn't quite know if he was Apache or white? Love was all very well and good, but practicalities remained to be considered, practicalities that she'd not thought about when she so impulsively demanded that her father let her marry. Suddenly Mackenzie wished there really was a spirit dwelling in Dragoon Springs, a higher, wiser power who could assure her that she had every right to follow her heart and ignore her head.

No spirit made itself known, however, as the sky grew lighter and lighter. Wispy clouds that streaked the sky above the mountains brightened from crimson to gold, and finally the sun itself made its majestic appearance, first as a molten sliver, then a luminous crescent. Rays of gold speared across the valley as far as she could see, touching the mesquite, the chaparral, the junipers, and the river with a moment of shimmering glory.

Set afire by one of those golden rays, a lone rider trotted toward Mackenzie, following the same route up the stream that she had ridden. She sprang up to fetch her rifle from its saddle scabbard. Then she recognized the intruder. California Smith. The Appaloosa gelding was distinctive, and so was the rider's carriage in the saddle—like a part of the horse. Her heart pounding in her chest, Mackenzie sat back and waited. Maybe the spirit had answered her after all.

Cal pulled the Appaloosa to a halt a short ten feet away from where Mackenzie sat. "Lu told me I might find you here. You're out very early."

"I couldn't sleep," she admitted.

"Neither could I." His eyes glittered with a steel-bright light. "Don't you think it's time we end this silly game?"

Mackenzie's heart jumped. "What game?"

"You know what game. We've got only so many days allotted to us on this earth, and I can't see wasting any more of them."

Mackenzie jumped to her feet when Cal kneed the Appaloosa purposefully forward.

"Make up your mind with a firm yes or no, Mac, because all your maybes could drive a man to do something careless."

Mackenzie wondered if he meant to do something primitive like scoop her up onto the horse and ride off with her. A ridiculous thought, especially after she'd been reflecting only that morning how civilized a man he really was. The situation suddenly struck her as funny.

"What do you think you're doing?" She dodged away, but the Appaloosa dodged with her. Answering the guiding pressure of Cal's knees, the horse expertly herded her toward the stream.

"This is ridiculous! Stop!" She couldn't sound at all serious with laughter bubbling up in her voice. "Think you've got me, do you?"

Cal answered with a wicked grin.

The years seemed to drop away as Mackenzie let the imp she'd once been take control. If Cal wanted a game of chase, then that's what he would have. She would show him he wasn't dealing with a pansy-picking parlor flower. But first she would even the odds a bit. Laughing, she broke into a run toward her horse.

"No you don't!" Cal admonished. The Appaloosa whirled and cut across her path, forcing her to retreat. Cal leaned over, untied Dolly's reins, wrapped them securely around the saddle horn, and gave the horse a smack on the rear. "Go home, girl." The mare trotted off in the direction of the barn.

"Traitor," Mackenzie called after her. "Yikes!" The Appaloosa started for her again. "You're being silly," she said as she dodged, then dodged again. "If that mare doesn't get back to the barn, I'm going to be mad as a . . . yikes!" She leapt the stream as Cal got too close, then took off running for the rocks where the springs issues. If she could climb to a spot where a horse couldn't follow . . .

Cal kicked the Appaloosa into a gallop, circled around, and cut her off. He could have easily overtaken her, Mackenzie knew, but he was enjoying the game too much to end it. "This really isn't necessary," she panted, dodging away yet again.

"Then stop."

She couldn't. They played a game, and yet the game encompassed a small element of fear and uncertainty that made Mackenzie continue to run. She wove a crooked path through the live oaks and junipers that bordered the stream; she ran through the wildflowers, the mares and their startled foals scattering before her, then back across the stream to dodge through the trees, and again into the grassy meadow. Working like a fine cutting horse singling out a straying heifer, the Appaloosa stayed with her in a slow, controlled canter, not bothering to overtake but simply herding her away from any avenue of escape—the rocks in one direction, the ranch in the other.

Finally Mackenzie could run no longer. She stopped and bent over, hands braced on her knees, gasping for breath. Even then she laughed softly. Cal reined the Appaloosa in beside her. Just as she'd known he would, he leaned down and lifted her onto the horse, setting her in the saddle in front of him in a position that left no doubt about his arousal.

"Game over?" he asked, his clear blue eyes burning as brightly as the early-morning sky.

"Yes. Game's over."

"Yes?"

"Yes." She smiled.

13

With Mackenzie in his arms, Cal slid from the Appaloosa to the ground. Mackenzie made no objection to being carried as he strode toward a little copse of trees. Cradled against his chest, she enjoyed the firm grip of his arms holding her tightly against him, the supple play of muscle beneath her cheek, the warm male scent that rose from his body. His heart pounded heavily, matching hers in a cadence of excitement. A sense of inevitability, of rightness, overwhelmed her.

Mackenzie knew suddenly that she'd been waiting for this moment not only for the weeks since Cal had returned, but for all the years he'd been gone. Something deep inside her had foreseen her surrender, feared it and longed for it at the same time. Now that the moment was here, she could only revel in it.

The grassy bank of the stream offered a soft bed. A stand of juniper guarded their privacy. Springwater rippled merrily over rocks in the stream, birds trilled a song to greet the morning, and in the pasture playful foals whinnied shrilly while chasing through wildflowers and grass. Mackenzie heard none of it. Her senses were full of Cal.

He laid her down on the grass and joined her there. Caging her beneath him with his arms, he kissed her fiercely, devouring her as a starved man might attack a feast. She met him with equal enthusiasm. Her mouth opened to welcome his invasion, her tongue sparring playfully with his. When they surfaced for breath, he tangled his hands in her hair and pulled it free of the bun that she'd hastily pinned it in that morning.

"You should wear it loose." Cal spread her hair in a bright fan on the grass. "Your hair is beautiful. You are beautiful."

Mackenzie lay in delicious anticipation as Cal unfastened the buttons of her shirt. She'd been in such a tizzy this morning that she had worn nothing beneath. Appreciatively, Cal parted the shirt to reveal rose-tipped breasts flattened against her chest. For a moment he simply looked, his eyes burning. Mackenzie could feel her breasts swell beneath his loving scrutiny. The ache within her grew almost unbearable. When he touched them, cupped their fullness in his callused hand, lowered his head and captured one nipple in his mouth to suckle, Mackenzie thought she would die from the joy of it. The rough texture of his face against her breast sent streamers of desire through her. His tongue played, stroked, and tickled until she clutched at his hair in desperation.

"Please! Oh please!"

Cal drew back scarce inches from her breast and met her eyes. "Patience, Mac. Let me show you how much I love you." His breath was a warm caress on her bare flesh. He moved a hand to assuage the ache between her legs. She arched up to meet him as he rubbed hard against the material of her trousers. The barrier that held his flesh from hers made the ache even sharper. A rush of warm moisture wet the cloth beneath his hand, and they both breathed in labored gasps of anticipation.

Impatiently he slid her trousers and panties down to her knees, parted her thighs and slipped a finger inside her.

"Oh, yes." She sighed, squirming with impatience as first one finger, then two plunged inside her in delicious invasion. Anxious for all of him, Mackenzie reached up and unbuttoned his trousers. He sprang free in raw masculine glory and moaned with pleasure as her hand closed around him. In desperate haste he pulled off her boots and trousers so he could fit himself between her legs.

She moved beneath him so that just the tip of his turgid organ tasted the sweetness inside. Cal closed his eyes, his fact taut. He grasped her hips and plunged home just as Mackenzie arched up to meet him.

Mackenzie stifled a gasp, impaled on pain as well as pleasure. She'd grown small and tight in the years of celibacy.

Breathing harshly, Cal stopped, his hands gripping her hips as if he would seal them together. "I should be more careful. I hurt you."

"No." Mackenzie closed her eyes. The brief pain of his hard intrusion was far overshadowed by the urgency of her own need. Even now it faded as the sharp ache of desire grew. "Please!" she whispered. "I need you." She moved beneath him, urging him to take more.

"Dammit, Mac. You make me so hot, I lost all control." He kissed her hard, then met her desire in a thrust of savage possession. Little cries of contentment escaped Mackenzie's throat, urging him on, faster, deeper. Body and soul he filled her, huge and rock hard. Small, soft, tight, but slick with passion, somehow Mackenzie's body accommodated all of him, closing about him as he plunged deep and pulling desperately at him as withdrew.

"Wrap your legs around me," he instructed.

She obeyed, delighted with how this new position snugged him into her. As he thrust again, Mackenzie squeezed herself around him possessively and heard him gasp in pleasure, so she did it again.

Mackenzie's response undermined Cal's attempt to be gentle. He thrust again and again, grinding his hips against hers, urging her thighs even farther apart so he could plunge deeper. His hands squeezed her buttocks and lifted her to meet him, plunging to the hilt in her tight, hot sheath, pumping with desperate, almost violent frenzy.

Mackenzie felt every ridge of the hard flesh that thrust into her; she felt impaled, possessed, conquered, and enjoyed every lustful moment of it. She enjoyed the coiled power of Cal's body, the taut, raw craving in his face. His mouth was a narrow slash of passion, his eyes blue flames burning into hers, insistently holding her gaze to share the intensity of his need. She grew impossibly tight with desire. With his every thrust she coiled tighter, her own body squeezing in upon itself as well as her lover. The flash of a knowing grin bore witness that Cal read her body as if it were his own. She ached, every nerve curled in a tension that craved release.

"Almost there," Cal told her hoarsely. "Almost there." He reached down between their straining bodies and found the center of her desire. The rhythm of his thrusting increased as he gently massaged that most sensitive, vulnerable little nub. A spear of ecstasy flashed through Mackenzie. Her body seemed to turn to water, then steam, then fire. Unable to breathe, her vision turning black, she burned in pleasure so sharp it was pain.

"Now!" Cal groaned. "Now. God!" He plunged into her with ferocious purpose, sealing her to him as if they were truly fused into one being. Mackenzie felt her body convulse, felt the hot spurt of his seed burn its way inside her. She clung to Cal's hard body, grasped the arms that caged her, wrapped her legs even more tightly around his lean hips—until the world faded and she felt them both float like windborne feathers into the air.

When Mackenzie finally opened her eyes both she and Cal were still on the ground. The stream still gurgled, the birds still sang, and the morning sun had climbed high above the mountains. The air shimmered with summer heat.

Cal still crouched above her. His body was moist with sweat, as was hers. He regarded her with a possessive warmth.

"I hope you listened to my warning. I won't let you go this time."

Mackenzie felt a bubble of contentment swell in her heart. "I'm not going anywhere. Neither are you."

"I never thought I was."

"Is that so?" She lifted one brow—though looking properly aloof was difficult lying naked on her back with a man comfortably riding between her thighs.

"Like I said, at some point in his life a man has to decide what he wants and go after it." He grinned. "You made me work hard enough for it, Mackenzie girl."

"Bullfeathers." She smiled beatifically and moved wickedly beneath him. "I'd like to make you work even harder." Mackenzie saw the beginnings of renewed desire light his eyes and felt a pleasant twinge between her legs.

"I don't know." He lifted one tawny brow. "The sun's getting awfully hot."

"The sun's not the only thing that can get hot." She slanted a glance toward the stream, then smiled innocently. "Do you suppose it's awfully wicked to make love while splashing around in the cool water?"

"Fish do it."

She reached out her hand and touched the male staff that rose between his legs. He was already hot, hard, and erect. Cal closed his eyes as she caressed him. "We might try to cool this off a bit," she suggested.

He rose abruptly, pulled her up beside him, and towed her behind as he waded into the little stream. Finding a comfortable stretch of soft moss, he pushed her down upon it and pinned her when the shock of the cool water made her try to jump up. "Maybe I'm not the only one who needs to cool off, you lusty little witch." He splashed her. She squealed, but her squeals turned to sighs when he stopped splashing and spread the water across her body with gentle strokes of his hands. Mackenzie once again helplessly surrendered to desire as Cal leaned down to suck the water droplets from the hollow of her throat, her breasts, and the little pool that collected just above her woman's mound. The water slipped around her, touching her intimately with cool, delicate fingers that made her long for a more substantial touch.

Cal didn't hesitate to fill her need. He spread her legs and without preamble drove into her. Mackenzie gasped with pleasure, and he smiled wickedly. "Anything a fish can do, I swear I can do better."

He proceeded to prove his claim.

The sun was at its zenith by the time they were sated. Her passion satisfied, Mackenzie regained a bit of proper modesty. Suddenly feeling a bit awkward in her nudity, she washed and dressed, then watched Cal do the same, not able to resist admiring the magnificent construction of his body as he unhurriedly pulled on his clothes. When he sat down beside her on the bank of the stream, she pillowed her head in his lap, yawned, and promptly fell asleep.

Mackenzie didn't wake up until the sun had started its downward slide toward the horizon. She wondered briefly what Lu must be thinking about Cal and her being gone all day together. Her stepmother probably hoped they were doing exactly what they had done. She looked up to meet Cal's eyes regarding her warmly. Sand clung to the tousled waves of his hair and a blade of half-chewed grass protruded from his mouth. Suddenly she wondered how she could have ever believed that she didn't love this man.

"You look mighty satisfied with yourself," he noted.

"I guess I am," she admitted with a smug smile.

He took the grass blade from his mouth, flipped it into the stream, and solemnly watched it bob and sway as it traveled over the ripples. "Mac. There's something I have to say; some air that still needs to be cleared between us. I've made a heap of mistakes in my life, but walking away from you six years ago was the biggest. I believed your father when he said you couldn't take being married to me. Figured he knew you better than I did. Turns out neither one of us knew you as well as we should have. I'm sorry. I really am."

Mackenzie sat up, rubbing the cheek that was dented from the seam in his trousers. She shook her head and looked at the ground. "I'm sorry I believed you could have ever deliberately injured my father. I was hurt and angry—just looking for an excuse to hate you."

The bitter memory showed on her face, and Cal's eyes darkened with regret. "Mac, you know it'll never be over. We'll always be branded by that day. We both did things we regret. The only thing we can do is try to forgive each other."

"Yes," she answered softly. The pain in Cal's eyes pulled at her heart. "You really did love my father, didn't you? That morning must have been as horrible for you as it was for me."

Cal shifted his gaze to the empty sky. "No day in my life has ever hurt more," he recalled. "Not when Daklugie died on the reservation, not when I left my home among the Chiricahua, not when Josh Cameron was killed in a skirmish with Juh and his platoon came back and booted me out of the cabin we'd been sharing. When you belong to two peoples who are tearing at each other's throats, there are lots of things that hurt. But nothing hurt so much as seeing Frank Butler shot down by an Apache bullet and then seeing you set the whole thing on my shoulders."

Mackenzie didn't know what to say. For years she'd been

licking her wounds thinking that she was the one wronged, not considering the hurt she'd dealt Cal. Indeed they both had much to forgive.

His gaze lifted to meet hers. "Maybe we should think about the future instead of the past. What are your ideas for the future, Mac?"

Mackenzie hesitated a moment. In the last few hours her world had changed so fast it left her dizzy. "My future is the Lazy B and Frankie . . . and you, if you choose to be a part of it. I love you, Cal. I never stopped loving you. Maybe that's why I hated you so much."

He didn't question the illogic of her statement. "Do you trust me?" he asked with soft intensity.

"Yes," she replied without hesitation. "I do trust you. I trust you with the ranch, with Frankie, with me."

"Mac, I can't promise you a happily ever after like those stories that you read to Frankie. It's an imperfect world, with imperfect people."

"It's a hell of world," she agreed vehemently. "But I'd rather live in it with you than without you." She regarded him suspiciously. "You claimed you were never going to let me go. You backing out now, Smith?"

Cal smiled. "No, Mac. I'm not back out of anything. I'm working up the guts to ask you to marry me."

She smiled. "I guess it's about time Frankie had a father."

"Any other reason besides getting Frankie a father?"

"How many times do you have to hear it?" she inquired impishly. "I love you, California Smith."

"And I love you, Mackenzie Butler." He grinned. "If I wasn't so hungry, I'd peel that dress right off your back and show you how much. But I can smell Carmelita's cooking all the way up here. Do you suppose they saved us some supper?"

They walked together to the Appaloosa and Cal hoisted Mackenzie up into the saddle in front of him. Mackenzie no longer found the position awkwardly intimate. The future looked rosier at that moment than it had in years. No more loneliness. No more bitterness. No more uncertainty. She loved California Smith, and this time they would have their forever.

But as they rode back to the ranch and the sun painted the sky a blood red, Mackenzie tried to push away the chilling thought that fortune and luck often had their own ideas about forever.

For the first time in years, the Lazy B Ranch hosted a Saturday-night barbecue to kick off the week of fall round-up. Most of the neighboring ranchers attended—with the notable exception of Nathan Crosby and Raitt Armstrong. A group of Tombstone citizens also came. Amos was there, of course; Ted Greene, his wife Samantha, and daughters Letty and Rosalie; Gus and Millicent Bigley; the Reverend Peabody from St. Paul's Episcopal Church and the Reverend Slater from the Methodist Church; Israel Potts, who had probably never in his life turned down a chance of free food; Nellie Cashman and three of her boarders; Judge Pinney from the county court; several of Lu's friends from the church sewing circle; and of course the Lazy B ranch hands, who made the party a bit more raucous than it might otherwise have been.

A barbecue spit had been set up in the pasture just north of the barn and a hog slaughtered to feed the crowd. Torches set around a large, carefully cleaned section of pasture provided light for dancing—two musician friends of Nellie's had volunteered their services on the fiddle and flute. The inner court and parlor would be used for sleeping when all had grown too tired to dance, eat, or visit, for no one could be expected to travel home until daylight could safely light their way.

As the sun dropped behind the Huachuca Mountains and the celebration began to hum, Carmelita came to the barbecue fire to relieve Mackenzie at basting the hog. "Is good to see so many people here, senorita," the Mexican woman declared. "We have not had fiesta in so long. Even our wild vaqueros are having a good time."

The hands were having a bit too good of a time, Mackenzie thought. They apparently found Carmelita's homemade cerveza to their taste, and they were loud in their appreciation. "I'd rather have them whooping it up here than getting drunk in town," she told Carmelita. "They'll be doing that soon enough when the cattle are all gathered."

"Le Senor California will keep them in line," Carmelita assured her.

The young Mexican woman was still sweet on Cal. Mackenzie hoped she would not be too disappointed tonight when Cal and Mackenzie made the announcement of their upcoming wedding. Lu and Amos were the only people they'd told so far. After the roundup the Lazy B would host another celebration—a double wedding. The thought sent a warm thrill of contentment straight to Mackenzie's heart. It would be lovely to acknowledge before one and all her relationship with Cal. After the wedding she would be able to put her arm around him—even kiss him—without anyone thinking a thing of it. They would have quiet evenings together, passionate nights, bright mornings. Mackenzie didn't care what people might say about Cal's Apache background. She'd lived in the shadow of disapproval all her life; there was no reason to change now.

This last week she had seen little of Cal. When she hadn't wanted him around, circumstances seemed to constantly push them together. Now, when she strained for sight of him everywhere she went, preparation for roundup and driving the market cattle to the railhead at Benson managed to keep them apart. Two nights before, they'd stolen a precious hour to be together in the barn, hidden from prying eyes in the loft. Lightning and Wind had dozed contently below while

Mackenzie and Cal had made love. Even then the workaday world had intruded upon their time together. At a most inconvenient time, Lu had walked into the barn looking for Mackenzie. Their hiding place had proved secure, however, and after her first startled panic Mackenzie had smothered her giggles until Cal loved her so breathless she could no longer laugh. She'd felt once again like the impish young girl who had left Boston searching for a new and exciting life. She'd found love, disaster, and now love once again. From here on out, Mackenzie assured herself, she was going to have the wind at her back and the sun shining down upon her head. With Cal and Frankie at her side, she could weather anything that life threw her way.

"Ah! There you are." Lu's greeting broke the optimistic train of Mackenzie's thoughts. "Frankie's in your room, dear, putting on her new dress. The hem needs straightening, and I told her you'd be in to take care of it." She gave Mackenzie a meaningful look. The time had come, Mackenzie knew, for Frankie to learn that she had a father after all. All week Mackenzie had looked forward to this moment and at the same time dreaded it.

Frankie was in her mother's room because her own didn't have a mirror. Most days Frankie didn't bother to look at herself. She didn't care if her face was smudged or her pinafore sash untied or her stockings wrinkled. But tonight she had a brand-new dress that Lu had made for her. Brand-new dresses were worth a look in a mirror, and parties with music, dancing, barbecued pork, and Carmelita's prickly-pear pie called for a clean face and neatly braided hair, even if such things were a bother.

"My hem is crooked," Frankie told Mackenzie as her mother walked into the room. The little girl pirouetted in front of the mirror and strained to see the new dress all the way around. "Gran said I shouldn't go to the party looking lopsided."

"I think we can straighten you up," Mackenzie said with a smile. "I brought some pins. Stand up straight and let me see what I can do." Mackenzie quickly pinned the crooked hem and helped Frankie pull the dress over her head. The little girl sat on the bed and bounced impatiently while her mother plucked the stitches from the hem and pinned the new one in place, threaded a needle, and began to sew.

"Frankie, you like Mr. Smith very much, don't you?"

"I like him lots," Frankie confirmed. "He's teaching me to ride Goldie without any hands. Will he be at the party?"

"Oh, yes. He'll be at the party." Mackenzie sighed. When she was a girl her aunt had scolded her again and again for her plainspokenness. Ladies learned to speak around awkward subjects, Aunt Prue had lectured her. A lady gets her meaning across without startling or in any way offending her listener. Her aunt had cited examples until Mackenzie was bored to tears. Now she wished she'd paid more attention, for this was certainly an awkward subject, and Mackenzie wanted wholeheartedly to avoid startling her little listener. "Frankie, I'd like to tell you something about California."

"You don't like him. I know. I heard you call him names."

Mackenzie felt herself flush. "I do like him. I like him very much."

"Then why did you call him names?"

Perhaps there was no better way to explain then to admit the truth. "I was angry at California for something that happened before you were born. He worked for my father—Grampa Frank—when I first came to Arizona. When your grandfather was killed, I was very sad and angry, and because I needed someone to blame. I blamed California and told him to leave."

Frankie's eyes were wide. "Did California kill Grampa Frank?"

"No, Frankie, of course he didn't. But because I was very

foolish and hurt I was mad at him anyway, and I was still mad when he came back."

"Are you going to make California leave again?"

"No, dear. California wasn't to blame for what happened to Grampa. I'm not mad at him anymore, and he's not mad at me either. California has decided to stay here, and we're going to get married." As she spoke the words to her daughter they suddenly became more real in her own mind, and she smiled with the wonder of it all.

"You're going to marry California?" Frankie squealed with delight. "That means he'll be here forever!"

"Well, almost forever," Mackenzie agreed with a grin.

Frankie bounced up and down on the mattress and clapped her hands.

"Just sit still a moment more, dear. There's something more I want to tell you." Mackenzie hesitated for a few moments, not knowing quite how to phrase the revelation. Frankie grew impatient and bounced up and down on the bed.

"I bet they've started dancing," Frankie finally hinted.

"There's going to be lots of dancing," Mackenzie reassured her. "And I'll bet California will dance with you."

Frankie's face brightened. "Do you think so? Can I go ask him?"

"In a moment, Sprout. California and I are going to tell everyone at the party tonight that we're getting married. And before that happens, I want to tell you that Cal is . . . is your father."

"Not till you get married," Frankie reminded her.

"Yes he is, Sprout. He's your *real* father. He's been your father all of your life."

Frankie's face went momentarily blank. "You said my pa was dead."

Mackenzie sighed. How did one explain a lie to a child? "That wasn't the truth, Frankie. I was terribly angry at California and thought he would never come back, that you would never see him. I was afraid that if you knew he was alive, you would always hope that he would come see you, and when he didn't, you would be terribly disappointed."

"Gran says it's bad not to tell the truth. *You* told me that too."

"I was very wrong to not tell you the truth. You have a right to be angry."

Frankie considered a moment, her brow puckering. "Are you going to send California away ever again?"

"No. I promise I'll never send him away again."

"And you won't lie to me again," the little girl said sternly. "Ever."

"Never ever."

A gleam appeared in Frankie's eyes. "And when Wind is big enough, can I ride him and make him my very own horse?"

Mackenzie raised a skeptical brow, and Frankie relented with a sheepish grin. "I guess I won't be mad at you. I love you a lot, Ma."

"And I love you."

Frankie bounced off the bed and gave her mother a hug. "I'm really glad California is my pa. Now I have a pa just like Issy, only mine's better."

"Well, I'll have to agree with you on that, Sprout, but don't tell Issy that your pa's better than hers. You wouldn't want to hurt her feelings."

"I won't tell Issy," she said with an impish grin. "Is my dress ready yet? I wanna go dance with my pa."

Mackenzie held it up. "All ready." She slipped the dress over Frankie's head, tied the sash in a neat bow, and straightened the ribbons on the little girl's pigtails while Frankie regarded herself appraisingly in the mirror.

"Does California know he's my pa?" she asked.

"Yes, Sprout. He definitely knows. He's always known."

"Does he love me like you do?"

"He loves you a lot."

Frankie smiled. "Good. Then he'll *have* to dance with me."

The party was a rousing success, a time of blossoming for Mackenzie. If the marriage announcement was met with only polite applause from many of the guests, and astonishment from others, those who really mattered were overjoyed. Amos led off the congratulations with a big hug and kiss, then scoffed at Lu's teasing that he didn't give his own betrothed such smooches. Nellie Cashman hugged both Cal and Mackenzie, whispering to Mackenzie that she sure had taken long enough to come to her senses. Gus Bigley surprised Mackenzie with a bear hug, and his wife Millicent gave her a reserved peck on the cheek and pronounced California Smith a good man "in spite of everything." Israel Potts shook Cal's hand and gave his blessing as if the deputy sheriff's approval were needed for the marriage to take place. Even Bay, Mahko, and Istee gave the couple good wishes. Their brown-skinned wives, hovering in the background, shyly came forward and, each taking Mackenzie's hand in turn said a few quiet words in their native language. Mackenzie smiled and thanked them, even though she didn't have the slightest idea what they said.

Dancing and eating continued while sparks from the huge bonfire swirled up into the sky to compete with the stars. Only a few hours before the sun was due to rise, the last of the guests gave up and found a place to sleep. The ranch hands slept very soundly indeed, having used the boss's marriage announcement as an excuse to consume enough of Carmelita's homemade cerveza to make a steer drop in its tracks. Mackenzie had let them have their good time; at least they had Sunday to recover before tackling roundup early on Monday morning.

Roundup. Mackenzie had always loathed the time of year when the herd was "worked." Every spring and fall the scattered herd was gathered, the mavericks and calves roped, tossed on their sides, branded, and earnotched with the Lazy B's identifying marks. In the fall, the market cattle were separated from the herd and penned, ready to drive to the railhead.

Roundup was the most trying time on the ranch. Cowboys were overworked and short-tempered, and the rank smell of smoke and scorched flesh permeated the air. The sound of calves bawling from the discomfort of their newly notched ears and seared flesh always made Mackenzie smart with sympathy. This year in particular would be hard, for she suspected Nathan Crosby was lying in wait like a coyote until they started bringing in the cattle with the changed brands and claiming them as Lazy B property.

The coming week, Mackenzie suspected, was going to be a hard one. But it would be better than the roundups of all the previous years, for this roundup week, Mackenzie wouldn't be facing the onerous task alone.

14

"There's going to be trouble, Mac. I want you to let me handle it."

Mackenzie folded her arms across her chest and lifted a brow. "Don't start acting the overbearing husband before we're even married, Mr. Smith. You're not boss-man here yet." She was dressed in rugged trousers and a soft cambric shirt. A kerchief wrapped her throat, leather gloves protected her hands, and a battered felt hat hid the fire of her hair—but not the fire in her eyes. "I've been worrying about the Lazy B for too many years to simply stay in the house baking pies while someone else shoulders the burden of the ranch." She gave the cinch of her saddle a determined yank, and Dolly whuffed so hard she scattered the husks of straw on the barn floor. "Really, Cal. You can't honestly expect me to stay home on the first day of roundup."

Cal sighed and unlooped Runner's reins from an iron hitching ring. "I suppose that is too much to expect," he admitted. "You've always been stubborn as a mule on a hot July afternoon."

She gave him an arch look as she led Dolly toward the door. "That's no way to talk to the mother of your child."

"It is if I want her to stay healthy enough to have more children."

Outside the barn, the morning was still murky gray. The Dragoons were a hulking black shadow crowned by pale-pink sky. By the arena, ranch hands moved about in a hushed manner that seemed to suit such a quiet, still morning. The men, like their mounts, stood with heads down, half asleep—Mackenzie suspected that most of them were still hung over from Saturday night's cerveza.

Mackenzie willingly let Cal take charge. She was quite content to let him call the shots. He knew cattle better than she did, and he certainly handled the men better. But she wouldn't stay home.

"Does everyone know where they're going?" Cal asked the men.

Sam Crawford spat into the dust. "Yeah. Bull and me and Gid, we're goin' north along the river. Skillet, Charley, George, and Harve are ridin' along the west hills, and the Injuns are takin' the middle ground."

"And we're bringin' in anything that we can tell is Lazy B, regardless of brand," Bull added.

Cal nodded. "If you see any Armstrong hands, or Crosby's boys, tell 'em they can see me if they have objections."

"No gunplay," Mackenzie interjected.

"Not unless they draw first," George Keller said.

"You heard Miss Butler," Cal warned. "Use your heads instead of your trigger fingers. I'll be riding the valley to make sure there's no trouble."

"Whatever you say, boss." Sam grimaced with an expression that was even more sour than usual. "But there's gonna be trouble. I can smell it."

Sam had voiced what they all expected—and what many of the hands hoped for. They were more at home punching cowpokes than cows, and their chief talent lay in throwing lead, not roping and branding beeves. As they rode beneath the Lazy B arch and headed for their assigned areas, Mackenzie wondered uneasily if she should have ignored Israel Potts's advice and pressed for the law—such as it was in the Tombstone area—to investigate the changed brands. Every week, more and more RA brands had shown up on the open range—all of them looking suspiciously like Lazy B's with legs attached to the lower part of the brand. Mackenzie had to gather them in. If all of the changed brands were eliminated from the Lazy B herd, the financial loss would make the coming year very hard indeed.

If trouble came, Mackenzie reflected stoically, then trouble came. She and Cal would handle it together. In past years few RA cattle had crossed the river to the eastern part of the valley, and RA cowboys likewise stayed west of the river. But lately her men had reported seeing a few RA hands mingling with Crosby men on the east ranges. Mackenzie didn't know exactly what was going on, but she suspected it didn't bode well for the Lazy B.

The week started smoothly. The weather was hot and dry, and the parched, brittle foliage made the cattle easy to spot. By Wednesday morning, almost half the herd was safely enclosed within Lazy B fences, and Mackenzie began to hope that they might get through roundup without incident. Though the crew had reported frequent sightings of Crosby men, no one had made trouble. Mackenzie prayed that the Bar Cross men would continue to go their way and let the Lazy B hands go theirs.

By Wednesday Cal also had relaxed his guard, for he gave

Mackenzie little argument when she suggested that they could check on the work much more efficiently if they rode their rounds separately instead of together. He appointed Istee to ride with her—a condition that Mackenzie willingly accepted.

She spent the morning with George Keller's group, scouring the arroyo-cut foothills of the Dragoons just south of the springs for cattle that might have strayed there from the valley floor. The hands were unhappy that, so far, all they'd had to do was chase strays out of mesquite thickets. They'd been looking forward to a little gunplay, or at least hurling insults back and forth with the Crosby crew—much more fun than eating dust all day and looking at a bunch of cows' behinds.

Mackenzie sensed the restlessness and decided she'd let some of the crew start branding tomorrow while the rest of the crew brought in the remaining beeves. By Sunday they would be ready to start driving the market cattle to the railhead in Benson, twenty miles to the north.

By early afternoon a line of thunderheads had built over the mountains and started to march across the valley. As big raindrops began to splatter into the dust, Mackenzie donned her slicker and listened to the men grumbling as they did the same. These spotty afternoon showers were an irritation—just enough to get a person wet and uncomfortable but not enough to do the parched vegetation any good.

"Let's head west," Mackenzie told Istee. The Indian sat impassively in the rain, ignoring the drops pounding down upon him. "I want to talk to Cal about starting the branding tomorrow." Mahko, Bay, and Gid Small worked the range between the hills and the floodplain. Mackenzie guessed that Cal might be with them. Istee nodded and without a word turned his horse toward the west.

They rode in silence, Mackenzie hunkered down under her slicker and Istee riding stoically beside her. Suddenly the Apache halted and wordlessly pointed. Mackenzie looked in the direction he indicated and spotted a group of five cows and three calves sheltering beneath a mesquite in a shallow arroyo.

"Let's go see." She kneed Dolly into a trot toward the little herd.

The cows all wore the RA brand, and by now, even Mackenzie could recognize the signs of alternation. The calves were unbranded.

"We might as well take these with us," she told Istee.

The Apache circled around the little group while Mackenzie untied the coiled rope from her saddle and began to wave it in the air. The cows looked at her with bored eyes, but they began to move nevertheless. Istee, Mackenzie noted with irritation, wasn't much help. He stared up the bank of the wash. She was about to rebuke him for inattention when a familiar rider appeared.

"Well, if it ain't my bossy stepsister playin' cowboy again." Tony Herrera reined his horse to a halt at the lip of the arroyo. "Only, I see now it's cowboys and Indians." He glanced contemptuously at Istee.

"Hello, Tony," Mackenzie greeted him calmly. "What brings you this far south? Most of Nathan's beeves are up north."

"Never can tell where a cow might take it into its fool head to wander." Behind Tony appeared four other horsemen, all men that Mackenzie recognized as Crosby hands. Together they slid down the muddy bank. The little bunch of cows and calves scattered as the newcomers cut through them. Tony looked at the animals and raised his brows in exaggerated surprise.

"Why, Mackenzie!" he exclaimed. "Don't tell me you're takin' these beeves in!"

"I am," she said in a level voice.

"These ain't Lazy B cattle. I knew you was havin' a hard

time runnin' the ranch, but I swear I never thought you'd stoop to rustlin' another man's beeves."

"You know very well these cows are mine."

Tony grinned maliciously. "Looks like the RA brand to me. Like I said, never can tell where a stupid cow'll take it in its head to wander."

"Raitt Armstrong can come get his cattle if he likes," she offered. "And at the same time he can explain why the RA brand on these animals looks more like a Lazy B with a few added legs than a genuine RA. In any case, I don't see that it's your business, Tony—unless you or your boss know more than you should about why these brands were altered."

Tony took off his hat and wiped his arm ostentatiously across his brow. "Whoooooee!" He grinned at the other Crosby men. "Guess I rightly been told off. You're gettin' mighty sassy since you decided to marry that yeller-haired Injun. He's teachin' you how to thieve cows, I guess. That's the only way an Injun knows how to raise beef."

Mackenzie glanced uneasily at Istee, who sat with his rifle across his lap, his face deadly calm.

"Yeah," Tony sneered. "We heard about you marryin' that sonofabitch Smith. Guess you'll do just about anything to keep a hired hand, huh, Mackenzie?"

"Get out of here, Tony," Mackenzie ordered in a tight voice. "I've got work to do. You can carry my message to Raitt Armstrong—and to your boss."

"Well, you can be sure they'll have some words to say about it." He grinned lasciviously. "Tell me, Mac. Is it true that Apaches put it to their squaws like a stud humping a mare? I figger you oughta know."

"Maybe she'd show us how it's done," one of the Crosby men suggested with a laugh.

"Hell no, she won't!" Tony replied. "My stepsis here saves it for Injuns."

"I could be an Injun if that's what it takes," another man volunteered with a grin.

"I doubt you have what it takes to be an Indian," a new voice called from behind the Crosby group. Mackenzie's rising panic subsided as Cal's Appaloosa slid down the side of the wash. The rain had stopped, but Cal still wore the Mexican poncho that was his only concession to bad weather. The rain had soaked through his headband and dampened his hair to a dark burnished gold. At that moment he was the most beautiful sight Mackenzie had ever seen.

Cal rode through the band of Crosby men, ignoring hands that moved to the butts of holstered pistols. "You hombres are making enough noise to scare every cow between here and the river." Cal wheeled the Appaloosa so that he faced Tony. "Kind of far off your herd, aren't you, Herrera? There aren't any Bar Cross beeves this far south."

Tony scowled. "There aren't any Lazy B cows either, Smith. These are RA. You're rustlin'. You Apaches may be used to stealing cattle for a living, but the ranchers around here won't put up with your thievin' their animals."

"I'd invited you to take your complaint to the law," Cal said with a cold smile. "But I figure you don't want the law looking too close at what you've been doing the past month or so."

"We don't need the law to see justice done. And even if we did, ol' Potts does what Crosby tells him to."

"Quit the act, Tony," Cal snapped. "We all know whose cows these are. If Crosby and Armstrong want to fight the Lazy B over Dragoon Springs, we'll fight, but let's not muddy the waters with this kind of stupid playacting. Crosby may find that he's bit off more than he can chew."

"Gettin' kinda big for your britches, aint'cha, Smith—talking like that when there's five of us and two of you."

"Three," Mackenzie corrected, including herself. Tony snorted scornfully.

"Just one more thing before you leave, Herrera," Cal continued as if he hadn't heard the threat. "The next man who threatens Mackenzie Butler in any way is going to find out what it feels like to be a gelding. I'll see to it personally."

Istee nodded approval. The four Crosby men squirmed slightly in their saddles and looked anywhere but into Cal's steel-blue eyes. The calm assurance with which he spoke the threat served to remind them of the cold practicality with which Apaches regarded mutilation and torture.

Only Tony seemed unimpressed. "You talk awful big, Smith. Think you can back it up?"

Cal's face remained stony and impassive.

"Seems to me what you do best, Apache man, is cause trouble. You're a goddamned pain in the ass, you know that? Occurs to me that Mr. Crosby might just give me a raise if I were to blow you away."

Mackenzie tensed, but Cal didn't flick an eyelash.

"I could do it," Tony declared arrogantly. "For all that everyone around here seems scared spitless of you, I'd wager you're faster with a bow and arrow than a gun." He flipped back his rain slicker to free his right arm. "And I ain't scared of you. Not one lousy bit."

Mackenzie looked in panic to Cal, then Istee. Neither one seemed concerned. She thought desperately of drawing her own rifle out of its saddle scabbard, but knew by the time she had it drawn and cocked, Cal might be dead. "Tony, for God's sake . . . !"

"Shut up, Mackenzie," Tony ordered. "This ain't a woman's conversation. Well, Apache man? You too chicken to draw?"

Cal smiled. "I think you rely too much on your fast gun, Herrera, and not enough on your head." He pushed aside the front of his poncho, and Tony found himself staring down the muzzle of a twelve-gauge shotgun.

"I'll be damned!" one of the Crosby men exclaimed with

an appreciative chuckle. "He got the drop on 'im." All four of them hastened out of the line of Cal's fire.

"Sometimes the victory goes not to the fastest, but the smartest," Cal philosophized with a grin.

Tony turned pale beneath his brown skin. "You yella sonofabitch. One of these days I'm going to make you sorry you messed with Tony Herrera."

"Keep acting like a fool and you might not live that long."

Tony spat into the mud, wheeled his horse, and curtly ordered the grinning Bar Cross hands to follow him as his horse lunged up the side of the wash. Mackenzie heard the Crosby men laugh at Tony's expense as they made their exit. She scarcely dared to breathe until the sound of their hoofbeats faded into the distance.

Cal lowered the shotgun. "I don't suppose I could convince you to spend the rest of the roundup in the ranch house."

Mackenzie took a deep breath. "Yes, I think maybe you could." As a prize target for Crosby's mischief, she was more of a liability than a help; the time had come for her to be smart instead of stubborn.

"The job's almost over, Mac. By tomorrow we'll have most of the herd in the north pasture and the branding can begin in earnest. You won't be missing much."

Mackenzie nodded. By Sunday the market cattle would be cut out and ready to drive to the railhead, and the following Friday she would gain a husband, for better or worse, for all the days that remained to them on this earth. Perhaps, she conceded, the time had come for her to behave more like a wife than a boss. "I'll go back to the ranch as soon as we get these cows back to the north pasture. You going to ride with us?" she asked, turning Dolly toward the north.

"Figure I will."

Cal fell in beside her as Istee flanked the little herd and got them moving. Mackenzie smiled. "For a moment there I thought I was going to lose you," she admitted. "I'm glad you're smart instead of fast."

"I was fast enough to catch you," he said with a grin.

"You didn't need to be fast to do that," she teased. "I didn't run very hard."

"You could have run like a jackrabbit and I still would have caught you."

Mackenzie grinned.

The next two days went smoothly. Sam Crawford and Gideon Small drove in the last of the cattle while the rest of the crew branded and earnotched calves, inspected the cattle for injuries and disease, and penned the market beeves together. By Friday night only a few mavericks were left to be branded and most of the market cattle had been cut out of the herd and penned. Just a few hours of work remained for the next day, so Mackenzie gave her hands the night off as reward for a job well done. The men drew straws to see who got stuck riding guard on the herd; Bull Ferguson and Skillet Jones stayed; the rest washed up, slicked down their hair, and headed for town.

Cal went with the hands, even though the last thing he wanted was to spend his evening in a loud, smoky saloon that smelled of rotgut and sweat. But he feared that Crosby might stage a confrontation in town instead of on the range. If the Bar Cross men came looking for a fight, he knew the Lazy B hands would be only too happy to oblige—and if the lot of them got thrown into jail, the Lazy B wouldn't be able to get the market cattle to the rail in time to meet their contracts. Keeping the crew on the ranch would have been the safest thing to do, but as Mackenzie had pointed out, they'd earned their night out, and if they didn't get it, Cal would be fighting the men as well as the cattle all the way into the railhead at Benson.

The town was quiet, however. At least, it was quiet by

Tombstone's standards. Though Tombstone was no longer the hotbed of bloody violence it had been in the early eighties, it was still a powder keg of miners, gamblers, whores, and cowboys—many of whom were rustlers or gunmen on the side. Hostilities between the Bar Cross and the Lazy B might just be sufficient to light the powder keg's fuse.

Cal spent the evening going from saloon to saloon, keeping his eyes on the Lazy B crew, who were restless and eager for action. Here and there he saw men from the Bar Cross, but they minded their own business. Knowing Cal had his eye on them, the pistol-happy Lazy B men minded their own business as well. But the tension in the air was as palpable as the August heat.

So Cal prowled the bars on Allen Street, sitting alone at his table, taking not more than a sip or two from the drinks he ordered. Occasionally he received a friendly greeting. At the Crystal Palace, Gus Bigley gave him a hello. In front of the Bird Cage Theater, Ted Greene greeted him and told him that he had a new-model Winchester rifle Cal should look at. A man as good with a rifle as Cal should have an interest in such a fine gun.

Trouble didn't raise its head until Cal arrived at the Bloody Bucket Saloon, a watering hole known as rowdy in a town where rowdy was the norm. Tony Herrera leaned on the bar drinking with Jeff Morgan and three other Bar Cross men. All of them had guns strapped to their legs and all were only a few drinks shy of being passed-out drunk.

"Well, looky who's here," Tony greeted Cal. "Didn't know they let Injuns in this here fine em . . . emporium."

Cal looked around the dingy saloon and was relieved that none of the Lazy B crew were here.

"Don't have a poncho to hide your damned shotgun now, do ya?" Tony challenged. "Why don't we just go outside in the street so I can show you what fast does to so-called smart. How smart are you gonna be with your brains splattered all over town, huh?"

"You're too soused to hit the side of a barn, Herrera."

A Bar Cross man—one of those that had been with Tony on the south range—snickered. "Learn your lesson, Tony. The man whipped your ass once this week. I hear he whipped it a coupla other times, too."

Tony's face darkened to an angry red. "We'll see what happens when he has to fight a man's way, goddammit! You comin' out on the street, or are you a coward, Smith?"

"Shut up, Herrera," Jeff Morgan interjected. "Don't be a fool."

Herrera slammed his whiskey glass down on the bar. "Whaddya mean, shut up?"

"You're drunk. You're gonna get yourself killed. Just cool down. You'll get your turn."

Cal left and let the two of them to argue the matter out. Tony was too drunk to be a menace, and Cal had other men to keep an eye on.

The rest of the night was relatively quiet. Cal did his rounds of Allen Street one more time. The job took a while, because the watering holes were many: the Eagle Brewery, French Rotisserie, Alhambra, Maison Dore, City of Paris, Grotto, Tivoli, Oriental, Brown's Saloon, Fashion Saloon, Miner's Home, Kelley's Wine House, and Judge Mose's Saloon—all within spitting distance of each other on the main street. Drinking, it seemed, was one of the Tombstone's favorite pastimes.

The trouble Cal anticipated never came to a head; the only hostility he encountered were the belligerent looks he got from those who didn't want a man who had once been Apache crossing their path. Cal was an easy man to recognize, and his manner of dress announced his Apache past with a pride that bordered on arrogance. Men bristled when he walked into the saloons and gambling houses. Women reacted also. The whores whispered to each other behind their hands, though many of the glances he got from that quarter were more inviting than hostile.

The hatred between Apache and white men seemed destined to live forever, and as long as one person in Arizona recognized Cal as the kid who had ridden out of Cochise's stronghold, California Smith would be hated. For himself he didn't mind. He was proud to be associated with a valiant people. But Cal wondered if he was being fair in marrying Mackenzie.

When Frank Butler had tried to send him away from the Lazy B, Cal had told himself that Mackenzie's father was right. But the old man hadn't been right; he had underestimated his daughter. Cal had underestimated her also. Mackenzie was as strong as a rock and just as unyielding when she wanted to be. She'd taken on a man's burdens when her father was killed—a woman's burden, also, spitting in the face of public censure to bear and raise Frankie without shame or excuses. Mackenzie would not be daunted by the glares of small-minded, fearful people who hated him because he had dared to survive and thrive among the Apaches, who hated him even more for refusing to be ashamed of his past.

Cal would not spare Mackenzie Butler the burden of loving him. She was the only boon he would ask of this damned world: a woman he loved to love him in return. Their love had lasted through six years of anger, hurt, and misunderstanding. Nothing would put out the fire now.

"Damm it to hell! Can't you even sit on your goddamned horse?" Jeff Morgan tried to prop Tony Herrera upright in his saddle, but his efforts were in vain, for the moment Jeff let go, Tony slumped forward over the saddle horn.

"I c'n ride," Tony slurred. "I c'n ride, dammit. Leggo. Lezz go."

"You fall off, I'm not pickin' you up," Jeff warned as he swung aboard his own horse.

"Lezz go, you ash . . . asshole."

They were fools to have come to town tonight, Jeff thought as they picked their way through the dark. The road out of town was muddy from the afternoon's thundershowers. Tony was dead drunk—and he wasn't much better. He doubted they would reach the Bar Cross until just before dawn.

Almost the entire Bar Cross crew had come to town tonight. Crosby had encouraged it. Go into Tombstone and blow off some steam, he'd invited—any man who was really a man had to let loose every once in a while. The old man hadn't been specific but there wasn't a man among them who didn't know what he meant—and they would've been happy to oblige with a good thrashing of the Lazy B boys if Morgan hadn't hinted that Crosby wouldn't go out of his way to help if they landed in jail. Although Crosby had Potts in his pocket, the town marshal was a crusty old coot who wasn't nearly as easygoing as Potts.

Jeff Morgan had worked for the Bar Cross only a few weeks, but already he didn't like the way Crosby handled himself. First there was the way he'd grabbed little Frankie and tried to use her to get to Mackenzie. Morgan didn't think for a minute that Crosby really would have hurt the kid, but the whole idea had stunk. The scheme to alter brands hadn't set too well with his conscience, either. Jeff knew how hard Mackenzie had worked to build her little herd of Herefords. He was convinced that she would be better off selling the ranch, but he hated to see her forced out of business by a thieving trick like brand-changing. Still, in the long run, almost anything that would make Mackenzie give up her foolish stubbornness and save her from that scheming, no-good California Smith would be justified.

"Are you coming?" Jeff snapped over his shoulder. Tony's

horse was traveling at more of a plod than a walk. "At this rate the sun'll be up before we get back."

"Just ho . . . hold yer goddamned horses! I think I'm gonna . . . gonna . . . "

The horse's slow shuffle stopped. Jeff heard the sound of heaving, and his own stomach roiled. He was tempted to leave Tony to make his own way—just because Herrera got stinking drunk didn't mean Jeff had to lose that few hours of sleep he might get before morning.

"You all right?" he asked as Tony's horse ambled up beside his.

"Sure."

"Feel better?"

"Oh yeah. Just great. Pukin' is one a my favorite ways ta have fun."

"Well, come on, then. Speed it up, will ya?"

"Awright, awright! That damned Smith ain't so tough," he grumbled. "One of these days I'm gonna nail him. Without him struttin' around the Lazy B, maybe you can go over there and screw my stepsis, huh? I figger you always wanted to."

"Shut up about Mackenzie."

"Don't see why. The bitch ain't exactly a pure and holy virgin, is she? Spreadin' her legs for that Apache man and birthin' his brat, not even pretendin' she has a proper husband."

"I said shut your filthy mouth!"

"Man, are you suckered!" Tony laughed, almost falling from the saddle in his mirth.

"Shit! Find your own way home, you sonofabitch jackass!" Morgan dug spurs into his horse. Startled, the horse kicked out and connected with the shoulder of Tony's mount. Tony's horse shied. The soft dirt at the edge of the road crumbled under the sudden weight. Panicky, Tony's mount struggled to regain its balance—too late. It toppled and rolled down into the wash beside the road, landing miraculously on its feet, saddle hanging askew.

Tony was not as fortunate. Five feet away from where the horse stood, Tony lay very still on the sandy bottom of the wash.

"Goddamn!" Morgan jumped from his saddle and scrambled down the side of the ravine. Kneeling beside the prone man, he felt for a pulse. "Shit. Oh, shit!"

Tony would never get to give California Smith his comeuppance.

By the time the sun climbed over the Dragoons the next morning, the air above the north pasture already smelled of scorched flesh and reverberated with the bawls of cattle. Two branding fires sent columns of black smoke toward the sky, tarnishing the morning freshness.

Even at the ranch house, a fifteen-minute ride from the pasture, Mackenzie could smell the stench and hear the beeves bellowing. For the last two days she had kept her promise to Cal and stayed at the house. To tell the truth, she didn't miss the branding. Roundup was not one of the things she liked about the ranching business, and she was grateful that today was the last day the branding fires would burn.

The horse part of the Lazy B was more to Mackenzie's taste, and this early morning she enjoyed herself by watching Lightning and Wind take their exercise in the arena. She remembered when the mare had first been turned into this paddock. Angry, frightened, desperate for freedom, she'd been a sight at once magnificent and sad. Now she seemed content with her foal at her side, his coppery red coat—just like his father's—gleaming in the morning sun. Lightning was no longer wild and splendid, but she was, Mackenzie decided, just as beautiful.

Lu came out of the house and walked toward the arena, an issue of *Godey's Lady's Book* in her hand. "Mackenzie, dear,

I've just come across the most splendid frock for Frankie to wear at the wedding, and I'm sure I can have it ready in time."

"With everything else you're doing to prepare for the wedding?"

"Weddings," Lu corrected.

"Weddings," Mackenzie agreed with a smile. "You're trying to do too much, Lu. Let me see the dress." She took the magazine from Lu's hand and studied the drawing. "Do you suppose I could make it up?"

Lu chuckled. "Mackenzie, dear—we don't want Frankie looking like a ragamuffin on the big day."

"I don't sew *that* badly."

"Yes you do. I have time to . . . " Lu turned to look toward the road beyond the arched Lazy B entrance. "Who's that coming? It looks like . . . My goodness! What's bringing *them* here together?"

"Whatever it is, it can't be good."

Riding through the Lazy B arch, Nathan Crosby surveyed the ranch compound as if he owned it. Behind him were four of his hands and three other men that Mackenzie didn't recognize. Beside Crosby rode Israel Potts. The deputy sheriff's face was set in a most officious expression.

"Morning, Israel," Mackenzie greeted him as the group rode up. "What brings you out here so early this morning?"

"Morning, Mackenzie. You seen California Smith?

Mackenzie's heart started to race. She didn't know what was going on, but she knew trouble was coming. "He's out at the north pasture taking care of the last of the branding."

"Good," Israel grunted. Nathan Crosby's eyes gleamed with satisfaction.

"Mind telling me what this is about?" Mackenzie asked.

Israel shot an uneasy glance toward Lu. "I suppose not," he said. "But I'm sorry to break it to Miz Andalusia like this."

"What is it?" Mackenzie demanded.

"We've come to arrest California Smith for Tony Herrera's murder."

15

Mackenzie was struck silent. Around her, the whole ranch seemed to grow still until the only thing moving in the whole world was her own racing heart. Even Lu, who had uttered a single gasp at the news of her son's death, seemed frozen into icy•immobility.

Tony murdered, and Cal the killer. The two men had argued often enough—even fought. Sometimes men died in the heat of a fight when tempers flared and weapons were at hand. Sometimes men had to defend themselves by deadly means. Tony might have provoked a fight; Cal might have had no choice. If something like that had happened, though, surely Cal would have told her. She had seen him in the barn early this morning before he and the hands had left to take care of the final chores in the north pasture. He would have told her then.

This was a bad dream. It had to be. Either that, or the whole world had gone mad.

"Well, Mackenzie?" From the look on Israel's face, Mackenzie guessed she had missed a question.

"Well what?"

Israel sighed impatiently. "Do you want to ride out with us to where Smith's working?"

Mackenzie cast a worried look at Lu, whose face was stone calm.

"Don't worry about me," Lu told Mackenzie in a quiet voice. "I guess I always knew someday that boy would get himself killed. And I don't believe for one minute that California Smith murdered him."

Mackenzie hesitated.

"Go straighten out this misunderstanding," Lu urged. "I can certainly take care of myself until you get back." She swept Potts, Crosby, and the entire posse with a cold glance.

"Make up your mind, girl," Potts said. "We can't lollygag around here all day."

"Israel," Mackenzie pleaded. "This is nonsense. Cal and Tony weren't on good terms, but Cal didn't have any reason to kill Tony unless he was forced to it in self-defense. Since when is that murder?"

"It was murder, all right," Crosby commented in his gravelly voice. "And Smith did it."

"Are you comin', Mackenzie?' Israel fidgeted on his horse, making the beast sidestep impatiently. "If not, we'll just go on up there and get 'im. If you want his side of the story, you can come to town and talk to him in jail."

"I'm coming," Mackenzie assured him coldly. "Just wait here until I change into some trousers."

Cal was dousing the branding fires when Mackenzie rode up with her official escort. The north pasture smelled of scorched hide and cattle dung. A temporary pen enclosed the beeves destined for market, and the other cattle were being scattered by the hands, back to the open range or to other grazing areas on the Butler property. Roundup was over for another year. What a way for it to end, Mackenzie thought with dismay.

Cal looked up from scuffing dirt over a damp fireplace. He glanced at Mackenzie's stricken face, then surveyed the others with her. "Potts, Crosby," he greeted them cautiously. "What's this?"

"You oughta know," Crosby grated. "I'm surprised you're still here, Smith. Either you have an ace up your sleeve or you're a lot dumber than I thought you were."

"Cal," Mackenzie began to explain, "Tony Herrera is . . . is dead, and somehow Israel's come up with the idea that—"

Israel interrupted sternly. "I'll do the talkin' here, if you don't mind, Mackenzie. Mr. Smith, where were you last night?"

"In town," Cal replied warily.

"Did you see Tony Herrera there? In fact, did you have words with Tony in the Bloody Bucket at about nine o'clock?"

"More like he had words with me."

"Where did you go after leaving the Bloody Bucket?"

"Around to some saloons. Then I rode home."

"Anyone ride with you who could say for sure you came right back to the Lazy B?"

"I rode alone."

Crosby looked smug as a cat who's cornered a mouse. "Let's get on with this, Israel. We've heard enough."

Cal's eyes narrowed. "What make you think I killed him, Potts?"

"A little after midnight, just a few hours after you two had angry words, Tony Herrera was shot riding from town to the Bar Cross."

"Shot right plumb between the eyes with a rifle," Crosby provided smugly. "You ain't been shy about showin' off how good you are with a rifle, Smith, and I don't know of anybody else who's good enough to make that kinda shot, 'specially at night with only the moon lightin' the target."

Mackenzie's heart sank. Shot between the eyes with a rifle. Not very many men could boast that kind of skill—but Cal could.

"You two duked it out often enough in front of witnesses," Israel added. "There's no shortage of men who can testify that you hated each other's guts, and everyone knows Apaches favor ambushes to take out their enemies. But the clincher is that we found something just down the gully from Tony's body that belongs to you, boy. Recognized it the minute Crosby found it. That damned medicine bag you wear around your neck. Notice you don't have it on this morning."

Mackenzie glanced at Cal's throat, where the little leather bag of Apache amulets had once rested. The medicine bag was indeed gone. Had he worn it when he left for town? Had he been wearing the bag at all these past few weeks? She couldn't remember—but she was being ridiculous! Cal would never strike at a man in such a cowardly way.

"Cal didn't do it," she declared. "He went to town to prevent trouble, not cause it! If he had wanted to kill Tony, he wouldn't have done it in a manner that pointed so clearly to him."

Israel spared her a sympathetic look. "Never can tell what a man will do once he's hot for another man's blood. You bein' a woman, you wouldn't understand."

"What I understand is that you're letting Nathan Crosby railroad you into arresting Cal on evidence that's nothing more than a coincidence! You can't—!"

"The deputy sheriff didn't ask for your opinion, Mackenzie." Crosby's harsh declaration cut across her defense. "Now, Smith, you gonna ride along with us peaceably, or are we gonna have to tie you across a saddle like a side of beef?"

"I'll ride," Cal said, his face like stone. He didn't look at Mackenzie.

"You make a break, we'll gun you down, boy," Israel warned as Cal mounted his Appaloosa. "There ain't no place out on this valley floor that you can hide."

Mackenzie's stomach knotted in frustration. Israel obviously was more than ready to believe that Cal was a killer. Probably half the population of Cochise County would feel the same way unless Cal could produce an alibi. As they started back toward the ranch compound, she pulled her horse beside his. "You must have been home before midnight," she told him hopefully. "Maybe someone saw you come in—perhaps one of the White Mountain men."

Cal shook his head. "Do you think anyone would take an Indian's word on it? Besides, I was still on the road at midnight."

"Then you must have heard the shot that killed Tony?"

"I didn't hear any shot," Cal denied. His voice was neutral, devoid of expression.

"Mackenzie, I'm gonna have to ask you to stay away from the prisoner for now." Israel wedged his horse between Mackenzie's and Cal's. "You notice he ain't denyin' anything. You're the only one denyin' it."

"Would you believe Cal if he did deny it?" Mackenzie demanded bitterly. "You're condemning him without a trial."

"He'll get his trial," Israel assured her. "Never you fear."

Crosby and Potts kept Cal between them for the rest of the ride back to the ranch house.

"I figure we'll just round up those Apache friends of yours as well," Israel told Cal as they approached the Lazy B archway. "They're a menace to the valley runnin' free out here. Wouldn't be surprised if they had somethin' to do with some of the rustlin' and brand-changin' goin' on in these parts. Ya cain't trust an Injun off the reservation."

"Hell," Crosby added. "You cain't trust an Injun *on* the reservation."

Mackenzie felt a painful knot of anger twist in her stomach. "Mahko, Istee, and Bay were here last night. I can testify to that. And you certainly can't have evidence that they've done anything against the law, because they haven't. They hardly ever leave the ranch."

"Just the same," the deputy said. "I wouldn't feel right leavin' them here when they could do you and Miz Andalusia harm. They're Apaches, after all. Never did understand why you didn't send 'em packin' back to the reservation when they first showed their faces on the Lazy B. It's a wonder your throat hasn't been cut while you were sleepin' and your whole place burned to the ground."

Explaining that the Apaches were the sanest and safest of her employees would be useless, Mackenzie realized. Cal was guilty because he'd once been Apache, and the White Mountain men were dangerous because they were Apache. Logic had no voice where such blind hatred existed. She wished desperately that she would wake up and discover this was nothing more than a nightmare.

"Where are those Injuns, Mackenzie?"

Lying would be useless. Mahko, Bay, and Istee were in the large pasture just west of the barn, working with the spring foals.

"No need to answer," Israel told her as they rode up to the barn. "I can see for myself."

As they reined to a halt, Crosby turned to Cal. "Get off," he ordered. Cal obeyed without a word.

"This might be a deal more peaceful if you just walked over there and told those Injuns that you had some work for 'em in the barn," Potts told Mackenzie. "That way we'd just round 'em up without a bother."

"They aren't that stupid," Mackenzie replied, a stubborn light in her eyes. Already the three Apaches were suspicious of trouble, Mackenzie was glad to see. They had watched Israel and his men like deer scenting the approach of a predator.

Suddenly Cal barked out a loud command in Apache. Instantly the three men fled. At the same time Cal darted into the barn.

"Get him!" Crosby ordered frantically.

Confused, the posse didn't know whom to chase, the Apaches or Cal.

"Get Smith, you idiots! Leave the damned Indians. Get Smith!"

Crosby kicked his horse violently in the flanks. It lunged forward toward the open barn door. Potts and two of the Bar Cross men tried to ride through the barn door at the same time and created a bottleneck that blocked their passage.

"Get out of my way!" Crosby cursed vividly in language that would have put even Mackenzie's hard-cursing men to shame.

By the time the posse sorted themselves out and managed to get into the barn, Cal was gone. They cantered back out the door, pistols in hands, looking frantically for their prey, but he had disappeared as only an Apache can. On the valley floor he'd had no place to hide, but here the jumbled Dragoons with their tortuous maze of canyons loomed invitingly close.

"He's headed for the mountains. You can depend on it," Crosby growled. "Get after him! The sonofabitch can't get gone far. He's on foot."

"Israel! Do something!" Mackenzie cried as Crosby and his men started their search. "They'll kill him without even a trial. They're not a posse! They're Crosby's men, with Crosby in charge. You're the law here! Control them, for God's sake!"

"Mackenzie . . ." Israel's voice trailed off uncertainly.

"There he is!" One of the posse pointed toward the mouth

of the mine drift that Frank Butler had driven through the foothills to the east—the tunnel that was Frankie's favorite place to play on hot summer days. "He's going into that old mine!"

"We've got him now!" Crosby exulted. "Go get him."

The posse hesitated. Even Crosby's own men held back.

"What the hell are you doing?" Crosby demanded. "Go after him!"

"On foot?" one man asked. "He probably knows that old mine like the back of his hand. He could turn around and ambush us in the dark and we wouldn't have any room to fight."

"Are you afraid of *one* man, you yellow bastards? Get after him, dammit!"

Crosby had done his work of painting Cal as a vicious savage all too well. The men squirmed and looked down into the dust, refusing to meet his eyes and at the same time refusing to follow his orders.

"You yellow-bellied bastards! You—!"

"Now, calm down, Nathan," Israel interrupted the stream of expletives. "They're right, man. Followin' Smith into that tunnel would be about as stupid as followin' a badger into a hole. Now, seems to me Smith's gotta come outta that tunnel on one end or t'other. I figure it must come out somewhere in those foothills, maybe not too far off."

Crosby glared at him. "How do you figure that?"

"Smith's no dummy. He wouldn't hide himself in a hole with only one way out."

Nathan considered. His gaze swung to Mackenzie. "Where's that mine drift come out, Mackenzie?"

"I'm sure I don't know."

"I'm sure you do know." Crosby's eyes narrowed dangerously. Mackenzie met his threatening glare with a glare of her own.

"Now, Nathan," Israel chided. "Don't get puffed up like a horned toad. Let me have a quiet word or two with Mackenzie about what's happenin' here." Israel dismounted and invited Mackenzie to do the same. "Come on, Mackenzie. Let's you and me just have a few words in the barn where it's cooler."

Mackenzie followed the deputy sheriff into the dim barn. Her eyes fell upon the ladder to the loft, where not too many days ago she and Cal had lain together in the hay, taking their pleasure together like naughty children while Lu searched down below. Her heart felt as though it was tearing.

"Mackenzie, I know you truly think this young man of yours is innocent, and it could be that he is. No one's ever been able to say that Deputy Sheriff Israel Potts hanged a man before all the evidence was in."

Mackenzie knew differently, but she held her silence.

"If Smith's innocent, the best thing you can do for him is to tell us where he's gonna come outta that hill and let us stick him behind bars where he's safe. Otherwise, gal, this valley's gonna be crawlin' with men who'd like nothin' better than to gun him down. And the law would be on their side, don'tcha see? He'll be brought down just like some wild animal."

"Nathan Crosby's likely to do that the minute he catches sight of him. Israel, don't you see what's going on here? Crosby thinks that if he can get Cal out of the way he can drive me off the Lazy B. Cal would never shoot a man in cold blood. Crosby's just grabbing any opportunity to find a chink in my defense."

"If the man's innocent, the judge'll set him free," Israel told her. "You let a manhunt get started in these hills, and the bullets will be flyin' before anyone ever thinks to ask Smith who he's killed and who he hasn't. The best thing you can do for that man is to help me bring him in."

"Crosby—"

"I'll control Nathan. That's a promise."

Mackenzie don't have much faith in Israel's promises, but

what he said had merit. Cal would be safer behind bars than hiding in the hills, and she could hire a lawyer to make sure Judge Pinney saw how ridiculous this murder charge was.

"Even if he did kill Herrera," Israel went on, "there's probably something that could be said in Smith's defense. Tony's been askin' to get hisself shot for a long time."

"That may be true," Mackenzie said, "but Cal didn't shoot him."

Israel waited.

"The tunnel comes out over by the dry springs in that big wash just below the Satler Mine."

"That's a good girl."

"If Crosby harms a hair on Cal's head, Israel Potts, I'll raise holy hell. I'll have the sheriff, the territorial governor, and the devil himself down on your back."

"I believe you would. I do believe you would."

Cal squinted into the bright morning sunlight as he emerged from the mine drift. The ravine that stretched away from the tunnel mouth seemed empty. Perched up on the hill, the played-out Satler mine was silent, its entrance haphazardly blocked by a barrier of rotted timbers. The only sound was the raucous cawing of turkey buzzards that circled on currents of air above the mine—probably some injured rabbit or deer was about to become buzzard breakfast.

Years ago, Cal had helped Frank Butler drive this tunnel through the foothills that backed up to the Lazy B. It's what had led to Frank's offering him work on the Lazy B, and now knowing the mine's ins and outs had saved his neck. His pursuers likely didn't know where the tunnel led. For the moment he was safe.

Safe. Cal's mouth twisted in a wry grimace. This morning when he awakened he'd had a future, a family—a place in the sun for the first time in his life. Now he was a fugitive. He had no doubt that these hills would soon crawl with men eager to boast that they'd rid the world of California Smith. They would be more interested in blood and glory than in justice. His only defense was to hole up in the Dragoons until the hunt had cooled down and then make his way to Mexico. Everything and everyone would have to be left behind—Mackenzie, Frankie, the Lazy B.

For a moment the loss threatened to overwhelm him, but he instinctively clamped down hard on his feelings. When he was just a child he had built a wall of reserve that kept the hurts of this life away from his heart. That wall had grown stronger with the years. Now it served him well. It blocked thoughts of Mackenzie and his hopes for the future, sealing them into a chamber of his mind where they could not intrude upon the task at hand, which was survival. Now was not the time for sorrow and regret. Now California Smith needed to once again become Goshk'an. Cunning and strength were his allies. Distraction could be his downfall.

Cal kept to cover as he made his way down the ravine, even though the hills seemed empty of threat. The very silence made him suspicious. The wildlife that usually populated the foothills—birds, squirrels, rabbits, lizards—were nowhere to be seen, as if they hid from intruders who had startled them before Cal's arrival. The hair on the back of Cal's neck began to prickle with alarm. Ahead the ravine narrowed and was choked with brush—a perfect ambush site. Even an Apache couldn't have chosen a better one. He looked carefully around him. There were no signs, no tracks, no clue. But signs could be obliterated. Every instinct that had been honed when he was an Apache warned of danger.

He turned back toward the tunnel with the certainty of danger chilling his heart. He had no gun and no horse. His only hope had been to lose his pursuers. If he didn't succeed in that . . .

A pistol shot exploded in the silence and a bullet ricocheted off a rock only a foot from Cal's head. He ducked and ran—not toward the tunnel, but up the hill toward the old Satler mine. Beyond the mine the foothills rose into the Dragoons in a jumble of terrain where only snakes and Apaches could survive. If he could lose his enemies just long enough . . .

A fusillade of bullets forced him to dodge and zigzag up the hill. There was no cover. Only his speed and the erratic course he ran kept him alive. Then his luck deserted him. A loose rock slid from under his foot. He sought a handhold on the hillside, grabbing a tuft of scrub grass that suddenly pulled free from the ground, roots and all. Unable to regain his balance on the steep incline, he tumbled, slid, and rolled. The sandy bottom of the ravine rushed up to meet him. He hit hard, the breath whooshing painfully from his lungs and the sunlight exploding into red and black spots that danced before his eyes.

When his head cleared, Cal looked up into a ring of pistols whose black malevolent muzzles stared down into his face. He froze. Behind one of the pistols, Israel Potts slowly came into focus.

"You just lie real still, boy. You've caused enough trouble for one morning."

"Careful, Israel," Crosby cautioned. "He's as full of tricks as a cornered coyote."

"Back off, Nathan. If you and your boys hadn't started shootin' back there, he probably would've walked right down the ravine and we could've taken him a lot more peaceable like."

"Bull! He'd already seen us. Woulda saved us a lot of trouble if at least one of us had better aim. He's hardly worth haulin' back to hang."

"Well, now, we're gonna haul him back, so don't get no notions otherwise. I never yet been a party to a lynchin', and I ain't gonna start now."

"He's guilty as sin," Nathan declared.

"We'll let Judge Pinney decide that." Israel motioned with his pistol. "Up, boy, real slow and easy."

The faces that ringed Cal were tense and wary. Even flat on his back without a weapon, he was an object of fear. The thought almost made Cal laugh. It also made him realize that if he made one suspicious move, the posse would fill him so full of holes he wouldn't even cast a shadow.

He got up slowly and carefully. Israel stepped forward to help him up, holding his pistol only a few inches from Cal's face. "That's more like it," the deputy sheriff said. "Don't throw your life away by doin' something stupid, boy. It's still worth something." At Potts's signal, two men broke from the posse and approached Cal warily. When it became clear Cal wouldn't struggle, they tied his hands behind his back and lifted him onto the horse behind Potts.

Crosby spat into the sand. "Your sweetheart told us right where to find you," he gloated. "Seems she's got more sense than I gave her credit for now that she sees what murderin' scum you really are."

Crosby's words pierced his heart, crumbling the wall of his stony reserve. Mackenzie's faith had been quick to collapse; once again she had assumed the worst of him. Was her love so fragile, so inconstant that it could be so easily swayed?

His mind suddenly filled with black, bitter anger at these cowardly, honorless men who surrounded him, and at fate itself. Israel Potts was wrong; Cal's life was not really worth anything anymore. But he would *not* live in captivity or let these jackals string him up for obscene display; he would escape or die in the attempt.

They rode southeast toward Tombstone. Cal was impassive, refusing to give his captors the satisfaction of his despair. The posse joked nervously, proud that they'd bagged their prey, but uneasy because they knew what Smith, even bound, was capable of. Crosby was ominously silent. Israel, his stout body swaying ungracefully in front of Cal, emanated the stink of nervous sweat. As the little cavalcade rode on, the jesting grew less loud and then sputtered into silence. Israel's horse, burdened with two riders instead of one, fell a short distance behind the others.

Cal saw his chance. He dug his heels sharply into the horse's sensitive flanks. The horse lurched in surprise and reared up onto its hind legs. Never a very accomplished horseman, Israel lost his balance. A bump from Cal sent him tumbling out of the saddle. Even before the deputy hit the ground, Cal propped his weight on his bound hands and pushed himself into the saddle, keeping his balance on the lurching horse from long practice and natural instinct. Guiding the horse with his weight and pressure from his knees, he turned it around and kicked it into a gallop toward the hills.

The break happened so quickly that before Crosby and the posse gathered their wits, Cal was galloping away in a flurry of dust.

"Goddammit! Get him!" Crosby yelled.

"Wait!" Israel shouted as the posse flew past him. "Don't leave me here!"

"Go to hell, you idiot!" Crosby shouted over his shoulder.

Israel tried to get to his feet, but his legs gave way beneath him. Face red as a beet and puffed with anger, he settled unhappily back into the dirt where Cal had dumped him.

Cal leaned low over his horse's neck, concentrating on his balance while letting the animal pick its way through the sage and mesquite. He was fortunate. Israel's horse—a big buckskin mare with long legs and a deep chest—was game, fast, and agile. With his arms tied awkwardly behind him, Cal needed all his skill to stay in the saddle over the rough terrain. He paid no attention to the shouting behind him, to the explosions of gunfire and the bullets kicking up spouts of dust on either side of him. All his energy was dedicated to urging the horse to greater speed and keeping his balance.

The foothills were close, looming closer. If he could just reach them, he'd be able to lose his pursuers. Crosby and his posse could search the mountains and canyons for days and never find him.

As the buckskin mare lengthened her stride, the ground seemed to fly beneath flashing hooves. The shouts and gunfire grew more distant, the bullets more erratic. The dull thud of hooves striking sand changed to the ringing impact of solid mountain rock. The hills ahead seemed to open their arms like a welcoming mother to enfold him in their protection.

Mackenzie's stomach was twisted into so tight a knot that she suspected it might never unwind, no matter the outcome of this day's events. She had sent Gid Small into town with instructions to report back with any news he heard about Cal, then she had forced herself to attend to business. Too many things called for her attention—getting the cattle to the railhead first and foremost. There was also the matter of finding men to replace the three White Mountain Apaches she had lost. When she had checked on their campsite their wives were gone, along with almost every trace that the Indians had ever lived there. She wished Mahko, Bay, and Istee well. For all her initial doubts about them, the three men had been faithful, reliable hands, certainly much less trouble than the white men who worked for her. She wished she'd been able to provide protection when they'd needed it.

Cal never left her mind. The injustice of what was being done to him—to them both—twisted her insides until she felt like doubling over with pain. Frustrated, she didn't know what to do. If only she could wake and find she was having a nightmare. If only she could go back in time twenty-four hours and keep Cal from going into town, keep him on the ranch where he would have had a foolproof alibi. If only . . .

Wishing and worrying didn't do a bit of good, but Mackenzie did it all the same. She went about the business of the Lazy B in a daze, her heart and her mind both elsewhere. She spent an hour talking to Lightning and Wind, alternately weeping and raging; she paced the length of the parlor until a path was indelibly traced in the rugs; she wandered the curved walkways of the court, pensively staring at the marigolds in the flowerbed. The rest of the ranch worried with her. Even her tough-minded, hardcase ranch hands were indignant at the turn of events. Carmelita went about her chores weeping. Frankie sulked and whined, feeling the tension but not understanding quite what had happened.

Of all the people on the Lazy B, Lu was most composed. She was, in fact, glacially calm. When Mackenzie attempted to put aside her own concerns and comfort her stepmother, Lu assured her she had no need of comfort.

"Tony was my son," she told Mackenzie. "Because he's my own flesh and blood, I loved him. But he was a bad seed, and I knew it from the time he was a boy. I always knew it, though I didn't know where the devil in his soul came from. His father was a good man. When he was alive he gave Tony a father's love, and I tried to be a good mother. But something inside him twisted." She shook her head sadly. "I don't know why. Only God knows why. Perhaps he will have mercy on his poor soul—and mercy on me, as well. I am sad for my son, but I can't grieve as a mother should."

At midafternoon the clatter of hooves outside brought both Lu and Mackenzie running out into the yard. The sight of Nathan Crosby riding under the archway with his "posse" made Mackenzie's stomach clench. She wanted to welcome them with Frank Butler's shotgun in her hands, but before she could duck inside the house to get it, Nathan hailed her with a greeting.

"Afternoon, Mackenzie," he said, just as if they were friendly neighbors. "Sorry to tell you that Smith escaped. We picked him up in the ravine, just where you said we'd find him, but on the way to town he attacked poor old Potts and got away. Israel came away with a broken leg."

Mackenzie's stomach twisted even tighter. "I'm sorry to hear about Israel."

"He'll be laid up for a while. Since I volunteered to be deputized on this matter, I'll be leadin' the posse that's goin' after that bastard Smith. I came to see how many men you can spare for a manhunt."

"I can't spare any men," Mackenzie said coldly, "and well you know it, Crosby."

Crosby grinned maliciously. "That's right. You lost a good part of your crew today, didn't you?"

"Even if I could, I wouldn't. If you think I don't know what you're up to, you're wrong."

"Since I seem to be the law right now, what you think doesn't really matter, does it?"

Mackenzie decided it was a good thing she didn't have that shotgun after all, because she might not have been able to resist deflating Crosby's ego with a few well-placed bullet holes.

"In any case," Crosby continued in a gravelly voice, "I figgered I'd stop by and warn you, since that white Apache's on the loose. I let it slip that you'd told us where to find him. He had murder in his face when he heard that. I know you and I don't always see eye-to-eye, girl, but I'd hate to see that sonofabitch slip back to this ranch with some Apache notion of revenge."

Crosby hadn't come to recruit men for the chase, Mackenzie realized. He'd come to gloat. Cal thought she'd betrayed him, and Crosby wanted her to know it and be afraid. Her reaction was sorrow, though, not fear. Once she had lacked faith in Cal and called him a murderer. Now he thought she'd done the same thing again. He had a right to be angry. Mackenzie wondered if she would ever get the chance to explain.

But that was of little importance compared to Cal's life. What chance did Cal stand in those mountains with no supplies and no weapons, hunted like an animal? Crosby and his so-called "posse" would ride after him and bring him back, but they wouldn't bring him back alive. Mackenzie was sure of it.

"You might wanna take some of your crew and set up a guard around your house until I can bring this renegade in," Crosby advised with mock concern. "Apache revenge is a nasty business, and they're not any more gentle with women than they are with men."

"Your concern overwhelms me," Mackenzie replied sarcastically.

Lu sighed as they watched Crosby and the posse head out the arched gateway. "I would feel better if more of those men were Israel's and fewer were Crosby's. I fear Nathan Crosby has little respect for the law, though he'll obviously don its mantle when it suits him."

A hot tide of rage and frustration flooded Mackenzie's heart at the same time a determined and quite unconventional resolve solidified in her mind. "I think Bull Ferguson is in the barn. Would you ask him to saddle Dolly for me, please?" Leaving behind Lu's puzzled look, she hurried into the house and called for Carmelita. "Pack me some food, enough for three or four days. And gather some blankets that I can use as a bedroll."

Lu marched in the house and confronted her. "What do you think you're doing, Mackenzie Butler?"

"I'm going with Crosby. Someone's got to make sure they don't lynch Cal the moment they see him."

"That's ridiculous! You can't ride off with a pack of men! That's not only dangerous; it's incredibly stupid."

"I don't give a damn!" Mackenzie said emphatically.

"Crosby will never let you ride with them."

Mackenzie fixed Lu with eyes as hard as cut emerald. "Just let him try to stop me!"

16

Mackenzie took off her hat and wiped her sleeve across her brow. All the years she had lived in Arizona and she still didn't understand how September—such a pleasant month in Boston—could be so searingly hot. The sun beat down like a white-hot furnace. Glaringly bright sand and rocks seemed to focus the heat directly on the line of seven riders who threaded their way through the gorges and over the jumbled rises of the Dragoons. Dust swirled from under the horses' hooves and hung in the still, hot air. Mackenzie itched where sweat trickled down her neck and back. Her shirt stuck to her skin uncomfortably, and her trousers chafed where no lady should be chafed.

Two days they had been on Cal's trail—two hot, uncomfortable, awkward days. The men of the posse treated Mackenzie like a skunk about to spray, which was no more than what she'd expected. She was a woman intruding on a man's territory, compromising their reputations—if these rough men had reputations to be concerned about—as well as hers. Nathan Crosby had spoken scarcely a word to her since their noisy confrontation when she had first caught up to the group. He'd been livid, and the language he'd used to express his feelings about her "foolishness" had burned even the posse's ears. He didn't limit himself to berating *her*. All females apparently shared her faults, stepping out of their place, pushing in where they weren't wanted, forgetting they were women, and failing to be grateful to men for protecting them from the world, putting clothes on their backs and children in their bellies.

Crosby ended his tirade by forbidding her to accompany the posse. When Mackenzie pointed out that there was little he could do to prevent her, he had merely laughed contemptuously. The rest of the day he had driven the posse at a pace that had even the men complaining, but Mackenzie kept up. When the sun set and camp was made, she cooked her own food and laid out her own blankets far enough from the men to provide a modicum of propriety. Next morning she had the campfire going before the men awoke.

Nothing more was said by Crosby or anyone else about her leaving the party. The posse—three Bar Cross cowboys and two other men that Mackenzie didn't know—seemed to accept that she was coming along. Crosby alternated between ignoring her and trying to wither her with black looks. He tolerated her presence only because he couldn't think of a way to get rid of her—at least not a way consistent with his role as acting lawman. Mackenzie was sure that he would have dearly loved to wring her neck.

Mackenzie had faced down Crosby's hostility, but now, as their second day on the trail drew to a close, she began to have doubts about the need for her effort. Over the last two days she had almost stopped being afraid for Cal and started feeling a bit of apprehension for the posse—and for herself as well. She'd heard the men's uneasy rumblings. The trail they followed through the rugged mountains was much too clear. California Smith seemed to be making no effort to hide his path. The posse followed him easily, though they never caught sight of him, and no matter how fast their pace, they couldn't quite catch up with him.

In the jumbled terrain where they rode, Cal's Apache-taught skills in stealth should have made him almost impossible to track. The posse knew it, and every one of them wondered suspiciously why their task was so easy. Who was in control—the hunter or the hunted? As for that matter, were they sure which of those roles they played?

Determined as she was to cling to her love for California Smith, to trust him the way she should have trusted him six years ago, Mackenzie found that the wildness of the country through which they road and the jumpiness of her companions made her uneasy and a bit fearful herself. When Dolly pricked up her ears and snorted at a shadow, Mackenzie's heart nearly jumped out of her chest. Her eyes roamed along the towering cliffs, peering up canyons with the same apprehension that the men showed. Several times she sternly reminded herself that Cal was not *her* adversary. She was on his side. They had made love, produced a child, declared their commitment to each other. She should be keeping a wary eye out for Crosby, not for Cal.

The sun was low when the posse came across a spring and stopped to water the horses. Mackenzie filled her canteens, then splashed as much of herself as she possibly could without sacrificing her modesty. While the others poured hatfuls of water over themselves and took care of personal business behind a mesquite, Mackenzie turned her attention to Dolly's feet. The mare's gait had been uneven over the past several miles. She found a small stone lodged in the right front foot and plucked it out. When she dropped Dolly's foreleg and straightened, Crosby was staring at her with undisguised contempt.

"She lame?" he asked.

"No. A night's rest will see her sound enough. She's a tough little mare."

He snorted. "Just like you, eh?"

Mackenzie didn't think that remark merited an answer.

"You start slowin' us up, I'll plum leave you behind. You can find your own damned way back through the mountains."

One of the posse who had earlier introduced himself as Adam Schenley strolled over to where Mackenzie and Nathan exchanged hostilities. "Why don't you leave the lady alone, Crosby? I'm beginnin' to think we ought to leave *you* behind."

Mackenzie almost laughed at the expression that flashed across Crosby's face. "Mind your own business," Crosby warned.

"I thought our business was bringin' in a murderer," Stan Beemer snapped. He and Adam, being the only two men on the posse who weren't Bar Cross hands, had become allies of a sort over the last two days. "Appears to me we're wastin' time sittin' here snarlin' at each other."

The Bar Cross men looked to Crosby for a signal to teach the two upstarts a lesson, but Nathan merely spat in the dust and growled. "Let's get movin'."

The posse took off at a determined gallop but soon slowed to a more sensible pace. Cal's trail led them through sandy gorges hemmed in by steep hillsides covered with prickly pear and Spanish bayonet. As the defile narrowed further, the posse grew even more uneasy.

"This is a damned good place for an ambush," Adam muttered. The canyon ahead was deep in dusky shadow. Boulders and thick brush covering the steep sides provided ample cover for anyone who lurked there.

"One man can't stage an ambush," Crosby scoffed. "It's time you boys remembered that Smith is running from us, not the other way around. I'm beginnin' to think we've got six women on this posse instead of just one."

The insult put a stop to the muttering, but not to the anxious glances with which the posse scanned the canyon walls. Soon the gorge grew so narrow that they were forced to ride single file along the trail. Even Mackenzie wished the narrow canyon would widen. Every shadow on the hillside seemed to have eyes that watched them.

Just in front of her, Crosby twisted in his saddle to look back over the straggling line of riders. "Tighten up the line, men. You're just askin' for—"

A sharp crack exploded on the cliff above. A rain of pebbles and dust showered the ground around them while high on the canyon wall the cracking and popping swelled to a loud rumble.

"Rockfall!" the man behind Mackenzie shouted. "Goddamn!"

The whole hillside above them seemed to shift and move. The earth roared. Dust was everywhere in a choking cloud that shivered in time with the canyon's vibrations.

"Go!" the rider behind her cried. "Let's get out of here!"

Even without Mackenzie's urging, Dolly plunged forward. Dust clogged Mackenzie's nose and mouth, and a deafening roar battered at her ears. The ground shook and heaved beneath Dolly's hooves as they fled. They careened around a bend in the canyon to relative safety, and Mackenzie pulled up sharply as Crosby slid to a halt in front of her. His cursing rose in volume even above the roar of the cataclysm.

Slowly the rumble quieted. The stray rocks bouncing down the hillside settled. Dust still hung in the air, as if frightened to settle back to earth. Mackenzie looked around her. Only four others had made it around the bend—Crosby and Hank Miller from the Bar Cross, Adam Schenley and Stan Beemer.

"The others . . ." she said, horror filling her throat like sickness.

A shout echoed around the canyon. It was the voice of Kelly Overmire, one of the missing Bar Cross men. "Crosby!"

"Overmire!" Nathan shouted back.

"We're caught behind the slide," came the answering shout. "Can't get over it. Have to go back."

"Damn!" Crosby cursed.

Mackenzie drew a breath of relief that the others were unhurt. The posse's size had been reduced by two.

"That fall weren't no accident!" Adam declared. "That were a neat job if I ever seed one. Split us in two like a knife."

"Probably meant to kill us," groused Miller. Crosby gave him a black look.

Mackenzie thought about Miller's statement and decided he was wrong. They had just cleared a narrow canyon where an avalanche would have proven far more deadly. No, the fall had been neatly set up so that the riders in front could escape around the bend, and any others could retreat back through the canyon to where a slight widening in the gorge gave them room to escape. If Cal had indeed started the slide, he could have picked a better place to kill them. Perhaps he'd merely wanted to separate them or frighten them into giving up the chase. Mackenzie refused to believe he would resort to wholesale slaughter, and she wouldn't even consider that Cal might condemn her to die along with his enemies.

Still, a hollow feeling of fear had settled inside her stomach. Apache revenge, Nathan had so gleefully reminded her, was a nasty and lethal business. Cal believed she had betrayed him. He might not be any happier with her at the moment than he was with Crosby.

The reduced posse continued on at a brisk pace. Mackenzie was pleased that Crosby was now outnumbered. Hank Miller was the only other Bar Cross man left, and Adam and Stan didn't seem to be overly impressed by the acting deputy's authority. In fact, the pose had tacitly divided into two camps: Crosby and Hank rode together in front, and Mackenzie, Adam, and Stan formed a trio behind.

Adam Schenley, Mackenzie learned, had been a hand at Henry Clay Hooker's Sierra Bonita Ranch in Sulphur Springs Valley until just a month ago, when he'd been bitten by wanderlust and decided the time had come to move on to less familiar pastures. Middle-aged and graying, his face was a wreath of sunburnt creases. In spite of rough, uneducated language, tobacco-stained teeth, and a body odor that was the accumulation of much more than two day's sweat and grime, Mackenzie liked him. His smile was an honest one.

Stan Beemer told her that he'd lost his job in the mine strikes the year before, and since then, he'd drifted around Tombstone doing odd jobs wherever he could find them. Younger than Schenley, he was elaborately courteous in an attempt to impress her. His breath smelled of liquor, and Mackenzie suspected he had a bottle in his saddlebags.

Both of them were unlikely allies, but Mackenzie hoped if this case came to a confrontation, they would stand with her against Crosby.

"Trail's gettin' fresher," Crosby noted. "We're gettin' close."

"The trail's too clear," Stan commented. "That damned Apache's leadin' us right where he wants us. Probably into another trap, if you ask me."

"Nobody asked you," Crosby told him.

"Ya know," Adam began in a conversational tone. "I came out to this country right after the war. Apaches were everywhere then. You couldn't make a move but some Apache was waitin' fer ya, ready to lift your scalp or hang ya head down over some fire. I came across one of them big freight wagon trains once. It was bound for Yuma with a load of miner's pay and cloth and whiskey and other stuff. Apaches got to it. The train was ripped apart, the mules had been hauled off, though a couple had been used for target practice, it looked like—and the drivers, every one of the poor bastards, was tied to one of those big wagon wheels upside down with their heads over a little fire. Boiled their brains while they was still alive. Skinned 'em, too. Those Apaches sure got imagination when it comes to killin' folks, I'll say that for 'em. Hope this California Smith fella's more white than Apache."

"California Smith's a white man," Mackenzie insisted. "He's *not* an Apache."

"That don't matter much. He was raised like an Apache by Cochise and his friends," Crosby growled.

Mackenzie decided the news that Cal had in fact been closer to Geronimo than Cochise while growing up would only worsen the situation, so she kept her peace.

When the evening became too dark for the posse to ride any farther, they camped beside a spring that bubbled out of the fractured rock of the hillside.

"Lordy, will a mug o' coffee taste good!" Beemer said as he dismounted.

"No fire," Crosby snapped. "You want to let Smith know right where we are?"

"Jesus!" Adam exclaimed. "Do you think he don't know where we are?"

"No fire," Crosby insisted.

They ate cold rations—salt pork and cold beans washed down with springwater and whiskey. No conversation relieved the tension in the camp. Everyone silently reflected on the myriad ways, in this rugged, inhospitable country, that the hunters could become the hunted. Enough had been said about Apache viciousness that day to fuel grisly imaginings for days to come.

Mackenzie forced herself to eat her supper even though it sat like a lump in her stomach. She spread her blankets closer to the others this night—sacrificing propriety to her jumpy nerves. While the men bedded down for the night, she splashed the dust from her face and hands with springwater that had gathered in a small pool. She then settled down with saddle for a pillow and two thin blankets to ward off the cool air.

The night was quiet—almost too quiet. The others tossed in their blankets. On a boulder overlooking camp, Hank Miller sat sentry with a rifle in his lap. Mackenzie saw the glow of his cheroot, a tiny red spot in the pitch-black camp. Above the earth, the vault of stars wheeled imperceptibly. Mackenzie closed her eyes and tried to sleep, but sleep wouldn't come.

For the hundredth time that day, she questioned the wisdom of her impulsive dash to Cal's rescue. She'd been convinced that Cal needed her help. Perhaps she'd felt just a bit noble in disregarding convention, propriety, and safety in riding to his aid; or perhaps some part of her—some foolish part—had felt that daring such a thing somehow made up for the way she'd treated him six years ago. Then there was the ache of frustration that wouldn't let her stand still while Cal battled for his life and freedom.

Now, facing harsh reality, she realized what a fool she was. Over the past two days Cal's ability to take care of himself without her help had become only too apparent. If today was any indication, soon what was left of Nathan's posse would be at each other's throats, and if not that, they would grow frightened enough that they would turn tail and head for home.

Then what? she wondered. Would Cal head for Mexico, traditional refuge for fugitives when the chase got too hot north of the border? Would he be on the run the rest of his life? Instead of joining in this dangerous, wild chase, Mackenzie should have stayed home and tried to prove Cal's innocence. Maybe she could have scraped together the funds to hire an investigator from the east—one of those free-lance detectives who worked apart from police.

On the other hand, she mused pessimistically, what good would a detective do? How could she prove Cal's innocence? His medicine bag had been found in the same gully with Tony's body, and he'd admitted he was in the right place at the right time when Tony was shot—shot with such deadly accuracy, at that. Any number of men might have wanted Tony dead: gamblers he had cheated, husbands he had cuckolded, men he had pushed and bullied once too often. But how many of those men had the necessary skill with a rifle to make such a shot?

One of them certainly did, Mackenzie assured herself. One of them *had* to. She refused to believe that Cal had killed Tony, not in such a premeditated, cold-blooded way. But even if she could somehow prove that he wasn't the murderer, would anyone in Arizona believe her? Cal carried the hated taint of the Apache. Most who knew his story were anxious to believe him a savage. No matter how long Cal lived with his own race, fearful whites would always reject him.

Mackenzie stared up at the cold stars and realized that she'd probably never seen California Smith again. Their story was over. Before they had reached their happily ever after, some capricious author of fate had changed the plot. Cal would always believe she had rejected and betrayed him, and if he escaped, she would always wonder where fate had led him. How would she ever explain this to Frankie? How could she explain when Mackenzie herself could scarcely accept that God would be cruel enough to allow her to lose Cal again?

Unable to face the cold indifference of the stars overhead,

Mackenzie turned on her side, curled into her blankets, and burying her face in her arms, silently wept.

Hours later, as dawn pinkened the sky, Mackenzie woke to the sound of Nathan's cursing and Hank Miller's strident shouts.

"It wasn't *my* fault!" Miller exclaimed. "Schenley relieved me halfway through the night. String *him* up if you want someone to blame."

"Hell's horns!" Adam Schenley replied. "I didn't see no one!"

"What'd you do?" Crosby demanded furiously. "Fall asleep, you sonofabitch?"

"I didn't fall asleep, dammit! If he got in here, he must be a ghost or one of those medicine-man witches the Injuns are so scared of."

"Well, he got in here," Hank Miller growled. "We're lucky he didn't murder us all in our beds."

Stan Beemer groaned, his first contribution to the exchange. "Killin' would be easier."

Mackenzie's eyes felt as though the lids were gummed with glue. Cobwebs danced in her head; she didn't understand anything of what was going on. Throwing back her blankets, she got up and stumbled toward the spring to wash her face. She splashed the sleep from her eyes and was about to take a drink when Adam Schenley shouted at her.

"Miz Butler! No."

"Huh?" she replied.

"The water! Don't drink it. It's poisoned."

The water poisoned? She noticed a cruel grin twisted Crosby's mouth as he stood silently and watched her. No doubt he'd hoped she would take a long, deep drink.

"I drank it last night," she explained. "It was fine."

"It's not fine now," Miller said with a humorless chuckle. "Look at Beemer."

Stanley Beemer's face was white as a fish's underbelly.

Looking miserably embarrassed, he turned away and vomited.

"The food he ate for dinner . . ." she speculated.

"Naw," Adam told her. "We got a sick horse, too."

"Yeah," Miller groused. "Mine. Beemer didn't tell me the water was bad before I let it drink this morning."

Mackenzie let the water drain out of her hands. Crosby looked disappointed. "That bastard snuck right past camp to get to the spring," he snarled, glaring at Adam. "And our damned sentry didn't see a thing."

"What makes you think *you* woulda seen 'im, old man?" Adam challenged. "Seems to me I heard a story about him walkin' right into your ranch one night not long ago and scarin' the crap outta you and all your hands. Jesus! I wouldn't talk if I were you."

Crosby and Miller both reddened, but Mackenzie wasn't paying enough attention to enjoy their discomfiture. Cal had been in camp the night before. To get to the spring he would have had to walk almost on top of her bedroll. The thought warmed and chilled her at the same time.

"I'm gonna die," Beemer complained. "I wish it'd been soon." His face grew tense. He flung Mackenzie a desperately mortified glance and fled for the nearest scant cover. Apparently his stomach was not the only part of him rebelling.

"You're not gonna die," Crosby shouted contemptuously after him. "At least not from pukin' and crappin' your fool guts out." He swung his saddle onto his horse's back and pulled the cinch tight. "Get ready to mount up," he commanded. "We've gotta get movin'."

"What about Stan?" Adam demanded.

"He can stay here with the sick horse. Hank'll ride his."

"We can't just leave Mr. Beemer here!" Mackenzie objected furiously.

"We'll come back for him," Crosby said.

"That's absurd! There's no good water here. You don't know how long it will be before we return. There might even be renegade Apaches still in these mountains."

"Well, there's one here for sure." Crosby punctuated his words by spitting into the dust. "And I aim to make sure he doesn't stay in these mountains—at least not above the ground."

"You can't leave Stan here," Adam agreed. "You might as well kill him as leave him here alone."

Crosby looked willing to consider the suggested alternative. "He can double with me," Adam said. "Miller can ride Stan's horse and we'll lead his horse behind."

"It'll slow us up too much," Crosby objected. "You wanna stay with 'im, go ahead. Miller and me'll ride on."

"To hell with you!" Adam snarled. "One man ain't worth this kinda chase. Herrera needed killin' anyway, if you ask me. I'm turnin' back with Stan."

"Have it your way." Crosby slapped his hat on his head and kicked his horse into a brisk trot down the canyon. Miller followed. Neither man gave the ones they left behind a backward glance.

Mackenzie looked frantically after the two departing men. There were few things she wanted less in this world than to be alone in the mountains with Hank Miller and Nathan Crosby. Yet to let them continue alone after Cal . . .

Cal could take care of himself, her good sense told her. Only the night before, she had reflected on the uselessness of her being here.

On the other hand, Crosby intended to put Cal under the ground rather than bring him back for trial; he'd as much as admitted it. If Cal killed either Crosby or Miller in defending himself, still another murder charge could follow him. If Mackenzie was there, she might be able to force Crosby to act like a lawman rather than a bounty hunter. The chance was slim, but could she ignore it?

She gave Adam an apologetic look and hefted her saddle onto Dolly's back. "I have to go with Crosby."

Adam grimaced darkly. "I wouldn't if I were you."

"I have to."

Adam shook his head, and Stan Beemer looked away. The sick man's skin now had a greenish cast. "Be careful," Adam warned.

Crosby and Miller were already mere dust clouds down the canyon. "I will," Mackenzie promised. "Take care getting him home."

"Yeah. Sure."

Mackenzie tightened Dolly's cinch, climbed aboard, and hastened to catch up with what she knew for sure was trouble.

Trouble was indeed what she got. Crosby and Miller cast her sideways glances when she caught up to them but didn't deign to otherwise acknowledge her arrival. Throughout the long day they ignored her. They hardly spoke to each other except to argue, disagreeing about their strategy, Cal's intentions, where to stop, and how long to rest the horses. Their tempers were so short that they would have disagreed about the color of the sky had the subject come up.

Cal's trail was fresh. He was just ahead of them, Crosby insisted, but they never caught up to him or even glimpsed a trace of him other than his tracks. Crosby declared they should circle around and intercept him; his trail led straight toward Cochise's old stronghold. If they rode hard they could wait for him in ambush. Hank Miller argued that Cal was trying to fool them. The fertile, well-protected valley that had been the Apache leader's hideaway was now a white man's ranch. Their prey would soon change direction and they would lose him for good.

Mackenzie thought Miller foolish for worrying about losing Cal. So far Cal had demonstrated more desire to harass and disable his pursuers than to lose them. But she kept her opinion to herself.

As darkness fell, they passed by an inviting spring-fed meadow to camp in a sandy gorge where high walls provided protection and no pond or spring made them vulnerable to poisoning. Mackenzie helped the men dig a hole in the sand to obtain water. The gorge was quite dry, and their little sand well measured three feet down before water started to slowly trickle in. Again Crosby forbade a fire for cooking food, but none of them was in the mood to eat anyway. As they settled into their blankets for the night, they all scanned the cliffs with nervous eyes. No moon lit the landscape. The gorge was inky black, and the cliff walls could be discerned only because they blocked the stars. The night was a perfect one for stealth, for silent mischief, for sneaking up on an unwary camp and wreaking havoc. Every one of them knew it.

Crosby took the watch. He sat on his blankets, leaned against a granite boulder, and cradled a rifle in his lap. Midway through the night, Hank offered to relieve him but Nathan refused. The old man's insistence on trusting only himself set Hank to muttering in insulted dissatisfaction.

Mackenzie courted sleep uneasily. A pistol kept her company under the blankets, and Dolly slumbered only a few feet away. The horse's movement would wake her if anyone dared come near. The precautions were against Crosby and Miller, she told herself—certainly not against Cal. She had nothing to fear from California Smith. She was on his side. He had to know that.

She lay on her blankets and stared into the black, silent night. Cal was out there somewhere, watching them. Mackenzie could imagine the burning blue stars were his eyes. She could almost feel his gaze, and couldn't decide if she was comforted or frightened.

Mackenzie was never aware of falling toward sleep, but sometime in the night, while Hank Miller snored and Nathan Crosby kept his watchful vigil, she did. When she woke she discovered a gift brought by the night—a slender, deadly-looking arrow stuck into the ground not two inches from the edge of her blanket. The startled gasp that escaped her lips woke Hank Miller. When he discovered an identical gift beside his bedroll, he cursed.

"Goddammit! Look at this! Crosby, how the hell . . ." Miller's voice trailed off when his eyes lit upon Nathan Crosby, gagged, trussed, and staked out like a hog ready for barbecue.

"My God!" Mackenzie threw off her blankets and ran to where Nathan stretched out on the sand, hands tied above his head and fastened to a stake buried in the sand, legs spread-eagled and fastened in a similar fashion.

Miller cut his boss free with a belt knife. Crosby ripped the gag from his mouth and stiffly got to his feet. He opened his mouth to speak, but the only thing his throat could produce was a dry croak.

"Here, drink." Mackenzie offered him her canteen. Crosby took a long swig, wiped his mouth upon his dirty sleeve, and glared at them both. Miller's mouth twitched upward in a grin, but he quickly squelched it.

"What're you smirkin' at?" Crosby demanded. "That bastard walked right past the two of you and you slept like babies. At least *me* he had to hogtie."

"He coulda killed us," Miller said soberly.

Nathan spat. "He's having too damn much fun makin' us look stupid. I'm gonna make that smart-ass Injun-lover sorry his mother ever gave birth. Saddle up!"

Miller scowled at the sand. "T'ain't no use, boss. We're never gonna get 'em, and sooner or later he's gonna get riled and stop playin'."

"What're you saying, Miller?"

"I'm saying I've had about enough. I'm tired of not knowin' who's chasin' who, and I sure as hell don't like the idea that Smith can walk into our camp any time he damn well pleases and stick us full of arrows. Where'd he get 'em anyway? He didn't have no weapons when he lit out on Potts's horse. He makin' these things in his spare time?"

"There's Apache caches all through these mountains," Nathan said. "Stands to reason he'd know where they are. He's probably armed to the teeth by now."

"Another reason to call it quits. You wanna get yourself killed, go right ahead. But I'm not fool enough or stubborn enough to keep on fightin' once I'm beaten." Miller turned his back on Crosby and went to saddle his horse.

"Never thought I'd see the day that Hank Miller turns chicken." Miller ignored him, and Crosby gave Mackenzie a halfway embarrassed glance. "Fine thing when the only member of a posse to stick it out is a woman."

"If you were smart, you'd turn back as well."

Nathan snorted. "I finish what I start. You go back with him. If you think your being here is gonna help your lover-boy, you're foolin' yourself. I'm the duly appointed representative of the law right now, and I'm gonna make sure justice is done to that yellow-haired savage."

Mackenzie glared. "Then I'll just tag along and make sure you stay within the limits of the law."

"You're a fool, Mackenzie Butler."

Hank Miller rode off without a word. Mackenzie hastened to roll her blankets and saddle Dolly, knowing if Nathan got a head start, he'd do his best to lose her. She filled her canteens at their little sand well, which was half full of dirty water. Nathan was still saddling his horse when she sought the cover of a stand of junipers and boulders for a necessary privacy. No matter how urgent the hurry, some things simply could not be ignored.

Buttoning her trousers and at the same time bending over to pick up her hat from the grass, she didn't hear the rattle until too late. Something sharp struck her arm, and the place where she'd been hit suddenly caught fire with pain.

17

A scream rang in Mackenzie's ears—a scream in her own voice, though she wasn't aware of screaming. She stumbled back. Suddenly the crack of a pistol explosion blasted the little composure left to her. She lost her balance and sat down hard on the rocky ground.

"That fixed him!"

Burning pain and shock made her head swim. "Wh . . . what?"

Nathan stepped across her and picked up the tattered, headless body of a rattlesnake. "Trust a woman to go beatin' around in the bushes without lookin' out for snakes. Got yourself bit, didn't ya?"

"I did?" The last few minutes were jumbled together in a chaos of confusion, but the pain burning in her upper arm confirmed Crosby's speculation. Mackenzie looked down the rapidly swelling flesh, and saw the twin puncture wounds and a double row of almost invisible pinpricks. Angry red streaks spread from the bite in an ugly starburst. Nausea swept her at the sight.

"Course, a smart lady like you knows how to take care of snakebite."

She did. Anyone who lived in Arizona Territory did, but she had no sharp knife, no boiling water, and how did one tie a tourniquet with only one hand? Her hands shook, and even sitting on the ground she was dizzy and light-headed. How fast did the poison spread? How long before it started to destroy her flesh, her blood? She had seen a rattlesnake victim once. His flesh had been pocked with blood blisters, and he had bled from every orifice of his tortured body. One hour after stumbling onto the Lazy B he had died in convulsions. The memory of his agony made her want to throw up.

She slowly got to her feet.

"Goin' back to camp?" Crosby asked with a chuckle. "Good idea." He took her uninjured arm and helped her stand. "I'll get you settled. Then I gotta be on my way. Got a full day's ride in front of me."

"What?" Mackenzie collapsed onto the sand where Nathan left her. "You can't leave!"

"Sure I can," Crosby said with a grin. "Gotta get back and tend to business now that you and that snake have won this little war for me."

"What do you mean?"

"Just this, little lady." Crosby looked as though he were enjoying himself. "California Smith has every hand in the territory against him. He can't go back to the Lazy B to make trouble for me. And now you've been obligin' enough to take yourself out of the picture. With you dead, your stepmother will sell the ranch to me without even a look back. She's got her sights set on bein' a wife, like a woman should. I'm gonna have everything goin' my way, Mackenzie. Your springs will see me through the drought, and your good pastureland will let me add another hundred head to my herd."

"You're leaving me here?" That one horrible fact sank into Mackenzie's brain. She regarded him with incredulous amazement.

"I'd stay awhile, but I hate to see a woman suffer. Even one who's been a pain in the ass like you."

"You bastard!"

"It's a rough country, lady. A man's gotta take care of his-self." He swung up into the saddle.

"Tell me before you go," Mackenzie demanded. "Did you kill Tony? Was all this just a setup for Cal?"

Crosby chuckled and shook his head. "I didn't kill Tony. I didn't kill you either, Mackenzie. You did yourself in with your own stupidity." He rode over to Dolly and took Mackenzie's rifle and the shotgun hanging from a thong looped around her saddle horn. "I don't figure you'll need these. But I'll leave you this." After emptying several shells out of the pistol, he threw her the gun along with a canteen. "That gun has one bullet in it. You might consider using it if the sickness gets too much for you." He grinned. "And if that Apache lover-boy of yours comes along, you better use the bullet on him, girl. He sure was mighty mad when I let him know you told us where to find him. I bet his Apache friends taught him some interestin' ways to get even with people he's mad at—especially a woman."

He gave her a long last look, as if savoring her helplessness. "Adios, Mackenzie. It's been an experience knowin' you."

Rage engulfed her as Crosby booted his horse into a canter down the gorge. For a brief moment she was tempted to use that one bullet to put an end to him. But she couldn't. She sat in the sand and felt sick despair sweep the last of her strength away.

"Damn him! Damn him to hell! And damn me for a stupid idiot!" Cursing made her feel marginally better. Mackenzie got to her feet and headed for Dolly. Gingerly, expecting her poisoned body to collapse any minute, she pulled herself into the saddle. The world started to tilt, and grasping the saddle horn to steady herself didn't help. Her scalp and lips were curiously numb, and a peculiar tic twitched her mouth and eye muscles. Insider her mouth she imagined she could taste her own tainted blood. Hopelessness overcame her determination as she realized she would never survive the ride home.

Dizzy from despair as much as snake venom, she allowed herself to slip from the saddle. There was nothing left to do but settle back and try to prepare herself for what was to come. She would stay in this gorge until she died.

As Mackenzie sat down heavily upon the sand, the numbness in her skin and face seemed to seep into her brain. She leaned forward and rested her head on her knees, thinking of Frankie—and of California Smith.

Cal squatted on the crest of a ridge, immobile as a rock. Bits of foliage were stuck in his headband to disguise the shape of his silhouette against the bright September sky.

Slipping back into his Apache identity these last few days had been almost frighteningly easy—a reminder that the civilized veneer that glossed over his savage upbringing was fragile indeed. Caches left long ago by Cochise's warriors provided him with all he needed: a knife, bow and arrows, rifle, ammunition, and even replacements for his filthy, worn clothing. An unlucky deer that happened across his path provided enough dried venison to last him for weeks.

As easy as it had been to once again become Apache, it was easier still to elude his pursuers and to lead them into traps that he hoped would make them turn back. He had no particular animosity for any of the posse—except possibly Nathan Crosby—and he didn't want to be backed into a situation where he was forced to kill or be killed himself. Once the posse had given up the chase, Cal planned to come out of the mountains and cross the open plain into Mexico.

He tried not to think of the life he'd been cheated of, for those thoughts filled him with bitterness and regret. Such emotional distractions were a luxury a man couldn't afford in this country, not if he wanted to stay alive. When he was safe in Mexico he could lament the life he had longed for, Frankie with her dimples and her wicked cherub smile, Mackenzie . . .

Mackenzie. The final bitter blow had landed when Cal spied Mackenzie riding with the posse. On seeing her with Crosby, Cal had been filled with cold, deadly anger. Mackenzie was as inconstant as the wind in the Dragoons's canyons, first whirling one way, then another. She claimed to love but didn't know what love was, faithless to herself as well as him. She wasn't worth the fear he felt for her safety among the rough men she traveled with; she wasn't worth his regrets; she wasn't worth the pain he felt at her betrayal.

Still, under the bitterness fostered by years of being hated, a wiser side of his nature wouldn't believe that Mackenzie would betray him. The evidence of his eyes couldn't convince his heart.

So when Cal sent a rockfall tumbling down a canyon wall onto the posse, he made sure that Mackenzie was in a spot where she could easily escape. When he added a dose of native bitter salts to the spring where the posse camped, he prayed that she wouldn't be the first to wake and go to the pool for a drink. And when just the night before he had visited the camp to demonstrate how easily he could take the lives of all of them, he had paused for a stretch of time to look upon Mackenzie's sleeping face, alabaster pure in the light of the just-risen moon. He wished he could see her smile again, the indulgent, maternal smile she sometimes gave Frankie, the seductive smile she reserved especially for him.

Right then, though, no smile had lit her face. Even in sleep she had looked slightly troubled and afraid. Who was she afraid of? Crosby? Perhaps Cal himself? He wanted to reach out and smooth the pucker from her brows and ease the tightness from her mouth. The last shred of anger slipped beyond his grasp. He didn't know why she rode with his enemies, but if he expected Mackenzie to have faith in him no matter what the circumstances, he should give her the same faith.

He'd stuck an arrow into the ground beside her bedroll, and wished desperately he could turn time around and go back to the night Tony Herrera was killed. His luck had run out at a crucial time, and he would pay for it the rest of his life.

At least Cal's demonstration of power with the arrows had produced the desired effect. As Cal squatted on the ridge and watched, Hank Miller had words with Crosby and rode off in a temper. That they all would turn back was too much to hope for, but Cal did regret that Mackenzie didn't leave also. Hank Miller was a hard case, but she would be better off riding back with him than continuing with Crosby. Besides, Cal longed to have Crosby to himself with no other eyes to watch a confrontation between them. Crosby was a man who needed a good, sharp reminder of his own mortality, and Cal was in just the mood to deliver it.

He continued to watch as Crosby and Mackenzie prepared to leave. Crosby looked ready to ride on without Mackenzie when she sought out a thicket for privacy. Then, unexpectedly, Mackenzie screamed. The old man reined his horse in, jumped off, and ran toward the thicket. A single shot echoed off the walls of the canyon.

For one horrible moment Cal thought Crosby had shot Mackenzie. Eyes blazing, he started to scramble down the steep canyon side, abandoning any attempt at stealth. Before he was a third of the way down the hill, however, Mackenzie and Nathan walked out of the thicket together with Mackenzie leaning heavily on Crosby's shoulder.

Cal stopped his descent and took cover. Crosby helped

Mackenzie to the shade of a large boulder, where she slid down into the sand. Though Cal was too far away to hear the conversation, he could see that they talked. Nathan strode away almost jauntily. He unloaded Dolly's equipment, threw Mackenzie a single canteen and a pistol, then spurred his horse up the canyon. Mackenzie mounted her horse to follow, but swayed uncertainly in the saddle. She slipped to the ground and onto the sand in what looked to be an attitude of exhaustion. The dust of Crosby's departure rose on the light breeze and slowly disappeared.

Cal frowned. Nathan Crosby was up to no good. That much was obvious. If the old man doubled back behind him, Cal might be in for a nasty surprise. Mackenzie might have been left in camp as bait to lure Cal into staying put.

The wise course of action was to go after Nathan, Cal told himself. The old grizzly had been asking for a showdown between the two of them, and Cal was more than willing to provide a showdown that would have the sonofabitch running back to the Bar Cross with his tail tucked between his legs.

Mackenzie was just sitting there in the sand, though. Such inactivity wasn't like her, even if she was exhausted. She made no move to remount Dolly, no move toward the canteen or pistol. Cal didn't like the slouched curve of her shoulders or the way her head rested on her knees without moving.

Cal was torn. His head told him to follow Crosby—losing track of the enemy had cost more than one man his life. Gut instinct, however, told him that something was terribly wrong with Mackenzie. He remembered his father Daklugie telling him that an Apache warrior did not let concern for a woman interfere with decisions or distract his concentration. It was not wrong to be concerned, the old warrior had told him, for a woman can be the very heart of a man's life. The wrong came when that concern made a man forget his training.

Cal watched for a moment more, then decided that in this case his Apache training would have to be ignored. One little finger on Mackenzie Butler's hand was worth more than Nathan Crosby and any danger he might present. Taking his rifle from its sling across his back, he made sure a cartridge was in the magazine and started down the hill.

Mackenzie's world was filled with heat and pain. Sweat seemed to boil out of her skin, and her heartbeat felt like the pounding of frightened wings in her chest. Eyes closed, she could see painted on her eyelids the hot scarlet heat that pulsed through her body. Her world had no room for thought, or even fear. Only heat and pain.

Something cool brushed against her skin. Her own cry filtered through the fuzziness of her mind, though she wasn't aware of making that startled, frightened sound. Again the coolness bathed her face, her neck, her arms, then washed across her breasts and stomach. Perhaps the coolness meant she was dying. Surely death was cold—dark and cold.

"Mackenzie, wake up."

The voice was familiar, but she couldn't quite place it. Thinking was so difficult.

"Mackenzie, do you hear me?"

The cool cloth swiped her skin again, taking some of the heat with it. The burning crimson field before her closed eyes cooled almost to black. Her mind cleared just a bit—enough to remember that the voice belonged to California Smith.

"Cal." His name came out of her throat as a croak. She opened her eyes a slit and tried to focus on his face. The world spun, and she with it. "Cal?"

"I'm here."

She raised a leaden arm to touch him. The skin of his cheek felt familiar against her fingers. "Cal."

Then she remembered. Fragments of images skittered across her memory—half dream and half thought. Cal's escape. The chase. Nathan Crosby laughing as he told her of Cal's anger, suggesting Cal might come back to get revenge . . .

She heard the gloating victory in Crosby's voice even now. What she couldn't remember was why she was lying here with California Smith crouched above her, why she was so weak that lifting her arm was a nearly impossible task, why her body throbbed with heat and spun in a vortex of pain. Was this part of Cal's revenge?

"Mackenzie, don't look at me that way."

Fear made her breath come short. She wanted to touch him, to bury herself in his embrace and cry out her pain. At the same time she wanted to run with a desperation that bordered on insane.

"Do you think I'd hurt you, Mac?" Cal asked sadly. "You really *don't* know me, do you?"

Her vision momentarily focused to sharp, hard edges. Cal's clear eyes looked down at her with no hatred, no anger, no hostility or gloating. Mackenzie had ever quite understood how eyes of such deep crystalline blue could be so warm, but they were warm.

"I didn't mean to betray you," she whispered hoarsely. "Oh, Cal. I thought they would hunt you . . . hunt you . . . like a wild animal. Israel . . . Israel said . . ." She hadn't the strength to finish her explanation. "Rattlesnake," she suddenly remembered.

"I know. I found it."

"Crosby . . . shot it."

"And then left you here." His voice was deadly.

"He's going back to tell Lu I'm dead. Buy the Lazy B."

"Lu won't sell it to him, Mac. Even if you were dead she wouldn't sell it to him."

Mackenzie wasn't so sure, but she also wasn't sure she'd live to find out.

"And if Crosby did somehow manage to get the Lazy B by leaving you out here to die, he wouldn't live long to enjoy it."

She saw the lethal glint in his eye. Apaches have interesting ways to get even with people. . . . That was what Crosby had said. She didn't know whether she felt satisfaction or pity. Suddenly, Cal gave her a little shake.

"Mackenzie, listen to me. Get the ghost look out of your eye. You're going to be back at the Lazy B before Lu has time to plan a funeral."

Mackenzie managed to smile, though she wasn't feeling either brave or humorous. "Rattlesnake," she reminded him.

"Do you want me to skin it and make you a belt?" he offered.

Dolt. She was dying and he was making jokes. Threats and jokes. Strange combination.

"Mackenzie, you're not going to die. You're going to be sick enough that you might want to die, but I won't let you. When I hightail it down to Mexico I want to know that you're back at the Lazy B taking care of our little Frankie. So don't you even try to die on me."

"Frankie . . ." she whispered.

"Yes, Frankie. Think of Frankie and how much she'd miss you. You're not going to die, Mac. I'll make you damned sorry if you do."

The worst of the sickness was yet to come. Before the day was out, Mackenzie discovered her own private hell. Cal applied a tourniquet to her arm, made clean, small slices into the puncture wounds, and sucked out what venom he could, but the poison had already spread. Almost too weak to move, she steamed in her own sweat and vomited until her stomach muscles ached from the violent spasms. Her arm hurt so much, she would have cut it off if she could. Blood blisters swelled, burst, and swelled again. Despite Cal's threat, he couldn't have made Mackenzie any sorrier about dying than she came to be about living.

When Cal loaded Mackenzie aboard Dolly she couldn't even manage to keep her balance. He mounted behind the saddle and wrapped a strong arm around her as Dolly moved slowly forward.

"Cold," she complained.

First she was cold, then hot, then cold. Blackness flooded her vision and the sounds of the world slowly faded. Surely she was going to die.

"Lean back against me and relax," Cal advised.

Her head lolled against his chest. "Back to the ranch?" she asked, struggling with the words.

"Soon. Right now we're just going up the gorge a ways to a spring. You'll be more comfortable where there's water and some cool grass."

With great effort, she smiled. "You didn't poison this spring, too?"

"Never use the same trick twice," he said jauntily. Suddenly serious, he told her, "That salted water wasn't for you, Mac."

She managed to give his arm a reassuring squeeze. "I know."

Cal stayed by her side for the next four days, leaving only to fetch his horse from where he had concealed it on the ridge. Over the campfire he boiled a vegetable-smelling poultice that made the pain of her arm fade to an almost bearable level. He forced her to drink what seemed to be gallons of water, to eat dried venison strips and fresh-cooked rabbit, even though the nourishment often came up almost before it went down. He washed her, helped her with embarrassingly intimate tasks, kept her warm at night with his body heat. When she raved in nightmarish delirium, Cal held her and talked comfortingly of how much he loved her, of Frankie, of a future together that both of them knew was a pleasant lie.

Much of the time Cal's voice and comforting touch scarcely penetrated the haze of her sickness. Her mind became a monster that used memories to torment her. She relived her father's death, first shouting for Cal to go and then crying for him to come back. Every distressing incident in her life, every stupid mistake, every disappointment paraded out in malicious detail.

Even in her lucid moments a pall hung over her mind, the snake's poison afflicting her spirit as well as her body. Mackenzie castigated herself for believing for even a moment that Cal had killed Tony. She berated herself for giving in to Israel and telling the posse where the tunnel outlet was. She convinced herself that this whole mess was her fault.

Cal tried to soothe her. "When Crosby told me you'd sent the posse to the tunnel outlet, I was mad as a hornet," he confessed. "When I saw you riding with the posse, I was even madder. I thought all sorts of black things about you before I realized that you had every right to believe I'd murdered Tony. Everything pointed to me as the killer. I couldn't really blame you for feeling betrayed. I was expecting you to have more faith in me than I was willing to have in you."

Mackenzie sniffed and wiped the tears from her face with the back of her hand. She hated crying. It was futile and a waste of time, but she hadn't the strength to hold back the tears.

"It's an imperfect world, Mac, with imperfect people. You can't expect yourself to do the right thing or make the right decision all the time. You've got to forgive yourself your mistakes and forgive me mine."

"We're both going to have to do a lot of forgiving in the years we live together." She almost managed a smile. They knew such a future was fantasy. Unless fate took an extraordinary turn, the time left for them to be together was measured in days, not years.

At the end of four days Mackenzie was sufficiently recovered to complain about her dirtiness. Cal had done an admirable job cleaning her more visible places, but there is only so much a sponge bath can accomplish.

"There's a pond over by the spring," Cal offered. "Do you feel up to a bath?"

"Just try to keep me from it."

The spring and its little pool was like a bright jewel set into a rugged setting of limestone and granite. Sunlight rippled off its surface, and although shallow, it was an inviting deep blue-green.

"Minerals," Cal explained when Mackenzie asked about the peculiar color. "You can see them coming out of the water over there." He set her down at the edge of the pool and pointed to where the spring trickled from the fractured canyon wall. The water had deposited solid globules of brownish white on the reddish native rock. Similar deposits surrounded the pool, which nestled in a shallow hollow at the base of the wall before overflowing into the little stream that watered their meadow. "The salts come out of the water when it flows out of the ground. If you drink too much of it you'll get a case of the trots."

"It looks like a porcelain bathtub. Just perfect for taking a bath."

Cal helped her peel off her clothes. Then he shed his own and assisted her into the pool. The water was lukewarm; the bottom of the pool cushioned their feet in slippery moss. Gratefully, Mackenzie sank up to her neck, keeping only her head and her bandaged arm above the water.

"It won't hurt to get your arm wet," Cal told her. "Let's take off the bandage. We'll wrap it again when it's clean."

He unwound the makeshift dressing that covered her injured arm. The bandage was a strip of cotton cut from his shirt. The rest of his shirt had been sacrificed to the same purpose. Mackenzie winched as he dunked her arm under water to soak off the cloth that had stuck to her wound. Finally, the bandage came gently away from her flesh. Cal lifted her arm above the surface of the pool and examined it with critical eyes.

"Ughh!" Mackenzie turned her face away from the expanse of destroyed flesh. The rattlesnake venom had worked like a slow acid to disrupt the flesh it attacked.

"It will heal, Mac. There's no pus. It's clean. No permanent harm done."

Hesitantly she turned her eyes back toward her arm. "It's ugly as sin." She was well enough recovered for vanity to get the best of her. "The scar's going to be awful."

"Your husband isn't going to mind," Cal said with a smile. "He thinks you're the most beautiful woman on the face of the earth, scar and all."

Mackenzie allowed herself to pretend the fantasy was true: the world was right again, and she would go home from here and plan her wedding to California Smith. But the truth intruded viciously. She had recovered; she would go home. But Cal would ride toward Mexico, and God only knew if she would ever see him again.

"I forgot something." Cal climbed out of the pool and, wet skin glistening in the sunlight, took his knife from its sheath on his belt, scrambled a short way up the canyon wall, and hacked at the Spanish bayonet plant. Naked as he was, he should have looked ridiculous, Mackenzie mused, but he didn't. Bronzed, lean, and fit, he could have passed for one of the Greek gods written about in the book Aunt Prudence had once caught her borrowing from Uncle Harold's library. Muscles in his back and arms rippled in a symphony as beautiful as any written by Hayden or Beethoven. His legs were straight, the calves corded with sinew and the thighs bulging with strength. His buttocks were lean, compact extensions of his thighs. Mackenzie felt a thrill of primitive pride that this man loved her, that even now he used his strength and wits to protect her.

In a few moments Cal slid down the wall—not even wincing as rough rock bit into his flesh—and came back to the pool. He proudly held up his prize for Mackenzie to see.

"Uh . . . nice."

He grinned. "It's soap. You wash with the sap from the root."

Maçkenzie had her doubts, but Cal was right. The sap didn't suds up like the dainty soaps her aunt had used or bite like the lye soap used on the Lazy B, but it left skin and hair feeling soft and clean. Cal took great care in cleaning her hurt arm, gently lathering and rinsing again and again until he was convinced the wound was thoroughly clean. Mackenzie winced and gritted her teeth, but put up with it. Afterward, he compensated her for the pain by washing every other part of her body with great attention to detail. His strong hands massaged her shoulders until the strain left her muscles. He caressed her breasts with soapy circles, then sat her on the smooth, mineral-encrusted edge of the pool so that he could lave her stomach, thighs, calves, feet and toes. She smiled when the rise and fall of his chest accelerated, guessing his labored breath wasn't from exertion. Closing her eyes and enjoying the wicked pleasure of his caresses, she wondered if this was the last time in her life she would know such joy.

"Rinse," he told her.

She obediently slid into the pool. His hand landed on her head and pushed her under.

"Don't you want to wash your hair?" he asked when she sputtered to the surface. Without waiting for an answer, he lathered the thick red mass that fell in tangled disarray over her shoulders. His strong fingers massaged her scalp in a way that made even her toes tingle with delight.

"Feel better?" he asked with a wicked grin.

She opened her eyes. "Um." She smiled dreamily. "You look like you want something."

He reached for her. She ducked. "I think you need a bath too," she said.

He submitted impatiently to her ministrations as her hands spread the gentle aloe lather over his neck, back, chest, and into his hair. When she reached his buttocks and thighs he grabbed her hands to stop them. "You're a tease, Mac." His voice was hoarse with a passion too long withheld.

"No, I'm not," she denied, blinking up at him in wicked innocence. "A tease is someone who promises, then doesn't deliver." She slid her hands over his flanks and trapped his engorged sex between her slipperly palms. "Do you need an engraved invitation?" she inquired in a mischievous voice.

"You're sick," he protested.

"Not *that* sick anymore, my love."

He closed his eyes as her fingers caressed him. "God . . . Mackenzie!" He swept her out of the water and laid her on the grassy bank of the pool. "Woman, you always get me so hot I can't take my time with you like a man should."

"I don't want you to take time," she told him. "Not a moment more." She wrapped her legs around his waist as he crouched between her open thighs. They both gave a cry of triumph as he plunged home. A warm rush of elation flooded through Mackenzie as Cal began to move—filling her achingly full, then withdrawing while her muscles tightened around him as if to prevent his escape, then thrusting again and driving the very breath from her body in joy.

Their coupling was short and violent. They'd been apart too long to allow the luxury of gentleness or patience, and the prospect of time closing in around them drove them to desperately seek solace and fulfillment from each other's bodies. They reached their peak in a climactic explosion of animal ecstasy combined with very human joy, and when their hearts slowed and their breathing once again became normal, they both knew that somehow, by some miracle, they had to find a way to be together. Their love had weathered too much to be sacrificed to a greedy old man like Nathan Crosby and something as insignificant and feeble as the law.

They lay together until the sun disappeared behind the canyon wall. As shadows merged into twilight and the day's heat faded, Cal gave her a final kiss and rose to wash their clothes in the pool. Mackenzie felt no shame in their nakedness as he carried her back to her bed and wrapped her in a light blanket. After a supper of squirrel, piñon nuts, and the roasted root of some plant—after tasting it Mackenzie didn't especially want to know which plant it was—they lay quietly together and talked.

In a couple of days he would take her back to the Lazy B, Cal told Mackenzie. By then she should be well enough to travel.

"What then?" She knew the answer but hoped that she might be wrong; that there might be another solution.

"I'll head for Mexico," he said sadly. "I figure it's that or the hangman's rope—or maybe some bounty hunter's bullet."

It was the answer she had expected, and dreaded. The trip into the Dragoons had started out as a nightmare and ended in a dream. She gave up the dream reluctantly. "I'm going to hire an investigator to prove that you're innocent."

"I'm not sure you can prove me innocent."

"Are you telling me that you *did* kill Tony?"

"No, Mac. There have been times when I wanted to kill Tony. But I didn't."

"Then I won't give up."

Another silence followed, both of them thinking of how nearly impossible the task would be.

"I wish I knew how my medicine bag got in that gully," Cal mused aloud.

"Were you wearing it when you went into town?"

"No. I lost it a few weeks before. Just suddenly noticed it was gone."

"You don't know where you lost it?"

"It could have been anywhere."

"I'm sure Crosby had something to do with this," Mackenzie said. "He practically boasted of it when he left me here. First thing I'm going to do when I get home is make sure that he gets thrown behind bars for leaving me out here to die."

"Don't get your hopes up. Crosby's good friends with the law, or at least what passes for the law in Cochise County."

"He tried to kill me. He would have succeeded if you hadn't come down from that cliff."

"He'll pay for that someday," Cal promised. "But I doubt it'll be the law that makes him pay."

Mackenzie heard the harshness in his voice. Was Cal's entire future to consist of hiding in Mexico and plotting revenge against the man who'd wronged them both? If that was the case, there was truly no justice in the world. "I wish I could go to Mexico with you," she said with a sigh. "But Frankie . . ."

"Frankie doesn't belong where I'm headed, and neither do you."

"I would go if it were just me," Mackenzie assured him. "Maybe I could sell the Lazy B and use the money to buy a ranch in Sonora. The pastureland is good in some places down there, according to John Slaughter. If we could buy a place where we could live decently . . ."

"Maybe . . ." Cal said. "Maybe."

They fell asleep entwined, clinging together like two lost souls looking for a way out of hell.

Mackenzie woke to look up at a bright-blue morning sky. The canyon was still in shadow; the meadow where they lay was blanketed with a faint mist of ground fog. She closed her eyes again, not wanting to wake and face the day, but after only a few moments she sensed that the canyon was quieter than the usual morning peacefulness.

She opened her eyes and turned over. The sight that met her eyes made her sit up so fast that her still-fragile senses whirled.

"Smile," Cal said very softly. "You're glad to see them." Still sitting beside her, he squeezed her arm reassuringly, but Mackenzie didn't feel the least bit reassured.

A small band of mounted Apache warriors regarded them with impassive faces from only ten feet away. At the forefront, Geronimo grunted in curt greeting. Mackenzie didn't need to understand Apache to feel the rebuke in his tone. The creases in the renegade's leathery face deepened into a scowl as he launched into a harangue in Apache that sounded anything but friendly.

18

Cal wanted to curse aloud at the fate that kept delivering hammer blows to his plans. Bad luck seemed to follow him like a black cloud hanging over his head. Dodging the thunderbolts coming from this particular storm cloud was going to take some fancy footwork.

Cal rose slowly, careful to show no alarm. Mackenzie struggled to get to her feet beside him.

"Your years with the *indaa* have made you lazy, blind, and deaf," Geronimo scoffed. "Is this the warrior I trained? A stupid boy who sleeps like the dead with no eye for who might come upon him?"

The rebuke was well-earned, Cal acknowledged. In his concern for Mackenzie and their future, he had completely forgotten to be alert. "You are right, uncle. I have grown soft living with the whites. I am fortunate that the warriors who surprised me are my brothers and not my enemies."

Mackenzie's hand clenched his arm in a hard grip. Cal

gave her credit for keeping her composure at the sudden appearance of the most feared savage in the southwest. Since Geronimo's conversation was in Apache, she couldn't understand what was being said—friendly greetings or a warning to prepare for death would all sound the same to her. Yet she stood beside him erect and proud, her face calm, her eyes surveying the band without alarm. Only Cal could sense the racing of her heart and the icy coldness of her flesh against his.

"This time you are lucky," Geronimo agreed, the seams of his face rearranging in to a faint smile. "Istee and Bay-chen-day-sen tell me that the white man has driven you out for killing one of them."

Another surprise. Cal looked closely at the faces of the men who ranged behind Geronimo. Istee and Bay were in the back rank of the band. Their expressions didn't change when their eyes met, but he sensed apology in their gaze.

"I found them traveling back to the reservation and told them they should fight like men, not run like little children. I knew you would like to fight also, so I came looking for you."

Another face caught Cal's eye. He tried not to show his shock when he recognized Yahnozha, his brother, the man he'd spared at the Lazy B six years ago, the man who supposedly had killed Frank Butler.

Geronimo noticed the direction of Cal's gaze. "Your brother will be glad to greet you. He also has lost everything to the white man. His first wife died of sickness on the reservation. His second wife was raped by a soldier and killed herself. His son prefers to stay on the reservation with old women and useless men. He will be happy to have a brother to fight beside."

"I also will be glad to give my brother greeting. I am honored that the great warrior Geronimo would let me fight beside him." There was nothing else Cal could say, not if he wanted to stay alive.

Geronimo nodded with satisfaction. "Good!" His gaze swung to rest appraisingly on Mackenzie. "It is good that your wife has the courage to come with you. Goshk'an's wife is not weak and foolish like other white women. She is wise and strong, like Apache women. She knows a man needs a wife, even when he goes to war." Suddenly he switched to English and addressed himself directly to Mackenzie. "Goshk'an's wife, is your daughter Fran-kee well?"

Cal felt Mackenzie start in surprise. He squeezed her hand in reassurance, not caring how un-Apachelike the gesture was.

"Frankie is well," Mackenzie answered in a voice that was studiously calm. "She is with her grandmother."

Geronimo nodded, satisfied. "Good!" He twisted in his saddle and gave orders to his band of Apache. The Indians dismounted and led their horses toward the spring. "We will eat and allow your wife time to pack your horses," Geronimo said to Cal. "Then we must go."

"My wife was bitten by a snake," Cal told him. "She is still too weak to travel, Uncle."

Geronimo gave Mackenzie a keen-eyed look. "You speak the truth. The woman is sick." He called to one of the warriors, who leapt aboard his horse and galloped away. Five minutes later the warrior reappeared with a little mounted cavalcade behind him—two youths scarcely more than boys, six women, and a little boy. As the group dismounted, Geronimo called one of the women over. In English he introduced her to Mackenzie. "This is Bi-ya-neta. You are sick, Goshk'an's wife. Bi-ya-neta will care for you. She is skilled in medicine."

Bi-ya-neta surveyed Mackenzie with eyes black and hard as marble, then reached out and took her arm. Mackenzie shot a desperate look toward Cal as the Apache woman tugged her in the direction of the other women. He smiled reassurance, trying to look more confident than he felt.

The group of Apache women closed around Mackenzie like the walls of a cage. Their black eyes regarded her with aloof, hostile stares until Bi-ya-neta spoke two short sentences in Apache. Then the women's faces relaxed. Three softened to the beginnings of a smile. The little boy, five or six years old at the most, stared at Mackenzie solemnly as he clung to the skirts of his mother.

"I tell them you are wife to nephew of Geronimo," Bi-ya-neta said.

"You speak English!" Mackenzie said, surprised.

Bi-ya-neta nodded. "Speak English good. Live on reservation. Talk with many whites."

"Oh. Good."

"Mackenzie is strange name. What name mean?"

"Well, uh, it means, uh, Scottish woman—my grandparents came from a land over the sea."

"Women from that land all have red hair like yours?"

"Some of them."

Bi-ya-neta seemed to consider. "Must be strange place. Husband say you bit by snake," she said on an abrupt change of subject. "Sick?"

"Not so much anymore. Just weak."

"Bite on arm? I look."

The other women gathered around even closer as Bi-ya-neta examined Mackenzie's arm, sniffed her breath, pinched her skin, and listened to her heart. They talked in rapid-fire Apache, each seeming to have an opinion on the patient's health. Finally, Bi-ya-neta silenced them all with a curt gesture. "You are getting well," she pronounced.

"Yes," Mackenzie agreed. She could have told them that without all the fuss. "I'm much better."

"I will watch over you as we travel."

"Thank you." Travel. Mackenzie's heart sank. Were they

prisoners? She'd hoped that Geronimo was simply paying a call, as he'd done on the ranch, and would soon be about this business, leaving them to be about theirs.

Bi-ya-neta shook her head as if she'd read Mackenzie's mind. "We all go with Geronimo. Don't matter if we want to."

Mackenzie gave her a surprised look. "You mean you are not here . . . willingly?"

"Geronimo raid our homes on the reservation. He very angry because we live on reservation without fighting. He kill many men, women, children, and take us back with him to be wives to warriors. Take young boys"—she nodded to the two youths who had ridden in with the band and were now with the men— "to learn to fight."

Mackenzie had never heard anything so atrocious in her life. She could understand Geronimo wanting to kill whites—after all, the Apaches had been driven from their homes and their way of life. But now he was killing his own people. "That's monstrous! How awful for you."

Bi-ya-neta shook her head. "Apache women learn to accept many things. You Apache wife now. Must learn to be strong." She pushed her way through the wall of other women. "Come. I will help you pack your horses. Soon the men will want to leave."

Mackenzie glanced at Cal, who was fifty feet away and deep in conversation with Geronimo. Cal's mouth cut a straight, tense line through this face. He was no happier about this than she was, Mackenzie realized, and he was just as helpless to keep it from happening.

By the time Bi-ya-neta had rolled up Mackenzie's blankets and tied them to Dolly's saddle, the band was ready to move on. Cal helped Mackenzie up onto the chestnut mare. "Would you rather ride with me than by yourself?" he asked.

"I'll be fine."

He gave her a worried frown.

"Really I will," she promised.

He mounted the buckskin mare he'd taken from Israel Potts. "We pretty much have to go along with this for now," he told her quietly as they rode out side by side. The band of Apaches surrounded them, and behind them rode the little group of conscripts from the reservation. "Geronimo is short of people—both men and women. To refuse to ride with him would be an insult. We can't risk getting him angry, Mac."

"I know you're doing what you have to do."

"I'll find a way to get you safely back to the Lazy B and Frankie."

Mackenzie's heart twisted with pain. Poor Frankie. She'd probably been told by now that her mother was dead. And Lu. Lu would curse Mackenzie for her foolishness, but she would grieve all the same. How long would it be before she got back to the ranch and let her family know she was alive? Or perhaps the more important question was: would she ever get back to the Lazy B?

By noon they had left the Dragoons behind them and had started south over the plain that led to Mexico and the rugged Sierra Madres. Geronimo's raiders were consummate horsemen. They covered territory faster than most white men believed possible. In a rare tolerant mood, the Apache leader slowed the pace in deference to Mackenzie's condition, but to Mackenzie's way of thinking they traveled very rapidly indeed.

She wanted to sit straight in her saddle and show these renegades that white women had as much stamina as Apache women. Just the day before, however, she had scarcely been able to stand on her feet. Staying in the swaying saddle of a horse required more strength than she possessed right now. All her muscles had turned to rubber—aching rubber, at that. Staying upright took all her concentration, never mind sitting tall and proud as the Apaches did.

After two hours of torture in the saddle, Mackenzie was

glad when Cal ignored her protests and slid her over to his horse to ride in front of him. His strong arm wrapped around her waist and steadied her. His broad chest, still bare from when he'd torn his shirt into bandages for her arm, was a bulwark of strength to lean against.

"Thank you," she whispered as she nestled against the comforting wall of muscle.

In answer Cal leaned down and kissed the top of her tousled head. Several warriors glanced at him in surprise at the un-Apachelike behavior. He didn't care. For the last few days in these mountains he had regressed to the Apache ways he'd learned as a youth, but now in the company of Apache comrades, he found himself uncomfortable. Listening to Geronimo and his band talk, Cal discovered the truth of the name they'd given themselves—*Indeh*, "the Dead." They talked and thought of nothing but death—the deaths of those they'd murdered and their own deaths, which they seemed to accept as an event that had already occurred. The cheerful bantering, the comradeship, the rough male humor that he remembered from his apprentice warrior days was gone. These raiders were solemn as the grim reaper himself, and Geronimo's eyes held the light of a zealot. Even Yahnozha, constant companion of Cal's childhood and youth, was a man who had been distilled down to nothing more than hatred and sorrow. After their first greeting, they didn't talk with each other. Once they had been brothers; now they were strangers with nothing to say.

Cal wondered if the Apaches had changed or he had changed more than he'd thought. Probably both, he concluded. He had finally become more white than Apache. Not that it mattered. The white world had thrown him out, and the Apache world was breathing its last painful gasp. California Smith was a man without a world, and if Geronimo suspected his true sentiments, he would end up without his life as well. If that happened, Mackenzie would be at the mercy of the renegades—a possibility that chilled his soul much more than the thought of his own death. He would sooner have Mackenzie die by his own hand than have her endure life in Geronimo's band.

By late afternoon they had crossed into Mexico. They rode on into the night without rest until reaching the Bavispe River. There they stopped for a few hours to rest the horses and eat jerked beef and venison. Beyond fear and pride, Mackenzie was asleep almost before Cal lifted her from his horse and set her on a pad of blankets. She didn't hear Geronimo tell him to leave her to the care of the women, nor did she hear Bi-ya-neta and the other women settle down around her on their own blankets to get some much-needed sleep.

The next day they mounted up and started south just as the sun rose above the horizon. The Bavispe was a string of jewels in the middle of the desert, its course a succession of deep pools and rippling falls of cool, pure water. The farther south they rode, the greener the valley became. Dense canebrakes choked the riverbanks. The rugged mountains through which the river cut were blanketed in grama grass and scrub oak interspersed with Spanish bayonet, mescal, and cactus. Deep, wooded canyons slashed through the terrain, and on the high ridges grew a green mantle of cedar.

The band grew more relaxed as they made their way south. This was home, the forbidding Sierra Madre that had sheltered generations of Apache raiders and had never been penetrated by the white man. At the end of four days, their little cavalcade had climbed high into the mountains along a trail that was as savage as the men who traveled it. Lava rock, sharp limestone, and unstable gravel paved the way. In many places the trail was just a narrow shelf on the edge of a precipitous drop. The way was littered with carcasses of cattle and ponies that had not survived the climb in months and years past. After what seemed an eternity of travail, Mackenzie began to wonder if she would survive, or be left behind on this unforgiving desert trail—just another dried-out carcass of a creature defeated by the mountain.

As they traveled, the Apaches frequently helped themselves to fresh supplies from well-hidden caches that had been stashed along the trail. Cal appropriated two lightweight deerhide shirts from one of the first caches they came across—one to replace the shirt he'd torn into bandages, and one for Mackenzie. Her own was threadbare and past the point where washings could remove the dirt and sweat. The deerhide shirt fell past her hips and had sleeves that covered her hands, but she solved those problems by slitting the sides and rolling up the sleeves.

After four days of hard travel, Geronimo finally called a halt in a narrow valley lush with grass and cool, pure water. That night the women built a big fire. After a meal of squirrel, rabbit, acorns, and wild potatoes, the men dragged a hollow log into camp and cut drumsticks from willow saplings. Playing the loyal Apache wife, Mackenzie helped Cal paint a fearsome horizontal slash across his face with red ochre taken from the banks of the river. Then she watched with the other women as he joined the other warriors in a violent dance around the fire.

The dance itself was almost as frightening as an attack. The hollow-log drum beat out a rhythm that pounded through skin and bone and forced the heart to beat time to its call. The warriors pirouetted and charged in all directions, dropping on one knee, then springing suddenly into the air, firing their guns, and chanting words that Mackenzie didn't understand.

"What are they saying?" she asked Bi-ya-neta, raising her voice to be heard above the racket.

"They sing of what great warriors they are. Tell of brave things they've done and enemies killed. Tell what cowards the Mexicans are."

"Why the Mexicans?"

"Tomorrow they attack a village of Mexicans. Geronimo wants more horses and cattle to take back to his camp, but even if they didn't have horses and cattle, Geronimo would attack them anyway. He likes to kill Mexicans even more than white men. Many years ago Mexicans kill his mother and his first wife—back when he was young."

"Oh," Mackenzie said lamely. Her heart went out to the poor Mexicans that would wake with the dawn, just as she had many years ago, to find their lives exploding in violence and blood.

When morning came to the little valley Mackenzie still hadn't slept. Cal and she had had words during the night. Mackenzie had begged him not to accompany the men on their raid, to find some excuse to stay in the valley. One didn't give excuses to Geronimo, Cal replied. The presence of one reluctant raider would make no difference at all to the Mexicans, and his refusing to go would make all the difference in the renegade leader's attitude toward Cal and Mackenzie.

Mackenzie had wanted to cry, to beg him to be careful for himself and not stain his hands with the blood of innocents. She held her silence, though. Over the last three days she had senses his growing uneasiness. These were no longer his people, and the pain of his loss shadowed his face and clouded his eyes. The friends of his childhood and youth had become strangers, their ways familiar yet no longer acceptable. Cal had lost a part of himself, Mackenzie realized, and regardless of what anyone thought of the Apaches, such a loss must be a painful wrench to one's soul. So she granted him her silence and spent the night praying against all hope that somehow they would be delivered from this road they followed into hell.

As morning dawned and the sun touched the valley with pale gold, the men ate a quick breakfast, checked their weapons one final time, swung aboard their horses, and with another great hullabaloo about what great fighters they were and how the Mexicans were going to run like rabbits, they galloped off to the west. The women were left in the little valley with a guard of two warriors and nothing much to do. At least Mackenzie assumed there was nothing much to do. She quickly learned that Apache women seldom were idle. As soon as the band was out of sight, they set about the task of gathering mescal and the fruit of Spanish bayonet plants for roasting. The women taught Mackenzie how to let a campfire burn down to hot ash and place the fruit of the Spanish bayonet plant in the ash until the fruit had cooked to just the right consistency. The roasted treat had a tangy, sweet flavor and slightly mushy consistency.

The mescal, an Apache favorite, took longer to prepare. It had to be cooked for several days between hot stones, Bi-ya-neta told her. Mackenzie was grateful to learn they wouldn't resume their breakneck pace immediately when the men returned. The rest would be a welcome respite.

While the Apache women worked, Mackenzie spent most of the day propped against a tree. When she wasn't being offered advice on cooking and other Apache domestic skills, she watched the birds play in the canebrakes by the river. Little sapphire-colored hummingbirds particularly caught her fancy. She found herself envying their carefree freedom as they flitted here and there. How would it feel to be that unfettered? Mackenzie had once believed that she was free to forge her own life, but everything she planned seemed to fall victim to the purposes of other people—her father, Nathan Crosby, and now Geronimo.

The sun set without bringing the men back from their raid. The women thought nothing of it, but Mackenzie worried. The Apaches seemed to regard death as an inevitable fact of life rather than something to be shunned. These men had little to live for. Their way of life, their families, their very honor had been taken from them. Perhaps, Mackenzie thought sadly, California Smith had little to live for as well. She wondered, if it weren't for Mackenzie needing his protection, would he, too, be seeking a glorious and quick end? Bi-ya-neta told her that the warriors probably had taken a very long way back to camp to throw any pursuers off their trail, but the Indian woman's matter-of-fact reasoning didn't stop Mackenzie from fretting.

At midmorning the next day Geronimo and his warriors returned to camp driving a herd of mules and scrawny cattle. None of the men were injured. All were in high spirits, shrieking cries of tribute to their success, firing their rifles into the air and jumping from their horses to gyrate in dances of victory. But Mackenzie sensed that Cal's joviality with the warriors was forced. When the celebration quieted and she went with him to wash in the river, he wouldn't talk to her about the raid, and she didn't press him. Some things were better left unknown.

After the warriors' victorious return, the rest of the day was much the same as the one before. When the women were not tending the roasting mescal, they taught Mackenzie how to build a wickiup. They stripped willow saplings of their leaves, anchored them in the ground, then bent them together and tied them with reeds and grass into a dome. This framework they interwove with green cane from the riverbanks and brush from higher on the valley sides. Hides obtained from the trailside caches finished the structure.

The women build three wickiups. One was for the warriors' sweat bath, and one was for the women and the little boy. The other was for Cal and Mackenzie, Bi-ya-neta told Mackenzie with a flourish. One of the Apache women, a young, comely girl scarcely out of her teens, remarked in hesitant English upon what a fine, handsome man Mackenzie had for a husband. The rest of the women chimed in with giggles of praise. Mackenzie was dumbfounded—not that they found Cal attractive, but that they giggled and gossiped just like white women. She was put to shame by their high spirits. Thesc women were prisoners as much as Mackenzie was. They were less fortunate, even, for Mackenzic at least had Cal to watch out for her. Bi-ya-neta and her Apache sisters had no one except the embittered warriors who had torn them from their homes and families. Yet they accepted their lot without complaint or self-pity.

Mackenzie thanked them for the gift of the wickiup in the few halting Apache words she had picked up over the last few days. She also tried to express her admiration for their bravery. Whether or not they understood her inadequate Apache, the women accepted her compliments with a solemn grace that would have passed for faultless deportment even in Aunt Prue's circle of society matrons.

Mackenzie was not so favorably impressed with the Apache men, however. The behavior they demonstrated couldn't pass for anything but barbaric. One of the mules stolen from the Mexicans was butchered for the evening meal. A young warrior, shrieking in a lust for blood that apparently hadn't been quenched by the attack on the Mexican village, started cutting meat from the unfortunate beast's flanks even before it was dead. Only a quick retreat to the wickiup saved Mackenzie from disgracing herself by throwing up. She could eat nothing that night, though the Apaches devoured the mule with relish. Even Cal seemed to find the meat to his taste. He was brought up on such meals, after all.

"It's not that different from eating a cow," he told her when she refused her portion of meat.

His words were reasonable, but still Mackenzie couldn't eat.

In addition to the mules and cattle, Geronimo's warriors had seized another prize in the Mexican village—tequila. Mackenzie watched in horror as after the evening meal, the twelve Apache men who sat around the fire consumed all three cases of the liquor. Soon laughter grew raucous, conversation slurred. Bottles were shattered gleefully against the rocks of the fireplace. One warrior staggered away from the fire to attend the call of nature and fell into the river. The task of pulling him from the water required four men, every one of them as drunk as the victim. Other warriors pulled the women into canebrakes or thickets to heed a different call of nature. Some were not so delicate and took their pleasure in full view of the campfire.

Mackenzie's stomach rose into her throat as the evening progressed, but she could do nothing to stop the drunken celebration. She sat like a statue beside Cal and tried to borrow his strength. He was her only anchor in a world of madness.

As the evening grew older Mackenzie began to hope that the drunken Apaches would be content to let Cal and her be mere spectators to the celebration. Her hopes were dashed when a young warrior by the name of Chaco pushed his way into the circle where they sat. He squatted down beside Mackenzie, his eyes fixing her with a hungry stare. His head wandered upon his neck as though he couldn't quite hold it upright, and his face was flushed from more than the heat of the fire.

Suddenly Chaco's intense gaze shifted to Cal. He slurred a few words in Apache that Mackenzie couldn't understand. Cal gave him an emphatic answer. Chaco looked at Mackenzie again, his eyes half closed in a sly look. He reached out a hand to touch the hair that fell over her shoulder in a thick braid. Mackenzie drew back instinctively. By this time the men who remained in the circle had given the trio their full, if somewhat woozy, attention.

The Apache snapped another few words to Cal. Cal snapped back with equal vehemence. Both men stood.

"Mackenzie, go to the wickiup," Cal commanded.

Mackenzie scrambled to her feet and retreated a few steps.

"Go!"

She turned to obey, but a brown, gnarled hand reached out to put a halt to her withdrawal. She looked up into the black, snakelike eyes of Geronimo.

"Stay," he ordered calmly in English.

Heart beating fast, Mackenzie looked back at Cal and Chaco, who had moved to the inside of the circle. They crouched and circled like two wolves thirsting for each other's blood. Then another warrior stepped into the circle, weaving unsteadily. He made a fierce declaration in Apache.

"Goshk'an's brother Yahnozha," Geronimo explained to Mackenzie. His words were clear and calm, though Mackenzie had seen him imbibe at least as much as his warriors had. "He fights alongside Goshk'an."

Yahnozha! The man Cal had spared six years ago. The man who had shot her father. He had to be the same; Geronimo had called him Cal's brother. Mackenzie felt herself go cold in spite of the warmth of the fire.

"Goshk'an fights for you," Geronimo told Mackenzie in a voice that sounded amused.

"Can't you stop them?" she pleaded.

The renegade leader didn't answer. Cal and Yahnozha were arguing in fervent Apache. Cal waved his brother away. Looking mortally offended Yahnozha stalked out of the circle. At the same time, Chaco lunged for Cal. The two of them grappled. The wrestlers moved with nightmare slowness, yet the strain of pitting strength against strength reddened their faces and made muscles bulge as though they would burst through sweat-slickened skin. Chaco stumbled and went down on one knee. Cal twisted, landing them both on the ground. They rolled a few times, then stopped with Cal on top.

Suddenly the glint of steel caught the fire's light. A knife appeared in Chaco's hand. Cal grabbed the Apache's wrist as the knife slashed upward. Again they strained against each other's strength, this time with life in the balance.

Geronimo grunted, then shouted a sharp command in Apache. Immediately the contest stopped. At another command from the renegade leader, Chaco dropped the knife and Cal climbed off his opponent's prone body.

"I have few enough warriors without them killing each other over a woman," Geronimo told them. Mackenzie knew he spoke in English for her benefit.

Chaco stared at the ground. Cal still looked angry.

Geronimo swept the circle of Apaches with a stern look. "Goshk'an's wife is one of us. She will be treated with respect like an Apache wife. The women we took from San Carlos will also be treated with respect. Choose them as wives if you wish. Otherwise, treat them as sisters."

Mackenzie thought Geronimo's protection came a little late for Bi-ya-neta and the others.

"It makes my heart sick to see Apaches acting like Mexicans and white men," he said as a final scolding.

The men within the sound of his voice scowled like sullen children. Geronimo grabbed a bottle of tequila and went back to his place by the fire to sit like a stone. The warriors took a moment to sulk, then continued drinking. Within an hour most of them were sprawled out upon the ground in a drunken stupor.

When Cal and Mackenzie finally retired to their wickiup, Mackenzie was still shaking. For the rest of the evening, every time an Apache warrior had staggered in her direction she had flinched. Drunken Apaches were no worse than drunken white men, she reasoned, but the Apaches approached drunkenness with the same zeal they gave everything else in their lives. They didn't stop drinking until every sense was obliterated, and while they still stood, their natural warrior aggressiveness erupted in shouting matches and fights. Geronimo didn't seem to care as long as no one killed anyone else. The whole night had been one upheaval after another.

"We're going to leave," Cal told her calmly once they were in the privacy of the little willow hut. His eyes were hard as flint in the dim light cast by the smoky torch he carried.

"How can we leave?"

"I'll find a way. You can't live like this." He grimaced. "I can't live like this. For years I've remembered being with the Apaches as the happiest time of my life, but now . . . Hell, Mac. This isn't the Apache life. This is . . . is . . ."

"I know," she said gently. Once she had hated Apaches just as most other whites in Arizona Territory hated them. But in the last few weeks, working with the Mahko, Bay, and Istee, meeting Bi-ya-neta and her fellow captives, and even riding with this band of desperate, murderous renegades, she had come to realize that there was much to admire about these wild people of the desert mountains. They had strength, resilience, intelligence, and a strict but peculiar sense of honor that she didn't pretend to understand. Sadly, though, as a people the Apaches were suffering the throes of an ugly death. It was painful even for Mackenzie to see, so she could imagine how Cal felt. These people were the companions of his childhood, his friends, his family. The world that had once been everything to him was dying violently, and he was forced to watch.

"Geronimo's lowered his guard," Cal told her. "He's decided to trust me, and he feels safe here in the mountains. There won't be sentries posted tonight. Everyone's too drunk except Mahko and Bay, and I have a feeling they'll want to go with us."

"You want to go tonight? So quickly?" Mackenzie asked breathlessly.

"We'll never get away if we wait until we reach the stronghold. Geronimo says he'll wait here another day to let the women finish roasting the mescal, but I don't trust him not to change his mind. We've got to leave tonight, Mac. It's tonight or never."

"What happens if we're caught?"

The only answer he gave was one raised brow. She got the message, successful or not, their escape would mean an end to life among the Apaches.

While Cal went to consult with Mahko and Bay, Mackenzie sat on her blankets and waited. She tried hard to believe that Cal was right, that the whole camp was dead drunk and no sentries would be posted. She didn't believe it, though. Since they had first met, luck had never favored them. Why should it change now?

The two White Mountain Apaches did want to go with them, Cal told her when he returned. They would wait a few hours yet. By then the few men still sitting around the fire drinking should be passed out and dead to the world.

"I'd just as soon get away without a fight," he said. "I don't want to kill my own people."

Mackenzie understood his feelings, but had her own reasons for avoiding a fight. She'd rather his people not kill them either.

"You're shivering," Cal said, lowering himself beside her on the blanket. "Are you cold?"

"Scared," she admitted.

"Mackenzie Butler scared," he said with a chuckle. "I'm glad to hear it, Mac. It makes me think you have some sense after all."

She cast him a doubtful look. "It's not so much the thought of getting killed. Everyone dies sooner or later. It's more . . . well . . ." She sighed. "I once saw a man and his family brought in after their wagon had been attacked by Victorio's warriors. They were on their way to California. They passed through Tombstone just a few months after Pa was killed, and I saw them in the mercantile. A day later their wagon was found. They'd been . . . been . . ."

Cal took her shoulder and turned her to face him. "Mac, even if we get caught leaving—which we won't—but even if we do, no Apache is going to touch you. I promise."

Her eyes questioned.

"I promise," he repeated. "No one will touch you but me."

She took a shuddering breath.

"Have you learned to trust me yet?"

"Yes," she said quietly. "You know I do."

"Then forget about what those poor people went through and try to get a few hours of sleep."

"I don't feel like sleeping." She reached out and touched his cheek. "I love you, California Smith. I'm glad we're together, even here."

He grinned. "I wish we were together somewhere else."

Mackenzie had to smile at his refusal to be serious—the granite-faced man whom she had prodded for weeks before he ever cracked a smile.

"If you really don't want to sleep," he offered, "I can think of another way to pass the time."

"In the middle of a camp full of Apaches?"

"That's what wickiups are for." He gently pushed her down on the blanket and propped himself above her. His closeness banished the chill of her fear. Safely caged in his arms, she could forget the menace that loomed outside the wickiup's brush walls. She had intended to ask him about Yahnozha, but now she decided to let the subject go. Too many things separated them already without bringing up one more issue to stand between them. Every moment left to them was too precious to tarnish.

"I love you, California Smith."

"And I love you, Mackenzie Butler." He took a kiss, his lips soft as a warm wind brushing against her mouth. "Let me show you how much."

19

The moon was dark as the four of them—Mackenzie, Cal, Istee, and Bay-chen-day-sen—led their horses away from the slumbering Apache camp. Squares of deerhide had been tied over the horses' hooves to muffle the sound of the animals' plodding, but the cautious measure was hardly necessary. The Apaches slept deeply and peacefully, their senses deadened by tequila.

Cal took the lead; Istee guarded their rear. Behind Cal, Mackenzie tried to be as calm as she imagined an Apache woman might be in this situation, but her heart pounded so loudly that she was sure the whole camp, drunk as they were, could hear it.

Mackenzie's heart thudded even more loudly when Cal signaled a halt, but she knew better than to break the silence by asking why they had stopped. Something was wrong; she could feel it in her bones. Out of the corner of her eye she saw Istee and Bay both reach for the rifles slung across their backs.

After a few silent moments of tension, a shadow detached itself from a clump of cedar and stood upright in their path. Istee and Bay both cocked their rifles, but Cal held up a hand to check their action. "Yahnozha," Cal greeted the shadow.

"Goshk'an."

Apaches did not call an individual by name unless a situation was very grave, Mackenzie knew, and the quiet greeting seemed to speak volumes more than just simple names. The tension between the two men fairly crackled through the silence. A shout from Cal's brother might only bring a few of Geronimo's men staggering out to witness the escape attempt, but it would undoubtedly bring a sufficient number to drag them back to face Geronimo's judgment.

Yahnozha did not shout, however. He spoke to Cal in a calm, cold voice that wavered only slightly with inebriation. Mackenzie slipped back toward Istee.

"What is he saying?" she whispered.

"He knew Goshk'an would leave. Goshk'an is no longer Apache, no longer has stomach for an Apache death. So Yahnozha say."

Cal answered in equal length in a voice just as composed.

"Goshk'an say he has more reason to live than die," Istee translated softly. "He tell Yahnozha that nothing ever stays the same. All things change. He change. Yahnozha change. The world change."

Yahnozha suddenly stepped forward and stared at Mackenzie. "You have a woman to live for," he said curtly in English. "She will breed you sons, white sons. More white men to trample the land."

Mackenzie wanted to retreat from his accusation, but she forced herself to stand her ground. Even in the darkness she could see the bitter gleam in the Apache's eyes.

"Why can the white man not live in his own land and

leave us in peace?" He addressed the question to Mackenzie, not Cal. "The white man is stupid. He has no honor. He kills the land with his tunnels and his cattle. The white man is worse than the Mexicans."

He looked back at Cal, glanced at the rifles ready in the hands of Istee and Bay, then turned his eyes once again to Mackenzie. Even in the darkness she could sense the sad resignation in his stance. "Goshk'an has yellow hair like the white man," he told her, "but he is my brother. Now he walks the white man's path, but I know he has honor because we were warriors together. He says to me that this red-haired woman has honor also."

The Apache stared at her for an unnerving length of time, then he spoke again. "My brother say I kill your father, white woman. I don't remember. I shoot so many white men, they all run together in my mind."

Mackenzie surprised herself by feeling only pity at this admission. What kind of existence must Yahnozha lead? What kind of devil ate at his heart to make him slaughter so many that the blood all ran together in one huge killing?

"I am sorry if I kill your father, red-hair, because you are my brother's wife. But now I give you your life in return for his."

His words carried a finality that somehow completed a circle in Mackenzie's soul. Six years ago Yahnozha had taken her life away as well as killing Frank Butler. Now he was giving it back.

"Go," he commanded.

Cal took Mackenzie's arm. Without a word to his brother, he turned and urged her down the valley toward freedom. She looked back to see Yahnozha standing atop a boulder watching them go. Silhouetted against the night sky, he seemed a very lonely figure.

"You didn't say good-bye," Mackenzie said to Cal.

"Yahnozha and I said good-bye a long time ago. The last

time I saw my brother was fourteen years ago, and I haven't really seen him since. The man who raided the Lazy B, the man who rides with Geronimo—that man is not the brother I grew up with."

Four tiring days later Mackenzie and Cal arrived at the Lazy B. Istee and Bay had traveled with them until midday the day before, then had gone their separate way toward the San Carlos Reservation. Mackenzie was sad to see them go. The two Apaches had become her friends—real people rather than just Indians. She offered them jobs on the Lazy B, saying she would intercede with both the local law and the San Carlos Indian agent. They politely refused; their wives awaited them on the reservation, and they were anxious to see if Mahko had made it back to San Carlos. Beneath their words she read that they'd had enough of the white man's world, and the renegades' world was no better.

"I suppose they're safer on the reservation," she'd commented regretfully once the two Apaches had left. "But it seems unfair."

Cal answered with a cynical smile. "Conquest is never fair. At least they'll probably live to have children and grandchildren who might see a better day." He left unsaid that many Apaches had chosen to die rather than live under the white man's rule. A way of life would die with them.

"Don't look so sad, Mac," Cal urged. "The Apaches are just as cruel to their enemies as the white men are to the Indians. More, maybe."

"So which are you?" she asked quietly. "White man or Indian?"

He shook his head. "Both, maybe. Neither. I don't know. But I'm not welcome in either world right now. Maybe the Mexicans can find some use for me." A ghost of a smile curved his life. "I've tried being an Apache, and I've tried being a white man, but I haven't tried being a Mexican yet. Maybe that'll work."

"You won't have to stay in Mexico forever," Mackenzie said defiantly. "I'm going to find a way to show Israel Potts that you didn't kill Tony—just as soon as I see Nathan Crosby slapped in jail for leaving me in the mountains to die."

Cal didn't answer. He thought she was whistling in the dark, but Mackenzie refused to believe that justice wouldn't win in the end. Fate meant for them to be together. She was sure of it. They'd been through too much to give up now.

George Keller and Sam Crawford were the first Lazy B hands to see them ride in. Two miles out from the ranch house both men greeted then with a loud hoopla.

"Well, glory be! We got out lookin' fer strays and look what we find!" Crawford's perpetual scowl didn't soften, but from the tone of his voice Mackenzie could have sworn he was actually glad to see them.

"You look like a damned Apache in that getup." Keller surveyed Cal's deerhide trousers and breechclout. "Course, you've always looked like a damned Injun. Cain't say but what I'd rather put up with you than some others I could name who're white men clear through to the bone, though."

Mackenzie didn't think she'd ever seen George Keller grin, but the lean, grizzled face split in a smile.

"You look a bit like an Injun yourself, Miz Butler," Crawford added. "Where you two been?"

"Crosby told us . . ." Keller began, but Mackenzie interrupted him.

"I can imagine what Crosby told you."

"Waall . . . He said you was dead from being snakebit."

"Yeah," Crawford added. "And that he liked ta got kilt by Smith and a bunch o' renegade Apaches. Said Smith'd gone native again and had sworn to get revenge on every white ranch in the valley. Figger we oughta warn ya, Smith. Potts says if you ever show your face around here it's gonna be lookin' outta one side of a noose."

"We'll just sec what Israel Potts has to say when I fill him in on his friend Nathan Crosby!" Mackenzie declared.

When the four of them rode under the Lazy B arch, Carmelita was leaning on the arena fence tossing scraps into the hog pen. The Mexican woman shrieked when she recognized Cal and Mackenzie. She continued shrieking, seeming unable to find a more articulate greeting. Lu appeared at the door of the ranch house, shotgun in hand, no doubt expecting to see raiding Apaches. She almost dropped the weapon in surprise.

"Mackenzie! Lord have mercy!" She rushed forward and practically pulled Mackenzie off her horse and into her embrace. "I don't believe it's you! Mackenzie . . ." She repeated the name again and again.

"And California Smith!" Lu released Mackenzie and stared at Cal. "You're supposed to be . . . My God! Look at you! Look at you both! If I didn't know who you were I'd think you were renegade Apaches who'd dyed your hair."

Carmelita stopped shrieking and ran to join the welcome. She gave Mackenzie a quick hug and Cal a long and very enthusiastic one. "I knew they would not catch you, Senor California. And I knew you would not let our little senora die."

"Carmelita," Lu snapped. "You're going to squeeze the very life out of the poor man. Release him." She turned back to her stepdaughter. "Nathan Crosby told everyone you were dead, Mackenzie. Where have you been? I can't believe you're here! And Cal! You get yourself in the house before someone sees you and decides to collect the reward that's on your head. Mercy! Listen to me babble! I just can't believe you're both here. You get in the house! Both of you. Mr. Crawford, please ride into town and tell Dr. Gilbert that I want to see him immediately. Not a word about these two being back, understand?"

"Nobody'll hear anything from me," he growled.

"Where is Frankie?" Mackenzie asked anxiously.

"She's in the tunnel, dear. She spends most of her time there since she heard . . . Well, she's been very upset. We all have. Carmelita will fetch her."

There was no need to fetch Frankie, for the next moment a miniature tornado tore down the hillside from the tunnel mouth and ran toward them as fast as her short legs would carry her. "Ma! Ma!" Frankie's high-pitched, joyful greeting preceded her.

"Frankie!" Mackenzie knelt and opened her arms. Frankie flew into her embrace.

"I knew you were alive! I told them, but nobody would believe me! I knew you would come back!"

Mackenzie buried her face in her daughter's bright hair. "We're both alive, Frankie."

"California!" Frankie cried. She bounced out of her mother's embrace and, still clinging tightly to Mackenzie's hand, wrapped one arm around Cal's deerskin-clad leg. "Issy's pa showed us a picture drawing of you! He said there's a reward for someone to find you." She wrinkled her nose. "It wasn't a very good picture."

Cal and Mackenzie exchanged a silent look of apprehension. Crosby and Potts hadn't wasted any time.

"Come on, now," Lu urged. "Everyone into the house. I want to hear what's happened to you two. Mackenzie, where on earth did you get that . . . interesting . . . clothing that you're wearing? Is that deerhide? I must say, it looks quite . . ."

The door of the ranch house closed behind them, and in the barn Gideon Small moved quickly to the tack room to fetch his saddle. Minutes later he rode quietly under the Lazy B arch, just as Sam Crawford had a quarter hour before. But Small, instead of turning south toward Tombstone as Crawford had, turned north—toward the road that led to the Bar Cross Ranch.

* * *

The evening that followed Mackenzie's return was a long one, full of explanations, revelations, and questions without answers. Right after supper was served, Amos Gilbert drove up in his one-horse buggy. After greetings were exchanged, they all sat together in the parlor. Even though the hour grew late, Frankie stayed awake on the parlor sofa, wrapped in her mother's arms and leaning comfortably against the soft pillow of her breasts. Mackenzie rested quietly against Cal's shoulder. Amos relaxed in Frank Butler's favorite armchair while Lu sat on a pillow at his feet and used his legs as a backrest.

"I've always thought that Nathan Crosby was a villain," Amos commented. "But I confess that this tale shocks me. I find it hard to believe that any man could stoop so low."

"He did come around a few days ago with an offer to buy the Lazy B," Lu revealed. "Of course, I wouldn't have sold it to him. He was quite understanding when I refused, though. Said I was still grieving and he'd be around in a week or so to discuss it."

"That bag of slime," Mackenzie said in disgust.

"Yes, well," Amos commented thoughtfully, "he has everyone believing that he's a hero right now, and I'm not so sure you'll be able to convince folks otherwise, Mackenzie."

"But . . . !"

"What's more, right now the valley's scared to death of Cal. The fellows who were on Nathan's posse have been spreading some pretty vivid tales about ambushes and poisoned springs and some other things that uncomfortably remind people of Apache tactics. That on top of Tony's murder . . ." He shook his head sadly. "I'd like to be able to say that Cal would get a fair hearing at a trial and Potts would be shown up for the idiot he is, but I'm not sure that would happen. I don't really think it's safe for you around here, Cal."

"I never thought it was," Cal replied. "I'm heading out for Mexico." He looked at Frankie snuggled in Mackenzie's arms. "Figured to leave as soon as Mac was safe, but I couldn't resist staying a few hours."

Amos regarded the three of them—the man who was supposedly the terror of the valley holding both mother and child in his arms. The doctor's mouth tightened to a line of regret. "A few hours together seems little enough to ask." He patted Lu's shoulders. "Maybe we should give these children some privacy, my love."

"Of course." Lu rose gracefully and took Amos's arm.

Amos turned halfway out the door to the court. "Cal, whatever we can do to help, you know we'll do it."

Cal nodded.

"Your stepmother and I have postponed our wedding until December, Mackenzie. Perhaps by then this mess will be straightened out and we can have our double wedding after all."

Mackenzie managed a weak smile. Everyone was spinning fantasies, but tomorrow when Cal left, all fantasy would come to an end.

"California! Are you going away again?" Frankie asked indignantly.

"Sorry, Frankie. I have to."

"Where are you going?"

"Mexico."

"When will you be back?"

"I can't say."

Frankie twisted in Mackenzie's arms to look reproachfully at her father. "You're not going off with the Indians again, are you? Issy's pa told me and Gran that you'd gone with the Indians and would never come back. Is Mexico where the Indians are?"

"There's Indians in Mexico, Frankie, but I'm not going to be with them again."

"You still look like an Indian," she insisted, as if his appearance made his words a lie.

Cal smiled. "Maybe it's time I looked more like a white man. What do you think, Frankie?" He untied the wide cloth of his Apache headband and pulled it from his head.

"You still look like an Indian," she declared.

"You know where your mother keeps her scissors?"

"Yes."

"Can you get them?"

Frankie looked dubiously at Mackenzie, who regarded Cal in surprise. "Can I get the scissors, Ma?"

"Carry the point away from you," Mackenzie instructed. She sent Cal a hesitant smile as Frankie scrambled down from her lap and headed out of the room. "I'm not sure I'd recognize you as a white man."

"I'm not sure I'll recognize myself," he said, a note of seriousness underlying the levity of his voice.

Frankie proudly carried the scissors from the desk in the office, point carefully directed at the floor. Feeling almost as if she were about to cut the biblical Samson's hair instead of Cal's, Mackenzie got a towel and a comb and set about to work.

Cal's hair was thick and wavy. Released from the weight of its length, the shortened strands curled around her fingers as if in caress. When she was done, Cal looked more different than could be accounted for by the shorn hair that now sprang from his head in thick waves. He looked younger, his eyes bluer, his whole face less stern. Perhaps he had truly shed his Apache identity along with his headband and hair. Life would be so much easier if he could shed the taint of his upbringing so easily.

Mackenzie put aside the scissors. "Done!" she announced, coming her fingers through the tawny waves. "Feel different?"

"You *look* different." Frankie measured the change in her father with serious green eyes. "Maybe now that you don't look like an Indian, you won't have to go to Mexico." She climbed onto the sofa beside him.

"I'm afraid I still have to go to Mexico."

Her lower lip shout out. "Can we go with you?"

"Not this time."

Frankie fixed him with a forlorn gaze. "I thought you were my pa. I thought you and Ma were getting married."

"I'll always be your pa, Frankie. Nothing will ever change that."

"Aren't you going to marry Ma?"

Mackenzie began a rebuke, but a quick shake of Cal's head stopped her. "It wouldn't be fair for me to marry your ma right now," he explained to Frankie.

"Why not?"

"Because—"

"Yes," Mackenzie interrupted, her brow puckered in a thoughtful frown. She looked Cal in the eye. "Why not?"

"You know why not," he said quietly.

"Because you're leaving? It doesn't matter how long you're gone, California Smith. You were gone for six long years and I never even looked at another man"—she smiled impishly—"even though I thought I hated you. I guess I'm just a one-man woman. I'm stuck with you."

"We don't know when we'll be together again," he objected.

Or *if* they would be together again, Mackenzie thought in silent pain.

"We'll be together again," she declared, holding his eyes with hers. "In my heart and soul I've been your wife since our first night together. Even when I thought I hated you, somehow I knew that we still belonged to each other. If that isn't being married, then what is?"

Frankie's eyes grew wide and excited. "Are you going to get married now?"

Cal gave Mackenzie a long look. "Do you know what you're getting into, Mac?"

Mackenzie smiled. "I do," she said, her words more than the answer to his question.

"Then come here." He took her hand and pulled her down beside him on the sofa. "Here, Frankie, hold my hand. You're part of this too."

Frankie giggled and squeezed between them. She appropriated one hand from each of them while they reached across her to interlock their fingers in a firm grip.

"This is for real," Mackenzie said quietly.

"This is for real," Cal agreed.

"I take you to be my husband," Mackenzie vowed. "No matter what comes tomorrow or all the days of the future, you will always have my love and my trust. What's mine is yours. My belongings, my body, my soul. Everything I am is yours."

Cal looked at her for a long time. His face was grave, but it wasn't the wooden Indian expression that Mackenzie had always hated. His eyes crinkled in a subtle smile, the line of his mouth was warm, and the rugged planes of his face softened in tenderness.

"You have been the wife of my heart since the first day I saw you," he told her. "It will always be so. My life and soul are yours. Without you, my world is empty."

"We are a family," Mackenzie vowed, squeezing Frankie's hand. "We will always be a family no matter how far apart we are."

They stayed on the sofa with hands joined for a long time. Finally, Frankie surrendered to a cavernous yawn.

"I think someone needs to go to bed," Cal said with a smile.

"I'm not tired," Frankie objected. "Really I'm not."

Cal carried his daughter to her room. She was asleep before he tucked her into bed.

"You're tired," Cal told Mackenzie when he returned to the parlor. "I'm surprised you haven't collapsed long before now."

"I'm not tired. Really I'm not," she echoed Frankie, but the denial ended in a yawn.

"I could carry you to bed too. Isn't that some sort of tradition on your wedding night?"

Mackenzie smiled. "Something like that."

Cal easily lifted her into his arms and strode toward the door. "You'll have to tell me where your bed is. I've never had the pleasure."

"Across the court. I'm surprised you don't remember," she chided gently. "You've been there with me in my mind almost every night."

Her bedroom was dark—even darker when Cal shut the door behind them with his foot. "I don't know if I remember how to make love on a bed," Cal said with a chuckle. "We've never been so civilized." He laid her gently on the feather mattress and sank down beside her.

"We'll manage, I think," she teased, unfastening the laces on his deerhide shirt.

Cal pulled the shirt over his head and tossed it aside, then took her hand and pressed it against his bare flesh. Crisp chest hair curled playfully around her spread fingers.

The finality of their situation flooded over Mackenzie in a rush of pain. "Every time we make love I think it's our last time," she whispered. "I wish this night could go on forever."

"Maybe it will." He kissed her gently. "Maybe there will never be a last time," he murmured. Again he kissed her, less gently this time. He nibbled and teased until her mouth opened under his. The taste of him sent a flush of erotic heat along her skin. "We don't know what lies in the future," he whispered against her ear. "Perhaps even death can't separate two people who love each other."

Mackenzie enjoyed the bunch and flow of hard masculine muscle under her hands as she caressed Cal's shoulders and back. Tomorrow was soon enough to face the harsh light of truth. For this last night she would enjoy the rapture of his possession without tarnishing their joy with reality. His kisses moved from her mouth to her eyes, then her throat. He lingered in the hollow of her neck, caressing with a warm tongue that drove all thoughts of the future from her mind.

Impatiently, she pressed herself against the hard thigh that lay between her legs.

"Not this time, Mac," Cal scolded gently. "Every time we come together you get me so heated up I take you like a damned rutting bull. Tonight we go slow. I'm going to have every inch of you. Every beautiful damned inch of you—if I have to tie you to the bed to keep you from making me lose control." He reached under her shirt to unbutton her trousers and slide them down over her slim hips. "I don't understand how you bore my child and still have the hips of a boy," he said with a chuckle.

He settled himself between her eagerly spread legs. The soft deerhide of his trousers, warmed by his flesh, wrenched a gasp of ecstatic anticipation from her throat as it settled against her soft, swollen flesh.

"That's right." Supporting most of his weight on his elbows, he stretched full length on top of her. "You get nice and warm and wet for me, Mac. This time I'm in control, and I'm not going to end it until we've both had a good long time to enjoy ourselves."

"Oh, you're cruel!" she accused, but her voice broke into laughter. "I'll make you sorry."

He rolled off her and at the same time pushed her shirt slowly up, baptizing each piece of newly exposed skin with a wet kiss from his tongue.

"Oh, that tickles! That . . . Oh, my. Don't stop. Please don't stop." Her plea ended in a sigh.

His tongue reached her nipples and laved them both in turn. Swirls of pleasure circled outward from each place his mouth touched. When she thought she would burst from desire, his hand smoothed its way over her belly and curled into the red-gold triangle between her legs. His fingers worked a wicked magic on her swollen, needful flesh that almost robbed her of the ability to breathe.

"Oh, Cal, please. You *are* cruel!"

He chuckled. "We Apaches are good at torture."

With a great effort of will, she pulled herself away from him. Breathing hard, she regarded him with green fire striking sparks in her eyes. "We'll just see who has the most endurance in this kind of torture, California Smith."

He reached for her. She scooted away, then surprised him by leaping forward and pressing his shoulders down on the mattress. "We'll find out how much you like a dose of your own medicine." She laughed softly. "Let's see, now. Where should I start?"

"Mackenzie . . ." he cautioned.

"I always wondered what it would feel like . . ." She pressed her mouth to his taut, masculine nipple and teased lightly with her tongue. Cal gasped, but she had scarcely started. His fingers dug into her shoulders as her tongue swirled, tickled, and teased its way down his chest to his navel, circling temptingly. She let her mouth dip lower, pressing against the soft deerhide laces that strained tautly over his swollen sex.

"Mackenzie!"

"Hmmm?" Her fingers slowly, tantalizingly unfastened the laces. Finally her lips touched swollen masculine flesh, wrenching a tortured groan deep from his chest. "Had enough?" she whispered, her breath quivering against his engorged sex. She looked up, one delicate brow arched wickedly. Her bare breast brushed softly against his groin, as if by coincidence.

"You little she-wolf," he rasped. "You have to have your way, don't you? Come back up here."

"I like it down here."

He took her shoulders, bodily lifted her up, and then tucked her beneath him as easily as if she were a feather pillow. "I'll show you where you like it." Every muscle in his body taut with need, he thrust inside her. She gasped with delight. "Is that what you wanted?" he growled against her throat.

"Yes. That's exactly what I wanted." She wrapped her legs around his lean hips and urged him even deeper. Teasing was forgotten as they both were consumed by the searing drive to fulfillment. Lost in passionate tempo of their mating, Mackenzie's world shrank to herself and the man joined with her. Her heart beat and her body breathed to the primitive rhythm of his loving. She was one with him, an extension of his desire, and he the fulfillment of hers. Together they burned, devoured by a fire that flared, ebbed, flared, each time hotter, brighter, higher until it exploded in an eruption of joy. Still swirling in the hot ashes of her own release, Mackenzie felt the powerful pulsing of Cal's climax. In that moment they seemed truly one, inseparable, joined forever in both spirit and body.

Perhaps that was the gift of love. Separation was only an illusion. A man and a woman truly in love were part of each other even hundreds of miles apart.

"Mac?" Cal's voice was hoarse, his breathing still rapid. "Mac, are you all right?"

Mackenzie released a long sigh of contentment. "I'm . . . wonderful."

"You are that."

She smiled—and prayed that the night would last forever. They had a lifetime of loving to crowd into a few hours of darkness.

* * *

The night was still dark when Mackenzie awoke. She had tried not to fall asleep; they both had tried. Through midnight and the hours when night rolled toward the dawn, they had talked, loved, talked, and loved again, by tacit agreement never mentioning the day to come or any of the days that would follow. They had no time for uncertainties. Nothing was so important that it couldn't be faced tomorrow.

But tomorrow came early. Mackenzie woke to a feeling of change. The hard masculine body she snuggled against was just as warm, and the September breeze that slipped past the shutters just as soft. The chill in the room had nothing to do with temperature.

Even before she heard the ominous drum of hoofbeats, the tension in Cal's body told her something was wrong. "Who . . . ?" She rose on one elbow and tried to see Cal's face in the dark. "Oh, Cal!"

His arm squeezed gently, but he didn't answer.

"I should have known this would happen. I never should have let you stay."

"I doubt you could have driven me away last night."

Mackenzie knew with sad certainty who visited them in the predawn darkness. Cal pulled on his trousers and reached for the shotgun that was propped in the corner.

"You can still get away," Mackenzie urged. "It's dark, and no one can sneak around in the dark like you can."

"Maybe. You stay here in this room."

"I will not."

A pounding shook the front door.

"Go out the pantry door and sneak across the yard to the kitchen. From there the guest house and smokehouse will block anybody's view of you making off for the foothills." Mackenzie grabbed a dressing gown out of her wardrobe, wrapped it around her, and followed Cal into the court. Two steps out of the room they both stopped. Frankie toddled sleepily along the brick pathway.

"The noise woke me up," she told them with a mighty yawn.

"Mackenzie!" came Israel Potts's voice from the yard. "You've got a fugitive in there. Turn him over or you'll be in a heap of trouble, girl."

Somewhere close by a warning shot echoed through the night. Cal sighed and set down his shotgun. "They'll shoot up this whole place trying to get me," he told Mackenzie. Frankie had tottered against his leg and now leaned there, half asleep. "It's not worth it, Mac." He rested a hand on Frankie's bright head and ruffled her hair. "It's just not worth it."

20

The sunlight in Tombstone seemed to be lacking in both brightness and warmth when Mackenzie pulled her wagon up to Nellie Cashman's American Hotel. Perhaps autumn was gaining ground on summer, or perhaps the pall was one of the heart. Mackenzie had felt nothing but emptiness since the predawn hour when Cal had been taken away, captured without firing a shot or swinging a fist in his own defense. Lu had wrung her hands, Amos had argued with Potts and Crosby, and Frankie had wept. Mackenzie had simply looked on in numb misery. If they hadn't all been in harm's way, Cal might have fought his way to freedom. He'd done it before, but he wasn't willing to risk the lives of those gathered around him.

Mackenzie cursed Nathan Crosby for a villain and Israel Potts for being in his back pocket. Crosby had paid one of her hands to spy, she had discovered. No one had seen Gideon Small ride out on his mission, but Skillet Mahoney and Bull Ferguson had seen him ride back in well after dark. With a little brutal persuasion by Bull, Gid admitted that Crosby had paid him to keep watch and report what he saw. Nathan hadn't thought Mackenzie would return, Gid told them, but the old man had hoped that Cal might come back for his daughter. Mackenzie had fired the traitor on the spot, but it had given her very little satisfaction. Getting her hands on Nathan Crosby might give her more.

"I'll tell Nellie that we'll be here for a few days," Lu said as she climbed down from the wagon. She lifted Frankie down as well. "I imagine you'll want to see Cal."

"Yes." Mackenzie motioned to Sam Crawford. "Will you take the wagon and team to the livery, Mr. Crawford?" While Mackenzie had been gone, Lu had appointed Sam foreman. He and most of the other hands had come along to show their support for Cal. The man they'd once hated was a hero in their eyes now that he'd run afoul of the law. "And keep the men out of trouble, please."

"They'll behave, Miz Butler."

When Mackenzie walked into the jailhouse, the town marshal was dozing with his feet up on his desk. "Marshal Creel?"

"What . . . huh?" The feet came down onto the plank floor with a thunk.

"Where is Deputy Sheriff Potts?"

"Oh . . . uh . . . Miz Butler. Israel said you'd probably be by. He's . . . uh . . . having' lunch."

"I'd appreciate it if you would go tell him I want to see him."

"Well . . ."

Her jaw squared ominously. "I'm not leaving until I see Israel, Marshal. So unless you want my company all afternoon, you'll go get him."

"Heck, Miz Butler. I can't very well leave you alone with Smith."

"What do you think I'm going to do? Break him out of jail in broad daylight? You want to handcuff me to the desk while you're gone?" She offered her wrist. "Or maybe you'd like me to come with you to fetch Israel."

"Now, Miz Butler . . . I don't think that'd be real proper."

So Israel was off drinking somewhere a decent woman shouldn't be seen. "I'm not leaving until I talk to Israel."

"Well . . . I suppose it'd be all right. I won't be gone but a minute." Creel ostentatiously took the jail keys from their peg on the wall and hooked them onto his belt. Then he locked the gun cabinet. "I'll be back in afore you can say boo," he warned.

"Boo!" Mackenzie said contemptuously as the door shut behind him.

When Mackenzie walked into the cell room, Cal had the old wooden Indian look on his face. He was gazing out the little barred window onto the street. The image that flashed into Mackenzie's mind was that of a caged wolf. He concentrated so on the outside world that he didn't even hear her come into the room, or so it appeared, but before she could greet him he spoke. "Mackenzie," he said without turning from the window.

"Cal." Mackenzie wrinkled her nose at the smell of the place. The adobe walls of the cells were stained with marks from prisoners who'd chosen not to use the slop jars. The thin mattresses on the cots looked as though they would momentarily be carted off by vermin. The cell bars were coated with dirt from the hundreds of hands that had grasped the cold, unyielding iron.

"You should have stayed away, Mac. They'll judge you guilty as they judge me—just by association."

"No one's going to judge you guilty," she declared. "After I talk to that idiot Israel I'm going to hire you the best lawyer I can find—that's if Israel still thinks you're worth holding after I tell him about Nathan Crosby."

Cal merely shook his head.

"California Smith!" she said in an annoyed voice. "I can't believe that you'd just buckle under to these villains! You've got to have some faith."

He turned away from the window. "You know damn well the white world has judged me guilty since I rode out of Cochise's stronghold as a kid. They never care guilty of what—just guilty. You think they're going to believe I'm innocent of killing Herrera?"

"There *are* people in this town who respect you." She gripped the bars of his cell as if she were the prisoner, not he. "And there *are* whites who are fair. My father was a fair man. Amos Gilbert is, too. Judge Pinney has a reputation as an honest judge. He won't convict you on the pittance of evidence that—"

"Mackenzie . . ." Cal put his hands over hers on the bars. One brow arched in gentle mockery. "I thought you didn't believe in magic any more. Isn't that what you told me?"

She smiled. "I'm willing to give magic one more chance. Or good luck, or miracles, or whatever it might take. How about you?"

"Well, now." Israel's voice intruded from the door of the cell room. "This is real sweet, Mackenzie, but I told Creel that the prisoner didn't get no visitors unless I gave my permission, and I don't recall saying that you could chat with him. You can't just bully your way in here and—"

"I have a thing or two to say to you, Israel."

"Well, now, I'm sure you do. But I'll ask you to do your talking in the other room. Smith here ain't gettin' another chance to light out on me. No, ma'am! And women who think they're in love don't have the sense God gave a chipmunk."

"All right, Israel, let's go in the other room and talk." Mackenzie squeezed Cal's hand and flashed him a grin. "Get ready for company in the next cell, Cal."

Israel hobbled out of the cell room after Mackenzie and closed the door with a bang. He limped over to his desk, sat down heavily in his chair, and waved his crutch in the air like an angrily pointing finger. "Well, now, what did you think was so all-fired important to send you in here bullyin' Marshal Creel into leavin' a prisoner unattended and draggin' me from my lunch?"

"Attempted murder. That's what."

Israel's brows shot up. "The only murder I know about wasn't attempted, it was real. And that fella in there"—he pointed to the door of the cell room with his crutch—"is likely the one who did it."

"I'm talking about Nathan Crosby trying to kill me in the Dragoons Mountains."

"What are you talkin' about, gal?"

"He left me to die, Israel. I was snakebit and he just left. He even bragged about how easily he would convince Lu to sell the Lazy B once I was dead."

Israel stared at her for a moment as if she'd gone mad, then his round face softened into bemused condescension. "Well, now, Mackenzie, I can understand how you'd be a little confused. Snakebite no doubt sent you right outta your head for a while. In fact, I'm amazed that you made it back. You've probably got some story to tell about that."

"Cal found me and stayed with me while I was sick. He was about to bring me home when we were taken by Geronimo and a band of his raiders."

"Now, that *is* interestin'. Nathan told me Smith had taken up with the Apaches again."

"It wasn't like that at all! Cal didn't 'take up' with them. We had no choice but to go along with the Apaches until we could escape. And Geronimo's men certainly never attacked Crosby. If they had, he'd be dead."

"Well, now—"

Mackenzie propped her fists on her hips indignantly.

"Nathan Crosby left me to die out there, Israel! Don't you think that constitutes attempted murder?"

"Well, now, I think maybe you're a bit confused, Mackenzie girl. Nathan told us you were snakebit. Says he kilt the snake and was about to tend to the bite when Smith attacked your camp. Nathan took after him, and Smith led such a chase through that rough country that he got turned around and couldn't get back to the ravine where you'd camped. So he came back here to get a search party to find you."

"That's a lie."

"I can see where you might think he up and deserted you out there, seein' as he didn't come back, but his intentions were good. I was on the search party myself, girl. Nathan was real concerned about you. We found the place where you camped, sure enough, but you was gone, and there was Indian sign. Figured if you didn't die of the snakebite you was killed by Indians. Nathan was real upset. He was mighty glad when he told me you were alive and back at the Lazy B."

"I'll just bet he was! Israel, nothing happened like he said it did. Crosby—"

"Now, Mackenzie. Calm down. When you're snakebit you can imagine just about anything. And besides, you sneakin' back here with a fugitive don't exactly give me a lot of faith in your objectivity. Not that I'm accusin' you of anything, but you can't tell me that you was fixin' to come into town and tell us that a wanted man was out at your ranch. Can you?"

"You're going to let Crosby get away with this?"

"I cain't see that he's done much of anything wrong. I know you think he did, but I cain't throw a man in jail because of what a sick woman imagined."

"You threw California Smith in jail because of some story Crosby cooked up."

Israel harrumphed indignantly. "Now you *are* stretchin'

the truth. That's different. You oughta be grateful this happened before you married the man, Mackenzie. There's one part of California Smith that's pure vicious Apache, and those devils don't balk at worse things than shootin' a man in cold blood. I'd hate to see you hitched to a man like that."

The effort was hopeless, Mackenzie realized. Talking to Israel was as effective as talking to a wall. She fixed him with eyes of glacial green. "When's the trial?"

"Judge Pinney set the date for next Wednesday."

Without a word she turned on heel and stalked out of the office. The door shut behind her with a slam that rattled the glass of the gun cabinet and almost lifted Israel out of his chair. The deputy sheriff shook his head with a sigh, pulled a handkerchief out of his pocket, and mopped at the beads of sweat on his brow.

Mackenzie had only a week and a day to find an attorney for Cal and help him prepare a defense—if defense was possible against prejudice that made guilt certain without conclusive evidence. She had told Cal she was willing to give magic one more chance, and for the first time in her life she wished desperately that magic and miracles really did exist. Mackenzie was going to need both if she wanted to keep the gallows in the courthouse yard from claiming Cal as a victim.

She spent the next day searching for a lawyer. Tombstone had plenty of them, almost all with their offices on Fourth Street around the corner from the county courthouse. None satisfied her. Most whom she talked to were not willing to take the case. The local newspapers—*The Nugget* and *The Epitaph*—had sensationalized Cal's story so that everyone had already decided his guilt. Few lawyers wanted to take on a case they already considered lost. Two were willing, but their idea of a successful defense was to try for a prison sentence instead of a hanging.

At the end of a discouraging day, Mackenzie didn't tell Cal of her failure, but he guessed anyway. His resigned acceptance of the situation only made Mackenzie more determined to succeed. Cal had already accepted that the verdict would be guilty, but Mackenzie wasn't willing to give up.

The next day she bought a stage ticket to Tucson—a seventeen-hour ride. The stage left at eight in the morning. While waiting at the depot, Mackenzie heard hammering in the courthouse yard. The gallows were being repaired—brought up to snuff for the anticipated hanging next week. The sound sent a chill of hopelessness up Mackenzie's spine.

On her first day in Tucson, Mackenzie was no more successful than she'd been in Tombstone. The few lawyers who were willing to take the case seemed more interested in the fee than the outcome. But on her second day in town she found an attorney fresh from New York City. In Arizona just a month, Walter Corby was full of liberal ideas, anxious to obtain justice for the victims of society's wrongs. Unlike Arizonans who had been in the territory longer, he considered Apaches the victims of an intrusive and rampaging civilization. Since California Smith was being persecuted because of his association with the "poor displaced inhabitants of this land," Mr. Corby was anxious to defend him. Mr. Corby was not only liberal; he was young, ingenuous, and inexperienced. But he was the best Mackenzie could find.

On the day of Cal's trial, Mackenzie arrived at the courthouse early enough to get a front-row seat. She wanted Cal to see her sitting there and feel her support. Frankie sat beside her, bright gold hair subdued into neat braids, impish face sober and big-eyed. Next in line on the bench were Lu and Amos. Amos's show of support for Cal would cost him patients, Mackenzie knew. She was moved that he thought the gesture worth whatever it might cost. Lu sat straight-backed and aristocratic, looking about the room with an expression that made clear she thought the proceedings a travesty. Beside Lu sat Nellie Cashman.

Cal had a few other supporters in the courtroom as well. Carmelita and her parents, three sisters, and one brother sat in the bench behind Mackenzie and voiced their opinion to everyone sitting around them that California Smith would have never chosen such a cowardly way to kill a man. In the very back of the courtroom were the Lazy B hands, squirming uncomfortably from being in a court of law, even though they were in the audience and not standing before the judge.

From what Mackenzie could hear of the conversations going on around her, she concluded that everyone else in the room was looking forward to a hanging. The buzz of voices in the courtroom was both eager and angry. When Cal walked into the room escorted by Marshal Creel and Israel Potts, the buzz changed to a murmur of surprise. With headband and shoulder-length hair gone, Cal didn't look the least bit like a murdering Apache—one of the descriptions an *Epitaph* reporter had used in an article earlier in the week. For the trial even his moccasins were gone, and in the place of his usual silent tread came the heavy step of white men's hard-soled boots.

The opening hours of the trial did not go well. Mackenzie's hope dimmed as she listened to Nathan Crosby describe Cal's retrieval of Frankie and fight with Tony. His version wasn't quite the truth, but it was close enough to be difficult for Walter Corby to refute. Crosby also told of finding the little leather Apache medicine bag in a copse of brush a hundred or so feet down the gully from Tony's body when he had examined the scene of the murder with Israel Potts. The prosecutor held up the bag for the judge's inspection as Crosby identified it as the same one he'd often seen hanging from a leather thong around California Smith's neck.

More witnesses testified to the history of animosity between California Smith and Tony Herrera. Israel Potts described their confrontation at the Fourth of July picnic, two Bar Cross hands told how Cal had gotten the drop on Tony during the roundup, and Jeff Morgan related how the two men had almost come to blows in the Crystal Place the night Tony was murdered. Haltingly, as if the story still gave him pain, Morgan described the ride home that night.

"What time was it when Mr. Herrera met his fate?" asked Mr. Daniel Peele, the prosecutor.

"A little after midnight, I'd guess. We stayed in town pretty late."

"Did you see or hear anyone else in the area?"

"No, sir."

"From your experience in this valley, would you have expected anyone else to be on or near that road at that time of night? Other cowboys? Maybe a saddle bum? Indians even?"

"No, sir. Most of the boys I know, at least the Bar Cross boys and the fellas from the Lazy B—they was still in town when we left. Indians don't much like to roam around at night, and any saddle bum out in that country at night would be outta his mind."

"Why were you out at night, then?"

"Tony was pretty drunk. I figured if I didn't get him started back to the ranch then, we'd never get there, and if we wasn't back at the ranch the next morning Mr. Crosby'd have our skins. Besides, I know that road so well I could ride it blindfolded."

"So you think whoever fired that shot was from around here? Someone who knew you would be traveling that road? Someone who rode out into the dark to deliberately lay an ambush?"

"Yessir. Most likely."

"Someone who went to all that trouble would have to dislike Tony Herrera quite intensely."

"Yessir."

"As Mr. Smith had demonstrated unmistakably."

"Did you see where the rifle shot that killed Mr. Herrera came from?" the prosecutor asked.

Morgan hesitated. He looked uneasy, Mackenzie thought. "No, sir. I didn't see. Seemed like it came from nowhere."

"And Mr. Herrera was killed instantly, without a chance to defend himself?"

"I guess you could say that. His horse spooked and stumbled down into a gully with Tony on its back. By the time I climbed down, Tony was good and dead."

"And where was he shot?"

"Uh . . . the bullet hole was in his head, between the eyes."

"An excellent shot, wouldn't you say?"

"Well . . . yeah."

Mr. Peele held up the medicine bag. "Do you recognize this?"

"Yessir."

"What is it?"

"It's an Apache medicine bag."

"Have you seen this one before?"

Morgan hesitated. "Mr. Crosby found it down the gully from Tony's body. I was there when he found it."

"Had you seen it before then?"

Again Jeff hesitated. His mouth worked uneasily. "Most Apaches wear a bag like that one."

Peele gave him a stern look. "Have you observed California Smith to wear this bag or one like it?"

"Yessir."

"Thank you, Mr. Morgan. Please stay in the courtroom in case I have further questions."

Morgan glanced at Mackenzie as he stepped down from the witness chair, but his eyes quickly darted away. Mackenzie watched him thoughtfully as he walked back to his seat. Jeff Morgan wasn't acting like himself. She'd never known him to be so uncertain in his speech and opinions, and never in their long acquaintance had he hesitated to meet her eyes, even after his huffy departure from the Lazy B.

She hadn't much time to think on the strangeness of Morgan's behavior, though, for Mr. Peele spent the rest of the morning calling witnesses—mostly townspeople who had been at the Fourth of July picnic—who testified to Cal's lethal accuracy with a rifle. Amos Gilbert testified to the nature of Herrera's injury. Israel Potts and Marshal Creel both confirmed that in their time enforcing the law in the San Pedro Valley, they didn't know of anyone who could match Cal with a rifle. Israel was also called upon to describe Cal's escape with the law attempted to bring him in for questioning, and Nathan Crosby recounted the sad adventures of the posse who had followed Cal into the Dragoons. He tried to imply that even Mackenzie's confrontation with the snake was Cal's doing.

When Nathan finished and left the stand, the prosecutor appealed to Judge Pinney. "Are these the actions of an innocent man? Escape from the duly appointed representative of the law? Attacks upon the brave, law-abiding men who attempted to bring him to justice?" He wrapped up with an elaborate account of Cal's background with the devil Apaches, concluding with a statement that Cal could hardly be blamed for being a mankiller when his temper was roused, considering his savage upbringing. "But is it fair to the citizens of this territory to leave such a man free? One can pity the baseness of a poisonous snake or a lethal scorpion. One can understand why nature made them dangerous. But the wise person kills such deadly creatures before they can do harm. Your Honor, I suggest that such a course might be the only solution here."

At the conclusion of the prosecution's presentation, court was recessed until the afternoon. Marshal Creel hurried Cal out of the courtroom before Mackenzie had time to say any words of encouragement.

"Tom just wants to make sure we don't have no trouble in the courtroom," Potts told Mackenzie. "Some of these people are pretty anxious to see California Smith get his due."

"They want a lynching, you mean," she accused.

"There's not gonna be no lynchin'," Israel assured her. He didn't have to add that there would be no need for a lynching. Judge Pinney would likely make hanging California Smith a matter of legal sanction.

"I trust you don't object to me visiting Cal over the noon recess."

"Cain't see why I should," Israel conceded with a generous air. "You might as well start saying your good-byes, Mackenzie girl."

Walter Corby was with Cal in his cell when Mackenzie arrived at the jailhouse, but Creel insisted that Mackenzie stay where bars separated her from the prisoner. "Ain't proper, you being in there with him," the marshal declared.

"At least give us some privacy," Mackenzie snapped.

Creel shrugged and left.

"I'll be going as well," Corby offered.

"No," Mackenzie said. "Please stay, Mr. Corby. How do you think it's going?"

"Well . . ." Corby hesitated. "Everything they've presented is circumstantial, you understand. The bag being found near the body is fairly damning, even though they can't prove positively that it belongs to Cal. And the public sentiment . . . I'd hate to think the law is influenced by emotion, but in this case, we can't be sure that it won't be."

Cal snorted. "We can be sure that it will be."

Corby shook his head sadly. "I have always been aware that the citizens of this territory hold the Indians in very low regard, but I'm surprised by the vehemence of antipathy and how these people let it color their reason."

"I'd like to testify," Mackenzie said.

Corby frowned. "I wouldn't recommend that, Miss Butler.

As a woman, you are too easily discredited, and your affection for Mrs. Smith is well known. The judge isn't likely to give much credence to anything you say."

"How about what Crosby did to me in the mountains—and what he said?"

"Mr. Crosby's story about what happened in the Dragoons seems to be generally believed. Besides which, even if you could discredit Mr. Crosby, that would have little to do with Mr. Smith's guilt or innocence. I'm afraid you would be subjecting yourself to an unpleasant experience for nothing."

Cal sent a stern scowl Mackenzie's way. "I want you to stay out of this, Mac."

"What do you mean, stay out of it?"

"If you won't think of yourself," he snapped, "then think of Frankie."

They exchanged glares for a moment, then Mackenzie's face crumpled. She took hold of the cell bar, and Cal covered her hands with his.

"Aren't you going to do anything to show that what Crosby is telling is a pack of lies?" she asked the lawyer in a trembling voice.

Corby's face flushed. He refused to meet her eyes. "I have several witnesses who will testify in Mr. Smith's favor this afternoon. We shouldn't lose hope."

Cal had lost hope days ago, Mackenzie knew. Corby was losing hope as well. Was she the only one who refused to buckle under to this injustice? She wouldn't let Cal hang; even if she had to organize a jailbreak, she wouldn't let him hang.

The afternoon was disheartening, even though Mackenzie was moved by the people who were willing to speak on Cal's behalf, and she could tell that Cal was surprised by the number of them. Ted Greene testified that Cal had fought Tony to defend his daughter. He also related how Tony and two other Lazy B hands had jumped Cal the night of the Fourth of July. "Smith's a man I wouldn't mind inviting into my home for supper. Hell, I'd trust him alone with my womenfolk and children. He's a good man. Out here, every once in a while a man has to fight. Herrera had it in for Cal Smith. There's no doubt about it. But I never did hear about Cal starting any of the trouble between 'em."

Others testified as well. Two saloonkeepers told the court that Cal more often prevented fights than started them. He'd been picked on and taunted more than once and usually handled the situation with glacial calm. Gus Bigley expressed his opinion that California Smith was a man of good character who had always been honest in his dealings at Bigley's gunshop. Amos Gilbert also stood behind Cal's character. But when Cal himself finally took the stand to protest his innocence, his lack of an alibi became painfully obvious.

"Do you know of anyone else in this valley who might have been able to make such a rifle shot?" Mr. Peele asked him.

Cal stated calmly, "I don't think I could have made that shot. Not in the dark. Not from a distance where Morgan wouldn't have been able to see where the shot came from."

"Well, Mr. Smith. Someone obviously did make that shot, didn't he?"

"So I'm told."

Peele met Cal's level gaze, smiled, and lifted the medicine bag as a killing blow. "Do you recognize this, Mr. Smith?"

"Hard to say."

"Feel free to examine it." He handed Cal the bag.

Cal opened the pouch and looked inside. "It's the medicine bag my father gave me when I left the Apaches with General Howard."

"It *is* yours, then?"

"Yes."

At the defense table, Walter Corby's face darkened.

"When did you last have it?"

"I don't remember. I noticed it was gone several weeks before Tony was killed."

"You don't know where you lost it?"

"No."

Peele's expression plainly conveyed his disbelief.

The judge's face was impassive. "Are you through, Mr. Peele?"

"No more questions." The prosecutor smiled in satisfaction and sat down.

"Court recessed until ten o'clock tomorrow morning."

Walter Corby looked discouraged. Cal's face remained impassive as he walked out in the custody of Marshal Creel. He didn't look at Mackenzie, though she suspected he was well aware of her eyes upon him. The crowd, all abuzz with their own opinions, filed out of the courtroom. Mackenzie sat where she was, staring dolefully into space and wondering if the Lazy B ranch hands were competent enough badmen to break Cal out of jail.

The weight of someone's eyes gradually distracted Mackenzie from her criminal musings. She looked up. A number of people still sat on the courtroom benches or stood in the aisle talking. A few curious glances darted her way, but it was Jeff Morgan's gaze that rested on her like a suffocating mantle. Their eyes met for only an instant before he looked away.

Morgan didn't look at her again. In fact, he seemed anxious to avoid her eyes. As quickly as he could, he left the room. She should ask Walter Corby to talk to Jeff, Mackenzie thought. Maybe her ex-foreman was the chink in the wall that might start the prosecution's case crumbling. If she could convince Corby . . . Mackenzie suddenly realized that once again her life was turning on other people's decisions. Why couldn't *she* get whatever needed to be gotten from Jeff Morgan?

Lu and Amos were a few feet away, talking to Ted

Greene. Mackenzie touched Lu's arm. "Would you take Frankie back to the hotel? There's something I have to do."

"Of course." Lu regarded her suspiciously. "Stay out of trouble, dear."

Mackenzie merely smiled.

Jeff Morgan was standing on the courthouse steps talking to Nathan Crosby. Mackenzie waited until they parted. Nathan headed for the Cosmopolitan Hotel. Jeff Morgan turned up the street and toward the Can-Can Restaurant. Mackenzie followed. When he changed direction toward the OK Livery, she changed direction with him. Finally, he stopped and waited for her.

"Mackenzie, what are you doing?"

"Following you."

"So I figured. What do you want?"

She put her hands on her hips and squared her jaw. "I want to know about Tony's death."

Morgan's mouth twitched. "I've told the whole town about Tony's death."

"Why didn't it sound like the truth to me?"

"Maybe because you've already made up your mind that the truth is what *you* want it to be, not what it is." He turned his back and walked off, as if that were the end of the conversation. She followed, hurrying to keep up with his long-legged stride.

"Jeff, I *know* California Smith didn't kill Tony."

"I didn't exactly say he did, did I? I guess that's up to the judge to decide."

"Why were you so nervous when you told the story of what happened?"

"Any man would be nervous when those fancy lawyers and judges get hold of him. Hell, God himself would be nervous." He turned up Allen Street.

"Where are you going?"

"To the Bloody Bucket to get a drink. Want to come?" he

asked sarcastically. "If you don't, then leave me alone, Mac."

She certainly didn't want to go to the Bloody Bucket, but she refused to let him go. Morgan crooked a brow in surprise as she followed.

All eyes in the saloon turned Mackenzie's way when she trailed Jeff into the bar. The place smelled of liquor, stale food, musky perfume, tobacco smoke, and sweat. Mackenzie steeled her senses and forged ahead. "Please, Jeff. Can we talk?"

The barkeeper scowled disapprovingly as Jeff sat down at a table and Mackenzie gingerly sat opposite him. He rounded the bar and started in their direction, but Jeff motioned him back.

"Mackenzie, I don't want to talk. I'm all talked out for today. Do yourself a favor and get outta here. This isn't a place for a decent woman."

"You know something about Tony's death that you're not saying."

He sighed impatiently.

"Jeff, you're not the sort of man who should be working for Nathan Crosby."

"What the hell do *you* know about what sort of man I am?"

"We've been friends for seven years."

"Friends? I worked for your daddy, and I worked for you. You don't know jackshit about me, Mackenzie."

His harsh tone and rough language took her back for a moment. They'd had plenty of differences, Jeff Morgan and she, but even when angry he'd never used such a voice. "Jeff," she finally said, "you're too good a man to be under Crosby's thumb. I know that Crosby put you up to something you're not comfortable with."

Morgan shook his head in denial. "You've got Nathan figured wrong. He's okay. Believe it or not, Mac, he's got your best interests at heart. Course, he's got his own interests in mind as well, but he's also doin' what's best for you."

"Then why did he try to kill me in the Dragoons?" Mackenzie asked with quiet conviction.

Jeff gave her a skeptical look. "You think he left you out there on purpose?"

"I know he did, Jeff. He told me so. He bragged about how easy it would be to buy the Lazy B from Lu once I was dead."

"Mackenzie, you were sick, imagining things . . ."

"I wasn't out of my head. I remember everything very clearly."

He snorted.

"Have I ever told you a lie, Jeff? In all the years you've known me, have I ever been false with you? Do you really think I would be so low to accuse Crosby of this if he hadn't done it?"

Morgan stared down at the table.

"Think about the other things Nathan's done to get the best of me, Jeff. He took Frankie—"

"He wouldn't have hurt her."

"You know better than that."

Silence.

"He's killed my cattle, almost ruined the springs, and changed so many brands to the RA that if I had believed his handiwork I'd be practically bankrupt. His men shot at me that day they drove the Bar Cross cattle onto my land, and they all but came right out and told me the next shot wouldn't miss."

Morgan still stared at the table, his mouth a tight line.

"Did Nathan kill Tony?"

Silence.

"Did he, Jeff? Tell me, dammit!"

"No." The tension in Morgan's posture broke. His shoulders slumped. "Hell no. Crosby didn't kill Tony. Tony killed

Tony." In rapid sentences he recounted the story of Tony's drunkenness, his horse shying into the ravine. Morgan had taken the body back to the Bar Cross, where Nathan had cursed and then laughed. The old man told Jeff that they were goin to get rid of that no-good yellow-haired Apache once and for all. The Lazy B would be without a foreman and Mackenzie without a sweetheart. On Crosby's orders, Jeff had retraced his steps over the dark road to show his boss where the accident had occurred. Nathan had propped Tony up in his horse's saddle, retreated a few steps, and sent a rifle bullet through Tony's head.

"Only one man I know of coulda made that shot from more than a few steps," Nathan had said with a chuckle. He'd shaken his head at the corpse. "At least the stupid bastard got himself killed in a way that's gonna do us some good."

Jeff lowered his face into his hands as he related Nathan's words. Mackenzie was silent for a moment while she digested the viciousness of Crosby's scheme. "What about the medicine bag?"

"It got torn off of Smith when he and Tony had a go-round the night Smith came for Frankie. Crosby pretended to find it in the brush when Potts came out with us to look at Tony's body. Figgered that would be the clincher."

Mackenzie exhaled a long, slow breath.

"Hell, Mackenzie. I know it wasn't right. But dammit! Someone's got to get you away from that savage. You'll be better off without the ranch and without him. He needs hangin'. It's just comin' six years too late."

She couldn't think of anything to say. Pain etched Jeff's lean face. "We've been friends for seven years, Mac. Friends. That's what you said. Didn't you ever realize that I love you? I've loved you since the first day you came to your daddy's ranch and stepped down from his wagon. You were wearin' a green dress and carryin' a parasol. And your hair was as bright as a sunrise . . ."

He trailed off, seeming lost in his own memories. Mackenzie's heart thudded. She truly hadn't known. She'd been so centered on her own plans and her own pain that she couldn't see anyone else's.

"I was too damn shy to tell you. Besides, I knew your daddy wouldn't approve. He thought a helluva lot more of California Smith than he did me, and he wouldn't let even him have you." He chuckled bitterly. "And Smith killed him."

"Cal didn't kill my pa, Jeff."

He regarded her with bitter eyes. Mackenzie wondered if Jeff's feelings for her might have colored his interpretation of what had transpired on the Lazy B that fateful day her father was killed. Had he, perhaps unconsciously, seen a way to eliminate the man who truly held her heart?

"You're going to tell this story to Walter Corby," she told him.

He sighed. "Yeah. I guess I can do that, at least. Mackenzie," he reached across the table and touched her hand. "I really did figure this was the best possible thing for you."

"I know you did, Jeff. But just once I'd like to make up my own mind about what's best for me. Let's go."

For once Mackenzie felt as though she were writing the story of her own life, and this time the ending was going to come out right.

The next morning Judge Pinney and the assembled citizens of Tombstone got a surprise. Stone-faced and staring into his lap, Jeff Morgan told his story. His voice was quiet, but after the first few sentences the courtroom was so hushed that his words were a shout in comparison. When Morgan's testimony was finished, Walter Corby asked for dismissal of all charges against California Smith. Judge Pinney raised his brows and looked at the prosecutor.

"No objection," Mr. Peele conceded.

"Case dismissed." The judge banged his gavel. "Deputy Sheriff Potts, I suggest you escort Mr. Crosby to the jailhouse until it is decided just what charges to bring against him."

For a moment stunned silence ruled. Then conversation exploded throughout the room. Cal turned in his seat and met Mackenzie's eyes, but their silent communion was cut short by the sudden flood of well-wishers that surrounded him. In the bang of a gavel he'd been transformed from a villain to a hero. Mackenzie tried to stand up, but her knees were weak, her hands trembling.

Suddenly one voice rose above the babble in the courtroom. Nathan Crosby bellowed like an angry bull. "Get your hands off me, Potts, you idiot! You believe that tail-tucked coward Morgan? He's been moon-eyed over that woman for years. She put him up to this!"

The attention of the crowd shifted from Cal to Crosby. All ears seemed to prick for the next bit of drama.

"This is a disgrace!" Crosby gravelly voice roared. "Look at him standin' there, a free man! You believe him instead of me? He's a bloody-handed savage, more Apache than any red bastard that's locked up on the reservation. He killed Frank Butler, Tony Herrera, and he tried to kill me—and every man in the posse that tried to bring him back. What're you doin' haulin' me off to jail when *he* stands there like he was a white man and not a devil Apache!"

Mackenzie held her breath as people frowned at one another, at Cal, at Crosby. Judge Pinney banged his gavel for order.

"Oh hell, Crosby! Shut up!" Ted Greene shouted. "California Smith's a good man."

"He's a better man than Crosby!" Someone shouted in

laughter. "He proved that in the mountains. Six men go after one, and all of 'em come back with their tails between their legs."

Someone else laughed—then the whole crowd.

Mackenzie saw the surprise on Cal's face. He hadn't expected anyone in Tombstone to back him up, and now the whole crowd seemed to be on his side. Hands clapped his back and reached out to shake his hand. The smile he offered these new friends had a trace of cynicism. He had a right not to trust the well-wishing of a fickle crowd, but perhaps the handful of friends who had gone against the tide and testified in his behalf would convince him that he had finally come home. Mackenzie hoped so, because she certainly didn't intend to let him get away ever again.

Though her legs still felt weak with relief, Mackenzie managed to stand. Frankie darted away, nearly knocking her mother over in the process, and attacked Cal around the knees.

"Can we go home now?" Frankie tilted her face almost straight up to meet Cal's.

"That's a good idea." He placed a hand on her hair like a man reaching out for a lovely dream to find that it's real.

"Looks like we'll have a double wedding after all," Lu said with a smile.

Cal caught Mackenzie's hand and pulled her toward him.

Amos chuckled. "I think we'd better have that wedding soon."

"Today," Cal said. "Let's have it today."

Frankie jumped up and down without releasing Cal's knees. "You already got married! I was there!"

"We're going to get married again," Cal explained to her. "Just to show everyone how much we love each other."

"Okay!" Frankie consented.

Nellie Cashman gave Mackenzie's arm a squeeze. "You'll have trouble keeping the whole town from attending. I'm afraid you've been promoted to Tombstone's favorite son," she said with a smile. "For today, at least."

"Let them come," Mackenzie said.

The well-wishers gradually drifted away. Lu and Nellie departed together with Frankie in hand, planning how to arrange Nell's boardinghouse to host a spur-of-the-moment double wedding. Halfway to the door, Frankie tugged on Lu's hand and turned back to Mackenzie.

"Is Issy's pa going to jail?"

"I think so, Sprout," Mackenzie confirmed.

"Who'll take care of Issy?"

The same question had lurked in the back of Mackenzie's mind during her campaign to have Crosby jailed. "Would you like Issy to visit us for a while?"

"Okay. Could she bring her pony?"

"I expect she'd like that."

"She could sleep with me in my room."

Lu put a fond hand on Frankie's golden head. "Come on, dear. I think your parents have things to discuss. Amos, are you coming?

"Be right there." Amos was occupied in serious conversation with Judge Pinney. Mackenzie heard her name mentioned along with Crosby's and suspected that the physician intended to make sure the incident in the Dragoons was included in whatever charges were brought against Crosby.

Right then Mackenzie didn't care. Her eyes were full of Cal's face; her arm tingled from his touch.

Cal's smile was lopsided as he pulled her into an embrace. "How did this happen?" he asked. "This morning I woke up in a jail cell, listening to hammers pounding on the gallows. A few hours later I'm a free man, one beautiful woman in my arms, another wrapped around my knees." He spared a glance for Frankie as she turned around and waved before following Lu out the door. "And you don't believe in magic!"

"I believe in you," Mackenzie whispered.

"Do you think anyone would mind if I kiss the bride-to-be?"

"I wouldn't mind." She grinned up at him. "And that's all that matters, isn't it?"

His lips came gently down on hers, caressing with chaste restraint. But a promise of passion made Mackenzie long for the privacy of night.

"I love you," she whispered to him. "I believe in you."

And magic.